Angel Harp

ANGEL HARP

A Novel

MICHAEL PHILLIPS

New York   Boston   Nashville

FaithWords
Hachette Book Group
237 Park Avenue
New York, NY 10017

www.faithwords.com

Printed in the United States of America

First Trade Edition: January 2011
10 9 8 7 6 5 4 3 2 1

FaithWords is a division of Hachette Book Group, Inc.
The FaithWords name and logo are trademarks of Hachette Book Group, Inc.

Library of Congress Cataloging-in-Publication Data

Phillips, Michael R., 1946–
    Angel harp / Michael Phillips.
        p. cm.
    ISBN 978-0-446-56771-8
    1. Widows—Fiction. 2. Triangles (Interpersonal relations)—Fiction. 3. Scotland—Fiction.
I. Title.
PS3566.H492A846 2010
813'.54—dc22

                                                                    2009044832

To
Stanley Jenkins,
God's man.

Contents

Acknowledgments

With grateful thanks to those who read the manuscript and offered their valuable input: Moira Legge, Brenda Mair, Catherine Mair, Rosanna Mair, Judith Johnston, and Stanley and Wilma Jenkins. Any errors or oversights that may have escaped us all, however, are mine alone.

Preface

Whenever one is blending fact and fiction, certain disclaimers and clarifications are necessary. Though my wife, Judy, might be said to be the "inspiration" behind a book about a harpist and harp teacher, this is not a story about *her* or anyone else. Everything that follows is fiction, the characters, the villages, the church, the relationships, the plot. While the setting of the story is reasonably true to the region of the Moray coast where Judy and I stay part of the year, most of the place names have been changed (and others retained) to reflect the fact that, after all is said and done, this is *fiction*, which requires adaptation even when based on reality. Those familiar with the region will recognize the location and layout of Castle Buchan as clearly distinct from Cullen House, upon which it is based, as are the local roads and certain other geographic details of the story. For reasons of my own, I placed the fictional "Castle Buchan" a bit closer to the Home Farm. That change required that the Home Farm be moved as well. I also took the liberty of slightly rerouting the A98, which I hope the road planners of Moray and Grampian won't mind. Experienced readers of fiction have no difficulty interweaving *fact* and *fiction* in this manner, having thorough acquaintance with the phrase "loosely based upon" as an undergirding principle of both historical and contemporary fiction. I clarify these points, however, for the sake of those readers for whom the taking of such literary liberties may be unfamiliar, and especially for our dear friends in Cullen and Portknockie.

An intriguing historical footnote may be of some interest. The *real* Buchan Castle—built in approximately 1574 two miles east of the town of Macduff at the site of the former farmhouse called

"Mains of Cullen"—was known by its official name, *Castle of Cullen of Buchan*. It was subsequently destroyed and nothing remains. What the historic connection is between "Cullen" and "Buchan" at this site east of Macduff I do not know. But perhaps the memory of the "Castle of Cullen of Buchan" can live on through this fictionalized story. Though there are some dozen current dukedoms in Scotland, the "Duke of Buchan" is an entirely fictional peerage.

About the characters, to use another phrase common in the fiction world, "any resemblance to real individuals living or dead is purely coincidental." The only actual person who might be found in the following pages is me. Judy often says that *all* my characters are me! Whether that is true in this present case, I am probably the least able to tell for certain. Though here and there I may employ the names of friends just for fun, the main characters are not based on any real individuals, "living or dead"!

A couple of final words...The use of the local "Doric" reflects the fact that most of the book was written in Scotland with an eye toward publication in that country. For American readers who find the dialect difficult at first, I would encourage you not to lose heart. As many have discovered with the occasional Scots dialect in the writings of George MacDonald, I am sure you will find yourself enjoying it soon enough.

As I write for readers in both the U.S. and the U.K., it probably cannot be helped that there will remain some spelling incongruities for one audience or the other (neighbor/neighbour). Though we try to catch these for the different American and British publications, I hope it will not cause too many bumps in the road where we miss them. A "Scots Glossary" is included at the end of the book to help those unfamiliar with the Doric dialect with some of its more commonly used words.

Michael Phillips
Cullen, Scotland
Eureka, California

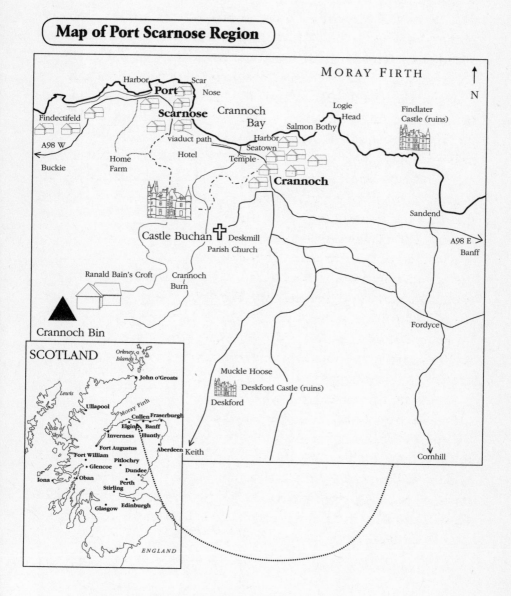

Map of Port Scarnose Region

MORAY FIRTH

N

Harbor
Scar
Nose
Port
Scarnose
Crannoch
Bay

Logie
Head

Findlater
Castle (ruins)

Salmon Bothy

Findectifeld

A98 W

Buckie

Home
Farm

viaduct path

Hotel

Harbor
Seatown
Temple

Crannoch

Sandend

A98 E
Banff

Castle Buchan ✝ Deskmill
Parish Church

Ranald Bain's Croft

Crannoch
Burn

Fordyce

Crannoch Bin

SCOTLAND

Orkney
Islands

John o'Groats

Lewis

Ullapool

Moray Firth

Cullen Fraserburgh
Elgin Banff
Inverness Huntly

Isle of
Skye

Fort Augustus
Fort William
Glencoe
Pitlochry
Dundee

Muckle Hoose

Deskford Castle (ruins)

Deskford

Aberdeen Keith

Cornhill

Iona
Oban
Perth
Stirling

Glasgow Edinburgh

ENGLAND

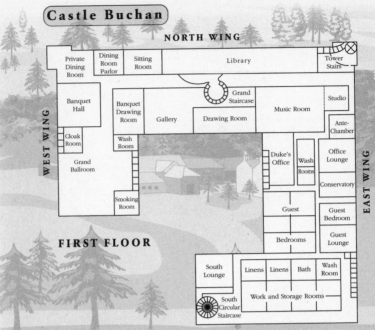

Castle Buchan

FIRST FLOOR

NORTH WING

WEST WING · EAST WING · SOUTH WING

Private Dining Room · Dining Room Parlor · Sitting Room · Library · Tower Stairs

Banquet Hall · Banquet Drawing Room · Gallery · Grand Staircase · Drawing Room · Music Room · Studio · Ante-Chamber

Cloak Room · Wash Room · Duke's Office · Wash Rooms · Office Lounge · Conservatory

Grand Ballroom · Smoking Room · Guest · Guest Bedroom · Guest Lounge

Bedrooms

South Lounge · Linens · Linens · Bath · Wash Room

South Circular Staircase · Work and Storage Rooms

GROUND FLOOR

NORTH WING

WEST WING · EAST WING · SOUTH WING

Formal Dining Room · Cloak Room · Entry Hall · Sitting Room · Great Room

Family Dining Room · Formal Lounge · Piano Room · Grand Staircase · Withdrawing Room

China Room · Wash Rooms · Drawing Room · Courtyard Sitting Room · Small Library · Guest Lounge · Coat/Hat Closets

Kitchen · Pantry · East Parlor · Wash Room · East Sitting Room

Food Storage · INTERIOR COURTYARD · Housekeeping Supplies

Breakfast Room · Larder · Laundry Room · Ironing Room

To Basement

Work Rooms

Maintenance and Work Rooms · Gardening Workshop

Garages · Tool and Equipment Room

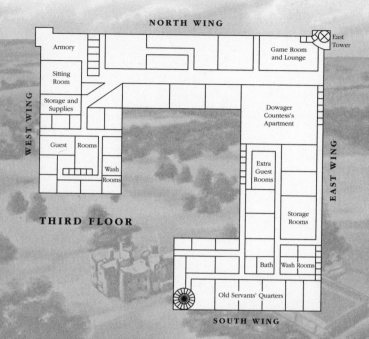

THIRD FLOOR

NORTH WING

Armory

Sitting Room

Storage and Supplies

Guest Rooms

Wash Rooms

WEST WING

East Tower

Game Room and Lounge

Dowager Countess's Apartment

Extra Guest Rooms

Storage Rooms

EAST WING

Bath

Wash Rooms

Old Servants' Quarters

SOUTH WING

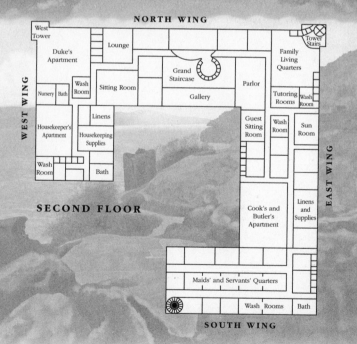

SECOND FLOOR

NORTH WING

West Tower

Duke's Apartment

Lounge

Nursery

Bath

Wash Room

Sitting Room

Grand Staircase

Gallery

Parlor

Linens

Housekeeper's Apartment

Housekeeping Supplies

Wash Room

Bath

WEST WING

Guest Sitting Room

Wash Room

Cook's and Butler's Apartment

Tower Stairs

Family Living Quarters

Tutoring Rooms

Wash Room

Sun Room

Linens and Supplies

EAST WING

Maids' and Servants' Quarters

Wash Rooms

Bath

SOUTH WING

ANGEL HARP

Chapter One

Dreams

By yon bonnie banks, and by yon bonnie braes,
Where the sun shines bright on Loch Lomond,
Where me and my true love were ever wont to gae
On the bonnie, bonnie banks o' Loch Lomond.

O ye'll tak' the high road and I'll tak' the low road
An' I'll be in Scotland afore ye:
But me and my true love will never meet again
On the bonnie, bonnie banks o' Loch Lomond.
—"Loch Lomond"

It is a terrible thing when dreams die.

I haven't cherished many dreams in my life. My dreams were quiet and personal. I usually thought of myself as a relatively simple person. I didn't care about changing the world or being rich, or even for that matter having a fancy home. I could have been content most anywhere.

Everyone wants to be happy, I suppose. I don't know if I would call that a dream.

There were a few things I *had* dreamed of, being loved by a good and worthy man and loving him in return, having children and raising them and loving them and being loved by them, growing old with my husband and watching our sons and daughters mature and blossom and raise children of their own. But one by one those dreams had been taken from me.

My husband is gone now. The circumstances aren't important. At least I don't want to dwell on them. They're too painful. Suffice it to say he is gone.

1

We had planned to have children, of course, but kept putting it off. First it was the money problems of newlyweds...thinking we needed a bigger house before starting a family...my husband's career...my own part-time work.

Suddenly years slip by. My husband died and there were no children.

I wasn't particularly old when I found myself alone, only thirty-four. Not even past my prime, as they say. But it's old enough to *feel* old if it comes before you're ready for it.

My friends told me I needed to get out, to see people, to start "dating" again. What a horrible thought! I could hardly imagine it. Good heavens, I already had a gray hair or two. My hair was either dark blond or light brown, whatever you want to call it, so it hid the occasional grayish strand pretty well. But I knew they were there. I also knew what they meant—that the clock of life kept ticking and I wasn't a teenager anymore.

It isn't as if a single woman, a *widow*—gosh, what a thing to call myself at thirty-four!—can just snap her fingers and suddenly find a line of eligible, successful, sensitive, handsome, *nice* men in their mid to late thirties lining up at her door. It doesn't happen that way. I had never considered myself that good-looking. I know men judge differently, but when I looked in the mirror I couldn't rate my looks at more than three-and-a-half or four.

Maybe four-and-a-half.

And when did four-and-a-half turn heads? Ten is the standard in our world.

I'd been told I had a nice smile, but it hadn't been seen much lately. The people at church told me I ought to go to the singles group. That prospect sounded as bad as dating. Sitting around with a bunch of twenty-somethings noodling on guitars, or with thirty-somethings checking each other out, obviously "looking"—no thanks.

I'm not exactly sure how the next few years passed. If time flies when you're having fun, it somehow also goes by when you're not. I continued to work half-days as a teacher's aide and threw myself into my music. Once a week I drove four hours for a lesson with the harpist I had studied under when I first took up Celtic music years before. I occasionally lugged my small harp to my second-grade class. From that a few private lessons resulted when parents called to ask if I would teach their children on a more regular basis. And when asked to play for weddings or garden parties or to provide background music for a social event or mixer, I usually accepted.

Over the years my little harp studio grew. I added students, then also gradually added harps until I had six in all.

It is hard to describe the personal bond a harpist feels with his or her favorite instrument. A harp is part of your very soul. Even though I had six harps, they were *all* favorites, for different reasons. Of course my big pedal harp, a Lyon & Healy 15, which I called the *Queen*, was the most majestic of the six. But my black twenty-six-string Dusty Strings my father had given to me for a birthday years before was perhaps the most special of all. After my husband died I named it "Journey." I don't know why—I hadn't called it anything before that. But a day after the funeral, realizing that this small harp had been with me for a long time and had been through a lot with me, I just started calling it *Journey*.

I had four other harps as well, two thirty-four-string harps called *Aida* and *Shamrock*, which I called by their model names. Then I had two small lap or ballad harps—a very small twenty-two-string Irish harp made by Walton which I called the *Ring*, and a twenty-six-string harp my husband had made from a kit, called the *Limerick*.

There is a story behind the Walton "Ring." When my husband proposed to me, knowing of my love for the harp, he asked me, "Would you like a diamond ring, or a harp some day?"

I'm no fool. I knew which cost more...by about ten to one. I chose the harp!

So as an "engagement ring" of sorts, he ordered the little ballad harp from Walton in Ireland, had it shipped to us in Canada, and surprised me with it before we were married. Hence, the name.

Five years later we were able to buy the *Queen* from another local harpist who had decided to sell it, and pay her over several years. Otherwise, at that time in our lives we would never have been able to afford a large pedal harp. We made the final payment just three months before my husband died. I had my two "rings"—the *Ring* and the *Queen*—but my husband was gone.

The other harps had come along gradually as I began to give more and more lessons.

What does one person need with six harps? I can imagine someone wondering.

For weddings and parties and church services I nearly always played on my pedal harp. Its sound was so full and large and rich it could fill a cathedral. That was the sound you needed on such occasions. And for outdoor garden receptions or open-air weddings, you needed large volume such that would carry without acoustics helping magnify the sound.

But obviously you couldn't wheel a sixty-nine-inch-tall, eighty-pound harp into a hospital room. My Dusty Strings portable level harp suited that purpose perfectly. I could carry it in its case with one hand, and it had a rich and vibrant tone that could easily fill a large room.

For my own purposes, the *Queen* and *Journey* would have been all I needed...along with my sentimental favorite—the *Ring*!

If you plan to give harp lessons, however, your students have to have something to play and practice on. Some people bought harps. But it is a huge financial commitment for someone to make before they are absolutely certain their initial love for and fascination with the instrument are going to last long enough to justify it. So I used the four others for loaners and rentals—the two larger student-size harps for older children and adults, the two ballad harps for younger children.

I loved teaching children to play the harp. That was the bright spot in my life. But was it enough in itself to give the rest of my drab existence meaning?

Turning forty didn't exactly wake me out of my lethargy. At first it just stunned me.

Forty! Good heavens, am I really forty? I thought.

Not that forty is really very old either. There are millions to whom forty would sound pretty good. But if you've never been forty, it's a milestone that means you're not *young* anymore. The years are beginning to tick by ever more steadily. Whenever that indefinable thing called one's "prime" is, anyone can be excused at forty for pausing to wonder if it passed by without their knowing it.

At first I became dreadfully depressed. If ever I'd had the chance to marry again, I had just wasted half my thirties doing nothing about it.

Gradually that phase faded. Then I went through a period of trying to deal with it by forcing myself to look the cold hard facts in the eye and accept them like a grown-up and quit being a crybaby. Every day I told myself, "You are forty, you are a widow, you are middle-aged, you have more gray than you can safely keep plucking out, you are going to live the rest of your life alone. Deal with it."

That was more depressing than telling myself I had just wasted six years! I quickly gave up that tactic, too. Even if my *you're-getting-old* mantra was true, I didn't have to keep reminding myself.

A day came I'll never forget, though I wouldn't mind forgetting it. It was a nondescript Sunday in November—gray, threatening rain, cold, dreary. I had nothing to do, nowhere to go. There were no lessons scheduled. I saw nobody. As dusk began to fall about five-thirty that afternoon, I realized the whole day had gone by and I'd not seen another soul all day. I was sitting on the couch of my living room, and from out of nowhere I just started to cry. For no reason, I just began to cry.

The sad truth had finally hit home that I was *lonely*. I was alone in the world...and it felt awful.

I cried myself to sleep on the couch, woke up about ten in pitch black, cold and hungry, and dragged myself to bed.

A week or two later I had a dream. I mean an *actual* dream, at night in my sleep.

I think my husband was the focus of it, but I can't remember. It's not important. You know how sometimes you have dreams and the story of the dream, if you want to call it that, fades but the feelings it arouses remain with you. This was one of those.

I woke up crying. The words were ringing in my head: *Don't let me die, don't let me die.*

I was *so* sad and lonely at that moment. Strange to say, I felt even lonelier than after I realized I would never see my husband again. I just lay in the dark and sobbed and sobbed until I could sob no more.

Finally I got up and went to the bathroom, blew my nose, splashed my face with cold water and tried to take a deep breath, then went back to bed. I turned the wet pillow over and lay down on my back and just stared up at the ceiling of my bedroom in the darkness.

The words didn't go away.

Don't let me die, don't let me die.

As I had returned to wakefulness a few minutes earlier, with fleeting phantasms of my husband evaporating like mist from my brain, I had the sense that he was calling out for me to help him, that I might somehow have been able to save him. No wonder such an uncontrollable sadness flooded over me. It was like blaming myself all over again for what had happened.

But gradually I realized that it wasn't my husband speaking at all. It was the dream itself. The *dream* was saying, "Don't let me die."

I had no idea what it meant.

After an hour or so, I began to doze. When I next came to myself, light was visible behind the curtains of my bedroom. It was morning.

Almost the moment I opened my eyes, again came the words from the middle of the night, though now slightly changed: *Don't let the dream die.*

I got out of bed and threw back the curtains. Yesterday's rain had passed and a brilliant pink-and-orange sunrise greeted me.

And I knew that it was indeed a terrible thing when dreams died. I had given in to lethargy and despondency and loneliness. I had let hope slip away. I had allowed my dreams to fade.

As I stood looking out on that bright sunrise, I thought to myself that maybe it wasn't too late.

Some of my dreams were gone forever. I could never get my husband back.

But I could not let them *all* die. There were still dreams worth dreaming.

Chapter Two

Bringing a Dream to Life

O sing tae me the auld Scotch sangs, i' the braid auld Scottish tongue.
The sangs my father loved to hear, the sangs my mither sung,
When she sat beside my cradle, or croon'd me on her knee.
An' I wadna sleep, she sang sae sweet, the auld Scotch sangs tae me.
An' I wadna sleep, she sang sae sweet, the auld Scotch sangs tae me.

Sing ony o' the auld Scotch sangs, the blithesome or the sad,
They mak' me smile when I am wae, and greet me when I am glad.
My heart goes back to auld Scotland, the saut tear dims my e'e,
And the Scotch blood leaps in a' my veins, as ye sing the sangs tae me.
And the Scotch blood leaps in a' my veins, as ye sing the sangs tae me.

—"The Auld Scotch Sangs"

New beginnings start one step at a time.

That day after my dream, the day of the sunrise, I made a decision. That sounds like a small thing. In fact, it's the most important thing in life anyone ever does. Making decisions is hard. You have to summon something from deep inside that . . . well, that takes courage in a way. I don't know whether I'd made a decision—a real, conscious, look-it-in-the-eye-and-decide *decision*—in years. I mean the kind of decision that might really make a difference, might change the course of your life in some way. No one can see the future, so you can't know. That's why decisions take courage. You can't see where they might lead. But I made one then, and it felt good.

I decided that on *that* day I would take *one* step toward *one* dream.

Maybe just a small step. But I would take some step, whatever it was, toward a future that I had some say in myself. Maybe nothing would come of it. But I would do it anyway. Prime or no prime, I wasn't going to sit around marking time while any more empty years floated past and left me behind. Life was too precious to let it drift along. I wasn't going to let life just randomly happen, taking the easiest path at every fork in the road. I was going to set my hand to the rudder, as they say, and make some of my *own* decisions about where I went.

When you let your dreams die, however, you also lose your ability to dream. You don't only lose the dreams themselves, you stop dreaming altogether. You forget that it's *possible* to dream, and that life's dreams are good things. After making what I call a decision, I found I couldn't even think of a dream I wanted to do something about. That scared me. Had I really sunk so low?

If that was true, then I hadn't only let my dreams die, I had allowed a part of me to die with them. I wasn't willing to accept that.

I determined that I *would* dream again.

It was during one of two afternoon lessons I had that day that I was reminded of a dream. I had been teaching one of the little girls who came to my studio after school a Celtic march called "Brian Boru's March." Suddenly as she was playing...I remembered!

One of the dreams my husband and I had shared was to take a sabbatical and make an extended visit to Ireland or Scotland or Wales, Britain's three Celtic regions. Maybe all three. It was a dream that hadn't evaporated completely, though it had faded so distantly into the past that, when I recalled it to mind, it came back into my memory slowly at first. Then gradually more images returned. We had talked about spending a summer traveling by car. We even fantasized about renting a little stone cottage in the Highlands and spending a year out in the wilds alone. My husband would write the great American novel—we still called it that even though we were Canadians—and I would write songs and play my harp.

Fanciful dreams. But maybe people need dreams to keep them going. Right then I needed to recapture mine.

I don't know why those Celtic countries had intrigued my husband. Though his name was Italian or French, I think he had Irish blood somewhere in his ancestry. He always talked about returning to connect with his Celtic roots, which for some reason intrigued him more than the Italian or French. My own introduction to those lands came through my study of Celtic music which I dearly loved. I had some vague sense that I possessed Celtic blood, too, on my father's side. Maybe that's why I liked the music. Something about the melancholy nature of Celtic harmony gets deep into your soul in a way other music doesn't. It has a nostalgic feel of something long ago. The haunting melodies and themes of its folk songs and ballads draw you in. It is music you *feel*, not just hear. You want to *be* there. It's music that makes you happy in a sad, quiet way, as contradictory as that sounds. At least that's how it affected me. And at this phase of my life, that sad, haunting, melancholy Celtic music perfectly resonated with everything that was stirring inside me, and it drew me even more than before.

Some people probably don't like those kinds of feelings. I've always thought that one of the reasons music gets so deep into the human consciousness is that people are "tuned" in certain ways like musical instruments. Different types of instruments, like different types of people, make different sounds. The sound of brass is not the same as the tone produced by a violin.

Some people have talkative, frilly personalities like a flute. Others stand out front as natural leaders like a trumpet. Others are gregarious like a clarinet. Others are more subdued like a bassoon. Others are full and complex like a viola or cello. Some are ordered and precise like a drum. Others are unpredictable like a French horn. And some are impossible to characterize and seem just a little different from everyone else, like an oboe.

In the same way, I thought all men and women possessed an innate personality that was tuned in either a major or a minor key.

That didn't mean some people were always happy and others always sad. Some of the world's most triumphant and joyous music is composed in minor keys. But there is an inherent difference between the sound and texture of the two that I think is replicated in people as well.

My personality was one that vibrated to the rhythms of life in minor keys. Celtic music stimulated the nostalgic melancholy harmonies of those chords inside. Its melodies resonated within me in ways I couldn't have explained. It could not be put into words. The music of personality was something each individual *felt* for himself. My husband would sometimes ask, "Can't you play something peppy?" Then I would try to learn a *peppy* song or two. But I would always gravitate back to ballads and airs.

So between my music and my husband's ancestry, and maybe my own, many things Celtic slowly got under our skin during our years together. We devoured Irish and Scottish novels. We read *How the Irish Saved Civilization* and *Angela's Ashes* and *How the Scots Invented the Modern World*. We were enthralled by the films *Braveheart* and *Local Hero*.

That's how our dream of visiting those places began.

I had not thought of going to the islands and Highlands of Britain and Ireland in years. But after my dream and the sunrise, it all came back.

I went into the living room and scanned the spines on my bookshelves. How could I have forgotten? There were Lillian Beckwith and Jessica Stirling and *A Scots Quair* and a few old-fashioned Waverly novels of Sir Walter Scott's. I pulled out one of Lillian Beckwith's novels and thumbed through it. Even as I saw the cover again after so long, and as my eyes fell on a few scattered words here and there, the memory began to return, like fragments of a dream flitting back into your brain after waking. I found myself smiling.

Gradually I remembered more.

I remembered talking wistfully about one day playing my harp on some lonely high-mountain crag, heather in bloom all around me, no one listening but a long-haired Highland cow or a handful of grazing mountain sheep. Or perhaps I would sit at the edge of a great cliff overlooking a wild rocky seashore with gulls rising and falling on the eddies of the sea breezes. I would play music of the soul, the vibrations of the strings of my harp intermingling with the whining of the wind and the gulls' cries and the crashing of waves on the rocks below.

Even if nothing came of it, just being reminded of that mental vision was invigorating. It was good to *think* again...to recapture hope...to dream of adventurous things.

Why not actually do something like that? I wasn't too old to travel, to see more of the world. What was stopping me?

Money was not a problem. I lived so simply that I tended to accumulate more than run out. I had no debts. If I wanted to, I could take two years off before having to worry about money. What was I hoarding my little nest egg for, anyway? Why not use it to live with rather than saving it to die on?

It would be good to get away, I thought, to see new places. I was in a dangerous rut. My life was going nowhere.

It was time to dream again. And not merely dream...to *live* the dream. Maybe I had more control of what happened in my life than I realized.

A small dream—a week or two, maybe a summer. It didn't have to be a whole year. But it was a start.

Maybe when it was over and it was time for me to return home, nothing in my life would change. Maybe I would resume my boring schedule and still be a middle-aged widow without much to show for herself.

But somehow, if I could just find that mountaintop—or that ocean cliff—I knew that something *would* change...inside *me*. My life might not look different from the outside, but I would be different. I would have *done* something that might mean nothing to anyone else. But it would mean something to me. It would be a connection—to the memory of my husband, to the music I loved, to a history and a land I didn't know much about but that nevertheless had once drawn me. I would have taken a step outside *myself*...into the great wide world beyond.

The most important thing that unknown mountain and that unknown sea cliff came to represent was simply the fact of my waking up and saying, "I am not going to live forever in this rut. I am going to let myself dream."

It was a simple dream. But it was my dream. That's what mattered.

I went to a bookstore that same day and bought a guidebook for Ireland and Scotland. Then I went to a travel agency where I picked up some maps and brochures about airline travel and car rentals and lodgings.

That was my one *first step*.

Chapter Three

An Adventure Begins

The heath waves wild upon the hills,
And foaming frae the fells,
Her fountains sing of freedom still,
As they dance down the dells.
And weel I lo'e the land my lads,
That's girded by the sea;
Then Scotland's vales, and Scotland's dales,
And Scotland's hills for me!
I'll drink a cup to Scotland yet
Wi' a' the honours three!

—"Scotland Yet"

Stepping off the train at Inverness, standing there with my suitcase in one hand and the harp case of my *Journey* in the other, looking around wondering what to do next, that's when the reality of what I had done hit home. Up till then—making plans, canceling lessons for the summer, actually setting out four months later and flying to London, somehow navigating the hopeless early morning confusion at Heathrow and taking a taxi into the city, asking a million questions wherever I went, then catching the all-day train north at King's Cross Station to Edinburgh and then Inverness—the excitement of what lay ahead had carried me along in a blur of anticipation.

Suddenly there I was. What next?

A train station has to be one of the most depressing places in the world. Everyone is bustling and hurrying and running. Then between trains suddenly it goes quiet and deserted—cold, silent, dirty, impersonal. What few people are about wander back and

14

forth making no eye contact. It would be different if I had someone to meet. But I didn't.

A wave of loneliness swept over me. With it came doubts: *What am I doing here?* There was no Celtic mystique. No music. No kilts. No Mel Gibson in his Braveheart getup. No bagpipes. No honeysuckle-covered stone cottages with sheep grazing beside them and heather in the distance.

Just a dreary, empty, lonely train station.

I found my way out front. There was a hotel adjacent to the station. But I'd made arrangements for a bed-and-breakfast from a travel guide. I looked around and found a taxi stand. It was gray and rainy, adding to the dreariness. Hearing the taxi driver's Scottish accent was a bit of a thrill. And he was so friendly! But he was no Braveheart. It was just a city, after all—not much romance in that.

I took the taxi to the bed-and-breakfast I had booked for the night. The lady was friendly enough, and showed me to a tiny bedroom. The door closed behind me and I sat down on the bed, again feeling very, very lonely. I was glad it was late in the day. Though I'd dozed on the train, I was exhausted from the trip and hoped a night's sleep would lift my spirits. It was a long way to come just to be depressed. I could be lonely well enough at home.

I went out for a walk, found a small grocery store, bought some cheese and oatcakes to eat in my room, then went back and, after my simple supper, got out my book and went to bed.

Why had I come here...to Scotland instead of someplace else?

I don't know, really. I had no idea where to go in either Wales or Ireland. The big Irish cities frightened me when I thought about traveling alone. I suppose it's better now that terrorism isn't as bad. But the idea of navigating Dublin and Belfast still made me nervous. I knew nothing about the outlying countryside of Ireland. And besides, Lillian Beckwith's books were set in Scotland, not Ireland. So gradually Scotland became the focus of my thoughts.

Actually, I felt a little like Lillian Beckwith, though she had more spunk than me. I wasn't really the spunky type.

I had looked over maps of Scotland. I wasn't especially drawn to the big cities, though the guidebooks said Edinburgh was one of the most spectacular cities in Europe. As I perused my maps, the name *Inverness* had a romantic sound to it. It looked like a good place from which to see the Highlands and the north of Scotland. So that's where I decided to go first. That's why I was here. No reason. Just a town picked from a map.

Everything I read about Scotland was full of history—kilts and tartans and swords, peat fires and stone cottages, battles and bagpipes, clans and castles and heather. It was exciting...alluring, I suppose, though I knew next to nothing about Scottish history. Yet gradually I became familiar with the high points and famous names—St. Columba, the ancient Picts, Robert the Bruce, Bannockburn, Mary Queen of Scots, the Jacobites, Bonnie Prince Charlie, Culloden, Robert Burns, Sir Walter Scott. And, of course, Mel Gibson or the warrior he played.

Honestly there were so *many* names and battles and high points that I couldn't keep them straight. I had no idea how they fit together. But slowly I found the history sort of getting *into* me in the same way the music did. The Scots were so proud of their past. I saw it everywhere almost immediately, in the gift shops and in the folk music I heard playing.

Just walking about on the platforms of the Edinburgh train station I had overheard from somewhere a haunting melody about the MacDonald clan of Glencoe—*Cruel is the snow that sweeps Glencoe, and covers the house o' Donald.* I couldn't get it out of my head for hours, though I didn't even know who the MacDonalds of Glencoe were. I thought I had known Scottish music from my harp playing, but soon realized how little of it I was aware of, and how oblivious I was to the link between Scotland's music and its history.

Having arrived in Scotland, I had no distinct plans. I'd brought books to read, maps and tour books, and my Celtic harp. I had reserved a rental car I would pick up on the day after my arrival. I intended to tour about, see the Scottish countryside, stay in B and Bs as I went, and see where it led.

I might have gone on an organized tour. I might have figured out every detail of my itinerary and made reservations for every night in advance, leaving nothing to chance. I wasn't really a random, spontaneous person. I usually played it safe, kept unknowns and contingencies to a minimum. It was out of character for me to strike out not knowing what I would do next, not knowing where I would stay from one night to another, not even knowing which direction I would point the car once I was behind the wheel.

I had "planned" it this way on purpose. I wanted to challenge myself. If this trip was going to accomplish anything, if I was going to discover new places of strength within myself, then I couldn't do everything the easy way. I wanted to force myself to wing it, so to speak. I needed to see if I had the courage to do things I had never done before.

Could I make decisions, fend for myself, strike up conversations, get myself out of awkward situations?

Was I even capable of having an *adventure*?

The whole prospect was intimidating, even frightening. I would either succeed or fail. But I had to try. If I didn't grow from this experience, what would I gain?

The morning following my arrival, after breakfast I walked the half mile or so to the center of Inverness and spent an hour just meandering about, listening to people, wandering into shops, absorbing a thousand new sensations. It was like any modern bustling city, I suppose, yet because it was Scotland, I found it exciting and wonderful. I was thrilled when a kilted man walked by. I walked slowly through the Victorian Market, then down and across the bridge over the river Ness and back. Finally I found a taxi, went back to the B and B to get my things, and from there went to the airport and made arrangements to pick up my rental car. I had reserved it for three weeks, just long enough to return to Inverness and take the train back to London for my return flight home.

As soon as I had my luggage and harp loaded in the rental car, I sat down behind the steering wheel. I took a deep breath, completely disoriented by sitting on the right side of the car, and said to myself, *Well, here you are! It's time for this adventure to begin in earnest.*

Driving on the left side of the road was one of the main challenges I had decided to confront. I could have traveled by bus and train. But I didn't want to play it safe. I was terrified of driving on the left. Everything felt backward! But I was determined. When it was over I wanted to know I had conquered some hard things.

I started the car and timidly inched through the parking area and then crept out of the airport at about two miles an hour. The airport was east of town. I thought I would first drive south along Loch Ness and down Scotland's west coast. It seemed more rugged and interesting. But to get to Loch Ness I had to go through Inverness, which I didn't want to do immediately. As I came out of the airport, instead I turned west and drove for a while to get accustomed to everything. It didn't take long before I began to feel comfortable enough. The roads were narrow and people were going way too fast. I constantly had a line of cars behind me anxiously trying to pass. Goodness, they drove fast for such narrow roads!

But after the terrifying thrill of several confusing roundabouts, and with constant traffic whizzing by, and a brief detour onto a side road, I pulled over for another look at my map to make sure I knew which road to follow. I reversed course back in the direction of Inverness, and then headed south toward Loch Ness and Scotland's west coast.

Chapter Four

The Tourist

I hadn't intended to write a travelogue and it's already starting to sound like one. But when a person is breaking out of a rut the way I was trying to do, everything is interesting because it is new.

I drove south beside the shores of Loch Ness and stopped at several touristy places where busloads of people were buying souvenirs and snacks and taking pictures. I hadn't realized Scotland was such a place for tourists. There were tour buses everywhere. But furry green little stuffed Nessie dolls weren't the reason I had come, and I moved on.

The little town of Fort Augustus at the head of the loch was fun. I stood and watched, fascinated, as a large boat went through the succession of locks from the higher level of the Caledonian Canal and down, finally drifting leisurely away into Loch Ness.

I stopped at a woolen and tartan store, with tea room, for lunch. I thought it more interesting than the Loch Ness tourist shops. Here I got another taste of what I was talking about before—the tartans and bagpipes and music and history. I wandered about in the shop for an hour, listening to the music, recognizing some tunes but mostly finding myself caught up in new feelings and sensations that were wonderfully haunting and melancholy, nostalgic for a past that was not completely gone. Robert the Bruce and Bonnie

Prince Charlie seemed to be the heroic figures most prominently emblazoned in legend, with Robert Burns and sad Mary Queen of Scots following close behind. I determined to learn more about them.

Driving on I found Fort William delightful. I walked the whole length of the town and back, glancing up occasionally at Ben Nevis, Britain's highest mountain, standing solemn guard several miles outside of town. I had to laugh to myself. They were so proud of this mountain. Yet I was from Canada where the Canadian Rockies would dwarf Nevis to less than a foothill.

Then I realized that another aspect of Scotland's magic was that very pride. The Scots were proud of *everything*—every hill, every town, every loch, each little glen, each brown peat-colored stream, every Pictish stone. Everything had a name. There were stories connected with every inch of Scotland. You couldn't turn around without encountering someplace that Robert Burns or Lady Caroline Nairne or Neil Gow or J. Scott Skinner had written a ballad about.

I perused a dozen or more shops with yet more tartans and kilts and woolens and folk music. Though I was only midway through my first day, I had already begun to recognize some things and know a little of what they meant. In every shop I recognized the bright red Royal Stewart tartan and knew that Mary Queen of Scots, King James who commissioned the King James Bible, and Bonnie Prince Charles Edward Stewart were all of the famous Stewart line of Scottish kings and queens. By now I had heard the ballad of the MacDonalds of Glencoe three or four times in various shops and was picking up more and more details about the clan rivalry between the MacDonalds and the Campbells and why the Glencoe massacre was such a prominent turning point in Scottish history.

I still wasn't sure who the Jacobites were, or what the Jacobite rebellion between England and Scotland was about—though I was pretty sure Scottish independence, Catholicism, Protestantism, and a dispute over Britain's monarchy were at the heart of it. I learned that it had culminated in a famous battle at Culloden near Inverness in 1746, led by Bonnie Prince Charlie for the Scots and the Duke of Cumberland for the English. I had been only a few miles from the battle site. If only I hadn't been in such a hurry to drive south the day before, I might have visited it. But then I had never heard of Culloden. I would have to stop there when I returned to Inverness in three weeks.

The more about Scotland's past I learned, the more it dawned on me that I had already played probably a third of the songs I was hearing and was even vaguely familiar with their words—*Speed, bonnie boat, like a bird on the wing, over the sea to Skye . . . carry the man who's born to be king, over the sea to Skye.* But I had known nothing of their significance. Now I knew that particular song was a ballad recounting Prince Charlie's dramatic escape to Skye after his defeat at Culloden.

It was amazing what you could learn from tourist shops and folk music and posters and maps and guidebooks.

In Fort William I bought several CDs and began playing them in the car as I continued my travels. After leaving Fort William, by the time I made my way into the desolate valley of Glencoe, with awe-inspiring peaks rising on both sides of me, I was ready to glean far more from the Glencoe Visitor Centre than I would have been able to even that same morning. Here I was actually at the site of the ancient home of the Glencoe MacDonalds whose ballad I had been listening to since my arrival. I watched the video about the massacre and the history leading up to it, and gradually more of the pieces of the intricate, fascinating, colorful puzzle of Scottish history began to fit together.

The first night of my travels I spent at a bed-and-breakfast in Oban, another memorable town.

I continued to make my way through the mountainous, watery west of Scotland, then east to Stirling, and again north through the middle of the country and the Grampian Highlands. I stopped at most of the tourist places because I thought I should—Bannockburn and Stirling, for instance, and several famous castles. It was good to continue expanding my sense of the colorful history the Scots were so proud of.

I was in no hurry. I stopped whenever the fancy struck me.

At Bannockburn I learned about the Scottish fight for independence led by William Wallace (aka Mel Gibson) and Robert the Bruce, culminating in the famous Battle of Bannockburn in 1314 when "the Bruce" defeated English King Edward. I was progressing geographically backward through history as I went—from Inverness and Culloden in 1746, to Glencoe where the massacre had taken place in 1692, to Stirling and the Battle of Bannockburn of 1314. But somehow the sequence of my travels didn't matter. I began to feel proud of myself as I was able to connect the dots and understand more and more of this fascinating history.

It was amazing to me how thoroughly the music—the songs of the people—told Scotland's story. I doubted you would learn much about U.S. history, for instance, no matter how many times you listened to "My Darling Clementine" or "The Yellow Rose of Texas" or "Swanee River." But if you carefully listened to the words of "Scots Wha Hae" or "Land o' the Leal" and the numerous ballads about Bonnie Prince Charlie, you *did* begin to gain a sense of the flow of the history of Scotland. It was folk music that, taken all together, told a cohesive story of a people and their land.

The drive back north from Stirling through Pitlochry and to Braemar and Ballater and Banchory along the shores of the river Dee toward Aberdeen was spectacular in its quiet and desolate grandeur. They were all lovely towns, and the constantly changing landscape was breathtaking. During this whole time, though music occupied such a pivotal place in my learning of the history of this land I was visiting, I did not take out *Journey* to play. It couldn't be just anywhere. I was waiting for the *right* time and the *right* place. Somehow I had not felt that yet. I was confident I would know when that time had come. I had dreamed of playing on that heathery crag or windswept cliff overlooking the sea, and I was determined that it be the perfect cliff or crag. Even when I was alone in my B and B room each night, something prevented my getting the harp out of its case and running my fingers up and down its strings.

For years this particular harp more than any of the others had been my comfort, my solace. I suppose I would say it was my truest friend, the companion I had known almost longer than anyone, though not longer than the *Ring*. Especially was that true now that my mother and husband were both gone and my father was half a continent away. I really was one of those people you hear about who are "alone in the world." It may sound strange, but my harp knew *me* more deeply than anyone, more deeply, I think, than even my husband had. The melancholy strains that came out of it were more than mere music, they were *me*. The music was an expression of the deepest places of my being. The music of my harp reflected the pulse of my personality as nothing else could. The first time I had set my fingers to a harp, before I knew anything about it, I knew I had discovered a musical soul mate.

Over the years the music of my harp had come to be *one* with the invisible undulations of my temperament. I was most completely myself, most deeply in harmony with everything it meant to be "me," when alone and quietly making soft melodies upon its strings. The music of the harp and my own depths of personhood, were of a single vibration. When they resonated together, I felt whole, complete, and one with life...one with myself.

Now my friend was silent. I didn't know why.

But I was content to let her remain silent until the time came for her to speak her melancholy mysteries once again into my soul.

Chapter Five

Port Scarnose

I sit on a knoll and I view the ocean;
My bosom is swelling with keen emotion.
And hear the lark trilling it high in cloudland;
The mavis' notes echoing through the woodland.

—Angus MacEacharn, "I Sit on a Knoll"

A week had gone by when again I found myself in the north, not far from where I had begun. I had driven through spectacular Highland passes and along desolate moors that stretched for miles. I had taken several long walks along rugged hilltops and through forests and along the loveliest peat-brown streams. I had seen numerous Highland cattle and sheep along the way.

But the moment I was waiting for with my harp had not yet come.

A third of my trip was over. I began to wonder if I was expecting some magical moment that was *never* going to come.

There was no place else I was particularly eager to visit. I suppose I could have gone to Edinburgh and Glasgow and Aberdeen and spent a week in the big cities. I might tour Scotland's dozens of famous castles and gardens and distilleries and more of its ancient historic sites. Culloden was still on my list, but not much else. I was ready to stop driving about. I had had my fill of being a tourist and going to visitors centers and shops. I wanted something deeper than superficialities. I wanted to *connect* somehow, though with what I wasn't sure—with the essence of this land I had come to explore. How could you connect in a tourist shop?

What was it that connected people with one another? Why were

24

some people lonely and others not? Lonely people lived in isolation. But if you were part of a community, there were connections...people connections. What is a community, after all? It's just a group of people that you care about and who care about you. When I was at school, either in the classroom or with the teachers and other aides, I was part of a little community there, too. Connections.

That's what I was missing in Scotland, the sense of community. How could a tourist experience that connection when speeding by, observing, taking pictures, buying souvenirs? There's no time to connect.

I needed to slow down, perhaps stay in one place for a while and just let whatever I had come for sink in. Maybe that's what you had to do if you truly wanted to know a place. But where? There was no *one* place, no perfect quaint little village that epitomized the essence of Scotland.

I realized that it wasn't possible to interact, to "connect," with a whole country all at once. I had been driving a week but had no sense of place, no sense of belonging.

Perhaps the specific place didn't even matter. To touch Scotland, maybe I had to touch some real place—it didn't matter where—and become part of it, for however brief a time. Fairy-tale places didn't exist in real life. I had driven down the winding road into Pennan where *Local Hero* was mostly filmed. But there was no connection there either. *Local Hero,* like *Braveheart,* was a movie.

But what about real life?

These towns and villages I was traveling through were like towns and villages everywhere. They were places where people lived and worked. They weren't Hollywood sets. They weren't plots from a book. They were communities.

I found myself along the coast between Inverness and Fraserburgh the day after leaving Pennan. It wasn't as desolate and wild as the western coast. But I liked it. Something about it drew me more than anywhere I had been up till now except for Glencoe. As

I drove through one after another of its coastal fishing villages, I realized I was no longer seeing tour buses. The region wasn't remote but was certainly off the most highly traveled tourist routes. Everything probably looked about the same as it had a hundred years before—gray stone houses, slate roofs, fishing boats in the harbor, little village shops. No malls, no motorways, no tour buses. People were just going about their lives the way people did everywhere.

Most of the sizable towns along the coast were really three towns in one—an old town, a sea town, and a new town.

The sea town usually sat at the water's edge and comprised small, unassuming former fishermen's cottages, all of nearly identical simple stone construction. Usually they were arranged in a hodgepodge, as if someone had built his house pointing in one direction, then someone else had built his pointing in another direction, then someone else had built another pointing in yet a third direction, with no planning, no streets, little semblance of order or uniformity, until there were two hundred houses thrown together without a plan. Then all were painted, or partially painted, with different color schemes, creating a random but peaceful chaos of disorder.

Rising above the sea town, statelier houses, often two story, of the same granite block, some of lighter quarried sandstone, rose in more orderly array and along recognizable streets overlooking the sea town. These houses were more varied and were rarely painted except for the stones about the doors and windows. They might be small or large, sometimes elegant, though always stark in the way granite cannot be other than stark. They might be as simple as a fisherman's cottage or have enclosed porches and gables and dormer windows. These were the former schools and banks and homes of merchants and the well-to-do.

Then farther up and away from the coastline were the suburbs, you might say—the newly constructed homes and apartment buildings—all probably nice and cozy inside, but uninteresting and unappealing with their modern plaster walls and orange roofs rather than the blue-black slate roofs of traditional Scottish construction.

From a distance, as you approached, you could usually see all three "towns" as clearly distinct groups of houses and buildings.

The day was advancing as I drove through one such village called Findectifeld. As I left the main road I made my way first to the sea town and along past its harbor, then up a steep street to the larger and more elegant homes of the old town. I think it was the prettiest little town I had seen yet. Gradually I climbed up the hill and back to the main road past the brick and plaster homes of the new town.

For some reason I did not want to continue farther west, and as I drove out of the village I circled back the way I had come.

Two or three miles on I retraced my way through a village called Port Scarnose. Driving now slowly through its streets for a second time, between stone houses of granite, everything clean and bright, most with colorful little gardens or flower boxes, I became enchanted. Blooming flowers were everywhere! Port Scarnose sat on a little promontory that jutted out into the North Sea. Within two or three minutes I emerged onto its coastal promontory called the Scar Nose perhaps eighty feet above the water. I stopped briefly and just took in the scene. The day was clear. Across the widening Moray Firth I could barely make out the hills of Sutherland in the distance.

I made my way on the coastal road along the headland above the harbor and to the end of the rugged point of the jagged promontory, then back and through every street of the village one after another. A girl with red hair scampered by on the pavement.

There sure were a lot of redheads in Scotland!

The girl's appearance and gait caught my eye. I slowed and watched her a moment. Even as I did, a huge black BMW came creeping along the street toward me. Its personalized license plate arrested my attention... B-U-C-H-A-N.

I did a double take and smiled. The car with the significant plate was bigger than any car I'd seen in Scotland. The sight caught me off guard and I stared at it briefly in astonishment.

Almost as if the car itself had been reading my thoughts, it slowed and stopped. I eased past it along the narrow street, glancing into its windows as I went by. They were tinted dark and I saw nothing. I had the creepy feeling *I* was the one being watched! As I drove on I glanced into my rearview mirror. The black limo still sat there. Perhaps whoever was inside was watching someone else. I saw the girl turn into a lane and disappear from sight. The next moment, the BMW inched forward, then gradually sped up and moved away in the opposite direction.

I continued to the end of the street and on through the town. I saw no more suspicious vehicles. It was a simple village. Wash hung out on clotheslines. People were walking their dogs. Women in aprons spoke to one another across low stone fences. Old men with ties and coats and caps and canes walked leisurely about or sat talking on various benches positioned at intervals along the headland.

There didn't appear to be a tourist for miles. Except me, of course.

It did not take me long to fall in love with this town!

I began scanning the streets for a B-and-B sign. Whatever else I was going to do, I knew I wanted to stay here at least for the night. As idyllic as it appeared, how could I possibly know that dark secrets were hidden behind the doors of this peaceful place, and that before I left Scotland I would be drawn into the very center of them?

I continued again through Port Scarnose's streets, seeing only two B and Bs in the whole village. As I came to the edge of town and was turning around, I saw a sign that read "Moray Coastal Trail" pointing to a walking path leading along the headland out of town. I parked nearby and struck out along the path.

The way led along the edge of the coastline away from the town west toward Findectifeld, which I had driven through twenty or thirty minutes earlier. I was perhaps twenty or thirty meters above the sea. The rocky headland jutting in and out, with boulders and caves all covered with colorful sea grasses and flowers, presented the loveliest picture to the senses that I think I had yet seen. Multitudes of birds flew about. Down in a little hollow halfway to the bottom two rabbits scampered through tufts of grass. The water of the sea was unbelievably clear and blue-green near the shore the way I imagined the Mediterranean. I'd always thought of the North Sea as gray and dreary and practically filled with icebergs. But this was a spectacular coastline.

I reached a little crest along the path. A bench sat overlooking the sea. I stopped and sat down. It was so peaceful and quiet. The sea stretched out in front of me in half a dozen distinct colors. It looked like an artist's canvas. Rain had been threatening all day. The sky was a menacing gray-black to the west where the sea was dark and foreboding. But as I cast my gaze east, the sky was brilliant, and the water below me many exquisite colors of blue and green, rich and translucent close to shore, fading to deeper shades farther out.

It felt so tranquil as I sat there. If anything could give me the same feeling of oneness with myself as did my harp, it would be the sea. I have always loved the ocean. Just being near it fills me with contentment—whether it is walking along a sandy beach, swimming in the surf where the water is warm enough, walking along a high rocky cliff, or just sitting and staring out at the constant ebb and flow of the tide.

So I sat and sat, taking in the peaceful panorama of the sea and its warm, fragrant breezes.

As I absently gazed about I could see the shadow of the black clouds moving toward me. In fact, the roofs and gray stones of Findectifeld were no longer in sunlight as when I had driven through. They were now engulfed in gray darkness. I looked out in the opposite direction. Port Scarnose was still bathed in sunlight, reflecting brightly off its stone and slate.

Suddenly a gull flew by in front of me. It was so close the motion startled me. As it passed, it turned its head briefly toward me. I almost had the sense that it was looking at me, as if it had been sent to give me a message, to tell me something.

Just as quickly it was gone, arching high then diving down over the cliff toward the water. What a magical moment!

I continued staring out over the sea. I knew right then that this was where I would play my harp.

But I hardly had time to ponder it further. I was jolted from my reverie by a gust of wind in my face. Suddenly it had become very chilly.

Again I glanced toward Findectifeld.

I was shocked to see the black clouds from the west directly over it. Slanting rain was pouring over the town in a torrent.

"Oh, no!" I shouted, jumping up. It was coming toward me, and fast!

I started running back down the hill toward Port Scarnose. Even as I ran the brightness faded. Wind whipped around my feet as I went. Within seconds the whole village in front of me turned dark gray. Offshore, what had moments before been a spectacular blue-green ocean had become a gray-and-black cauldron covered with whitecaps churning its surface into a frenzy.

I glanced hurriedly back, almost as if being chased by some dream-monster. The bench where I had been sitting was engulfed in the downpour!

The storm was coming more rapidly than I could run. I laughed in terror and tried to hurry faster.

Then it came. Rain poured down upon me in buckets. I had known it could really rain in Scotland. But I had never experienced anything like this!

I reached my car seconds later. Already I was soaked to the skin, and laughing in pure delight.

I climbed inside, panting from the run, and tried to catch my breath. Water dripping from my hair and down my face, I started

the car and drove to one of the B and Bs I had seen. I parked in
front, and went up to the door and rang the bell.

A lady answered, looking a little surprised as I stood there, my
hair a mess and my clothes hanging limp all over me.

"Hello," I said. "I am looking for a room."

"An' hoo lang will ye be stayin', lassie?"

Lassie . . . I liked the sound of that!

"I don't know," I replied. "Maybe a day or two . . . or maybe even
three," I added, laughing.

"Ah richt. Then intil the hoosie wi' ye. Luiks like ye'll be needin'
some dryin' oot as weel."

Chapter Six

Journey Comes Home

How contented was my lot,
In the lang, lang syne,
In my cosy Highland cot,
In the lang, lang syne,
When wi' shoeless feet, I strayed.
—"The Lang, Lang Syne"

The day after my arrival it rained nearly all day. Even the rain could not dampen my spirits. Though I spent most of the time in my room reading a Lillian Beckwith book, I got out for short walks whenever the downpour let up for a while. I thought that everything seemed changed now. Having decided to stay a few days, I looked at people with different eyes. Did they seem friendlier because of a change in *me*, because I was more cheery? Or was there some other difference here from where I had been earlier?

Maybe both. I didn't know.

The next morning dawned without a cloud to be seen anywhere. The storm had passed in the night and left not a trace behind except sparkling wet ground. The streets and gravel paths were mostly dry by midmorning.

At eleven the sun was high and warm and I was ready to go out with my harp. I took it out of its case for the first time and tuned it. Then I drove to the edge of town and struck out on the path along the headland, lugging my harp case in my hand. The last time I had been here I had been running for my life to escape the rain. But today I was in no hurry.

I sat down on the same bench as before. I was glad no one was around. Today I needed to be alone. I gazed out on the gorgeous blue North Sea in front of me, so peaceful and fragrant and colorful once more after the stormy tumult of two days earlier.

At last I took a deep breath, then removed my harp from its case and attached its short legs. I set them down on the ground and pulled the top of the harp to me. I set my fingers to the familiar strings and slowly began to play, softly at first, then gradually gaining assurance and allowing the music to come.

I played a few chords and random arpeggios at first, just feeling the music of the moment. Gradually some of my favorite Celtic melodies began to come out through my fingers—"Loch Lomond," "Will Ye No Come Back Again," "Road to the Isles," "Skye Boat Song," "Wild Mountain Thyme," "Dark Island"...they poured out in succession as if being drawn from the harp by the land and the sea and the mournful, musical, melancholy history of this place.

Then suddenly as I played, the lonely, shrill cry of a gull pierced the air from somewhere out over the edge of land. Almost the same instant the crash of a wave echoed off the rocks at the shoreline below.

My fingers stilled. The music had entered my heart, and it was enough.

I sat in silence. After several minutes I realized I was weeping.

I almost felt as if *Journey* were saying through its music, "I am home at last."

Chapter Seven

Gwendolyn

Gaily through the scented wood
Pass'd a maiden smiling sweetly –
Graceful, happy, fair, and good,
Stole she there my heart completely.

—"Maiden by the Silver Dee"

After the day with my harp on the headland trail, and the release of emotion that had surged from within me, all thoughts of leaving Port Scarnose were gone. I knew where I would spend the rest of my time in Scotland. I had no desire to travel anywhere else.

This was where Scotland's soul had touched me.

Over the following days I walked the streets and familiarized myself with every inch of the village. I got to know every path along the sea in both directions. I continued past the bench of the rainstorm where I had later played my harp, all the way to Findectifeld and back. I also walked and explored to the east. I discovered Bow Fiddle Rock and the Whale's Mouth and Jenny's Well and the Preacher's Cave and Florimel's Rock and the Bore Crag and Duncan's Dune, and eventually walked along the beach past the rocks known as the Three Kings to the neighboring village of Crannoch and back on the old railway viaduct.

The rugged end of the Scar Nose promontory where the village sat was only a stone's throw from the B and B. I walked along its cliff, looking down on its huge rocks and caves and the little cove at the base of the town, several times a day. I never tired of it. What a spectacular setting for a town—right above the water's edge. When it rained I played my harp or read in my room, or

34

drove to the headland and sat relishing the view of the tempestuous sea, as beautiful stirred up wild by a storm as it was on a bright sunny day.

I visited more and more with the lady who owned the B and B, and she invited me to have supper, or "tea," with her for as long as I was here. I greeted neighbors whose faces were becoming familiar as I passed with more regularity on my walks. The lady at the market, whose nametag read Cora MacKay, began to recognize me and asked why I was here and how long I was staying. After that we began chatting like old friends. I suppose I didn't *really* know anyone, but I began to feel somehow part of the little community that was Port Scarnose. Whether I was really part of it I almost didn't care. It gave me a feeling of security, of belonging.

The Doric dialect of the northeast was difficult at first—especially when people spoke among themselves. I couldn't make out a word of it! But once I opened my mouth and they heard *my* accent, most people slowed down and spoke "English" to me, though still so heavily accented by Scots that it often took me twice through to understand.

I soon realized that Cora at the market had two distinct modes of communication—the one she used with locals and friends, and the one she used with me. A lady came in when I was looking over the different varieties of oatcakes from the local bakeries—one from Portsoy, another from Huntly, and others. Though the conversation at the counter, as I overheard it, sounded intriguing, even mysterious, I could make out only about one word in ten:

"...sax 'ear syne the day...ne'er forget that day...an ill-end that wis..."

"Aye, peer Maggie...ne'er got ower it..."

"...an' why for no...as bonnie a lass like her Winny...she was aye ill-fashed ower it..."

"Aye...but haena ony mither the richt tae greet..."

"...tae gang oot ilka 'ear wi' flo'ers...tis a fearsome place tae gang alane, ken...wadna mysel'..."

"...they say the ruins is full o' the ghaists o' pirates wha were ill-cleckit..."

Suddenly they both went silent as the door opened and the bell rang. A woman walked in. I glanced toward the door but couldn't see her face. All I heard was, "Fine day, Olivia...," followed by more Scots I couldn't make heads or tails of. When the woman who had just come in left a little later, the two women resumed, though in low tones.

"...haena doubt *she* kens the day weel enouch..."

"...there aye wis bad bleed atween them twa..."

"...Maggie had aye nae eese for the likes o'..."

But then several more people came in and that was the end of my eavesdropping.

I was out on the same bench again with my harp the next afternoon. By then I had taken my harp to play along the shoreline at a number of places. But this would always be my favorite special place.

I hadn't noticed anyone about, but the path was a well-traversed route and the Scots were great walkers. As I sat facing the sea and playing, I heard footsteps running along the trail behind me. I paused and turned around toward them. A girl of nine or ten, with bright red hair, was running toward me with an uneven gait. I thought she might be the same girl I had seen on the walk the first evening I had driven through the village, but I couldn't be sure. There were redheaded children everywhere.

She slowed as she saw me look at her, a bashful look spreading over her face. Slowly she continued her approach.

"What's that?" she asked, speaking slowly.

"It's a harp," I answered. "Have you never seen one before?"

"No. You sound funny."

I couldn't help laughing. "That's because I'm not from around here," I said. "I come from far away. I'm visiting."

I had already detected, from her look and the sound of her voice, that something was wrong with the girl. I couldn't tell if she was ill or a bit slow. Her body seemed to move in an odd way, almost as if she had had a stroke and was partially paralyzed, though she seemed too young for that. She looked at me a few seconds, still puzzled by my odd accent, then glanced at my harp. Throughout our brief conversation she had been inching closer.

I played several chords and ended with a big swooping glissando. Her face lit up.

"That's bonnie," she said. "That's rale bonnie!"

"Would you like to try it?" I asked.

Her eyes lit up again. She looked up into my face as if to see if I meant it. I nodded and smiled. Tentatively she stretched out a pudgy forefinger and plucked at one of the strings. The sound of it almost seemed to frighten her. Quickly she pulled away, though never once took her eyes off the strings. I waited. Gradually out came her hand again like the shy head of a snail creeping from its hiding place. This time she reached out and pulled her finger along the strings toward her, creating her own improvised little glissando.

She giggled at the sound and again drew back into her shell. But her face was bright. She was obviously enchanted by what she had done.

More footsteps and a voice interrupted us.

"Gwendolyn, come away!" it said. "Don't bother the lady—come here."

I turned and saw a woman about my own age, perhaps a few years older, hurrying toward us with a look of annoyance on her face. As she reached us, she looked me over briefly. She seemed to be looking more deeply inside me than I was comfortable with.

"I'm sorry, missus," she said. "She's much too forward. She's always running off and making a nuisance of herself.—Come, Gwendolyn."

She took the girl's hand and pulled her away. The girl made no objection and went with her compliantly.

"It was really no trouble," I said. "I don't mind. If she would like—"

"No, missus. She has to learn to mind her own affairs."

The woman hurried the girl off down the path toward Port Scarnose. I began playing "Will Ye No Come Back Again," hardly thinking of the significance of it. As the sound reached her, whether she understood the words or not, the girl turned and cast one more glance back toward me. I smiled again. The next moment the path took them round a high bush of gorse and they disappeared from sight.

All that day, and the next, I was haunted by visions of the sweet little girl called Gwendolyn. The expression of joy on her face from the simple motion of drawing a solitary finger across the strings of my harp was testimony both to the magic of music itself, and to the mystery of the harp as mankind's most ancient instrument by which to express that music.

I dearly wanted to see her again and set her mother's mind at ease. I continued making my little pilgrimage out to the bench, more frequently now, several times a day, hoping to find them out again.

Finally I saw them. They came walking toward me, hand in hand, this time just leaving Port Scarnose. The moment the girl saw me on the bench, she pulled her hand loose and dashed up the path.

"Hello, Gwendolyn," I said.

She seemed startled to hear me call her by name. She stopped abruptly and stared at me. Within seconds the woman came up behind her.

"She has been talking about nothing but the harp lady ever since that day we saw you," she said.

"I hoped I would see you again," I said.

"May I play your bonnie thing again?" the girl blurted out.

I saw the woman begin to object, but I smiled quickly. "Please," I said, "I don't mind. Would you really like to, Gwendolyn?" I asked, turning to the girl. Her eyes were as wide as two saucers.

"Come here," I said. "Stand in front of me."

I took her hand and pulled her toward me and made room for her to stand between me and the harp with her back to the bench. I reached my arms around her. As I did, she relaxed back into my embrace. I pulled the harp back to us.

"Now then," I said, "put the fingers of your left hand here—"

With my own left hand I set her tiny little fingers on the strings.

"—and your right hand here."

I did the same with her right. With my own fingers I strummed a few strings randomly to show her what to do, then pulled my hands away.

"Now you do it," I said.

Without a moment's hesitation, her little fingers began to pluck at the strings. For a minute or two the sounds were random and dissonant. But almost as if there were eyes in the tips of her fingers, she seemed to sense the tones of the different-colored strings of the scale. In all my years of teaching youngsters I had never seen such a thing. She began plucking individual strings, then two or three at a time, making actual chords. Within another minute or two actual melodies and harmonies were vibrating from the soundboard.

I listened awestruck. I wish I could have seen her face. But sitting behind her I couldn't, and I did not want to disturb the magic of the moment. Even without seeing her, I could tell from watching her fingers that inside she was absorbing the mechanics of the instrument in a way that transcended logic. She wasn't *thinking* about what she was doing. It was just *happening* from deep within her subconscious. Her fingers were finding and playing genuine *music*.

She played and played, her fingers growing more comfortable all the time, her head gently rocking back and forth to the music she was making. I sat in a trance.

By this time I had all but forgotten her mother where she stood beside us. I can only assume that she was as astonished as I was. When at last I remembered her, I glanced briefly toward her. I expected to see tears in her eyes, but instead she just stood stoically, apparently unmoved.

Gradually Gwendolyn's fingers began to slow, then they fell silent.

"That's all," she said. "The song is over."

"That was beautiful, Gwendolyn," I said. "What song was that?"

"I don't know. Gwendolyn just played it."

She wriggled out from behind the harp and returned to the woman's side. The woman just stood, then slowly shook her head but said nothing more and turned to go. The expression on her face was impossible to read.

"I am staying at Mrs. Gauld's bed-and-breakfast," I said. "I would like to see you both again."

The woman nodded but without indication of a smile, then took Gwendolyn's hand and they continued on their way. I sat for a while longer but did not play again. At last I packed up my things and left. It didn't seem fitting to play again right then. Gwendolyn's music needed to linger in the air. I was positively enchanted with the girl!

I took my harp back to my room, then went out for a long thoughtful walk along the coastline in the opposite direction beyond Crannoch. There I discovered the trail I had read about past the pet cemetery to the Salmon Bothy. Finally I returned on the headland, beside the caravan park and along the viaduct back to Port Scarnose.

Chapter Eight

The Man's the Gowd

Is there, for honest poverty,
That hangs his head, and a' that?
The coward-slave, we pass him by,
We daur be poor for a' that!
For a' that, an' a' that,
Our toils obscure, and a' that,
The rank is but the guinea's stamp,
The man's the gowd for a' that!

—Robert Burns, "A Man's a Man for All That"

In the same way that Gwendolyn's fingers seemed to unlock the music in the strings of my harp, listening to her play unlocked something inside me.

Something had happened deep in my soul. I greeted people differently after that, not as a visiting stranger but as someone who had a reason to be here.

That reason, strange to say, was innocent little Gwendolyn.

I didn't even know her last name. Yet I felt that I had come here for a purpose. And whatever it was she was part of it.

I don't know how word spread, but gradually people seemed to know about me. When I was out walking, or when I nodded and smiled in the market, they occasionally said things like, "You must be the lady with the harp."

After returning from a walk, Mrs. Gauld handed me a note with a name and a phone number.

"Adela Cruickshank cam roon," she said. "She heard ye were bidin here. She has always wanted tae play the harp, ye ken. She wondered gien ye wud gie her a fyow lessons while ye were here. An'—"

She paused. An embarrassed look came over her face.

"What is it, Mrs. Gauld?" I asked.

She smiled and glanced down. "I dinna like to ask," she said. "But my mum's in hospital. She isna so weel and I wondered, that is gien ye dinna mind, gien ye might play a wee sang or twa for her. She loves music, ye ken, an' I'm thinkin' it micht cheer her up."

I smiled. "I would be happy to."

That same afternoon I went with Mrs. Gauld when she drove to see her mother at the hospital about five miles away. I took my harp into her mother's room and played for perhaps an hour. Finally I got up to take a break and stretch my legs. The door of the room had been open. When I walked outside the corridor was filled with people listening, nurses and doctors and patients in wheelchairs they had brought out of their rooms so they could hear. When they saw me, some of them began clapping, then everyone joined in. Though I thought I had been playing just to Mrs. Gauld's mother, half the hospital had been listening! Several asked when I would be back.

The next day, Adela Cruickshank came to the B and B for her first lesson.

"Don't I recognize you from somewhere?" I asked as Mrs. Gauld introduced us.

"Aye, mum, I wark at the post, ken," replied the lady I had just met as Adela. "I hae seen ye a time or twa."

"Yes, of course—that's it," I said.

Adela was so thrilled she asked if she could come the next day and practice what I had shown her.

All this time I hadn't seen little Gwendolyn again.

That afternoon, about the same time as on the two previous occasions when they had been out for walks, I again sought my favorite bench with my harp, hoping for another encounter that might prove as magical as before.

You might think I would tire of playing. But I never did. I had enough songs to occupy me that I could play for hours without repeating one. Even if I had repeated, it wouldn't have mattered. Music *itself* was its own delight.

It was a sore temptation to try to recall to mind and re-create what I had heard coming out of my harp beneath little Gwendolyn's fingers. But I did not want to spoil the memory by trying to capture something that wasn't mine at all. To try to lay hold of it would have been as futile as trying to snatch hold of a passing breeze upon my face uplifted from the fragrant currents of the sea. Gwendolyn's unknown random music had been a melodic zephyr blown ethereally from unknown regions to enjoy for a moment and then to remember with wonder.

. I had been working on a new song of my own since my arrival in Port Scarnose. Its melodies were still coming to me in bits and pieces, as new songs do. They rarely reveal themselves complete and fully formed. Tunes, like words, come in phrases, sometimes in sentences, very occasionally in whole paragraphs, but never in complete chapters. You have to play them over and over, massage them and try out little differences and changes until you've got them just right. As I continued to work on my song, now and then a few notes and phrases crept in that reminded me of that magical passing breeze. I did not try to remember its melodic fragrances, but when such fragments came I allowed them to sprinkle my own song with mysterious hints that maybe the music was not entirely my own but was coming from someplace that even I did not altogether understand.

It's difficult to name a song before it is ready. It seems presumptuous to give it a name when it remains nebulous and unformed. But the song that was forming during those days had named itself.

It would be "Gwendolyn's Song."

I sat down to play. It was a different kind of day than most—clear but still and calm. Not a breath of wind disturbed the surface of the sea. Out beyond the shore break, the gentle swell rose and fell as if it were an undulating liquid surface of rich blue-green glass. If ever there was a day to spy dolphins breaking the surface, today would be that day. The air was heavy and sultry. It felt like a calm before an invisible coming storm, though I could see no hint of weather on the horizon anywhere. Slowly I began to play. The strings seemed to vibrate with added energy from the dense atmosphere. I felt the sound carrying on the air, almost echoing back upon me as if I were in an outdoor amphitheater with very strange acoustics.

How could open air have acoustics at all? Yet somehow that's what it felt like.

I played with vigor, enjoying the full sound, hoping maybe that little Gwendolyn, wherever she was at that moment, might hear and might persuade her mother to come find "the harp lady" again. I was haunted by what had happened with her. I was eager to put those little fingers at my harp again. If indeed she was one of those rare ones endowed with the mystical gifts of the *savant*, someone should know so that it could be explored further.

I don't know how long I played, thinking of little Gwendolyn and working on my own song that she had inspired. Probably thirty or forty minutes.

Gradually my fingers fell quiet. Perhaps that sounds funny to say, as if my fingers were thinking for themselves apart from my brain, as I had said about Gwendolyn's. But in a way that's not so far wrong. When I am making up tunes, I play spontaneously as I feel. Sometimes it comes, sometimes it doesn't. Music flowing from within is like that—unpredictable. Sometimes I have the feeling that as they move along the strings my fingers are more in tune with the music that is struggling to find expression than is my brain. Perhaps that was Gwendolyn's secret too.

As my hands quieted, I realized that Gwendolyn's song had revealed all it had to give for the moment. I knew there was more. But I was not meant to hear it yet. It would come in its own time and its own way.

I sat quiet and peaceful. Sensing a song rising up from deep places inside you is an emotional experience that, while causing a rush of exuberance also brings a depletion of creative energy that leaves you happily weary. Afterward all you can do is sit and relish the moment.

On this occasion I didn't have that luxury. Suddenly I was shocked out of my reflective silence by a man's voice.

"That was truly beautiful," it said, softly but loud enough that I could hear.

I spun around, thinking someone must have crept up the path behind me. But no one was in sight!

More surprised than frightened, I turned around frantically. Where had the voice come from! Thinking I had imagined it, all of a sudden a man's head rose fifteen or twenty feet in front of me from down over the cliff. Its owner turned to face me, then scrambled up over the steep grass and rock and jumped onto the level where I sat watching him in amazement. He was slightly taller than average with fair skin and a full head of bushy red thatch, of stocky though well-proportioned build, probably in his early forties and dressed in blue slacks, a blue plaid wool shirt, and walking boots.

"I can't remember when I have heard anything so perfectly one with its natural surroundings," he said, "so in harmony with God's creation." What Scottish accent the man possessed was subdued, refined, intermingled perhaps, though I was certainly no expert, with educational influence from south of the border.

"Where did *you* come from?" I asked, staring blankly back at him as if he were an apparition that had appeared out of thin air. "I had no idea anyone was within miles!"

Reading astonishment and shock on my face at his unexpected appearance, the man smiled broadly, then broke into a gentle good-natured laugh.

"I apologize. I see that I startled you," he said. "Like you, I had no idea anyone was nearby. When you began to play I did not want to disturb you. So I remained where I was and allowed the wonderful music to flow over me."

"But...I still..." I began. "Where *were* you?"

"Just there, down over the edge," he said. "In my own private little hideaway."

"Oh, like this bench is for me," I said.

"Is this where you come to be alone?" he asked.

"In a way," I replied, at last beginning to relax. "It's not exactly private, but it has become a special place for me. This is where I first played my harp in Scotland."

"You are visiting the region, I take it?"

"You can tell I'm not a native?" I said.

"I confess"—he nodded with an engaging smile—"there is a little something I detect in your accent that gives you away. American?"

"I'm from Canada...Alberta."

"Ah, right...America of the north. Of Scottish descent?"

"I think possibly. I know many Canadians are, but I know little about my roots."

"How long are you here...are you traveling about?"

"I'll be here another week-and-a-half. I traveled at first, but I plan to remain in Port Scarnose until it's time for me to go."

"Well, perhaps we shall meet again. We must think alike since this same spot on the coastline draws us both."

"I still cannot see where you were," I said. "It looks as if the cliff drops off all the way to the water."

"Some time ago, I discovered a little crook or hollow in the rock," said the man. "It's nicely padded by thick tufts of shore grasses...just down over there," he added, pointing to where he had appeared. "It's the most marvelous little spot. It reminds me of old hymns like 'Shelter in the Time of Storm' and 'In the Cleft of the Rock.' From it I command a stunning view of the entire coast, as well as the rocks and shore below. I nestle into my little cliff-hole. The birds fly about, sometimes so close I can nearly touch them. It is perfectly secluded. People pass by along the path, but no one suspects the existence of my small sanctuary. I come here regularly to sit, to pray, to think, to read, sometimes to write."

I glanced down and now saw the slender volume in his hand. "What were you reading today?" I asked.

"Oh, this," he said. "An old fifteenth-century devotional book— Kempis's *The Imitation of Christ.*"

"Oh . . . well I certainly never dreamed anyone was around!" I laughed. "Otherwise I would never have played so freely."

"Then I am glad I did not reveal myself! It was magical. There I sat gazing out over the sea. Slowly, as if out of the very heavens themselves, I found myself enwrapped in the most angelic music I had ever heard. Imagine *my* shock! It had to be as great as yours. I knew somebody was making music, and nearby. I simply took it as a gift. Nor did I recognize the tone at first as that of a harp. I didn't know what I was hearing. Of course, that makes it all the better—the aura of uncertainty adding to the mystery. What kind of harp is it?" he asked, looking it over.

"A folk harp," I answered. "Here in Scotland you would call it a *clarsach.*"

He nodded, examining it with interest. "Tell me, what was that tune?" he asked. "It truly carried me away. I could have listened forever."

"Just something I am working on," I replied, embarrassed at his lavish praise.

"Your own composition!"

I nodded sheepishly.

He stared at me a moment, his mouth open just a crack. "I am stunned," he said at last. "It really was most extraordinary."

He paused briefly. He seemed to be thinking.

"Would you . . ." he began after a moment, "—would you consider playing for our local congregation?"

"I'm afraid I don't understand," I said, puzzled.

"In church, I mean. Sometimes the organ music Sunday after

Sunday, it can be monotonous. I am always looking for something fresh. I know everyone would enjoy it. More than enjoy it—they would be thrilled."

"Are you the music director or something?" I asked.

"Actually, I am the curate. Iain Barclay at your service," he said, reaching out his hand. I shook it, though I have to admit I was startled all over again to discover that I had been speaking to a minister. He certainly didn't look like one! "The invitation is sincere," Curate Barclay went on. "I would love to have you play for us. It would be wonderful."

"I don't know," I said hesitantly. "I'm not sure I would be comfortable playing in church."

"Why not?"

The question was simple enough, but it caught me off guard.

"I, uh...I'm not a church person."

"A *church person*," he repeated. "What exactly do you mean?"

"A believer, I guess...I don't profess, that is, I don't think I would call myself a Christian—or at least a practicing one."

"Oh...hmm, I see," he said, nodding slowly. He seemed surprised. "From listening to your music," he added, "I assumed otherwise."

"Why would you think that?" I asked.

"It's just that I felt the Spirit of God in your music."

"I doubt if it was that," I said, half laughing. "God and I aren't exactly on intimate terms."

"He could still make music through you. His Spirit resides in all men and women, whether they acknowledge it or not."

"I doubt that's true in my case," I said. I probably sounded a little cynical.

"Well, no matter. I'm not bothered. My invitation still stands."

"Even if I don't go along with what the church stands for? You would still want me to play?"

"Absolutely. I would be delighted. I believe that all music is God's. After all, where does music come from?"

"I guess you would say it comes from God."

"Of course. Music is a reflection of God's goodness and joy. Cows don't make music, or zebras or monkeys or any other animal. Hmm...there are birds—maybe that destroys my point! But I think I would still maintain that man makes music because we are created to express God's goodness and joy."

"Maybe it's because we are thinking, intelligent, creative beings. Music is just a natural expression of who we are."

"I agree completely," rejoined the curate. "And who are we but beings created in God's image? Man's creativity couldn't have come from nowhere. Every note of every song that comes out of us is a reminder that we are made in the image of God."

"I still think you are reading too much into it," I insisted. "I was just making up a song."

"Perhaps you were praising him without knowing it," persisted the minister. "Now that I learn it was your own composition, I am doubly convinced that God's Spirit is in you. If such music is in your soul, he must be there, too, giving birth to your music."

This was getting to be too much! I had a religious fanatic on my hands. Though I must admit, he was not like any Christian I had ever met. He was so full of enthusiasm but didn't seem anxious to convert me or convince me to his point of view. Strange as it is to say, he didn't seem to care whether I believed in God or not.

"Do you believe that *everything* good, like music, comes from God?" I said after a moment. "Even from people who don't believe in him?"

"Of course—absolutely," he answered with that same happy enthusiasm. "Where else would the good come from? God is the Author and Creator and Composer," he added with a grin, "of all the good in the universe."

"If you say so!" I laughed. "I must admit, I have never heard a minister talk quite so...I don't know, with such optimism about, you know, about God and the world and religion and Christianity.

It seems they're usually more intent on sin and hell and the wrath of God and getting people saved and all that."

He threw back his head and roared with laughter. The man called Iain Barclay continued to be full of surprises.

"Not enough of the hellfire in me to suit you?" he said, still laughing.

"It's not that," I said. "It's just different from what I've been exposed to."

His laughter slowly subsided and the smile gradually faded from his lips. He grew thoughtful.

"A common misperception of the Christian faith," he said. "Sadly, what you have voiced *is* what most people are exposed to rather than the *true* essence of Christianity. There are those of my own congregation, too, who find me as disconcerting as you do. The dour face of Scottish Calvinism persists. They don't want their Christianity quite so embracing as mine. They like to talk about God's love, but with long faces. They recognize that there is such a thing as the joy of the Lord, but they never forget that it is reserved for only the elect...the joy of the long face I call it. They like their curates sober minded."

"Well, I can see that they got more than they bargained for in you!" I laughed. "So how do you handle it?"

"Just keep being myself. And I preach what I consider the true essence of Christianity. If those who find me a heretic oust me from the pulpit, then so be it. My nature is not to contend but to enlighten. That I will continue trying to do, whether in the pulpit or out of it."

"You don't really mean that there are some who consider you a heretic?"

"Oh, absolutely. Too much goodness in the gospel is heresy, don't you know. Believe me, Calvin's roots run deep. You have to remember that were it not for Scotland's role in the Reformation, Calvinism might never have gained the doctrinal stranglehold it did throughout the rest of the church."

"Why Scotland?" I asked.

"John Knox exported Calvinism from Geneva here to Scotland. It took over the religion of the entire country. Scotland in the early seventeenth century provided the greenhouse, so to speak, from which Calvinism spread worldwide."

"Ever since I came," I said, "I have been learning about Scotland's history. But I guess I haven't paid much attention to its religious history."

"Scotland's history, at least of the last five hundred years, *is* religious history. Religion is the engine that has driven everything else."

"I didn't realize that."

"*Everything* in Scotland goes back at some point to religion. This is where Calvinism's roots remain deepest. But..." he said with a little laugh, "I didn't mean to start a church history lecture. As you said, you're not a 'church person.'"

He grinned, as if to reassure me that he meant nothing but good humor by the comment.

"And it really doesn't bother you?" I asked.

"That you're not a church person?" he rejoined.

I nodded.

"Not in the least. People are people. They're not divided into church people and not church people. Every man or woman I meet has something I can learn from. I like people. I don't try to categorize and pigeonhole them into this group or that group or this belief or that belief, but to find out what I can learn from them. Actually, if you want me to let you in on a little secret, if I had the choice to spend the afternoon talking theology with a group of *church* people or with a group of intelligent and logical agnostics, I would pick the agnostics any time. They're often more interesting!"

"Maybe you *are* a heretic after all," I laughed again.

He glanced at his watch.

"Oops!" he said. "I've got to be somewhere. One final plea—at least do this for me, come visit the church. During the week, I mean, when no one is there. Bring your harp and play for a while. I will leave you alone if you like. You may have the place to yourself without fear of heretical redheaded curates popping up from out of nowhere. Just play and see if you do not feel a majesty, a reverence...maybe something like what you feel here. Our church is a wonderful place, twelfth century...the acoustics are marvelous. You will think you are in Westminster Abbey! It's just a small country parish...but, well, just come and try out the church before you decline my invitation."

He was looking at me with such a childlike expression of expectation, how could I refuse?

At last I smiled and nodded. "All right," I said. "I will agree to that."

"Good. Here's my card and telephone number. Ring when it's convenient for you. I will come collect you if you like—where are you staying?"

"At Mrs. Gauld's bed-and-breakfast."

"Ah, right. The church is a mile from town, in the country, and somewhat difficult to find the first time. How is tomorrow?"

"Fine," I nodded.

"Good, give me a ring then."

He took several steps along the path, then paused and turned back.

"Oh," he said with a sheepish smile, "—if it is not too presumptuous of me...might I ask your name?"

Chapter Nine

Confusing Roots

Michael, row de boat ashore,
Hallelujah.
Michael, row de boat ashore,
Hallelujah.
—"Michael, Row the Boat Ashore"

My parents were hippies of the 1960s, my mother Canadian, my father from the U.S. They went to Woodstock and traveled around in a VW bus plastered with bumper stickers about Vietnam and Nixon and Whales and Tibet and Authority. I've seen pictures. They got "saved" and then became part of the Jesus Movement, which was sort of the hippie version of Christianity at that time. In those days hippies named their children with trippy Mother Earth designations. Then the Bible-carrying parents of the Jesus Movement went to the other extreme and gave all their children biblical names. A flood of Rachels and Sarahs, Davids and Jonathans, Ruths and Rebekahs joined Generation X along with Sky, Clover, Moon, Fawn, and Willow.

My parents sort of split the difference and named me Angel Dawn Marie. I was never quite sure if my roots were in the hippie culture or in the Jesus culture. It seemed as if they couldn't make up their minds and so threw in a little of everything, with an extra name to boot. The result was that I didn't feel I belonged to either culture—or to any other for that matter. I never had a sense of belonging.

The whole thing was cumbersome and I hated it. The "Angel" added such a subtle pressure to be a "good girl," a perfect little child—"That's a good little angel!"—that sometimes I couldn't bear it. From before I could remember I vowed that when I grew up I would drop the *Angel* the first chance I got.

And I did.

When I went away to college, I told not a soul my full name, including the college admissions office. I kept the change secret from my parents because I didn't want to hurt them—they were good parents and had no idea how I felt—but I filled out all my college papers *sans* Angel. I didn't blame my parents. It wasn't their fault how I had reacted to a name that I'm sure meant something very special to them. They didn't know and didn't need to know. It was something I had to work through myself.

My mother was sincere, but I have the idea the "Angel" was her idea. All through the years I was growing up, there still lingered about her the aura of hippiedom. She was notoriously disorganized, was invariably late, tended to dress with a peculiar flair, and was always taking up the banner for some oddball cause or another. She was utterly mistrusting of government. When Ralph Nader came along, she was all over that, even though she couldn't vote in the U.S. elections. I think she may have even contributed to one of his campaigns.

I don't know how to describe it...she just seemed like one of those people who never outgrew the sixties. My father was a lawyer so it was different for him. He sort of by definition became part of the establishment. But my mom never really was able to mainstream.

After being away a few years, and coming home to visit mostly on holidays, and at first for the summer, though that gradually gave way to two- and three-week visits, suddenly it dawned on me, *Gosh, my mother's a space cadet!*

Perhaps it's the swing of the generational pendulum, but I tended to be fastidious in how I dressed and orderly in my whole outlook on things. I suppose you would say I was conservative and intellectual in my approach to life. I wasn't an intellectual, a "brain." But I tended to process information intellectually and rationally.

After I began playing the harp in connection with music studies in my second year away, the irony of it could hardly escape me— that within a year of dropping the name *Angel* I had taken up the very instrument associated with angels! But it was coincidence, nothing more. It only deepened my resolve to never let my given name pass my lips again.

Good heavens, what was I going to say, "Hi, my name's Angel. I play the harp"?

No way.

Coming out of the Jesus Movement, my parents were of that broad general classification of Christians called evangelical. Such I always considered myself, too. I hadn't thought much about my beliefs. I just adopted what the church taught and what everyone else believed. I suppose that's what most people do. I "accepted the Lord" when I was thirteen at a church camp. I was baptized. I went to Sunday school and church and youth group and knew all the songs and slogans and catchphrases and doctrines that evangelical young people were taught. Gradually I thought of that teaching as what I *believed*. It never occurred to me that there might be a difference between being taught a bunch of doctrines and real personal *belief*.

When I went to college, I started attending a church near the school where many of the Christian students went. Everything continued on as before, though as I said I was then going by a different name.

I met my future husband—his name was Edward—in my last year of school and we were married two years after that. He made no profession of belief. He was a thorough secularist. The fact that I became involved with him, accepted his proposal, and then married him, without worrying too much about our different outlooks, probably says something about the lazy nature of my own belief system. People can make of it what they will.

I suppose loss of faith comes slowly.

I said earlier that making concerted, definite *decisions* is hard and takes courage. That's the opposite of what happens when you lose belief.

Does anyone suddenly *decide* to stop believing?

I don't know. I sort of doubt it. That isn't what happened to me. I just gradually drifted away from beliefs I thought I held. I don't know when it started, or when it ended. It was gradual, invisible. I just slowly stopped believing. And if my beliefs had just been learned from what others taught me, maybe it was no great loss. If they were really the beliefs of *other* people that I had just latched on to and pretended to believe, how could I sustain them anyway? Maybe I'd never really *believed* at all, only had held to some religious culture of ideas that were current among the people I was around.

If making decisions is hard, mental drift is just the opposite. It's lazy. When you *don't* summon the courage to do hard things, and instead allow yourself to be carried along by the current, taking what comes, that's the lazy way. I have the feeling that's how most loss of faith comes—from laziness rather than decisiveness. That sounds flaky. More like my mother than me. But there is a lot of our parents in us, probably more than we want to admit. Maybe in the drift that occurred I was my mother's daughter more than I knew.

When I went away to college and dropped the name whose implications were so burdensome, I didn't immediately also drop the Christian faith of my upbringing. That came more slowly. But I think that's when a few cracks began to develop in my belief system.

Asserting my independence in such fashion with my name, and asserting it *against* the familiar persona I wanted to wear no longer, was an act that had implications, too. Maybe deep in my subconscious, saying "I don't want to be called *Angel* anymore" led also to, without my stopping to think about it, "I don't want to be called a *Christian* anymore."

But I am guessing. It's hard to know ourselves accurately. That being we know best will always remain a mystery.

The bottom line is this: Because I had never thought deeply and concertedly about what I believed, or thought I believed, and because I was spiritually more lazy than courageous, when the drift away from my shallow beliefs began, I never even knew it.

Edward and I were married for seven years. He was a good man, entirely faithful, loving and kind and considerate. He provided for me, made me feel safe and secure. He believed in me. Actually, he was far nicer than many Christian men I knew and had dated. I kept going to church after our marriage, which he encouraged. But he had no interest in it himself. Neither of us really minded that our beliefs were different. We got along and respected one another in spite of our differences. We had a good relationship and a good marriage. Somehow belief never entered into it.

My friends and acquaintances at church, however, were concerned about my being "unequally yoked" with a nonbeliever, as the expression goes. They were always praying for my husband's salvation. I prayed for him, too, in my own way. But it was difficult for me to share their anxiety about his soul. Maybe I should have. Perhaps that shows how weak my own faith had become, I don't know. I'm not sure why I kept going so regularly—it seems odd to me now.

But honestly, my husband was kind to me and we loved each other. Somehow I found it difficult to fret about his lack of spirituality. Especially so in that at the women's prayer meetings and Bible studies I attended every week, half the time was usually taken up with everyone's complaints about their husbands—their Christian husbands.

The way the other women talked, I wouldn't have traded places with any of them. Three of the most outspoken members of the group were divorced. One woman was on her third marriage. The leader of the Bible study was divorced and remarried, and both her husband and ex were active in the church. Her ex had remarried, too. All these women were eager to counsel me about *my* marriage. They felt sorry for me because my husband wasn't "saved," yet I wasn't sure I didn't have the best marriage of the lot. My husband was a good, nice, gracious person. It seemed that should count for something. It meant the world to me.

But in their eyes such human qualities didn't matter. Only salvation. What someone was like *as a person* had nothing to do with it. It was something about the Christian outlook I never could understand. None of them had the slightest interest in *knowing* my husband, or knowing what I saw in him. Their inconsistency—can I go so far as to call it hypocrisy?—bothered me more than I realized at the time. It wasn't until later that I realized how shallow it made them all seem, not only as women, but spiritually shallow, too. They didn't really *care* about people. How could that not make what they called their faith seem superficial as well?

When my husband died my world was shattered. By then my mom was also gone, one of the millions who make up the breast cancer statistics of those who *didn't* benefit from early detection. My dad, still with dual citizenship, eventually returned to Oregon in the United States and went on with his life. I hadn't seen him since Mom's funeral, and he was too busy when my husband died to come to his. His lack of compassion hurt, and communication between us, never the best, drifted toward nonexistence.

During those two years of my life I discovered how little faith I had left. In fact, I began to wonder if I had really ever possessed true *faith* at all. What had it *ever* meant? I had just gone along with what everyone else believed. I had prayed to "invite Jesus into my heart" at thirteen because I knew that's what you were *supposed* to do.

It isn't that I had faked it. When you're young you *think* you're sincere. But how capable are you of knowing your deepest self, of gauging true sincerity? As time goes on, you're taught what to believe. Gradually you just accept things without thinking about them. It becomes more a *system* of belief than anything very personal. You learn the pat answers. You memorize the doctrine. You catalog the Bible verses that confirm and validate all the points of belief so there are no cracks in the system. Somehow you flatter yourself that you *know* the Bible, when in fact you've actually read probably about one two-hundredth of it and haven't a clue about its overview and bigger picture.

Of course I could remember constant talk about one's personal relationship with Jesus. But all that meant was that at some point in your life you prayed a prayer whose words someone told you to say. Where's the personal relationship in that? I was never taught how to *live*, how to *behave*, only what I was supposed to believe. How *personal* is it when you're taught exactly what to think?

I never considered any of these things when I was in the church. I just went along. It was only later, in retrospect, that I began seeing it with different eyes—seeing that the talk of *personal relationship* was really masking a pervasive blanket of conformity that actually *prevented* much personal expression of belief. At least it did in my case.

I had one weird quirk to my personality that I never quite understood. It didn't seem to fit with the rest of the me that I knew. In the same way that perhaps I had more of my mother in me than I realized, this quirk probably came from the same gene pool that led my dad to become a lawyer, to chase lost causes, to stand up for the underdog, to try to right the world's wrongs.

As contrary as it sounds, because they obviously pursue such a career for what would seem to be a love for children, teachers can be remarkably clueless to the true dynamics at work between the youngsters in their classrooms. I have worked as an aide with several teachers through the years who seemed completely taken in by their cutest, smartest, most "in" students, while remaining utterly oblivious to those less-fortunate boys and girls with real needs who were right before their eyes every day. When I started working in classrooms, and often being given playground duty, I always sought out those boys and girls on the fringe, those with special needs, even those who were looked upon as troublemakers. Once they realized that I genuinely cared about them and would listen, such children flocked to me during every recess. Most of the regular teachers had no idea why.

I certainly wasn't a campaigner for right and truth or anything else. I was generally soft-spoken. But a sense of justice for the underdog was always with me. And there came times in my life when a great sense of anger and indignation would rise up unpredictably within me against something I perceived as unfair or simply *wrong*.

Probably my interest in the unpopular children as a teacher's aide grew out of my own experience on the playground when I was young and that unpredictable Don Quixote complex suddenly came over me, and against all odds I would speak my mind without considering the consequences. Usually those consequences weren't good. Who pays attention to the shy girl on the playground who suddenly takes it upon herself to get in the face of the class bully for being cruel to one of the other children? I got more than one bloody nose and skinned knee for my trouble. It was very confusing to my sense of youthful justice to realize that not even the teachers cared about *why* I did what I did. They put the blame on *me* for causing trouble, and I, not the class bully, was the one who had to stay in at the next recess.

Fortunately, as I grew older I learned to control my occasional outrage rather than make a scene and do something stupid I would later regret. But there was one incident that occurred when I was a senior in high school that I've never forgotten and that cost me a friendship. Two of my good friends, Betsy and Clarissa, planned to go to the senior prom together and have just as much fun even though they had no dates. I didn't have a date either, but I didn't expect to and had no interest in going to the prom. Then suddenly, two days before the prom, Clarissa was invited out by one of the school's most popular guys, a football player no less, whose own girlfriend was out of town. Clarissa accepted. Betsy was terribly hurt and left out in the cold and didn't go to the prom at all. Maybe in retrospect I overreacted—who can blame a girl for accepting such a high-level date? But it was one of those times when that weird sense of justice rose up inside me and I couldn't keep my mouth shut. I angrily told Clarissa I thought what she had done was horrible. I didn't speak to her for the rest of the year. When she gave me her class picture, I tore it up right in front of her face.

Okay, it wasn't very nice of me. Was Clarissa's treatment of Betsy any worse than *my* anger and unforgiveness toward her? Obviously not. As I look back, I regret how I handled it. But it was one more example of that uncontrollable urge welling up inside me, *compelling* me to lay aside my normally reticent nature and charge forward on a white steed of truth toward some windmill of injustice that was actually none of my business.

Was it a character *strength*...or a character *flaw*?

I suppose even all these years later, I'm still not altogether sure. It's one of those double-edged swords of human nature, with a side that can be used for good, and an opposite side that can do far more damage than good. It all depends on how wisely we use such impulses.

After the incident with Betsy and Clarissa, my father, by then an attorney with a reputation for windmill-causes of his own, said to me: "Don't charge off condemning someone, or *defending* someone, unless you know the whole story. You may find yourself defending someone you wish you hadn't and who isn't as innocent as you first thought, or condemning another who isn't as guilty of wrong as you assumed. Drawing conclusions too soon, and without full information, will only result in your getting egg on your face. Nothing in human relationships is as clear as it seems."

"But I *do* believe Clarissa was wrong, Dad," I said.

"Fine. Then maybe you did the right thing, though it sounds to me like you overreacted just a tad. My only point is to look at *both* sides of anything. Then if you're sure, do what you have to do....or in the words of good old Davy Crockett—be sure you're right, then go ahead."

I probably rolled my eyes and mumbled something about how he never understood me. *Davy Crockett...good grief!*

I'm not quite sure how this personality quirk fits with the gradual loss of my faith. If I was so intent on *truth*, how did I allow myself to fall out of belief? I think that is the point—I *wasn't* that intent on truth so much as that periodically I would become very angry against some perceived injustice. That is a common thing in the world—people will fight tooth and nail against something, or give their lives to a cause without ever considering larger questions of universal truth. It is obviously foolish to try to set the world right by waging war on the evils around us, if at the same time we neglect the only part of the world that we are really capable of influencing and where our real business ought to lie—our own character, belief, and conduct.

The loss of my husband revealed how far I had already drifted. My faith *wasn't* personal. I needed faith then more than ever, but nothing was there. Rather than turning to God for comfort and consolation, I found myself throwing out to an empty universe all the bitter *whys* that are voiced at such times of loss and pain: *Why me...why him...why now...why, God, why, why, why?*

But no answers came. Heaven was silent.

I began to wonder if it was silent because it was empty.

I found no consolation at church. I couldn't bring myself to keep going. I knew my church acquaintances—it suddenly became difficult to think of them as *friends*—felt doubly sorry for me now because not only had I lost my husband, but with his being a nonbeliever, his fate was now the proverbial fate worse than death.

But no one wanted to actually talk about *that*. The big H!

What comfort could they possibly offer me, what hope? I knew they were avoiding me.

Once the funeral was over, no one reached out. None of them called. None came to visit. They all sent cards, of course—cards that spoke of *hope* and God's *love* and *mercy*, with appropriate bland passages of Scripture.

It was a little game played by Christians at the death of non-Christians, tossing around soothing words of supposed comfort, when down inside they were really thinking, *If only he had accepted the Lord before it was too late. But now there is no hope. The poor sinner is in hell being tormented forever.*

I don't know any other time when Christian hypocrisy is quite so blatant and visible as at death.

I never went to church again. I hadn't planned it that way. I just couldn't pretend that I believed in God's goodness when I saw no goodness in what had happened. I certainly found no "goodness" in the pat answers I knew I would get if I went back to church.

If so much as *one* person had called and expressed compassion, had invited me back, and been glad to see me, I probably would have resumed a life in the church. I was lonely. A genuinely compassionate friend would have meant so much. Whether that would have been enough to rescue a fading faith, who's to say?

It doesn't matter anyway. That one call never came.

The drift away from what I had once believed was gradual, but eventually complete. I didn't even have to cut the lines. They had just frayed over the years until my connections with the Christian faith were severed without my doing anything about it.

When I actually stopped believing, I don't know. There was no moment. There was no decision to reject the Christian faith. I simply woke up to the gradual realization that my belief had died long before.

Chapter Ten

Small Parish Cathedral

Oh, I'll tak' my plaidie contented tae be,
A wee bittie kilted abune my knee,
An' I'll gie my pipes anither blaw,
An' I'll gang oot ower the hills tae Gallowa'.
—"The Gallowa' Hills"

The curate's question was still ringing in my head:

"If it is not too presumptuous of me...might I ask your name?"

I shook myself back to the present. For an instant the license plate I had seen earlier flashed through my brain, and why I had reacted when I saw it.

"I'm sorry," I said. "I spaced out for a minute. No, of course not—it's Marie...Marie Buchan," I said, for some reason giving my maiden rather than my married name.

"Well, Marie Buchan," said Iain Barclay, "I am happy to officially know you at last!"

He reached out his hand almost like a formal diplomatic gesture and we shook hands.

"*Buchan*, that is an interesting name," he said. "Do you know its history?"

"Not much."

"It's Scottish."

"I knew there was a Scottish connection of some kind. I saw the name listed and Buchan tartans and everything in some of the shops. But I know nothing about it in relation to my family." I didn't mention the mysterious BMW that had passed along the street my first day in the village.

"It is as Scottish as MacDonald or MacGregor or Barclay."

"Really—that's great! Maybe I am connected to Scotland more than I realized."

"There's more. The name is associated with this very region of Scotland along the Moray Firth. This area used to be called Buchan."

"No kidding! That's really nice, since this area seemed to draw me."

"Half of Scotland, they say, immigrated to Canada in the nineteenth century," Barclay went on. "Your father is Canadian, I take it?"

"Actually, no," I replied. "My mother was. My father is from the States."

"Well, no matter. Many Scots relocated to the U.S. as well. But whenever it happened, I would give high odds that some ancestor of yours was from this area at one time.—I'm sorry, I really have to run...literally."

At last Scottish curate Iain Barclay left me and hurried down the path toward Port Scarnose. I was left with many new things to think about.

I did telephone him the next day and made arrangements for that same afternoon. Even as we walked from the parking lot toward the small building with its single steeple rising into the air, I felt a sense of quiet descending over me. The ancient stone church was surrounded by grave markers, so old and dilapidated and broken that you couldn't even read the inscriptions on most of them. Many looked well over a century old. The setting of the church, too, was unusual—out in the country a half mile, or so it seemed, from any other building.

Curate Iain Barclay led me inside. I knew instantly that he was right. It was wonderful—so old and tranquil and majestic. The architecture was the same as all the architecture of the region—sandstone and granite. But with its pillars and stained-glass windows, and its tremendous age, it was indeed like being inside a tiny country cathedral. Mr. Barclay showed me around, then said I could set up my harp anywhere and play for as long as I liked.

"I'll go outside and do some work around the garden and grounds," he said. "That won't bother you, will it?"

"I really don't mind if you listen," I said. "Music is for everyone, isn't it? Come and go as you please. It's just...well, as I told you, it will be a little strange for me to play here. I haven't been inside a church in years."

He disappeared and I saw nothing more of him. I walked around for a few minutes soaking up the atmosphere. It felt so different from any church I had been in in America or Canada. So stately. The walls were lined with plaques and engravings and monuments, large and small, to the lairds and dukes and earls of the past— Ogilvies and Grants and Sinclairs and Buchans of the region. Many of them, I presumed, were buried behind their monuments. The pews were of dark wood, old, straight, and looked uncomfortable. A balcony ran around two sides, which the curate had said was the fishermen's loft. Along an opposite wall was perched an ornately carved private miniature balcony, or box, with a single pew that looked as if it might hold six to eight people. I asked about it later. The minister said it was the duke's private box but that no one had been in it for years, not since the old duke's death.

Finally I was ready to play. I found a place near the center of the church where it seemed the acoustics would be best, and got out my harp. The moment I began I was transported into another world. It was peaceful, almost regal, as the curate had promised.

And the acoustics! I scarcely had to touch the strings and they exploded with sound.

My anxiety about playing in a church vanished in an instant. I played for more than an hour. I had such a good time. I think I enjoyed it almost as much as playing out by the sea.

When I was through I went in search of Mr. Barclay. I found him down on his knees outside, planting some flowers in a border alongside one of the church walls. He glanced up as I approached.

"You win!" I said. "It was lovely."

"I'm so glad you enjoyed it. I couldn't help hearing you all the way out here. I don't know that I've ever heard such sounds coming from within the church."

"I had decided I would make a deal with you—to play if you would tell me where the girl called Gwendolyn lives."

He climbed back to his feet, looking at me in surprise.

"You know little Gwendolyn, do you?"

"Only briefly," I answered. "She and her mother were out walking when I was playing my harp. At the bench, you know, where I saw you."

"That woman is her aunt. Gwendolyn's mother is dead."

"Oh, that's too bad. What about her father?"

He did not answer. An odd look flitted momentarily across his face, a look of pain, I thought. Quickly it passed.

"You said you *had* been going to make that deal with me," he said. "Did you change your mind?"

"In a way, I suppose. I didn't think it would be fair to place conditions on it. I will play for your service if you still want me to."

"Wonderful! This Sunday—that is only three days from now. Will that give you time to prepare?"

"It will have to be this Sunday. I will be gone in another week."

"Oh, yes, of course...I had nearly forgotten. Then this Sunday it is. And I will see if I might help you with your request," he added after a brief pause. "Gwendolyn and her aunt are in my parish, of course, but it would be awkward were I to be involved directly. I presume you go out walking in the village...let me suggest that you take your way along Fordyce Street. There are really many lovely homes there. I am confident you would enjoy it."

"Thank you, I will do that," I said. "I have just one more question—what kind of music would you like me to play...hymns, Scottish music, contemporary, traditional?"

"Whatever you like—mix it up," replied the curate enthusiastically. "I will have you play, if you don't mind, as people are coming in, then during the offering, as well as one special piece. Do you know many hymns, not being..."

"A church person?" I laughed. "Yes, I know a good many hymns."

"Ah, I see.—I have the feeling there is more to your history than you have let on."

"Perhaps."

"Then I shall look forward to hearing about it should you ever feel so inclined."

"I will keep that in mind!"

As we left the church fifteen or twenty minutes later and walked back to Iain Barclay's car, behind a high stone wall I noticed what seemed to be a huge and ornate building. I hadn't noticed it earlier, and now realized that the church wasn't altogether isolated. All I could see was portions of the top of whatever it was through the trees, and what looked like spires and turrets.

"What's that?" I asked, pointing toward it.

"That's the castle."

"What castle?"

"Castle Buchan," replied the curate. "It's where the duke lives."

Chapter Eleven

Village Gossip

Hush ye, my bairnie, my bonnie wee dearie;
Sleep! Come and close the een, heavy and wearie;
Closed are the wearie een, rest are ye takin' –
Soun' be yer sleepin', and bright be yer wakin'.

—"Hush Ye, My Bairnie"

Three days later I again found myself in the old twelfth-century church of Deskmill Parish, doing the last thing I had anticipated when I made plans to visit Scotland—playing my harp for a Presbyterian Church of Scotland worship service.

I must say, however, that I enjoyed it. I hadn't played some of my favorite old hymns for years before dusting them off in preparation a few days before. And for reasons I can't quite explain, it felt good to play them again. The people were warm and gracious and appreciative. After the service eight or ten women clustered around and introduced themselves and welcomed me to Deskmill and Port Scarnose.

I felt more a part of the community than ever.

I think it was sometime that afternoon when the realization hit me—suddenly the days were winding down. My return flight to Toronto was approaching fast.

Yet I didn't want to leave!

It was a gorgeous day and I went out walking. I passed several people who stopped and said they had seen me at church and how nice the music was.

I walked along Fordyce Street from one end to the other, keeping a look out for Gwendolyn or her aunt. But I saw neither of them.

Late that afternoon Iain Barclay came by the bed-and-breakfast for a brief visit to thank me for playing that morning.

"You were really a hit," he said. "People have been telling me all day how much they enjoyed it."

"They've been telling me, too!" I laughed. "I'm glad they liked it. I did, too."

He turned to go, then paused.

"Would you be interested in having tea with me tomorrow evening?" he asked. "Nothing fancy, just a light supper at my house."

"Uh, sure—yes, I'd like that," I answered.

"I'll come by for you. Say, around five."

"I'll be here!"

He left and I felt . . . well, happy. I don't know why. Goodness—of all the weird things in the world—I had a date with a minister!

I went out again after supper. It was a warm evening. At that time of the year in northern Scotland it didn't get dark until after eleven. *The gloamin'* it's called. There's really nothing like it on a warm night.

I walked back and forth along the headlands, first toward Crannoch, then toward Findectifeld. The waves continued flowing back and forth against the rocky shore more gently than at other times, almost as if responsive to my quiet mood. Gulls were flying about. Did they ever sleep?

As the evening advanced the sounds from the village gradually quieted and I felt alone. The air was still and fragrant, the long, slow pink of the sunset painting half the sky in gradually fading colors of the rainbow.

The events of the day, especially the church service, went round and round through my mind. I felt strangely at peace. I don't know why. I couldn't believe it had anything to do with the service. Yet as I sat that morning listening to Mr. Barclay preach, and joining in the singing of the hymns that were nothing like most of the music I had heard in any church back home, something had stirred within me.

Was it a spark of the faith I had once had coming back to life?

It was something new, something *different* from what I had known in church before.

I made my way back toward Mrs. Gauld's about ten-thirty. The whole village now seemed asleep. I wasn't afraid in the least to be out late and alone, as I would have been to walk the streets of downtown Calgary at that hour. It was *different* here. I was walking slowly, in no hurry. It was eerie in a way, so late and so quiet, and with the dying pinks and oranges of sunset still suspended out over the horizon.

As I went, I saw a sign in the window of a small cottage: "Self-Catering, For Rent—By Week or Month."

I paused and stared at the sign a few moments, then peered in through the darkened window. It seemed like a nice little place, furnished and cozy. The wheels of my brain got busy.

The next day Miss Cruickshank came for another lesson. We chatted for a while afterward. Then Mrs. Gauld fixed us tea and the three of us sat down in Mrs. Gauld's kitchen and visited for another hour.

I asked them about Gwendolyn. The two women looked at each other with expressions that both seemed to say, "Hoo muckle suld we tell her?"

"What is it?" I asked.

"It's jist, she's no weel, dear," replied Mrs. Gauld hesitantly.

"What do you mean?" I said. "Is she slow, or sick?"

"Nae body kens richt. Ever since...weel, syne the beginnin', she's..."

She looked away and didn't finish.

"She's jist nae athegither *richt*, dear," added Miss Cruickshank. "Why are ye interested in Gwendolyn?"

"I've seen her twice out walking. She played my harp for a few minutes. I think she has musical gifts."

Again the women looked at each other.

"It might be best, dear," began Mrs. Gauld, "—that is, as ye're only here a fyow mair days, nae to see her again."

"But why? I *want* to see her again."

"'Tis said she has pooers, dear—pooers best kept away fae."

"What kind of powers?"

"*Dark* pooers...fae the ither side."

Before I could reply, the kitchen door opened and a lady walked in carrying a cloth satchel. Mrs. Gauld glanced toward her.

"Oh, Tavia," she said. "I'd maist forgotten ye were comin'."

The newcomer greeted Mrs. Gauld and Miss Cruickshank.

"Tavia, this is Marie Buchan. She has been bidin' wi' me for a few days. She is fae Canada.—Miss Buchan, this is Tavia Maccallum, wha helps me wi' the cleanin'."

"Ye maun be the harp lady," said Mrs. Maccallum...or *Miss*, I didn't know which. She was stout and short, with short-cropped blond hair, full of animation and energy and with one of the prettiest smiles imaginable.

I smiled. "I suppose I am."

"Ye can start wi' the upstairs," said Mrs. Gauld.

The lady started up the stairs as we resumed our conversation, though I saw her hesitate as I spoke. She was obviously listening.

"I am still perplexed about what you were saying about Gwendolyn," I said. "You can't be suggesting...surely you're not saying that she's demon-possessed or something? Surely people don't take that kind of thing seriously, not today. She's just a sweet little girl."

Miss Cruickshank clicked her tongue knowingly.

"Things are different here, dear," said Mrs. Gauld, speaking to me almost as if she were instructing a child. "This is the land o' the Celts. The auld ways haena died oot here like they hae in much o' the rest o' the warl'. Ye've heard o' the second sicht?"

"Vaguely."

"Aye, weel young Gwendolyn has it, ye ken, an' 'tis a weel-known fact. Wi' the second sicht comes mair besides. 'Tis not always weel for those standing too close, ye ken. She had a frien', the wee lassie wha lived next door. The puir lassie was hit by a lorry oot ridin' her bicycle."

"Do they think Gwendolyn had something to do with it?"

"Oh, nae, naethin' so dreadful as a' that. Gwendolyn wasna even wi' her at the time. 'Tis jist that her aunt said that the nicht before Gwendolyn lay awake half the nicht moanin' and carryin' on, wi' visions o' a child cryin' oot, an' then the next day her wee frien' was deid."

I was getting goose bumps as I listened!

"Be that as it may," I said, "I would still like to teach her as much of my harp as I can, though I don't think she needs to be taught. She has a gift and I would like to see what she might be able to do with it."

Gradually the subject changed, and I was glad. I asked about the town and its history. Another thirty minutes flew by.

When Miss Cruickshank got ready to leave, she asked me how much I charged because she wanted to pay me for the two lessons, since I was leaving in a few days. But I couldn't take her money. Being here the way I was, meeting people, almost like part of the community in a small way, I felt so much richer than when I had arrived. There was no way I could charge her.

When I told her I almost thought she would cry. As appreciative as she was, however, every time I saw her after that, there seemed to be a change in her demeanor toward me.

Somehow I knew it was because of what I had said about Gwendolyn.

Chapter Twelve

Growth

When I've done my work of day, and I row my boat away,
Doon the waters o' Loch Tay, as the evening light is fading,
And I look upon Ben Lawers, where the after glory glows,
And I think on two bright eyes and the melting mouth below.
She's my beauteous nighean ruadh, my joy and sorrow too,
And although she is untrue, well I cannot live without her.
For my heart's a boat in tow, and I'd give the world to know
Why she means to let me go, as I sing ho-ree, ho ro.

—"Loch Tay Boat Song"

My "date" with Iain Barclay was as low-key and relaxed as every other time I had seen him. He had the table spread out with meats and cheeses and crackers and scones. As he made tea I couldn't help thinking how comfortable he seemed in the kitchen. It was a well-appointed kitchen, too. Just the way he moved around in it, opening cupboards and taking things down and setting the tea-kettle on the stove, it was clear that he spent time there. Whether he was a master chef, I didn't know, but he appeared to be a man who did his own cooking and enjoyed it.

The whole house was tidy and attractive and homey. Iain was good-looking, intelligent, educated, engaging, warm—everything a woman could ask for. I couldn't imagine why there was no *Mrs.* Barclay. Maybe curates weren't in demand as husbands in Scotland. I didn't know. I certainly had no intention of asking.

When everything was ready we sat down. I was a little surprised that he didn't pray. I didn't know what his normal habit was, but he was obviously trying to put me at ease. I wouldn't have minded. I was used to that sort of thing. It was another one of those little indications that he was...well, just a nice man. He wasn't so tied to his own traditions that he couldn't be as comfortable *not* praying so as not to embarrass someone who wasn't a Christian.

There was nothing about him that made any *show* of his religion. So he just poured out tea for us and began sipping at his cup without formality as I helped myself to oatcakes and a slice of cheese.

We talked and ate. It was relaxed and easy. Every once in a while I would stop and remind myself that I was sitting having a good time with a minister!

Iain Barclay was one of those rare individuals who was more interested in learning about others than in talking about himself. I didn't think of myself as a particularly talkative person. In groups I hadn't been one of those who monopolized conversations and turned every point on to myself. I tended to be a listener. But with Iain, after a while it began to dawn on me that I *was* doing most of the talking. He asked probing questions that drew me out. He was *interested* in me. He made me comfortable in responding and sharing what I was thinking and feeling.

Before an hour had passed, I had told him more about myself than I had anyone since my husband. It was natural. It felt good to have another person value me. It was not something I had felt much recently—valued, just as a person, as *me*.

Although I didn't tell him about my name.

The most amazing thing was that he didn't speak a spiritual word the entire time. Even when I told him about my own past and my struggles with belief and why on the day we had met I'd said I wasn't a Christian, he took it all in without a preachy response. He just nodded and replied now and then with a kind comment or another question. I could tell he was feeling with me the frustrations and uncertainties I had been through. He was empathetic, not judgmental. Not a hint, no tone or expression of criticism. Only kindness and understanding.

It was cathartic and healing, in a way, to tell the story from my husband's death till the point when I realized I no longer believed, especially to have it received so graciously. I hadn't told anyone the whole thing before.

It would be dangerously easy to become attached to such a sensitive and caring man. I told myself that I had better watch my step. *Don't forget, Marie . . . this guy's a minister!*

Finally it grew silent. I realized I had said just about everything there was to say. I drew in a deep breath and exhaled slowly. Revealing my past had felt like reliving the past ten or fifteen years all over again.

"I appreciate your being so open with me," said Iain after a quiet minute. "I can see that it was difficult for you. It's not hard to see why you decided to leave your faith."

"You don't think I was wrong?" I said.

"Right, wrong—who am I to pass judgment without having walked in your shoes?"

"That's not how most church people would respond."

"Hmm . . . perhaps," he said. "But life is a journey, a quest for truth and understanding. We are all on individual journeys. We have to find our own way. What you have told me is part of your journey, and I am sure it is not over. Neither is mine. Hungry, truth-seeking people grow and change and develop. That's what life is. So no, I do not think you were wrong. You responded to the circumstances that came to you in the way you felt best at the time. I admire your courage in trying to grow through them."

"I had not thought of it that way before," I said.

"That's what I was thinking as I listened—that you were trying to grow through your grief. I think that does take courage."

"*Grow* . . . even in losing my faith?"

"Growth is individual. Growth has no straight paths. Sometimes there are detours. But I'm sure you will get there in the end."

"Get where?" I asked.

"Where you are going." He smiled.

"That seems an unusual response for someone in your profession," I said.

"I told you I was unconventional."

"Aren't you worried about me, concerned for my soul?"

"Not a bit!" he laughed.

"Most Christians would be."

He grew serious again and thought a moment.

"You're probably right," he said, nodding slowly. "I suppose it all comes down to one's view of God."

I was surprised that he stopped and said no more. He was so reluctant to preach at me. Rather than put me on the defensive, he whetted my appetite for more.

"And?" I said after a bit with a questioning tone. "Surely you're not going to leave it at that!"

"All I meant," he said, "was that if your view of God is as a judge, then I suppose everything tends to revolve around who's saved and who isn't, and how God is going to judge you if you aren't."

"And...?" I said again.

"I *don't* view him that way."

Once more he stopped and didn't appear to be going any further. Again I laughed lightly.

"And...?" I repeated a third time.

He smiled and grew thoughtful.

"Would you like to hear how I see God?"

"I would."

He drew in a breath and thought for a few seconds.

"All right," he said. "I view God in the way that Jesus spoke of him—as a good Father waiting with open arms to receive us back home, and to love us and tell us everything is going to be all right, because he is going to make it all right."

"That's nice," I replied. "If only that was all there is to it. But even to me, someone on the outside, I have to admit that it sounds simplistic."

"Do you really think so?" said Iain in a genuinely thoughtful tone. "I think its simplicity makes it profound. Suddenly all the doctrinal complexities are swallowed up in the simplicity of a Father's love."

"If only that could be true," I said, almost wistfully.

"When I hear something like the story you've told me," Iain went on, "I feel a little of the compassion I think God feels toward all of us. It makes me realize how much he loves you. He feels the pain you have been through as only a Father can to see one of his children suffer."

"If he feels that," I said, "why did he take my husband from me?"

"Oh, Marie!" said Iain, and I could feel the pain in his voice. "*God* didn't take him from you."

"Who did then?"

"No one *took* him from you. Things like that happen. The world is full of pain and heartache. God doesn't cause it or orchestrate it. He is our refuge *from* it, but not the cause *of* it."

I heard him say the words, but they hardly penetrated. I had, I suppose, been subconsciously blaming God all this time. I said I didn't believe in him, but that didn't mean I wasn't capable of also blaming him. Mine was the schizophrenic and irrational reaction of accusational unbelief.

So it would take me some time to get my head around what Iain had just said.

In his sensitive way, Iain saw that my circuits were overloaded. He said no more in that vein. The conversation gradually drifted in other directions. I told him of my talk with Mrs. Gauld and Adela Cruickshank about Gwendolyn. He shook his head in annoyance when I told him what they had said.

"The auld wives," he muttered.

"What do you mean?" I laughed.

"A Scottish term for busybodies," he replied. "All that about Gwendolyn—it's a load of rubbish. You're absolutely right, she's just a sweet girl, a poor, sweet girl."

"Why do you say *poor*?"

He was quiet a moment. He seemed to be wondering whether he had inadvertently said more than he should have.

"It's not widely known," he said at length, "but she has a rare degenerative illness, some form of lymphoma, I believe."

"Oh, that's horrible!" I said. "Is that why she looks...I mean, is she slow?"

"No, nothing like that, though people sometimes make that assumption. It is simply the way it affects her. The disease is gradually taking its toll on her brain along with the rest of her body—you may have noticed she walks a little unevenly."

"Yes, I did."

"It is almost like the long-term effects of a degenerative stroke."

"Is there nothing that can be done?"

He shook his head. "I'm not intimately familiar with the details," he said. "Her aunt doesn't keep me well-informed because...well, that is another story we need not go into. I do know that early in her life Gwendolyn was taken to the best specialists in London. They were uniform in their prognosis that nothing could be done to reverse the progression of the disease. As far as I am aware, there have been no medical breakthroughs to alter that view."

"What is the prognosis, then?" I asked.

"It is not very pleasant," replied Iain with a sad smile. "Her body is slowly dying. She had no chance from the day she was born."

"That is heartbreaking! I had no idea. What is her life expectancy?"

"As far as I know, the median is usually about fourteen or fifteen years."

I couldn't prevent a shocked gasp escaping my mouth. My hand went to my lips.

"But she looks to be, what, almost ten already," I said, feeling a little faint.

"Actually, she is eleven, and on the long side of it. She will be twelve in another three months."

It was worse than I had imagined.

"Will it be...I mean, what..."

I didn't even know how to finish what I was trying to ask.

Slowly Iain shook his head. "No one really knows what to expect," he said. "Most of what I have heard, as I say, is secondhand

rather than through Mrs. Urquhart, Gwendolyn's aunt. As I understand it, the doctors say the end can come suddenly or gradually,
that there can be a slow deterioration or that she might one day
simply not wake up."

"That is *so* sad!" I said, slowly shaking my head in disbelief.
"Does Gwendolyn know?"

"I honestly have no idea. Children have deeper instincts than we
give them credit for. I'm sure she knows that she is different from
other children."

"What about the second sight?" I asked.

"There may be something to that," replied Iain. "I would prefer
simply to call it a keen intuition. What a child like Gwendolyn sees,
what she feels about her own future, those are questions we will
probably never know the answers to. When a child is faced with
mortality—and I think Gwendolyn must sense it, whatever she has
been told—I think it opens them to realms we are unaware of. But
as for the other nonsense that goes with it, pay no attention to it."

"You mean the dark powers and all that."

"Yes. That kind of talk infuriates me. She is simply a child dear
to God's heart. But people talk. Most of the children of the village
won't go near her. They are frightened that if they speak to her they
may wind up dead like poor Sarah MacLeod, who was hit by the
lorry. One thing they told you is true, however. This is still the land
of the Celts, and there remains more superstition floating in the air
than is healthy. People will latch on to any silly rumor if it has a
whiff of superstition or the second sight about it. Then they begin
to believe it. But they don't have the good sense to keep ancient
Celtic sorcery where it belongs—in legend."

"After what you've told me," I said, "I am more certain than ever
that I want to give her the chance to play my harp again."

Chapter Thirteen

Change of Plans

The mellow mavis tunes his lay, the blackbird swells his note,
And little robin sweetly sings above the woody grot.
There's music in the wild cascade, there's love amang the trees,
There's beauty in ilk bank and brae, an' balm upon the breeze.

—"Morag's Faery Glen"

The next day I spent the latter half of the morning walking along Fordyce Street. At last my efforts were rewarded. I saw Gwendolyn bound out of a house about fifty meters ahead of me, followed a minute later by the lady I now knew to be her aunt. I didn't feel that I should invite them to Mrs. Gauld's, after what she had said. So I would invite myself to their house!

I walked toward them. "Hello, Gwendolyn," I said as I approached.

"Hi, Harp Lady," she said. "You don't have your harp today."

"It is back where I am staying.—Hello, again," I said as her aunt came up. I reached out my hand. "My name is Marie Buchan, we saw each other the other day."

"Yes, I remember," she said, shaking my hand a little reluctantly it seemed and staring through me with a penetrating gaze. "I am Olivia Urquhart." Her voice was different from before—slow, measured, almost mesmerizing. I almost had the feeling she was trying to hypnotize me with her eyes and voice.

"Would you mind...I mean, I would like to let Gwendolyn play my harp again," I said a little uneasily. "She seemed to take to it so quickly. Would you mind if I brought it over and let her play for a while?—That is, if you would like to, Gwendolyn," I added.

81

"Oh, yes!" she exclaimed, her eyes bright. "Please, Mummy, please, may I, please!"

"I don't suppose there would be any harm," said Mrs. Urquhart slowly, obviously thinking the thing through. "We were just going out for a walk—Gwendolyn needs exercise and fresh air. She must get out of doors every day. Perhaps you could come this afternoon?"

"Yes, I would like that very much."

"Can the harp lady come with us, Mummy?" said Gwendolyn. "Come with us, Harp Lady. We are going for a walk."

I glanced toward Mrs. Urquhart. She nodded though without a smile. She was obviously not eager to have me come along.

Gwendolyn reached up and took my hand, and off we went toward the bluff and the sea.

The time passed quickly. I learned no more about little Gwendolyn than Iain had told me. She chattered away, but her aunt volunteered no additional information. I had the feeling she was subtly examining me as much as I was Gwendolyn. The more I saw of the two, the more mysterious both girl and aunt became. On our way back an hour later, I left them and returned to Mrs. Gauld's. Mrs. Urquhart told me to come to their house in about two hours, after Gwendolyn had had lunch and a rest.

When I left the bed-and-breakfast carrying my harp in its case I didn't tell Mrs. Gauld where I was going. I knew she wouldn't approve.

I reached the Urquhart house again and walked to the door. I didn't even get my finger to the doorbell. Gwendolyn had been watching for me. She opened the door before I reached the porch, then yelled back into the house, "The harp lady's here, Mummy!"

"I'm afraid she didn't have much of a rest," said Mrs. Urquhart, a little more warmth in her tone as she walked forward and invited me in. "She was too excited about your coming."

"Hello, Gwendolyn," I said. "Do you think you would like to call me Marie instead of the 'harp lady'?"

"I could if you want me to. But I like to call you Harp Lady."

"Then you may call me that, too. But my name is Marie."

Mrs. Urquhart showed me to a chair and I got out my harp. Gwendolyn's eyes were alive as she watched me pull it from the case and attach the legs and set it on the floor. I could see her fingers twitching in anticipation. I asked her to get another chair and sit down beside me. I told her a few things about the strings and how to hold her fingers. I couldn't help it—it was the teacher in me.

But I needn't have bothered. Gwendolyn was not going to be like any student I had ever had. With her, everything would be intuition. I might as well save my breath about elbows out, wrists in, thumbs up, and all the rest. She was going to play as she *felt*.

After a minute or two, I placed the harp before her, helped her get her hands around it and her fingers resting on the strings, and showed her how to lean the harp toward her. Then I scooted my chair back and waited.

Just as she had before, she began gently plucking a few individual strings, as if getting to know how it felt again. Within minutes she was beginning to play a melody and move her hands more freely. Across the room, Mrs. Urquhart stood watching. Neither of us said a word. When I snuck a peek at Gwendolyn's aunt some time later, she seemed deep in thought.

Gwendolyn played for an hour. It was absolutely magical. Not a hint of the former melody emerged in all that time. But I heard enough to convince me more than ever that nothing short of musical genius was at work. *Something* wonderful and mysterious was happening here. I sat mesmerized. The sound, the style, the intricate yet simple tunes and melodies that flowed in and out, appearing and disappearing like a constantly moving tide, were like nothing I had heard in my life.

I asked Gwendolyn's aunt if I could come back again the next day about the same time. She nodded. She seemed grateful but said nothing to encourage or discourage me. She was willing but not particularly eager. I hoped she had been touched, but she was a woman who did not allow her emotions to show.

That night, with memories of Gwendolyn's music swirling in my brain, I reached the decision I had been thinking about for two days.

I could not go home now. I just couldn't.

I needed to stay in Port Scarnose awhile longer. I didn't even know for how long. But suddenly I had a purpose. I would let Gwendolyn play on my harp every day if I could. I wanted to bring what joy was possible into her life.

I would cancel my return flight and stay in Scotland for . . . well, for a while.

The next day after making the call to the airline, I went out to the self-catering cottage I had seen. I had thought it vacant, but this time I saw a light in the window and a car in the drive. I went to the door and rang the bell.

It opened a moment later. I saw standing before me a distinguished-looking man, perhaps in his late sixties, dressed casually and wearing blue jeans. He was holding what appeared to be a Bible in one hand, with a finger between the pages where I had apparently interrupted his reading.

"Hello," I said. "I wanted to inquire about the cottage for rent. Are you the owner?"

"No," he replied. "We have just been staying here for a time."

"Oh, I'm sorry. I didn't know whether the cottage was occupied. I didn't mean to disturb you." I turned to go.

"We will be leaving day after tomorrow," the man said after me. "Would you like to come in and have a look around?"

"That is kind of you," I said. "I suppose it would be nice to see the place from the inside."

"In fact," he added with a friendly smile, "my wife will be back shortly. She just went down to the market. Why don't you come in and have tea with us? My name is Stanley Jenkins."

He was so gracious and his invitation so warm, how could I refuse?

"I am Marie Buchan," I said as I shook his hand, then followed him inside.

The next hour was one of my most enjoyable since arriving in Port Scarnose. When Mr. Jenkins's wife, Wilma, returned, I found her as friendly as her husband. Both sang the praises of Port Scarnose. When I explained my situation they encouraged me to stay longer, insisting that I couldn't do better for a place as long as I was there.

"If you like it so well," I asked, "why don't you live here in Port Scarnose?"

"We took this cottage only temporarily," replied Stanley. "We returned to Scotland recently from New Zealand and will be living in Inverurie. But our place there wasn't quite ready for us yet, so we took this cottage."

After an hour's visit I knew that I had made two more dear friends for life. I left with the owner's telephone number. I walked to a phone booth and called right then. The lady who owned the house lived about twenty miles away. I told her that I had met the Jenkins and would be interested in the house when they were gone. We made arrangements to meet.

"You probably have no towels and linens?" she said.

"No, I'm sorry, I'm afraid I don't. I didn't think of that."

"Nae' bother. I will bring some for ye. Hoo lang will ye be wantin' it?" she asked.

"I don't know," I said. "A week at least, maybe two...maybe even a month. I just don't know. I have no definite plans when I will return to Canada. I hope that will be all right."

"Of course, dear. Ye hae my telephone number. Ye can let me know."

I told Mrs. Gauld that I had decided to stay and had booked a self-catering place. She was happy for me and told me to come by if I needed anything or just to visit.

I had not seen Iain Barclay in several days. I had to tell him about my change of plans. But I felt strangely timid to see him. What would he think? Would he think I was staying because of him?

And...*was* Gwendolyn the only reason I had decided to postpone my trip home? I couldn't think about that right now!

I went to the Urquhart house every day the rest of that week. Gwendolyn's aunt, while not making a point of inviting me to come back, seemed willing enough for my visits to continue.

Within a day, word about my teaching Gwendolyn the harp began to get around town. I wasn't really *teaching* her. I wasn't even trying to. But when I walked up Fordyce Street, I was aware of stares. And when I looked out the window when Gwendolyn was playing on the third day, I saw a few people clustered about the street. I opened the front door so they could hear. No one smiled, but they listened.

As excited as she had been, I never heard from Adela Cruickshank again. Maybe she thought my harp was haunted now.

Finally I got up my courage and walked to Iain's house. It was Friday morning. Somehow I knew he would ask me to play in church again.

I was nervous. What was wrong with me? I felt like a schoolgirl!

I took a deep breath and walked to the door and rang the bell. It seemed like forever that I heard nothing. I began to hope he wasn't home and that I could dash away. I would talk to him later.

Then I heard footsteps inside and knew it was too late.

The door opened.

"Marie!" exclaimed Iain with a great smile on his face. "Come in!"

My heart was beating. I'd forgotten how red his hair was. It was all messy and uncombed, and looked wonderful.

"I'm so glad to see you," he said, leading me into his sitting room. "I'm sorry I haven't been by. I had to run into Aberdeen for church meetings two days ago. I spent the night at the home of a friend. We had meetings most of yesterday, then a dreadfully boring dinner last evening with speakers and presentations. I didn't get home until after eleven. I'm afraid I only just got up. I haven't even had my tea yet. Will you join me?"

"I don't want to intrude—"

"Intrude!" he interrupted. "Good heavens, I thought we were beyond that! If I remember correctly, you're leaving tomorrow, so this might be my last chance. Please join me."

"Well, all right. But actually—"

I hesitated as I followed him toward the kitchen where he began filling a kettle with water for tea. He turned toward me where I stood in the doorway.

"—Actually," I continued, "I'm moving out of Mrs. Gauld's this morning."

It hadn't come out exactly as I had intended.

"Oh, no!" exclaimed Iain. "You mean you're leaving today? I had hoped we could have another visit, maybe this evening."

"No, that's not exactly what I meant," I said. "I mean, what I came by to tell you . . . the thing is, I saw a place down in the lower part of town, a self-catering cottage for rent. I called about it, and I've decided to take it. So I'm moving over there this afternoon."

"But, I don't . . ." he began, staring at me with the kettle still in his hand and a look of bewilderment on his face.

"I canceled my flight home," I said with a sheepish smile. "I postponed my return. I decided to stay for a while."

His mouth opened in surprise. The next instant he bounded toward me in three great strides. Before I knew what had hit me, I found myself swallowed in an unexpected bear hug.

"That's great!" he exclaimed. "I'm so happy—"

Suddenly I gave a little cry. A shot of wet cold had flooded my back.

Iain stepped away, then, seeing the kettle still in his hand, he realized in the exuberance of his embrace that he had emptied half of it onto my dress.

"Oh, no!" he cried. "What an idiot I am—I'm sorry!"

He ran across the room, threw the kettle down and hurried back with a dishtowel in hand. He spun me around and set about patting me down. By now I was over the shock of the cold. Getting doused by a kettle of water was almost a relief. Now I didn't have to deal with the aftermath of his sudden embrace!

Poor Iain was embarrassed beyond words.

"It's all right, really," I said, starting to laugh at his frenetic activity. "It's a warm day—that's why I didn't wear a coat. I'll dry out in no time. Put the kettle on and let's have some tea."

Gradually he calmed down, muttering about what a clumsy oaf he was. But within a few minutes he was relaxing and setting the tea things on the table.

"I am sorry," he said for about the fifth time. "I was excited. It's such good news that you're staying! There's so much I want to talk to you about."

"Like what?" I said.

"I don't know, nothing definite. I didn't mean it like that. I just, you know—I hadn't...well, I hadn't had *enough*, I suppose."

"Neither had I," I said. "I haven't had enough of Scotland or Port Scarnose, and guess what? Since I saw you last I've been going over to the Urquharts every day. Gwendolyn's been playing my harp. I can't wait for you to hear her. You won't believe it! Maybe you could come with me this afternoon. I usually go over around two o'clock."

He wasn't as overjoyed about the prospect as I had expected.

"I'm not sure that would be a good idea," he said. The smile disappeared from his face.

"Why not? I want you to hear her."

"I'm sure I shall. All in good time. There are, shall we say, some difficulties between myself and Mrs. Urquhart that would be best for you to remain uninvolved in. In the interest of your work with Gwendolyn, it would be expedient if you were not to mention me at all."

I stared across the table, puzzled. I could see that Mrs. Urquhart might be considered hard as a twenty-minute egg. Yet who would not like Iain Barclay? But I asked no more questions. His tone did not invite them.

"But," he added on a more cheery note, "now that you will be here, how about playing for church again on Sunday?"

Now it was my turn to grow pensive.

"I don't think I will," I said. "Not two weeks in a row."

"You said you enjoyed yourself."

"I did, very much. I can't explain it, I just don't think I want to again so soon."

"That's fine, suit yourself. When you are ready, please tell me. I don't want to pester you by asking you every week. The invitation is a standing one. Everyone will enjoy it immensely. As will I."

I nodded and forced a smile. Funny feelings were coming over me.

"I hope you will feel welcome to attend the service," added Iain, "even without your harp. Yours truly will be occupying the pulpit again."

I couldn't help laughing.

"I will feel welcome." I smiled. "Though no guarantees. I'm still not—"

"I know, I know. You're not a church person. Disclaimers duly noted!"

Chapter Fourteen

Mysterious Churchyard

This is my Father's world, and to my listening ears,
All nature sings and round me rings, the music of the spheres.
This is my Father's world, I rest me in the thought
Of rocks and trees, of skies and seas—his hand the wonders wrought.
This is my Father's world—the birds their carols raise;
The morning light, the lily white, declare their Maker's praise.
This is my Father's world! He shines in all that's fair;
In the rustling grass I hear Him pass—He speaks to me ev'rywhere.
—Maltbie D. Babcock, "This Is My Father's World"

I left Mrs. Gauld's about four o'clock on the afternoon of my move with hugs and well-wishes and promises to come by every day. She had not seemed as disturbed about my involvement with Gwendolyn as Miss Cruickshank, though I detected a slight pursing of her lips when I told her.

After being in small bedrooms for almost three weeks, it was strange at first to have a whole place to myself. All my possessions were stuffed into one suitcase, and here I was moving into an entire house.

To have a kitchen of my own again—for a while at least—and a sitting room with a wonderful fireplace! I couldn't have been more excited. The first thing I did was move my few clothes into the dresser and wardrobe in the bedroom while the water was boiling on the stove. Then I made a fire, struggling a bit with the coal, fixed myself a pot of tea, and sat down with a book.

I thought I was in heaven!

After a while I went out for a walk. By this time I knew all the streets and lanes of Port Scarnose. It was like getting to know them all over again with a new place to come back to that I called home.

My decision felt so right. I was happy!

I had already decided to have a talk with Mrs. Urquhart. The next afternoon while Gwendolyn was playing, I got up from the chair where I was sitting and motioned her into the kitchen.

"I wanted to talk to you," I said, "about Gwendolyn."

She looked at me without expression.

"You might want to think about buying a harp for her," I went on, "so she can continue after I am gone. I could help you locate one that would be right for her if you like. I know they are expensive, but I think it would really help her."

"*Help* her?" said Gwendolyn's aunt. "What do you mean?"

"With...you know, in coping with her condition," I answered. "It seems that it would help take her mind off her sickness."

"What do you know of her sickness?" she said a little irritably.

"Nothing, really. Mr. Barclay just told me that she isn't well."

"Iain Barclay ought to keep his interfering nose out of other people's affairs. He had no right."

"He meant no harm," I said. "I asked him about Gwendolyn. He would have said nothing otherwise."

"He still had no right."

More and more I was picking up hints of some secret hovering over the community. There was more involved than mere rumors about Gwendolyn's second sight. Whatever it was had to do with Gwendolyn *and* Iain Barclay!

I didn't see Iain all day Saturday. Sunday morning came. I couldn't get my mind off him. I pictured him in his house getting ready for church.

I wondered what a minister thought about on a Sunday morning. Did he think of it as a workday? Or did his anticipation build with excitement to be in church and to see all the parishioners again?

Would he be nervous about his sermon, or eager to mount the pulpit to speak? I had never wondered about such things in my life.

But then I had never known a minister quite so well before either.

In the midst of my reflections, the shocking realization occurred to me that I was thinking about a man like a high school girl. What had come over me? And a *minister*! I had to get over this!

The whole thing was really strange. I had considered myself a nonbeliever for the last few years. I'd never gone quite so far as to admit to being an atheist. Though practically speaking maybe that's what I really was. In either case, here I was obsessing about a minister for whom talking about God was as natural as talking about the weather.

How weird was that!

The morning advanced. A few fleeting thoughts plagued me about going to church after all. But somehow I just couldn't do it. Having my harp to play before had been the ideal excuse, a perfect crutch. I had walked into the church without having to wonder about everything the church stood for, without having to think about what it all *meant*. I was there to play. That was enough.

But if I went today, I would have no crutch, nothing to fall back on, nothing to help keep my distance from that meaning. I would have to walk in and sit down in a pew and wonder what people were thinking, and wonder what I was thinking!

I wasn't ready to face all that. Not yet. And besides, I would be going for the wrong reason—just to see the minister. The *meaning* of the church, and the *implications* of my preoccupation with the man in the pulpit...those were things I couldn't face just yet.

Then why hadn't I just said that I would play again?

I wasn't sure. Something about it wasn't right. Once—that was okay. I had done that as a favor to Iain. But to keep doing it—when I knew, even if the people listening didn't, that I didn't believe in what it was all about, didn't believe in the words of the very hymns, I couldn't do it. It would have been hypocritical.

Having tea and talking to Iain Barclay was one thing. He was pleasant. No pressure. No expectations. I enjoyed him. Why not admit it? I liked him.

But sitting in the church without an excuse, naked, exposed, vulnerable—that meant having to deal with God, with whether he existed, or whether the church and all it stood for, including a nice man like Iain Barclay, was just a sham.

With God—if he was real—there was no place to hide. There were no excuses, no crutches.

It was just you and him.

No, I wasn't prepared for that. I didn't want to pretend I was something I wasn't.

About ten-fifteen I heard the church bells ringing in the distance. The sound made me feel lonely in my new little Scottish cottage. I felt like I *ought* to be there. But I didn't *want* to be there. That's where people were—life, singing, happiness...and Iain Barclay's cheerful smile and exuberant enthusiasm for everything the church stood for.

And here I was alone.

I went over to my harp where I had set it up in a corner and tried to play. But something was missing. I couldn't stop thinking about the church service and the fact that I wasn't there. I pictured Iain standing in the pulpit. I wondered what he was talking about. Were people paying attention or sleeping?

I hate to admit it, but I wondered if he had thought of me at all during the morning the way I was thinking about him.

The hour dragged slowly by, more slowly than if I were actually sitting in a boring church service, though I doubted if any of Iain's were boring. It was a relief when eleven-thirty came and I knew the service was over. Yet I still felt out of sorts.

I tried to read, I tried to play my harp, I fixed myself a light lunch, I tried to take a nap, I went for a walk. But nothing worked. Something didn't feel right. I couldn't escape the feeling of being drawn by the church even though the service was over and I hadn't gone.

About three that afternoon I took my harp out to my rental car and drove out of town. I knew where I had to go. I had to make right what had been wrong all day.

I drove toward the small Deskmill church, relieved that there were no cars about. There wasn't a sign of life anywhere.

I parked and got out, quietly taking in the scene. I felt calm inside, at peace for the first time that day. In the same way as on the first day I had come to Port Scarnose when I had known I would play my harp above the sea, I knew that I had to play again at this church.

I had to play today.

I made my way around the church through the broken and dilapidated grave markers, collecting my thoughts. Something here made me feel peaceful and calm. I returned to the car, got *Journey*, and walked again toward the church. I tried the front door. It was locked and I was disappointed. I went around to the side door, but it was locked, too.

I looked around and found a sturdy-looking horizontal slab of stone. Surely it would hold me. I took out my harp, screwed on the legs, set it on the ground, and slowly began to play.

The first notes that came out were from the opening line of the old hymn "This Is My Father's World." I hadn't planned it. My fingers just played.

I loved that hymn. It had always spoken to me so deeply about the wonders of creation.

As I played, a completely new thought crashed into my brain like a wave breaking on the jagged rocks of the coast at high tide.

Who was I playing for *right now*?

Was all this just for me? If so, then why the old churchyard? Why had I come *here*? And why an old hymn about God?

Was I as alone as it seemed? Was there really no one else to hear me?

Or might I be playing for someone Else?

If I was playing for *Him*—if he *was* up there somewhere and by some chance could hear me, that was a thought altogether too big to take in.

A few goose bumps crept up my spine. Maybe I believed in God more than I thought.

I tried to shake such questions from my mind and just enjoy the music.

I suppose it should not have surprised me that what came out of my harp continued mostly to be hymns. I was surprised how many I knew from memory. The sound didn't carry the same as inside the building, yet there was something eerily wonderful about sitting on a gravestone playing all by myself in the middle of an ancient church cemetery. I was surrounded by dead bodies lying under the ground all around me. I remembered a Bible verse, something about a cloud of witnesses. I found myself wondering peculiar things like whether the souls of any of these people whose bones were here might be hovering about listening to me. It was a little spooky.

Maybe I was playing for a congregation after all, a congregation of dead people. If there were harps in heaven... *if* there was such a place as heaven... I wondered what my feeble little earthly harp sounded like to the spirits who might have come down and listened to me.

After a while my fingers stilled. It was deathly quiet. It was almost as if the birds in the trees had all left, or had stopped singing so they could listen, too.

I sat for a minute or two just drinking in the silence.

Suddenly I heard a crack, like the breaking of a twig. It had come from across the churchyard. I glanced toward the sound but saw nothing. My first thought was of a large bird—hundreds of crows lived in the surrounding trees—or perhaps a deer in the woods.

Then I heard footsteps. Still I saw no one. The sound must be coming from the other side of the stone wall bordering the church property. Whoever it was walked quickly away and the footsteps faded. Several seconds later came a few steps crossing gravel, very faint in the distance, and the dull thud of a door closing.

Then silence returned.

I got up, left my harp by the stone, and crossed the churchyard to the wall. It was six and a half or seven feet tall, too high for me to see over even if I jumped. I climbed up on one or two of the horizontal grave markers like the one I had been sitting on. All I could see were the few parts of a roof—turrets and towers and such—on the other side that I had seen before.

By now my curiosity was up. If someone had been listening to me from over the wall, I wanted to know what kind of place it was!

I walked along, inspecting the wall to see if there were any breaks where I could get a glimpse through to the other side. There weren't.

At last I came to a section of the wall where the overcoating of mortar and plaster had aged so much that it was falling away, revealing the rough stones beneath. I stretched my hands to the top of the wall, which I could easily reach, then put one foot on one of the stones and tried to pull myself up. I managed to keep my foot on it and slowly climbed up the rough stones of the wall, hanging on to the top with my hands and elbows. After a good amount of work, and a few scrapes on my forearms, I succeeded in getting my head up to the top of the wall, just high enough to peer over.

The sight that met my gaze took my breath away.

Stretching out in all directions was the most beautiful park and grounds imaginable. Nicely trimmed lawns and gardens and hedges and ponds went on, it seemed, for acres. Widely spaced majestic oaks and beeches spread out great huge branches like a giant canopy over portions of it. In the middle of it all rose the most spectacular stone castle, looking like something out of a fairy tale. Its roof comprised steep angles and towers and turrets and parapets running all the way around. It was a U-shaped building like many of the castles I had seen, taller than it was wide, of light sandstone blockwork, austere yet somehow inviting. It was not a fortress, but a Disneyland castle.

Quickly my arms became tired holding on to the top of the wall. I jumped back to the ground and returned to my harp with much to think about. My playing at the church was done for the day.

It didn't cross my mind until I was getting ready for bed that night that this was supposed to be the day I spent on an airplane between London and Toronto.

Chapter Fifteen

Invitation

Has your dearest friend beguiled you?
Wife or sweetheart looked askance?
Has the gossip's tongue reviled you?
Drown the thought with song and dance.

—"Hark! How Skinner's Fiddle Rings"

Two days later, the Tuesday when I should have been back in Canada recovering from jet lag, I was in for the biggest surprise yet of my trip.

I take that back, my second biggest surprise, following closely on the heels of Iain Barclay's red head popping up near where I sat on the bench overlooking the sea.

At eleven in the morning a car drove up and stopped in front of my little cottage—an expensive car. Sleek and black, it looked like someone's personal limousine. I had the curtains drawn and was playing my harp in the window, where I could just catch a glimpse of the sea through the houses on the other side of the street. I kept playing until the car drove up and caught my eye.

I had seen that car before!

A man stepped out, dressed in a chauffeur's uniform, complete with black-billed cap. He walked to my door and pressed the bell.

I got up to answer it, *very* curious and a little spooked by seeing the car again.

"Good day, ma'am," the man said in perfect polished Queen's English, like nothing I had heard in Scotland. "You are, I believe, Miss Buchan."

"Yes," I said slowly.

"If you will forgive the liberty," he said, "I called for you at the bed-and-breakfast, where Mrs. Gauld was good enough to direct me here."

"I see."

"I have come from Castle Buchan on behalf of the duke. He has learned that you are a harpist. He asked me to deliver this."

The man handed me an envelope.

"It is a request to play for him at the castle tomorrow," he went on. "He asked me to convey that he would be most appreciative if you would accept, and to tell you that I will return for you tomorrow at this same time for your answer, and, if you consent, to take you to the castle. You will be remunerated, of course."

Castle *Buchan*, I thought to myself. That explained the license plate I had noticed on my first day.

The man nodded, then turned around and walked back to his swank BMW and drove off, leaving me standing a little bewildered with the unopened envelope in my hand. Before I could read what was inside, I saw Mrs. Gauld hurrying toward me along the walk. On her face was an expression of urgent anxiety. I waited and smiled as she came up.

"Fit did that man want?" she asked.

"He gave me this," I said, showing her the envelope. "Apparently the duke wants me to play for him at the castle. Who is he, anyway?"

"Naebody ye want tae be foolin' wi', dear," said Mrs. Gauld. " 'Tis why I came, tae warn ye. I suspected somethin' like this the moment ye took up wi' the wee bairn. Naethin' guid can come o' it."

"But what is it all about, Mrs. Gauld?"

"Jist that wee Gwendolyn is the duke's daughter."

I stared at her with eyes wide in amazement.

"Though some fowk say different," Mrs. Gauld went on, inching closer to me and lowering her voice. " 'Tis nae evidence in the ither direction except the color o' her hair. That winna go far in court.

An' I say that fitiver po'er the girl's got comes fae her father, wha's in league, they say, wi' worse than fallen angels. 'Tis the curse that's the root o' it—the curse that came when the lassie's mither died, an' was passed tae her fae him."

"Why does she live with Mrs. Urquhart?" I asked.

"She is the duke's sister. She grew up as a lassie in the castle but married a man in the village, wha the duke had nae use for. The moment the lassie was born he disowned her. Wi' his wife deid, puir lass, he was bitter an' a' kennt immediately there was somethin' wrong wi' her. The bairn nearly died, too, that verra nicht like her puir mither. Whether it was fae the sickness or the red hair, which she had fae the first, he refused tae hae anything tae de wi' her. Her aunt took her in. He hasna laid eyes on her sae lang syne."

"That's terrible," I said. "So the poor girl has no mother and a father who has disowned her?"

"Ay, he's an ill man. He owns half the town an' makes nae frien's wi' his high rents. But we canna stan' here talkin' aboot sich things on the street, lass. Invite me in for a cup of tea, an' I will tell ye the rest. I said naethin' afore because there wasna need for ye tae ken. But wi' the evil man trying tae get ye into his lair, if somethin' was tae happen tae ye I wadna forgie mysel'. Ye're a nice lass. Someone's got tae tell ye."

Chapter Sixteen

No Audience

Sure, by Tummel and Loch Rannoch and Lochaber I will go,
By heather tracks wi' heaven in their wiles; if it's
thinkin' in your inner heart
Braggart's in my step, you've never smelt the tangle o' the Isles.
Oh, the far Coolins are puttin' love on me, as step I wi'
my cromak to the Isles.
—"The Road to the Isles"

I didn't learn much more from Mrs. Gauld than what she had already told me. That was astounding enough. Now I had more reason than ever to continue visiting little Gwendolyn with my harp.

After she was gone, I opened the envelope and took out the card, gold embossed on front with what I assumed were the duke's initials: *A T R*. Inside I read a simple typed message:

It would bring me great pleasure for you to play your harp for one hour at Castle Buchan, twelve o'clock, noon, the eighth of July.

A. T. R., Duke of Buchan

Even after what Mrs. Gauld had told me I saw no reason not to accept, though from the little I had learned I was prejudiced against this man *A T R*, whoever he was. Furious would be more like it.

But why turn down a paying gig? How much trouble could I get in? The chauffeur had seemed nice enough.

Maybe it would pay for another few days in Scotland.

Perhaps if I played at the castle I would get the chance to tell him what I thought of a man who would refuse to see a daughter as sweet as Gwendolyn who had an incurable disease.

If only I could get to the castle and back without anyone in town knowing about it. I didn't want to become the object of village gossip *myself*!

I was already discovering, however, that such a luxury would probably not be afforded me.

I went to the Urquharts again that afternoon. I couldn't help looking at both Gwendolyn and her aunt differently after what Mrs. Gauld had told me. But I said nothing about what I had heard. I did tell them, however, that I would be away the following day and would not be able to come, but would resume the day after that.

Even though I was technically booked only from twelve to one, I thought it best under the circumstances not to have two engagements, so to speak, back-to-back. Though playing when I was by myself energized me, I found that playing for others exacted an emotional, even a physical, toll. I always needed some downtime afterward to mentally relax and regroup.

Later that afternoon I went through my music notebook to gather together and brush up on an hour's program of music. I had no idea what kind of an audience I would be playing for the next day—the duke and a few friends, the duke alone, in a formal setting or providing informal background music for a garden party. So I selected an assortment, mostly Scottish dances and ballads, a few familiar classical pieces, and two or three pop tunes that always seemed to liven up an audience, either from the Beatles' repertoire or Hollywood themes. I put together about an hour and a half's assortment of music, knowing that I would make my final selections as I felt suited the occasion.

By eleven the following morning I was sitting in the living room at the window, in my nicest shoes and dress, my hair styled as neatly as was possible, my harp tuned and in its case, waiting for the black BMW to arrive. I didn't want to waste any time once the chauffeur appeared. I didn't know if Mrs. Gauld took her duties as "auld wife" seriously enough to spread word of the invitation around the village. I had fantasies of people standing behind curtains watching my little cottage from every window up and down the street! I had a good idea Mrs. Gauld herself would be watching. No doubt the duke's car was instantly recognized wherever it went.

The black BMW limo came into view and stopped on the street in front of my house at eleven-thirty. The chauffeur wasn't halfway to the house before I was out the door with my harp. I wanted to give the neighbors as little opportunity for gawking as possible.

He nodded as he saw me, then turned halfway up the walk and led me back to the car without a word. He opened the trunk, or boot as they call it, and helped me set the harp and my bag of music and supplies inside. Then he opened the back door for me, I got in, he returned to the front seat behind the wheel, and we were off.

We drove down the street, then he turned and made his way through the village and out toward the main road. Of all the routes we might have taken, with chagrin I saw that we were driving right past Mrs. Gauld's bed-and-breakfast! As I expected, there she stood in her yard at the gate.

I shrank down in the seat even though the windows were tinted. As we passed I could almost feel her eyes squinting at the duke's car. From the direction it was going, I knew she knew I was inside.

I hadn't taken her advice. I had the feeling I would hear about it sooner or later.

From the route we followed, I would never have expected to wind up within miles of the Deskmill Parish Church. Our way led out of town, along the main road a short distance, then off on a single-track road through fields where pigs were rooting or grazing or whatever it is pigs do. On the other side of the road stretched lush green fields of growing grain of some kind.

We passed the buildings of a large farm, continued to wind through planted fields and pastureland, the pigs giving way at some point to cows. We crossed a stone bridge, turned sharply and entered a dense wood. We wound through trees for perhaps a quarter mile before the gardens and parkland I had seen from the other side of the stone fence opened in front of us. There stood the castle majestically in the midst of the grounds.

The sight was all the more stunning from this direction. That we were anywhere near the church I found remarkable. Yet to my right I saw the stone wall bordering the castle grounds. I could just make out the familiar steeple of the church through the trees on the other side.

The car pulled into a gravel entryway, the tires crunching like the footsteps I had heard on Sunday afternoon. We came to a stop directly in front of the castle. The chauffeur got out, walked around and helped me from the car, got my harp from the boot and, carrying it for me, led me toward the huge oak front door.

I glanced about feeling entirely awed. Up close the castle seemed even more from a fairy tale than it had from over the fence a hundred yards away.

As the door opened we were met by a woman about my own age. As her eyes rested on my face, for the briefest moment I saw a flicker of what almost looked like relief. But just as quickly she pulled it back inside and it was gone.

"This way, miss," she said in a friendly though reserved voice. "I will show you where you may put your things and set up your instrument."

She led the way and I followed, with the chauffeur and my harp bringing up the rear. I found myself walking through a wide entryway that alone would have swallowed my little self-catering cottage, up a wide and majestic circular wood staircase, then left into an expansive corridor running the length of the first floor. We passed a set of ornate oak double doors on my left, then slowed as we approached another similar set of doors to my right. The lady opened them and showed me into a grand room that looked like it might have served as library and lounge or even a music room. Two walls were lined from floor to ceiling with books. All about the room were couches and easy chairs, various desks and lamps and settees, and a grand piano. It was a long rectangular room, at one end of which a series of tapestried dividers were spread across the width of the room, dividing the far quarter from the main room. What was on the other side I could not tell, though several enormous tapestries were hanging on the walls above the height of the dividers. I could only make out the tops of them.

"You may put your harp here, miss," said the woman, indicating a straight-backed chair next to a lamp and a small wooden table where sat a pitcher of water and a glass. "Is there anything else you need?"

"I don't think so," I replied. "Will I be playing here?"

"Yes," she answered, then glanced at a large grandfather clock against one wall. "You may begin playing as soon as you are ready."

The chauffeur had set down my harp on the carpet, handling it with uncharacteristic gentleness, I thought, for a man who, I presumed, had had no experience with harps. He then left the room. The woman now left me also, and I was alone.

I found myself a little intimidated as I glanced about. I couldn't help staring. The place was absolutely stunning, every bit the equal of anything I had seen in the few castles I had toured during my first week in Scotland. The paintings and tapestries and books and antique furniture, not to mention the grand piano, in this room alone must have been worth a million pounds!

It was silent as a tomb. Yet what a setting to play my harp in.

I still had no idea who I would be playing for. But I had been in similar situations before where they wanted music in progress as the first guests began to enter. So I got out *Journey* and put on the legs and set up my music stand and set the notebook I had put together for the day on it. Then I set about tuning.

When at last I was ready I glanced at my watch. It was five minutes till noon.

I started with "The Road to the Isles." I realized I was just playing to myself for the moment, but I wanted to be well into the rhythm and flow of it when people started coming in.

During my second time through it, I paused while the grandfather clock went through its Westminster sequence, then emitted twelve somber chimes. I continued, then followed my first selection with "The Dark Island" and "Will Ye No Come Back Again." There was still no sign of anyone.

This was a little strange, I thought. But I kept going.

Fifteen minutes later came the quarter-hour Westminster tune and I was more bewildered than ever.

By twelve-thirty I was thinking that it was more than a little strange...it was *really* strange. I was playing to an empty house!

I went through my songs one by one. At least it was a good practice session, although I hardly needed to get dressed up in my nicest outfit for this. By quarter till one I was seriously wondering what was going on, whether I'd misunderstood something. But I knew I had the time right, and the lady had told me to start playing. So I kept on.

At one o'clock on the dot, I heard a door open and close somewhere. I glanced toward the sound as I kept playing. It had come from the end of the room screened off with the tapestry dividers.

Almost the next instant, the door I had come through opened and the lady walked in. She waited until I had finished "Eleanor Rigby," hardly an appropriate song to end with, and difficult enough on a lever harp with all its accidentals, but that's what I was playing at the time. Then she walked toward me.

"The duke thanks you very much," she said. "You may gather your things. Nicholls will be with you in a moment to help you down to the car and take you home."

She turned and left without another word. I saw nothing more of her.

A minute or two later the chauffeur came in and picked up my harp case, and I followed him with my bag from the room and downstairs and outside.

Three minutes later I was again riding along the wooded drive, this time away from the castle, wondering what this had all been about, and if I would ever see the place again.

I had come to Scotland to have an adventure. This certainly qualified! I would be able to get a lot of mileage out of this story. But whoever this duke was, I was more irritated at him now than ever.

Nicholls—it was nice to be able to call *someone* connected with the castle by name—stopped in front of my cottage. He got out, carried my harp to the front door, set it down, and handed me an envelope. I waited until he was gone and I was inside before opening it. It contained two one-hundred-pound notes.

Whatever it had been about, it was certainly the best-paying gig I'd ever had.

This was three times my going rate!

Chapter Seventeen

Wakings

I love a lassie, a bonnie, bonnie lassie,
She's as pure as the lily in the dell,
She's as sweet as the heather,
The bonnie bloomin' heather,
Mary, ma' Scotch Bluebell.

—"I Love a Lassie"

I half anticipated seeing Mrs. Gauld walking along the pavement as we drove up, descending upon me like a stern mother-priestess of rebuke. Even after I was safely inside, I kept expecting to hear her at the door any minute wanting a full report. But no inquisitorial visit came.

I sat down in an easy chair and sighed, trying to take in what had happened. Even though I had had no audience, at least not one I had seen, I still felt drained. Uncertainty and confusion can be as taxing as physical exercise. Gradually I dozed off.

When I woke up I was ready to get out into the fresh air and put the morning behind me. I changed my clothes, munched down a couple of oatcakes, then grabbed my harp and set out. I hadn't been to the bench on the bluff for almost a week. I drove to the edge of town and from there set out along the familiar path.

Strange to say, as I played I felt soothed, the familiar peace of this place returning to me. No Gwendolyn appeared. No red-haired curate popped up from out of nowhere. Just the fragrant sea breeze and gulls and the North Sea spreading out before me.

I could not be in this spot, however, without thinking of Iain Barclay. This was Wednesday. I hadn't seen him since Friday. I *wanted* to see him. I wanted to ask him about Gwendolyn and the duke. I wanted to tell him about my strange experience at the castle.

He was not the kind of man from whom you could hide things or keep secrets. I knew that if I saw him I would feel compelled also to tell him that I had gone to the church on Sunday afternoon, had played in the cemetery, and had had the odd sensation that I was being listened to—by God or dead spirits or somebody. For some reason, I was shy about telling him all that. It would open up too many of my own uncertainties about where I stood with God. I wasn't ready for that.

After playing for a while, then taking a drive along the coast toward Fraserburgh, I had barely reached my cottage when the doorbell rang.

Oh, no, I thought. *Mrs. Gauld! Here comes the third degree about my jaunt out to the castle.*

I drew in a deep breath and went to the door.

"Iain!" I exclaimed when I saw him standing there. The relief and delight on my face must have been obvious.

A smile spread across his lips. "Wow!" he said. "That is quite a greeting, more than I expected!"

"What do you mean?" I said, laughing lightly.

"I thought maybe you were upset with me."

"Why would I possibly be upset with you?"

"I don't know—I haven't seen you for so long. Here," he said, handing me a tiny bouquet of white and purple, so small I hadn't even noticed him holding it. "I brought you this as a peace offering."

I took it and held it close. "They're lovely, thank you," I said. "It looks like . . . is it heather?"

"The genuine article—*erica calluna vulgaris.*"

"But it's so early, it's only July. I've seen no hint of the hills blooming yet."

"True, mostly it's a month or two away. But if you know where to look, and get down on your hands and knees, a few early varieties are beginning to poke their shy heads out. That's why the bouquet is so small—there isn't much of it."

"That makes it all the more special. Thank you! But what do you mean, a peace offering?"

"I just hadn't seen you. I didn't know what to think."

"I'm sorry," I said. "I wasn't upset about anything, believe me. I was a little embarrassed about not going to church. I felt funny, like I should have. I thought you might be disappointed with me. Then—"

I stopped and sighed.

"—Then something came up and...it's a long story. I've been distracted for a few days. But come in. Would you like some tea?"

"That sounds great. So, what has been going on, anything you'd care to tell a friend about?"

He followed me into the house and on toward the small kitchen. I put water on to boil.

"I suppose I would," I said in reply to his question. "Mrs. Gauld would probably like me to tell her. But I think I'm in her doghouse."

Iain roared. "In the doghouse with one of the locals. Ha, ha! That is hilarious!"

"Why hilarious?"

"It just struck me as funny. In a place like this—where half the population lives within a few miles of where they were born, you're always bound to be stepping on *someone's* toes. The roots of everything go deeper than meet the eye. Wheels within wheels, you know. I'm *always* in somebody's doghouse."

"You're a minister, that's different. I'm just a visitor."

"Not anymore. If you've managed to offend one of the stalwarts of the village like Mrs. Gauld, you've graduated beyond visitor to the status of incomer. But please, it's my turn to set the record straight, too. I was *not* disappointed with you for not playing or attending church."

"I knew you weren't, not really," I said, glancing down, embarrassed now that I had said anything. "You...well, I just knew that you wouldn't be. Yet I couldn't help feeling that way. You know how sometimes you *feel* things that you know logically aren't true?"

"Sure, it happens all the time. But just so you will know beyond any doubt—whether someone goes to church or not, I cannot tell you of how little consequence that is to me. Especially if I am preaching."

"I'm not sure I understand what you mean. Why when you're preaching?"

"Only that I've never been overly impressed with my own importance," replied Iain. "As a minister, my job is to *serve*. What do I think, that my golden words are so important that people have to come every Sunday and hang on my every word? I don't take myself that seriously! Mostly I just want to be there for people—like I said, to serve."

"*Serve*...how do you mean that exactly?" I asked.

"A good question," Iain replied. "I might have to think about that one for a while. Off the top, I would say that my desire is to help people in their own personal spiritual journeys. Of course, service has its practical element—cups of cold water to the thirsty, blankets and clothes and food for the needy. That is an integral part of the church's role, too. But I have always found the greater challenge is waking people's spirits to seek God for themselves. Waking people out of spiritual lethargy—that is no easy matter. If I can help do that, then to me that is true service."

If I let them, his words could hit close to home. I knew he wasn't directing them at me, but I could hardly help making the connection.

"In doing that," I said, "aren't the words you speak in church important?"

"To a degree, of course. But a sermon Sunday morning in a church has to be one of the worst possible settings for helping people come awake. Overall, I rate my sermons just about at the *bottom* of the list of important things about my job. My expectations in church itself are limited. If I can plant a few seeds that stick, I will be pleased."

"What would be a better setting than church?"

"It's different for everyone. Growth within the human heart is completely individual. God is in the business of waking people up. It's all about finding truth, walking in integrity, becoming who we're meant to be, discovering who God is. Those are the things that matter, not whether we're in church from Sunday to Sunday. If church helps someone get there, if anything I happen to say or do helps someone get there, then I am happy. Getting there is the goal, not the particular pathway one person or another happens to take along the way.

"Of course," he continued, "I would love to have you play for services again. But as far as the rest, your own journey of faith or belief, or whatever you want to call it, I respect that individual process too much to interfere with it. I am honored that you have shared with me what you have. You have allowed me to be part of that journey with you. I hope you will never think of me as a minister who is urging anything upon you. I hope you will think of me only as a friend."

I did not know how to reply. This man continued to surprise me! That he was sharing so personally about his own perspectives on belief, when I had as good as told him I didn't believe in any of it, was remarkable. I hadn't thought about these kinds of things for a long time. And I certainly hadn't talked so much to anyone in years—especially a man. But it felt good to talk and think. I suppose in a way I was emerging from the fog I had been in for the last six years.

"Uh...thank you," I said, trying to smile. "You've helped me already. It's been good just to be able to talk about things of belief again, without any pressure, and to try to put my past into some kind of perspective."

"You'll have to tell me about that past someday, *if* you want to. I am intrigued. But now do you want to tell me why you're in Mrs. Gauld's doghouse?" asked Iain.

I laughed at his abrupt change of subject. He was determined not to force the conversation toward spiritual things unless I initiated it.

I told him about the invitation to play at the castle, and Mrs. Gauld's visit, although omitting what she had said about the duke and Gwendolyn. The moment I mentioned the duke, Iain's mood seemed to change. He grew quieter and more thoughtful. I wondered if he was going to give me the same dour warnings Mrs. Gauld had.

"What happened?" he asked.

"I decided to go anyway," I said. "I couldn't help it—I was curious. To play in a castle...that kind of opportunity doesn't come along every day. So I went."

"How was it?"

"Weird!" I laughed. I told him about the concert with no audience.

He nodded, looking as if nothing I was saying surprised him.

"The duke is something of a recluse," he said. "I have no doubt that he was listening to you from behind the dividers."

"Do you really think so?"

He nodded. "Actually, I know the castle fairly well," he said. "I am familiar with the room you were describing. There is a separate sitting area on that far side of the room with its own private entrance. Unless the entire room is needed for a large gathering—and to my knowledge there has not been anything like that for years—it is usually partitioned off exactly as you saw it. The duke was no doubt sitting out of sight sipping a whisky and soda and able to hear you perfectly."

"That's a little creepy!" I said. "I had no idea. Why is he like that? He sounds like Howard Hughes or something."

Iain did not answer immediately. He glanced away. "Like I said," he responded after a few seconds, turning back toward me, "in a small village like this...wheels within wheels."

Somehow I knew his cryptic answer had to do with Gwendolyn. But something kept me from probing further right then. Again Iain turned the conversation quickly in another direction.

"Have you done Aberdeen?" he asked.

"What do you mean, *done* it?"

"You know—walked the mat as they call it, explored the city, toured it?"

"No," I replied. "When I was driving about before, I was nervous about the cities. I didn't go near Glasgow or Edinburgh and got out of Inverness as soon as possible."

"Aberdeen is wonderful! How would you like to drive in with me on Saturday? It's only a little over an hour. We'll make a day of it. I'll show you around, we'll walk Union Street and have an early tea and be back home by eight, in time for me to get my beauty sleep before church the next morning."

"Ministers worrying about their beauty sleep!" I laughed. "Now I've heard everything."

"A bad figure of speech!"

"You don't have to work on your sermon on Saturday?"

"I don't work on sermons. I have an idea of what I think God wants me to say and a general outline of my progression of thought. Other than that, I let the Spirit lead, as the saying goes. So what do you say...Aberdeen?"

"Yes—that sounds like fun. I'd love to."

Chapter Eighteen

Picturesque Guide

Oh, the auld hoose, the auld hoose,
What tho' the rooms were wee,
Oh, kind hearts were dwelling there,
And bairnies fu' o' glee.
And wild rose and the jessamine
Still hang upon the wa'
Hoo mony cherished memories
Do they sweet flow'rs reca'.

—"The Auld Hoose"

I'd bought most of the postcards and guidebooks and local para-phernalia that I had seen in the various shops of Port Scarnose and Crannoch. Not only were the Scots proud of their history, they were proud of their towns. Every village boasted posters and mugs and booklets and pens and keychains and maps and fridge magnets as if it was Britain's number one tourist destination. Yet down the road five miles was another village with its *own* range of touristy, historical products making the same claim! I had never seen anything like Scotland's extreme pride of place—*every* place—in Canada or the U.S.

There was, however, something distinct about Port Scarnose and Crannoch. The presence of Castle Buchan and its historic role in Scotland's past, along with the "Auld Kirk," gave a stature and prestige to the region that was unique. The beautiful coastline, with its impressive bay and beach suitable for swimming and dolphin watching, completed the package. Ever since my arrival I had been perusing my stack of local books—*Leisure Trails Around Port Scarnose*, Duncan Wood's *Crannoch, A Pictorial History, Heritage*

Tales, More Heritage Tales, Recollections of the Past, and James
Addison's wonderful walking CDs and pamphlets.

The Crannoch, Deskmill, and Port Scarnose Heritage Group,
who had published most of the books, had been busy!

Because of my love for the sea, nearly all my walks had been in
one direction or another along the coastline. When I woke up the
next morning to a warm sunny day, however, the fragrance of newly
cut hay and straw from inland drew me. While still lying in bed, I
heard the far-off lowing of a cow. I knew that the harvest would
soon be under way on the farms throughout the region. The fields
of grain were rich with golds and yellows and browns. I decided
that on this day I would strike out on one of the inland trails
toward the three local "bins," or hills, that stood overlooking the
three coastal villages—Little Bin, the Bin of Crannoch, and the Hill
of Maud.

None of them were high. The tallest, Crannoch Bin, was only a
thousand feet above sea level with an easy walker's trail circling
around to the top. Yet the brochure said it was high enough to
command a view along the coast of the Moray Firth all the way
from Lossiemouth to Logie Head, and on a clear day across to the
northernmost reaches of Sutherland on the far side of the firth.
With binoculars on the right day, some said, you could even see the
Orkneys.

I set out about ten. As I left the village, walking toward me was
a lady whose plump frame and blond hair I thought I recognized.

"Hello," I said, slowing as we reached one another, "aren't
you . . . it's Mrs. Maccallum, isn't it, from Mrs. Gauld's."

"Yes, mum—I'm Tavia Maccallum." She nodded, and immediately
I remembered her smile. "An' ye're Miss Buchan—I mind meetin' ye.
But I'm nae *Mrs.*, ken—I'm nae married."

"And I'm not *Miss* either." I smiled. "*Or* a missus. I'm a widow,
actually. My husband died several years ago."

"Oh, I'm sorry, mum."

"Thank you. Were you out for a walk?"

"Jist up tae the cemetery, there up the main road, ken," she said, glancing behind her. "I was jist puttin' some wee flo'ers on the stanes o' my daddy's grave. 'Tis his birthday the day."

"Oh, I see. How long has he been gone?"

"Mony a year, ken. He died fan I was yoong. But I mind his birthday ilka year. Ye're oot for a walk yersel'?"

"Yes"—I nodded—"I usually walk along the headland there, between Findectifeld and Port Scarnose. Today I thought I would go the other direction and see some of the farmland and hills."

"Oh, aye, 'tis a fine day for it. It wid be bonnie fae the Bin the day. But mind yer step as ye gang—tis a crazy man wha bides jist this side o' the Bin in a wee hoosie wi' a curse on't. Ye dinna want tae gang near *him*. His lassie deid mony a year syne, an' he's niver been o' a richt mind syne. Cursed wi' the livin' deith, they say... waitin' a' these years tae exact his due, they say. Beware o' a man w' deith tae avenge... or on yer ain heid he'll seek revenge."

I did a momentary double take at the odd rhyme. I almost didn't realize it was a rhyme at first. I was still struggling to understand the thick Scottish dialect and didn't always grasp what was said to me the first time. But as the words sank in, I realized that the *avenge* and *revenge* had been intentional.

"Well, I will try to be very careful," I said. "How will I know this man?"

"Nae ither body bides on the Bin, Miss Buchan, 'tis nae ither hoose for miles. But dinna gang near him. Naethin' but ill comes tae them wha speiks till him."

"Well, thank you for the warning," I said, and we parted.

I left her and crossed the main A road, and then headed inland along the private road leading past the Home Farm of the castle and the duke of Buchan's estate. I recognized the woods of the castle grounds to my left from the drive the day before. After about a mile, I left the road on a public footpath that veered off through cultivated fields, guided by a moss-covered wooden signpost with an arrow pointing the way toward the Bin of Crannoch. In the distance a combine was harvesting either barley or wheat. Cows grazed in the field next to me. A mile ahead, the slopes of the Bin were dotted with white sheep. Occasionally a rabbit scampered out of the underbrush, ran along the path a ways, sometimes stopped a moment to stare at me, then disappeared. The air was still and fragrant with an entirely different range of smells than I encountered on my walks along the sea—green grass and mown fields and an occasional whiff of manure, which, strange as it is to say, along with the other smells of farming life, was appealing in its own way.

After another three-quarters of a mile the path began to steepen. I left the fields, climbed a stile over a fence, and entered a wooded area. I loved the Scottish coastal woods—fir and pine and birch trees, thinly spaced, nearly always with a thick blanket of moss underneath, a perfect fairy-tale setting for nice Narnian creatures like fauns and friendly trees. They were so different from the thick, dark, desolate, spooky forests of the Canadian Rockies, where you would be more likely to encounter bears or nightmarish Middle Earth beings with horrible names.

After I'd walked ten or fifteen minutes through this delightful wood, the trees gradually thinned and I found myself in bright sunshine with the loveliest grassy expanse of fields spread out around me. I would almost call it a meadow, for it seemed like one, surrounded as it was by woods and coming upon it suddenly as I had. But it was too large for a meadow, and sheep were grazing everywhere. It was a *field*, not a meadow, a field full of sheep. I knew I had been climbing, but as I looked around I realized these were the same sheep I had seen before from lower down. There was the peak of the Bin ahead of me. I had already worked my way halfway to the top!

The next stile I encountered had been built over a low stone wall, a dry stane dyke as it is called. I climbed over it and set out across the green sheep pasture. Slowly as I went the path I had been following blended into the grass and became less and less visible. I didn't notice at first because I was enjoying the walk so much. The sheep didn't seem to mind my being among them and kept grazing as I strolled past. I continued on in the direction of the great hill in front of me. By now I was breathing a little more heavily and was definitely climbing a serious slope. I came to another dry stone dyke, but this time there was no stile over it. Now I saw for the first time that I had lost the path.

I stopped and glanced about. Where could I have gone wrong?

Below me was the wood I had come out of. Beyond and over it I had a panoramic view of the sea in the distance and the village of Port Scarnose. I wasn't exactly lost. But my path had disappeared.

I made my way along the dry stone dyke all the way to the right until it intersected with another just like it, but there was no hint of how to get over it. I found myself blocked by two right angles of stone wall four or five feet high.

I could climb over it. But I was afraid of dislodging the loose stones and sending them toppling down. I didn't know exactly *how* to climb over a dry stone dyke.

I turned and made my way along this new wall more or less in the direction I'd come from. As I was looking around I saw in the distance, across two more stone dykes, what looked to be a cottage. You saw stone cottages everywhere throughout Scotland in the most solitary places—I had seen dozens. Some were so dilapidated there was nothing left but two end walls, others might have all four walls and a caved-in roof. Once I had seen stones piled in a heap with nothing left standing but a fireplace and a chimney. When the old stone farms and crofts that had been scattered across every hill and valley were abandoned, their former inhabitants just left them to the wind and the rain and the snow. The roofs of timber and thatch and turf were always the first to go and deteriorated rapidly. But the stone walls might remain standing for a hundred years as sad, silent monuments to a time when the Highlands of

Scotland were peopled with thousands of families trying to coax a living out of the harsh northern environment. Now it was families of sheep that inhabited the Highlands.

I walked all the way to the far end of the stone dyke and still saw no way over it. I turned and looked all around yet again. I still could not imagine where the path had gone. I was too far on my way up the Bin to turn around. Slowly I continued down the hill through the sheep pasture, glancing to my right and left. But ten minutes later, after backtracking nearly through the entire pasture, I still had not found so much as a hint of a trail.

Suddenly a figure appeared about fifty yards in front of me, walking out of the same wood I had come through, then climbing up the stile over the stone wall. I stood a moment and stared, not sure if I was dreaming. He was a picture out of a book! He wore blue dungarees, a bright red plaid wool shirt with the sleeves rolled halfway up his arms, and sported a ragged wool cap on his head. A full bushy beard of white was all I could see of his face. His right hand grasped a tall staff with a crook end, and with his left he held the four legs of a sheep that was draped around his neck and over his shoulders, bleating frantically.

The moment he was over the stile, he knelt down and let the sheep to the ground, swatting its rump as it ran off toward the others, then stood and continued toward me.

"Best o' the mornin' to ye, lassie," he said as he approached. "Fine day for a ramble."

"Yes, it's beautiful," I said, smiling. "But I'm afraid I've lost my way."

"Whaur is it ye be wantin' tae get till?" he asked.

"I was following the footpath up to Crannoch Bin," I replied. "At least I thought I was. Then I got to the end of this field and couldn't find a way over the stone wall. That's when I realized I must have gone wrong."

"Ye didna ging so far wrang as ye may think, lass. Gien ye'll jist follow me a wee while, ye'll be on yer way soon enouch."

I turned again and he led me through the meadowy field, now for my third time. With his staff, beard, and old hat and boots, I felt as if I'd time-warped to the Swiss Alps and just met a cheerful version of Heidi's grandfather!

"Am I still on the footpath up to the Bin?" I asked.

"'Tis mony a way o' gettin' tae the top," replied my strange guide. "Maist fowk nowadays come at it fae the ither side, through the woods tae the south. But ye're still on the auld footpath."

"I see no path at all."

"'Tis nearly gone fae disuse."

We reached the stone wall at the other end, not far from where I had been before.

"Noo, lass," he said, "here in the wa' ye'll see these protrudin' stanes for steppin' ontil. Dinna fret—they're buirdly enouch. I mortared them in mysel'."

He took three steps up over the stone wall as if he were climbing a ladder, then reached back for my hand and helped me up and over after him.

"I hadn't even noticed those stepping-stones," I said. "I was worried about knocking the rocks loose."

"'There wis a wood stile here for mony a year. When it finally gave way, I thoucht stanes in the wa' wud be better, an' as nane but me made much use o' it, I re-did a wee bit o' it wi' the flat stanes as wee stairs like."

"You must walk here often if you took the trouble to make a new stile like that."

"I dinna walk here, lass," he said, laughing. "I live here."

"Where?" I said, puzzled.

"In yonder cottage," replied the man, pointing toward the stone house I had seen. "'Tis my croft, all o' this, an' my sheep. 'Tis my lan' ye're walkin' on, so it behooves me tae keep my dykes in gude repair."

"Oh, I saw your house, but I didn't realize anyone lived there. You don't mind if I keep walking up the hill, do you?"

"Mind?" he repeated. "Why wud I mind, lass?" he said, now laughing again. "Ye're welcome tae roam aboot whaur ye like. 'Tis a public footpath an' ye got the richt o' the law wi' ye tae cross onybody's land whereiver a footpath gangs. But even gien there wasna, gien ye'll jist tell me yer name, then ye'll be welcome as a frien'."

"It's Marie," I said. "Marie Buchan."

"Weel, then, Marie Buchan—gie me a grip o' yer han'," he said, holding out his right hand. "I'm Ranald Bain."

I shook his hand and he smiled warmly.

"Noo," he said, "ye winna find much o' a path the rest o' yer way. But diagonal across this meadow jist there," he added, pointing up the hill to my left, "ye'll find yer way over anither wooden stile, an' fae there hold till the edge o' the wood till ye come oot intil a clearing. Bear left an' ye'll join the path fae the south I telt ye aboot. Then the way till the top'll be clear enouch."

"Thank you, Mr. Bain," I said. "I don't think I could have found my way without your help."

"Ye can thank me proper," he added with a friendly twinkle in his eye, "by stoppin' in at the cottage on yer way back doon an' haein' a drap o' tea."

"Oh, that is very kind of you," I replied. "Maybe I will—if I can find my way!"

Chapter Nineteen

Tales of a Historic Land

Hark when the night is falling. Hear, hear! The pipes are calling,
Loudly and proudly calling, down thro' the glen.
There where the hills are sleeping, now feel the blood a-leaping,
High as the spirits of the old Highland men.
Towering in gallant fame, Scotland my mountain hame,
High may your proud standards gloriously wave,
Land of my high endeavour, Land of the shining river,
Land of my heart forever, Scotland the brave.

—"Scotland the Brave"

I found my way to the top of Crannoch Bin and the view, as I had expected, was spectacular. Mostly my thoughts remained occupied, however, with the old man I had just left. And with an invitation pending to visit a genuine old-fashioned stone shepherd's cottage, I didn't spend more than five or ten minutes at the top surveying the plaque with its arrows pointing to the surrounding towns and bins and coastal landmarks. I was anxious to see if I could find my way back along the same route I had come.

It wasn't difficult. I had to look carefully where I needed to leave the main trail for the wooded area that would lead me back to the meadows where I had encountered Mr. Bain. But once I was again traipsing down through the trees, the way was easy enough. Before long I could see the sheep through the trees in the distance. Ten minutes later I was climbing the wooden stile into the first of the stone-fence-enclosed fields through which I had come earlier. There was no sign of Mr. Bain.

I paused to get my bearings, then struck out toward the stone cottage about a quarter mile away. I had to cross two more stone dykes. As I drew closer a few distinct pathways became clear and the stiles over them were easy to manage.

Sheep munched on the grass everywhere. A few paid no attention, others scattered, bleating and baaing as I made my way through them. As I neared the cottage I saw that it was nicely kept and tidy. It was surrounded by both a flower and a vegetable garden, and a large cultivated field of potatoes. Two sheepdogs started raising a ruckus as I walked up, though they didn't run to bother me but scurried around worrying the sheep seemingly just for the fun of it. Maybe they were showing off.

The door of the cottage stood open. I knocked, and poked my head inside.

"Hello," I said.

"Ah, lassie, come in, come in!" called the familiar voice of the old man from inside. A moment later the bearded and white-topped head, now without hat, appeared to welcome me.

"I was aye haupin' ye'd stop back. The water's het an' ready tae pour."

As I entered I saw a table already set with two places on a nice white tablecloth. A plate of biscuits and little cakes sat in the middle of the table next to a vase of wildflowers.

"You look like you were expecting company!"

"Aye, I was—yersel'."

I laughed. "You were that sure I would come back?"

"Reasonably so. It's nae second sicht that made me think sae, but I haup I ken somethin' aboot fowk, an' I read on yer face ane wha's yea is yea an' wha's nae is nae. Fan ye said ye micht come back, I took ye at yer word, an' hauped it would be sooner raither than later. 'Tis few enough visitors that pass by, I maun seize ilka chance I get. Sit ye doon, lass."

I did so and five minutes later I was enjoying tea and lively conversation with one of the most interesting people I had met since arriving in Scotland.

"I take it you live here alone, Mr. Bain?" I had just asked.

A shadow crossed Ranald Bain's bearded face. The brief silence that followed gave me the chance to take in his features more thoroughly. He was not a tall man, probably about my height, five-six or five-seven, and thin and wiry. When I had seen him before I sensed energy about him from the way he walked that seemed undiminished by his years, which I judged to be perhaps sixty-eight or seventy. His beard, as I said, was white, his eyes a deep blue, his complexion tanner than you often saw among the fair-skinned Scots. He was obviously a man of the earth who had lived most of his life out of doors.

"I do, lass," he said, nodding slowly after a moment or two. "I lost baith my wife an' my dochter tae the sea."

"Oh, I am sorry," I said. "How did it happen...were they on a ship or a boat?"

Again the shadow briefly clouded his bright blue eyes. "There's mony ways the sea has o' claimin' the life o' those wha bide along sich rocky shoals as this coastline," he said. "Nae, it wasna a boat gaun doon, though mony o' the fisher families o' the north hae lost sons an' brithers an' men fowk that way."

"How long has it been?" I asked.

"Oor dochter was but a lass. 'Twas thirty or mair years syne. My wife was lost but six years syne."

"Again, Mr. Bain, I am so sorry. I lost my husband six years ago as well."

"I am aye sorry tae hear it. But fretna yersel' aboot me, lass," he added, smiling and now pouring more tea. "We had a gude life, my Maggie an' me. I hae nae regrets. Nae that I dinna miss her, but we winna be parted sae lang."

"Have you always lived here," I asked, "up on the slopes of the Bin?"

"A' my life, as did my father, an' my gran'father an's his father afore me. The croft has been in oor family fae the days o' the bonnie prince. Course the families had mony bairns an' 'tis but a wee croft that wi' cattle an' sheep an' what they cud grow cud but barely keep food in the mouths o' ane family. Sae as they grew the brithers an' sisters had tae seek their fortunes elsewhere, an' some became fishers an' fisher wives, some warked the lan', an' some went tae the cities, an' some went abroad tae Canada. But always there was ane fa remained tae work the croft an' raise his ain family right here, an' sae it went generation after anither, an' noo here am I, the last o' the line o' the croftin' Bains, alane wi' my sheep."

"What will become of your land and home?" I asked.

"I dinna ken, lassie. It will pass back till the duke an' perhaps a few years later the roof will collapse an' it will become like sae many ither crofts. But all things o' this warl' are passin'. E'en families come tae their earthly end."

"Do you have other relatives?"

"Nae doubt. But no that I ken. The lan's the duke's anyway, no mine, sae till him it will gang an' he'll do wi' it what he will."

I munched on an oatcake and took a sip of tea.

"Why is Bonnie Prince Charlie so famous?" I asked. "It seems that half the folk songs I hear are about him. And you made it sound as though your family had connections to him."

"Aye. The Bains fought wi' the prince. That was after they fled fae Glencoe fifty years afore. Sae they were Jacobites afore the Bonnie Prince was e'en born."

"Who are the Jacobites?" I asked, laughing. "I am having a hard time figuring out Scotland's history, though it's all around me."

"Aye, lass, 'tis a mite confusing on account o' the Scots bein' divided in their loyalties—Catholic or no, Jacobite or no. But 'tis simple, too. 'Tis aboot Scotland's independence, Protestantism an' Catholicism, an' the monarchy o' Britain."

"Those things sound complicated enough."

"Ye'll get a grip o' it in five minutes, lass, gien ye want an auld crofter tae tell ye the auld sang, as we Scots say."

"Oh, please, Mr. Bain. I would love to have you explain it to me."

"Then hae anither drap o' tea," he said, reaching for the teapot, "an' ye'll soon be an expert yersel'."

"I doubt that!"

"Weel, lassie," he began, "it all begins wi' the people o' this lan' o' the north. Different races came till England an' Scotland. They shared this big island, ye ken, but they were different people. 'Course 'tis all mixed up noo, like it is all o'er the worl'. But in the beginnin', the Scots were maistly a Celtic race, an' the English were Anglo-Saxons—twa peoples, twa races, twa separate countries. An' that's hoo it remained for mony centuries. The Romans came an' conquered England, but they couldna conquer the Picts, which is what the Celtic people o' Scotland were called back then. Sae the stories gang that they painted themsel's an' were fierce warriors, an' were ruled by matriarchal lineages—the kings comin' doon through the lines o' their women, ye ken. Isna athegither a healthy thing, in my opinion, for God ne'er intended women tae rule. The Buik says't as plain's can be. But some fowk see it differently, especially noo in these modern days fan feminism's takin' o'er mair an' mair o' the culture an' feow ken the mortal danger o' whaur it's led ilka culture that's ta'en that road. But 'tis anither story, that—fit I was tellin' ye is that England an' Scotland remained twa separate countries an' twa separate peoples for centuries.

"But as time went on, all o'er the worl', as some countries an' people became mair po'orful, they wanted tae conquer an' subdue their neighbors an' take their lan' for themsel's. 'Tis a natural thing, though sinful an' greedy. But 'tis hoo people's an' nations are. Sae as the years went along an' England recovered fae Roman rule an' strengthened itsel', its kings began tae luik at the lan' o' the Scots tae the north thinkin' they'd like tae hae that land for themselves. All through the Middle Ages, the twa countries fought back an' forth, whiles one gettin' the upper hand an' whiles anither. An' as England was bigger an' stronger, there were times when it subdued the Scots right proper an' when Scotland was nae better than a northern province o' England.

"But e'en during sich times, the prood Scots ne'er forgot their Celtic roots an' their independence. They may hae been ruled by the English for a season, but they ne'er gie up the independence in their herts. They ne'er forgot that they were Celts. They werena Anglo-Saxon nor English.

"Then came a climax. 'Twas late in the thirteenth century during a period o' English rule that was grim an' cruel for the Scots. The auld Scots king had deid, ye see, wi'oot a clear heir tae the Scots' throne. English King Edward had come north an' used the opportunity o' confusion in Scotland tae place it under his ain rule, an' Scotland was in a sorry state. There were some wha tried tae rally the Scots tae rise up an' throw off Edward's rule, men like William Wallace. But they werena strong enough an' Edward squashed them under his thumb."

"William Wallace," I said. "He was the one they called Braveheart. I know about him from the movie."

"I dinna ken aboot that, lass."

"It's not important. Please, go on."

"Then came a day when a man called Robert Bruce, wha's father an' gran'father hae been earlier claimants tae the Scots throne, began tae raise a secret army throughout Scotland. In time he raised a big enough army that the Scots were ready tae take on Edward an' all the might o' England. Fit the Wallace couldna do, the Bruce was ready tae try again. The year was 1314 an' the twa armies met at Bannockburn jist outside Stirling. Hae ye heard o' Bannockburn?"

"Yes," I answered. "I visited there, before I came up here."

"Aye, then ye'll ken a' aboot it. 'Twas the greatest battle in all Scottish history. King Robert the Bruce defeated King Edward an' sent him back south across the border tae England. An' the independence o' the Scots was guaranteed for anither four hundred years, or close till it."

"No wonder Robert the Bruce is so famous."

"He's aye the greatest hero in the history o' Scotland for his defeat o' the English at Bannockburn."

"What about Bonnie Prince Charlie?" I asked. "I thought *he* was the most famous Scot."

"He's comin' in his time, lassie!" laughed Mr. Bain. "Jist be patient. By the 1600s, though Scotland an' England were independent countries, the dispute between nations all oor Europe had changed. It wasna jist aboot land sae muckle as afore, an' stronger nations bein' greedy for their neighbor's land. Noo 'twas aboot religion, too, on account o' the Reformation. Noo Catholic nations wanted tae impose Catholicism on ither countries, an' Protestant nations wanted tae impose their beliefs. An' though both England an' Scotland were Protestant, Anglican, an' Presbyterian, 'twas still a dispute aboot Catholicism that led tae the Jacobite rebellion. An' there were an unco heap o' Catholics in Scotland, too, which added tae the problem.

"What happened was this, ye see—in the 1680s, James II became king o' England, an' he was a hated Catholic. Noo the English lords couldna bide a Catholic on their throne. So they said tae William o' Orange fae o'er in Holland, 'Will ye come tae England an' be oor king instead?' 'Twas an invitation William o' Orange couldna refuse. He sailed for England an' became English King William II."

"That doesn't sound right," I said. "He wasn't even an Englishman."

"It wasna richt. But the English lords preferred a Protestant Dutchman on their throne tae the richtfu' heir wha was Catholic an' a Scot. William's wife Mary was English, sae they justified it till themsel's. 'Tis the way the English think, ye see. They pride themselv's o' being a nation o' law, but gien they dinna like what the law says they change it. No that the Scots are ony better in the matter o' the kings o' its history, but they arena sae high an' mighty aboot it like the English.

"Sae William o' Orange became king. But the Scots didna like it—no on account o' their bein' Catholic but because James II was a *Scot*, the great-grandson of Mary Queen of Scots, an' was also the king o' Scotland. The leaders o' England, in offerin' the crown tae William o' Orange, had also offered him the kingship o' Scotland as weel. Ye see, e'er since the time o' Mary's son James, England an' Scotland, though separate countries, had had the same king. He was already King James VI o' Scotland. But when Queen Elizabeth died in 1603, he became heir to her throne as weel, as Mary an' Elizabeth were cousins. Sae King James VI o' *Scotland* became King James I o' *England*. An' after that, in what's called the union o' the crowns, the twa nations had the same king."

"I am afraid I am getting very confused!" I laughed. "I'm not used to keeping so many kings and queens straight in my head."

"Weel, maybe it isna sae important that ye mind ilka one, but the bigger story they tell. Ye see, there were mony Scots, maistly in the Heilands whaur the Catholics lived, wha werena aboot tae boo the knee tae William o' Orange. In their minds, their king was still James, no matter what the law o' the land said. That's hoo the Jacobites came into bein'. They were loyal tae the hoose o' Jacobus or *James* in Latin—the Stewart line that had been on the Scots throne syne the 1300s. But James had fled into exile in France when the Parliament invited William o' Orange tae be king. The opposition tae his kingship in some parts o' Scotland was sae great that William set oot tae crush it. He ordered a' the Scottish clan chiefs tae take an oath o' allegiance tae him.

"But in the Heilands, whaur the loyalty tae James was strongest, many refused. William increased his demand, threatenin' deith tae any wha refused. The last clan chief tae take the oath o' allegiance was MacDonald o' Glencoe. But because his oath was late in reachin' the king, William ordered ilka MacDonald o' Glencoe tae be put tae the sword."

"I thought they were killed by a rival clan."

"Aye, they were, but the Campbells was under orders fae King William."

"I don't understand. Why would one Scottish clan fight against another?"

"Ah, lass—fightin' among themsel's, 'tis the history o' Scotland itsel'. Rivalries atween clans meant more tae some than the nation as a whole. Kings secured loyalty hoo they cud, wi' money, wi' power, wi' special favors, wi' land. An' the Campbells were loyal tae the English king, e'en gien he wasna English at all. Scotland was split, ye see, atween Protestants loyal tae the new king William, an' Jacobites an' Catholics loyal tae ousted King James. It wasna sae easy as jist Scots on one side an' the English on the ither."

"What happened at Glencoe, then?"

"Whan MacDonald o' Glencoe was late wi' his oath o' allegiance, King William—that's William o' Orange, the Dutchman, ye ken— sent the Campbells tae Glencoe tae carry oot his terrible order. An' that they did early one cauld snowy February mornin' in 1692. They roused the MacDonalds oot o' their beds an' the dreadfu' slaughter began."

"That's awful."

"'Twas horrible indeed, though many escaped, includin' my own ancestor, cousin tae the chief MacAonghais wha fled Glencoe wi' his son John. 'Tis hoo the Bains came tae settle in this region. The lad John Bain became a man an' settled in Portsoy whaur he worked in the marble quarry."

"What happened to James?" I asked. "Did he ever regain the throne?"

"Nae, nae. The massacre o' Glencoe was the end o' all hope o' Scottish independence an' a' hope o' the Stewart king rulin' either England or Scotland agin. After the massacre naebody dared oppose King William. He was grudgingly acknowledged as king in Scotland. But the Jacobites kennt in their herts that he wasna the true king. When James VII died in France, the French king proclaimed his son James Francis Edward Stewart the rightful king' o' England, Scotland, an' Ireland. The French, ye see, was always bitter enemies o' the English, an' 'twas in France among the exiled English an' Scots that the Jacobite spirit remained stoot. James VIII tried tae start a rebellion tae put the Stewarts back on the throne in 1708, after the Act o' Union, but it came tae nothin'."

"The Act of Union?"

"Aye, the end o' Scotland as a nation. Scotland's Parliament was disbanded an' Scotland was swallowed up intil England."

"How sad."

"Aye, but the Scots had only their ain lords an' leaders an clan chiefs tae blame, always fightin' amongst themsel's. They ne'er realized fit they were givin' away one step at a time through the years, until it was too late an' they woke up tae realize they'd given away the whole o' Scottish independence one wee concession after anither."

"But I thought there was a Jacobite uprising that almost succeeded."

"Aye, but it came later, in 1715."

"What happened then?"

"By that time, William o' Orange was deid an' Anne was queen. Fan she deid in 1714, when the English lords made a German fae Hanover king o' England, Scotland, an' Ireland. The indignity o' a foreigner on the throne in place o' the rightful Stewarts became e'en greater in Scotland. George I was a man wha couldna e'en speik the English tongue an' had ne'er set foot in England. That's fan the Jacobites rose under the earl o' Mar an' James VIII sailed frae France tae reclaim the Stewart crown in place o' the German George."

"You sound like a Jacobite yourself!" I said, laughing.

The old man was thoughtful and quiet a moment, then slowly nodded. "I believe in right," he said. "I'm nae Catholic, an' I'm nae rebel an' I hae nae ill will toward England. But the fact is, James VII was the *rightful* king according tae law, nae William o' Orange. That made his son, James VIII also the rightful king, nae George I. The Stewart line was the rightful line o' the monarchy, an' still is— nae a Dutchman, nae a German. Gien that makes me a Jacobite, perhaps ye be in the right."

"I am still confused," I said. "Who is Bonnie Prince Charlie?"

"He was the *next* heir in line tae the Stewart throne—the son o' James VIII, the grandson o' ousted James VII. That's why he was called the prince—he was son o' him the Jacobites saw as the rightful king. When the uprisin' o' 1715 failed, then Jacobite hopes rested on the prince."

"Did he make an attempt to take the throne back, too?"

"Aye, he did—in 1745. That's when the *third* Jacobite uprising took place. Prince Charles sailed fae France an' landed in the western Heilands an' rallied support among the Heiland clans. Afore long he had a huge army an' marched south intil England. An' he was almost successful in retakin' the English throne. He came jist sae close. His army marched all the way tae Derby."

"What happened then?"

"What ye must remember, lass, is that Bonnie Prince Charlie was only twenty-four at the time. He wasna a skilled general. He was jist a romantic figure that captured a'body's imagination. But as a leader o' an army, the fact was, he was jist a lad. Wi' a mair skilled man in charge, they might o' succeeded in puttin' the Stewarts back on the throne. But the puir bonnie prince made one blunder after anither an' the hale uprisin' was doomed fae puir leadership. When the English Duke o' Cumberland raised an army tae stop Charlie's march toward London, instead o' fightin', Prince Charlie turned aroun' an' retreated back tae Scotland. What advantage he had was lost right then. His army was tired an' hungry an' demoralized an' began tae disintegrate. As he went the duke's army grew stronger an' Charlie's army shrank. Cumberland chased Charlie a' the way up England an' a' the way through Scotland until finally there was nae mair place for Charlie tae run an' maist o' his army was gone.

"The twa armies finally met outside o' Inverness on the great moor o' Culloden. As a general, puir Charlie kept blunderin' an' blunderin'. He's the romantic hero o' Scots ballad an' sang, but Charlie wasna muckle o' a hero at a'. The puir lad was o'er his head. His bad decisions cost thousands o' Scots their lives. The Duke o' Cumberland ran roughshod o'er Charlie's army like 'twas child's play, an' sent them fleein' a' through northern Scotland, wi' the duke an' his men chasin' an' killin' an' massacrin' all o' Charlie's men they could fin'. 'Twas a dreadfu' thing, as bloody an' fierce an' inhuman as Glencoe. Charlie may hae been foolish, but the Duke o' Cumberland was ruthless an' evil. The Scots hae ne'er forgiven him for the senseless blood he shed long after he had the victory won. My ain ancestors fought for the prince an' had tae flee for their lives."

"What happened to Prince Charlie?"

"He fled frae the battle an' went into hiding. He was hid in ane place after anither, wi' the duke's men chasin' him through the Heilands, wantin' naethin' mair than tae run him through wi' their swords. But finally he escaped by night in a wee boat across tae Skye, an' fae there back tae France, whaur he lived oot his days."

"Hmm...over the sea to Skye," I said softly. "And after Culloden, there were no more Jacobite uprisings?"

He shook his head. "Nae mair. 'Twas the end o' it. King Geordie in England an' the English lords, they were determined tae crush a' Scottish hopes after that. They outlawed the kilt an' the tartan an' the bagpipes."

"*Outlawed* them!"

"Aye. 'Twas the lowest time in a' Scottish history. The Scotland o' the past was deid. Fit the English couldna kill was Scottish pride an' the spirit o' the Celt. It *couldna* be killed, no matter fit they might du. In the words o' the Savior, they might kill the body but they cudna kill the soul. But after that, the soul o' Scotland didna come oot in battles an' uprisings an' rebellions, but rather in poem an' sang an' ballad. Burns an' Scott gave a rebirth tae Scotland's heritage wi' the pen instead o' the sword."

The small cottage fell silent. I took another sip of the tea in my cup. It was cold. I hadn't realized how long I had been sitting there!

"I think I ought to go," I said. "I don't want to take up your whole day, and—"

"Dinna ye fret aboot my day!" Mr. Bain laughed. "Back when I was a younger man an' had fifty head o' Heiland coo tae look after an' crops tae tend, I may hae been a mite concerned wi' my wark. But in this modern age o' social benefits, e'en an auld crofter like me gits his wee pension ilka month. I live simply an' hae nae wants. The Lord's been aye gude tae me. Sae when ye visit Ranald Bain's croft, ye need hae nae worry aboot me. An' I hope ye will visit again. Be welcome onytime, an' as often as ye like."

"Thank you very much." I smiled. "I have enjoyed myself immensely. And you have given me much to think about! Maybe I am *beginning* to understand the words to some of the songs I play. Now I want to visit some of the places like Glencoe and Stirling all over again."

I stood up. As I began making my way toward the door, I glanced about the interior of the cottage. We had been sitting in a large room, where the table stood sort of between the kitchen at one end and a sitting room at the other. I now saw that the sitting room was in the shape of an L and extended around the protrusion of a wall, leading to that portion of the house where I presumed there were bedrooms. For some reason this time I walked around the table in the other direction from which I had entered. Looking into the interior of the cottage, I was now able to see partway into the far L of the sitting room. What I saw there took my breath away.

I gasped and half ran toward it.

"What is it, lass?" said Mr. Bain, rising and following me, having no idea what could possibly have caused such a response in me.

"It's a harp!" I exclaimed, slowing as I approached. "A beautiful Scottish harp."

"Aye," said Mr. Bain, coming up behind me, still not understanding what the fuss was all about.

"Why it must be . . . what, fifty or more years old," I said, reaching out reverently to touch it. I didn't recognize the wood, but it was light in color. The shape, too, was unlike anything I had ever seen . . . old, classic, Celtic. Most of the strings were still in place but loose, some dangling and not even attached to the soundboard on the bottom. Others were frayed from age. "It's wonderful!"

"Actually 'tis a mite older than that," he said. "'Twas my gran'father's, an' I'm thinkin' it came tae him fae his father."

"When was it last played?" I asked.

"I couldna say, lass. I remember my gran'father strummin' it an' singin' the auld Burns ballads. He was the bard o' the Bains an' played an' sang for the laird. But it's nae been played mony a year syne that I recall, no by me or my Maggie."

"Well, it might actually be that having strings on it all this time is what saved it." I continued to examine the old harp. "Do you mind if I pick it up?"

"Nae at a'."

I looked it all over and ran my eye along the soundboard. I saw no sign of cracks or warping.

"Why div ye say bein' wi' strings saved it?"

"Because the tension of the strings actually holds the wood together. Harps don't last indefinitely like violins and other stringed instruments. You rarely find a hundred-year-old harp in such fine condition. Oh, I would love to hear what this lovely instrument sounds like!"

"Ye seem tae hae mair than a passin' knowledge o' the harp an' its workin's."

I turned back toward him and smiled. "I play the harp," I said. "I have one almost exactly the same size—though of course much newer—down in the village where I am staying."

"Hae ye noo! Ye're a harper?"

I nodded.

"Then I would aye love tae hear ye make yer music on this one. My gran'father called it his *auld mither*, though I ne'er kennt why. I think it had tae do wi' a favorite book o' his. I might e'en dust aff my auld fiddle."

"You play the fiddle?" I said, now expressing my own astonishment.

"Aye."

"That's great! It would be such fun to play together."

"Bein' a bard, my gran'father played a' the instruments—box an' fiddle an' tin whistle, though no the pipes. 'Tis his fiddle, too that I play, an' 'twas him that taught me. The fiddle he called his *auld wife*. But can onything be dune for the puir thing?" he added, looking down at the harp.

"If you would like me to, I will put new strings on it and we will find out."

"Aye, I wud!"

"Then I will bring up a set of strings."

"Weel, Marie Buchan, I see 'twas the hand o' God that led yer steps tae me this day. Ye had made an auld man happy indeed. Whan ye're gone, I may jist get oot the auld wife an' remember the baroness o' Nairn an' her frien' Gow for a spell."

"I would love to hear you play," I said.

"Gien ye dinna mind, lass, what I'm feelin' in my hert this day I maun let oot alone. 'Tis a matter o' the hert, ye ken. 'Tis my way o' makin' worship in my soul."

I smiled and nodded.

"I understand perfectly, Mr. Bain," I said. "It is exactly the same with my harp. Sometimes I have to be alone when I play. The music is too deep, it doesn't feel the same with someone else listening."

"Aye. But we will join the sound o' oor strings one day."

"One day soon, Mr. Bain. I promise."

I walked toward the door of the cottage, then turned back again. "Thank you for everything," I said. "I enjoyed myself more than I can say."

"Fan ye come agin, gien I'm no here, I may be oot ae place or anither, jist gie a loud ring o' this bell here, ye see, abune the door.—Ye can fin' yer way doon tae the village?"

"I'm sure I can," I said, smiling and reaching out to shake his hand.

"God be wi' ye, lass, till we meet again." He leaned forward and kissed me on one cheek, then on the other.

"Good-bye, Mr. Bain," I said.

As I returned down the hill I recalled the warnings Tavia Maccallum had given me. She was obviously mistaken about there being only one house on the slopes of the Bin. I was certainly glad I had not encountered the crazy man she had told me about.

Chapter Twenty

Face-to-Face

A prince can mak a belted knight,
A marquis, duke, an' a' that:
But an honest man's aboon his might,
Gude faith he maunna fa' that!
For a' that, an' a' that,
Their dignities an' a' that,
The pith o' sense, an' pride o' worth,
Are higher rank than a' that.

—Robert Burns, "A Man's a Man for All That"

Another surprise was waiting for me back in the village.

When I reached my cottage again later that afternoon, weary from the long walk but happy and aglow from the day's experience, I found an envelope on the floor beneath the mail slot. Since it had no stamp, it obviously had not come by post but had been hand-delivered. I stooped down to pick it up. It was the same monogrammed envelope: *A T R.*

That brought me suddenly back to reality!

I'm afraid my first reaction was pretty caustic, especially as I remembered everything Mrs. Gauld had told me about Gwendolyn.

You can forget it if you think I'm going to play for you again, Mr. A. T. R.! I said to myself. *Not even for two hundred pounds! What is it with you, anyway?*

I tossed the envelope on the coffee table and tried to ignore it. I read awhile, dozed, then played my harp, then checked my string supply to see if I had a complete extra set. I always carried some with me because strings could break without warning. But if I strung Mr. Bain's harp with my extras, I would have to order

139

another set quickly. I went through my papers and files to find the number of a harp maker in Ballachulish I'd heard of. I could call the next day to order a set.

It wasn't until some time later, after I had taken a shower and settled in for the evening and was heating up a can of Baxter's Highland Broth for supper, that I remembered the envelope.

I retrieved it from where I had tossed it and opened it. There was a card identical to the other. By now my agitation from first seeing it had subsided. I assumed it was probably a thank-you note equally impersonal to my reception at the castle.

I was certainly not prepared for what I read inside!

Dear Ms. Buchan,
Please forgive my liberty in contacting you again, and for making no appearance yesterday. Rest assured that your music was appreciated more than you might imagine. Forgive me also for presuming upon your kindness a second time, but it would give me great pleasure to meet in person the woman whose music has already meant so much to me on the two occasions I have been fortunate enough to hear it. Would you consent to coming to the castle tomorrow, Thursday, for lunch? Your reluctance under the circumstances would be understandable. In the event, however, that you will agree, I will send Nicholls round to you at 12.30. You may either accompany him, or communicate your disinclination at that time.
I am,
Sincerely yours,
Alasdair Timothy Reidhaven,
Duke of Buchan

I set the envelope down thoughtfully. This was certainly unexpected! A dozen thoughts ran through my brain—why to accept, why *not* to accept. And of course Gwendolyn sat right in the middle of those thoughts. I wasn't going to miss my visits with her twice. The way things stood at this moment, my loyalties were with her, not this duke who had such an odd way of doing things. I found myself getting irritated at him again. Why would I want to go? And what was he talking about—the *two* times he had heard me?

When the next morning came, however, I woke up thinking about what I ought to wear. *Why shouldn't I accept?* I thought. I didn't *really* know anything about the man. Maybe Mrs. Gauld wasn't even right about Gwendolyn. She also tried to warn me about ghosts and dark powers and spooky stuff like that and I didn't believe a bit of it. Her reliability as a purveyor of information wasn't all that high. The connection between Gwendolyn and the duke might be nothing but "auld wives' tales."

There was no doubt the man was strange. Keeping himself cloistered away in a castle like a hermit. Inviting people to come play for him, then not showing his face.

But if he hadn't wanted me to see him when I was playing, that was his right. He had paid for the performance. I was working for him. He could do as he liked. What business was it of mine if he happened to be socially challenged?

I *would* go. As for what to wear, it totally went against the grain to wear the same outfit a second time so soon. But I only had one really nice dress with me. The duke hadn't seen it. Nicholls probably wouldn't notice. The lady would, of course, but she didn't strike me as the type who would blab it about that I wore the same dress every day. So if I wanted to look my nicest, I had no choice—the blue and yellow it was.

I was sitting and waiting by the window at twelve-fifteen. Luckily I hadn't seen Mrs. Gauld in two days, though she was probably watching my every move.

The man called Nicholls drove up in the black BMW at twelve-thirty on the dot. I walked out the door and toward the street. He nodded as I approached and opened the door for me. He didn't look as if he had expected me to convey a *disinclination* to accept, as the invitation had said.

Without my harp as a crutch, my security blanket, I was more nervous than the day before. Yet the familiarity of the exercise—the car appearing in front of the house, Nicholls and his old-world formality, the drive out of town and through the countryside, the long entryway through the trees, the first sight of the castle, then pulling up and stopping in front of the door—it had a calming effect on me simply because I had been there before.

I think, too, it had begun to dawn on me that this was a special thing. From the sound of it, I took it that most of the people in the village had *never* been to the castle. Here I was on my way to a second visit in three days. This was an experience to savor.

I didn't even try to shrink down out of sight when we passed Mrs. Gauld's bed-and-breakfast leaving Port Scarnose. She was nowhere to be seen, though I had visions of her peeping out from behind her curtains. Today I didn't mind. Let her eat cake if she didn't like it. In spite of what I'd heard, and even in spite of the peculiarities of my first visit here, I couldn't help myself—I was enjoying this. I'd come to Scotland to have an adventure, and I was having one!

Nicholls opened the door for me and led me inside where, again, I was met by the lady. If she took note that I was wearing the same dress, she had the courtesy not to show it.

"Hello, Ms. Buchan," she said. "I am Miss Alicia Forbes, the duke's housekeeper. I will show you to the dining room."

I followed her in a completely different direction than before, turning right before we reached the grand staircase and walking what seemed to be most of the length of the ground floor. We made two or three more turns, and by the time we arrived I doubted I could have found my way out by myself.

Miss Forbes stopped in front of a set of double doors. She placed her hand to the door, then paused and glanced toward me. There was that look I had noticed in her face before, almost, strange to say, of relief and gratitude.

"*Thank you*," she said in little more than a whisper. "Thank you *so* much for coming!"

Just as quickly as she had dropped it for those two or three seconds, the mask of her station and position returned. She opened the two doors, and stood aside. "You may go in," she said in a professional tone. "The duke is waiting for you."

I walked in, tentatively I must admit. Even if it hadn't been for all the mystery leading up to it, the fact was, I had never met anyone as important as a *duke* in my life. And in a fairy-tale setting like this—a real *castle*!—I suddenly felt very small and intimidated.

My first glimpse inside showed a lavishly appointed dining room, not so huge as the other room but full of tapestries and paintings, antique furniture against the walls, including several ornate sideboards. In the center, running three-quarters of the length of the room, stood a long oak table that looked as if it could seat twenty-five or thirty. Only two places were set, on opposite sides of one another in the middle. It was an incongruous sight, the two place settings dwarfed by the enormity of the table.

At the far end of the room, a man stood at a window with his back turned. He wore a dark blue suit, and all I knew of him at first glance was that he had a full head of black hair that showed some gray around the edges and ears. I was beginning to feel as if I had been dropped into the middle of a Gothic novel. At the sound of the door, he immediately turned and walked toward me.

He smiled as he approached and held out his hand. Nothing can prepare you for a moment you've built up in your mind. What exactly I had been expecting, I'm not sure. I suppose I had an image of what he would look like, and it was shattered in an instant.

I don't know if I had been expecting the Beast or Prince Charming. But he was neither.

Actually—this sounds very weird!—maybe he was a little of both.

He was tall, broad-shouldered, and large. I don't know that I would call him heavy, but he was a big man. His face, too, was large and somewhat irregular, with a strong wide jaw and low forehead. He was not a handsome man...plain, almost homely. I wouldn't call him ungainly, but he certainly wasn't dashing or suave. Kind of a "gentle giant," to use a cliché. But being prepared after all that had happened for him to be standoffish and proper and modern and sophisticated, and expecting to dislike him, I was disarmed by his simple smile of almost old-fashioned welcome. It wasn't a gregarious smile, just a nice, simple one. Even as his hand came toward me, I noticed that it, too, like the rest of him, was huge, like the paw of a bear. It was a hand that could crush mine in a single grip!

"Hello, Ms. Buchan," he said, his voice a deep bass, "I am Alasdair Reidhaven."

"I am Marie Buchan," I said, returning his smile and reaching out my hand. He took it and shook it with a gentleness that was in such contrast to his almost lumbering gait. I wasn't really prepared to like him yet I found his touch almost a relief.

"Come, please sit down," he said, extending one arm and leading me to the table. He pulled one of the chairs out, helped me scoot in, then walked the long way around the head of the table in his somewhat uneven gait and sat down opposite me.

"I realize this may be awkward for you," he said, picking up a bottle from the table and pouring half a glass of wine into each of the two goblets in front of us. "But I hope you will find it pleasant enough."

His voice as he spoke, in contrast to its depth, was subdued and soft. He spoke slowly.

"It is awkward for me, too, I confess," he went on. "I have few visitors because I keep mostly to myself. The villagers consider me a recluse and most hate me. But I cannot help it—I am a private man. I would not socialize even if I lived in more modest surroundings. But as I am a duke, and I live in a castle, whatever I do leads to talk."

At last I found my voice. "Why did you invite me, then?" I asked.

"Because..." he began, then hesitated and glanced away. "Because your music moved me. I wanted to meet you. I had never heard a harp, up close, by itself, before last Sunday when you were playing in the churchyard. I heard the sound from my window. I hurried downstairs and outside, curious to know where it was coming from. I crept toward the stone wall around the church grounds and listened. The music was magical. It possessed a quality I cannot explain. It aroused deep feelings within me. So I instituted inquiries to see what I could learn about you."

Before either of us said anything further, a side door opened and a man dressed like a butler came in carrying two bowls of soup. He set them before us and left. Slowly we began to eat, though I cannot say I was very hungry. I was feeling too jittery.

"I felt the same enchantment listening to you play day before yesterday," said the duke.

"You were listening from behind those tapestry dividers?" I asked.

He nodded.

"Most people seem to find the harp as intriguing to watch being played as to listen to," I said.

"Perhaps I was shy to show my face," he said, almost with a sheepish expression. "I think I built you up so in my imagination that I—"

He hesitated and drew in a breath.

"I don't know," he said. "I apologize if it was difficult for you. I promise that should I ever be so fortunate as to hear you play again, I will listen in the open where I can see you and you can see me. And I would, I confess, like to *see* your harp as well, now that I have heard it."

The meal progressed, slowly and with light conversation that remained a little stiff. He asked me about how I had come to play the harp and why I was here and how long I would be in Port Scarnose. I managed to answer his questions without bringing up Gwendolyn, though she was on my mind. My anger toward him softened. He was not the kind of man you could easily be angry with. He seemed insecure, shy, lonely. I felt, I don't know—almost sorry for him.

When we finished with lunch, he showed me around the ground floor of the castle. We walked slowly and the conversation remained formal. I never did completely relax. Neither did the duke. He continued to move a little awkwardly, never seeming to know what to do with his two large hands. He appeared unsure of how to conduct himself with a guest. Or maybe it was that he felt awkward in the presence of a woman. But he played the role of host bravely, if woodenly. He told me about various of the antiques and tapestries and of the identities of the men and women in the paintings, and I nodded and commented. I might as well have been on a tour of one of the castles I had seen earlier with the duke as a tour guide in training.

We walked past a great pendulum clock on a wall and it began to strike the hour of three. Suddenly I remembered.

"Oh, my goodness!" I said. "I'd forgotten, the time got away from me. I need to get back to the village. I have been taking my harp to a little girl to play in the afternoons—"

I paused for a second.

"Her name is Gwendolyn," I added. As I did, I glanced at the duke out of the corner of my eye. But if the name meant anything to him, he hid it well. "I'm already late."

"I will show you to the front door and have Nicholls drive you home," said the duke, then turned and led the way. Whether it was the mention of Gwendolyn or the abruptness of my departure, the suddenness of the change seemed to throw him.

"I appreciate your coming very much," he said as we reached the main front door. "Very much indeed." He turned and disappeared back inside, while I followed Nicholls out to the car.

Chapter Twenty-one

The Look

Maxwellton braes are bonnie,
Where early fa's the dew,
And 'twas there that Annie Laurie
Gave me her promise true.
Gave me her promise true,
Which ne'er forgot will be,
And for bonnie Annie Laurie
I'd lay me doun and dee.

—"Annie Laurie"

My visit to the Urquharts immediately upon returning from the castle seemed different. Probably only to me.

Having a secret changes you inside. I now had two secrets I was withholding from Gwendolyn and her aunt—what I had heard about them from Mrs. Gauld, and that I had twice visited the castle to which, if Mrs. Gauld was right, they both had intimate connections.

I would have to mention it sooner or later, if only to find out whether what I had heard was true. But I didn't feel I could bring it up out of the blue. I was still very much aware, in spite of what Iain had jokingly said, that I was an incomer, a stranger. I did not really know these people and their ways.

Gwendolyn was happy to see me as always. She played with abandon and seemed particularly receptive to the small doses of instruction I gave to guide her technical progress. Mrs. Urquhart seemed more distant than usual. It might have been my imagination. But it seemed plausible that she might have heard rumors about my going to the castle. She had probably also by now heard that I had seen Iain Barclay on a number of occasions. It was clear enough she didn't like him.

As I was leaving I asked about a plan I had been revolving in my mind.

"Gwendolyn," I said, "would you mind if I brought a tape recorder and recorded you playing the harp?"

"What is a tape recorder, Marie?" she asked.

"It is like your CD player," said Mrs. Urquhart. "She has a CD player," she added to me. "She plays children's CDs."

"Yes, it's like that, Gwendolyn," I said. "Except that it will make music of *you* playing."

"That will be fun! May I listen to it?"

"If you like."

I left their house and went straight to Iain's. I didn't want to have secrets from *him*. I hadn't told him everything about myself, but I knew I needed to tell him about my second invitation to the castle. I owed him that much.

He invited me in for tea and we had a nice visit. As always when the duke came up in conversation he was quieter than at other times. I guess *he* had secrets, too.

I had only a little pocket cassette recorder with me. I took it to Gwendolyn's the next day and was so pleased with the result, though the quality wasn't very good, that I determined to try to find something that would make a better recording.

On Saturday Iain picked me up about nine-thirty and we drove into Aberdeen. I had a great time. It was nice to be a passenger and not have to worry about roundabouts and narrow roads and parked cars—especially after we got into the cobblestone streets of Aberdeen's Auld Toon.

By now we were comfortable enough with each other that conversation flowed freely and we were able to laugh and have fun together. I hadn't enjoyed a man's company so much since my husband was alive. I found a good compact recorder with an electronic microphone for making higher-quality recordings of Gwendolyn.

Iain took me all around Aberdeen. We walked the cobblestones of the Old Town where he told me stories of his university days. We browsed in a used bookstore at the top of the hill on the edge of the college grounds where Iain said he used to spend most of his spare money as a student. We went to dinner about five at a little bistro off The Green.

It was as we were sitting across from each other waiting to be served that I realized this thing had progressed beyond the level of mere friendship.

A lull came in the conversation.

I was fiddling with my napkin in my lap. As I looked up, Iain was staring straight into my eyes across the table with the most intense expression full of unspoken feeling.

My heart skipped a beat and I quickly looked away.

His look unnerved me. I knew that look. I knew looks like that were not the kind he would give passersby on the street or the men and women in his congregation.

When I dared glance at him again, he smiled. His expression had returned to normal. But something changed between us in that moment.

I think that's when we both *knew*.

The drive back from Aberdeen to Port Scarnose was quieter than any hour during the day. I suppose we were both tired after a long day. Sometimes you just run out of things to talk about.

But there had also been that look.

Iain dropped me off. He let me get out of the car by myself and did not walk me to the house. I think he sensed the potential awkwardness of it. We both stumbled over our good-byes with many pleasantries about how we had enjoyed the day and that we should do this again soon. Iain didn't say a word about church, as I knew he wouldn't.

Even as I was getting ready for bed an hour later, reflecting on the day and all that had happened, I had already decided to attend the service the following morning.

Chapter Twenty-two

Follow Me

When we ponder o'er the past,
And the reckoning day at last,
We are lost amid His wondrous power and love,
Let us dream among the flowers,
Mid the scented birchen bowers,
Till He draw us in a fond embrace above.
—"Where the Roses Blush and Bloom"

The Deskmill Parish Church was laid out in the shape of a cross, with rows of pews in each of the four arms of the cross facing the center. The raised pulpit stood against one wall in the center facing diagonally the nave where the four sections of the cross met. From where he stood on any Sunday morning, Iain could see to the end of two of the alcoves, but not the other two. The bottom end of the longest, where the main door opened, was especially obscured from his line of vision since the pulpit pointed away from it.

That's where I had decided to sit. I did not want to distract him. Nor did I want to be distracted myself. If I was going to church, I wanted to be there for the right reasons, to see if there was something I was meant to learn, to find out, to get from it, not to see Iain, or for him to see me.

I drove into the parking lot about five minutes before ten-thirty. A few people were still walking from their cars to the church. Most everyone was already inside.

I sat and waited.

The second set of bells echoed into silence at ten-thirty on the

150

dot. I got out of my car and walked slowly toward the church. The front door was closed and I heard the organ prelude coming from inside. It was about two minutes past ten-thirty.

Gingerly I opened the door and slipped inside. Having to crowd past several people, I found a place securely in the next to last pew. Iain was just walking up into the pulpit.

By the time the sermon came, my thoughts were calm. I tried to listen quietly and thoughtfully. Hearing Iain's voice without seeing him, knowing that he didn't know I was there and was, in a sense, talking to everyone else *but* me, was an odd sensation. It was like being able to observe him while remaining invisible, like a fly on the wall as the saying goes.

"My friends," he began, "I would like to call your attention this morning to one of the singular encounters in the New Testament—that between Jesus and the man we call the rich young ruler. You know how it goes—the young man asks Jesus what he must do to be saved, and Jesus replies, *Keep the commandments.* The young man says he *has* kept them. Then Jesus tells him he is still lacking one thing. *Sell all you have,* he adds, *and give to the poor, and you will have treasure in heaven. Then come, follow me.* We all know the conclusion: *The man went away sorrowful, because he was very rich.*

"I am especially fond of the version of the story that appears in Mark's Gospel," Iain said. "As the encounter begins, Mark says, 'Jesus, looking at him, loved him.' The Lord's prescription for happiness was founded in no legalistic religiosity—it was founded in love. Jesus *loved* him. That is why he made the demand he did. That look of love is the foundation of this story's importance. Jesus did not tell him to give up his possessions to be critical or because he did not want the young man to be happy, but because he loved him and he *did* want him to be happy. Jesus knew there was only one path to that joy. And he told the young man what it was."

Iain stopped for a moment. The congregation waited in silence.

"Let me suggest," he went on, "that we are all like the young ruler, each in our own way. We have certain possessions that are dear to us. I do not necessarily mean *material* possessions. Material possessions, money, mammon—of course these *may* prevent us from drawing close to God. But in the majority of cases, these are not the chief culprits. I would say, rather, that it is private and *internal* possessions that cause us to keep God at arm's length. We each have things that keep us from following the Lord all the way, that hinder us from heeding his, *Come, follow me*. They may be possessions of the mind and the intellect. For many they are possessions of the heart. They may be ideas, doctrines, intellectual crutches. For some they may be ideas of disbelief. For others they may be ideas of doubt. We cling to them and they obstruct our growth. They keep us from true happiness and fulfillment, yet we cling to them for dear life. It is a curious thing, is it not—that we hold fast to the very things that *prevent* the deepest fulfillment in life.

"What are your reluctances? What are mine? What are our secret, hidden treasures?"

Again the church went silent. It was some time before Iain resumed.

"I will share with you one of mine," he said at length. His tone was soft, thoughtful, and deeply personal. "I think my chief reluctance is fear," he went on, "fear for what the Lord might ask me to give up, to sell, to lay down, in order to follow, fear that he might require of me something I cherish no less than the young ruler treasured his wealth. In my own case, I do *not* mean possessions. I cannot think of anything I own that I would be unwilling to let go of. But what of other things of heart and mind? What if, like the ruler, I do not want to part with the very thing standing in my way?

"And why do I fear? He asks in love. 'He *loved* him,' Mark says. And he loves me as he asks if I, too, am willing...as he loves you when he asks if you are willing to obey the, *Come, follow me*.

"There can be no fear in love. So why do I fear when it is only my good that he desires? This is the great struggle of humanity—one which, to its shame, Christianity has not adequately addressed—the realization that it is only our *good* that God desires. *Everything* he does is for our good, because the Father of Jesus is our good and loving Father.

"Now clearly, you and I are here this morning in church because we have followed. We have come partway in answering the Lord's summons. The rich young ruler, too, came partway. Mark says he ran up to Jesus and knelt before him.

"But then comes the summons to follow *all* the way. And that the young ruler was unable to do.

"What about us? Are we content to be halfway followers? Or, having come to him—as those of us here this morning have come—are we willing to follow *all* the way?

"My friends, it is not usually the selling of our possessions he requires, but the giving of *ourselves.* You and I must therefore isolate our own invisible reluctances, our own encumbering possessions of heart. Because it may be one of these that keeps you or me from obeying the Lord's timeless, *Come, follow me.* When he looks you deep in the eye, when he *loves* you, what is it that he will require of you, that *you* might follow?"

With the words, *When he looks you deep in the eye,* my thoughts drifted away.

Iain's voice grew faint.

Suddenly I could think of only the look Iain had given me the day before in the bistro. I knew it had been a look of love. Suddenly I realized that perhaps I had mistaken the reason for the look, the source of that love. Had he been looking at me with the look of Jesus to the rich young ruler, or the look of love between a man and a woman?

For the first time, the thought crossed my mind that with Iain Barclay, perhaps the two were one and the same. For him, to love meant *all* that love could mean. For Iain Barclay, perhaps *man's* love and *God's* love could not be separated.

I didn't know what to do with a thought like that!

Did it make Iain's love—if it had indeed been *love* that I had seen in his eyes—greater, or less?

Iain's sermon was winding down. But my thoughts were spinning. I scarcely heard the rest of what he said.

We rose for the final hymn. I knew as soon as it had concluded that Iain would say a final prayer then descend from the pulpit and walk down the center aisle to the door, where he would greet everyone as they left the church.

I couldn't face him like that.

I couldn't stand in line, knowing that he would probably see me, then wait till my turn came and I would shake his hand and mumble, "Nice sermon, Reverend," along with everyone else.

I turned and brushed past the people standing and singing, trying to smile and apologize as I inched by. Then I made for the door.

Seconds later I was running back up the lane toward my car, wiping my eyes.

Chapter Twenty-three

Music on the Bin

Haud the pen sae gracefu' guidin',
Or across the violin glidin',
Tunefu' harmony providin'
That fills my soul wi' joy for ever.

—John MacLean, "Hee oro, Though We Maun Sever"

What I needed to recover from the service was a good long tiring walk, and something to take my mind off the unexpected emotions I was facing. It wasn't even noon when I got back home. I had the whole afternoon before me.

I changed my clothes, gathered up a set of harp strings and a few other things in my backpack, and set out for the slopes of Crannoch Bin. No more emotions today! No Bible, no parables, no sermons, if anything just another talk about Scottish history or harps...*whatever*, just so long as I could keep my heart out of it.

The walk did me good. How can you be out in the fresh air, smelling the fragrances of growth and life, the wind on your face, looking to the sea in the distance, the blue overhead with fleecy clouds drifting weightlessly through it, and not feel your spirits buoyed and invigorated?

I reached Mr. Bain's cottage but found him nowhere around. The door was ajar. I knocked and called out, but no answer came.

For the first time I was aware of how still and quiet it was. How much different it was here than along the sea where the rhythm of the waves, even if you weren't consciously thinking of it, was always in the background. Now, too, I realized that I had encountered no sheep as I made my way through the two grassy fields between the edge of the wood and the cottage. Every living creature had disappeared.

I glanced about, then remembered the bell.

I grabbed the little rope hanging from it and gave it a whack. The bell exploded with such a huge sound that it nearly knocked me over, shattering the peace of the hillside.

Even as the metallic echoes were still dying away, in the distance I heard a dog bark. The baaing of a few sheep followed it.

Four or five minutes later, the baaing increased and a minute after that I saw what must have been fifteen or twenty sheep running and skipping and waddling noisily toward me. Within no time I was surrounded by a crowd of dirty wool, nudging up to me, sniffing and baaing and bumping against my legs where I stood at the cottage door. Their shyness from the other day had completely disappeared. The bell must have worked some kind of magic. I reached out and ran my hand through their shaggy, oily, dirty wool coats. None of them seemed to mind.

What a delight!

Fifty yards away I now saw bearded Ranald Bain walking toward me, staff in hand, surrounded by another group of twenty or more sheep scampering about, with the two sheepdogs running alongside and in and out among them.

"Hello, lassie!" he called as he approached. "Ye've made some new wee frien's I see!"

"Mr. Bain...hello! Why are they so friendly today all of a sudden?"

"They heard the bell an' are expectin' a handout. Come tae the byre an' gie them a wee snackie o' oats."

I followed him to the pens and barn to one side of the cottage. A minute or two later I had a dozen sheep clustered about me fighting for the chance to nibble the oats out of my hand.

"Ye've made them yer frien's for life," said Ranald. "They winna forget ye noo."

Leaving the sheep to a sprinkling of oats in several troughs, I
followed Ranald Bain to the cottage.

"I brought a set of strings for your harp," I said. "Would you like
me to try to restring it and see what we can do with it?"

"Oh, aye! I been thinkin' aboot naethin' else since ye was here,
haupin' that maybe ye'd teach me tae play a wee."

"I would enjoy that," I said. "First we have to see if your harp is
strong enough after all these years to hold the tension of the
strings. From what I saw the other day, I think it will, but you never
know for certain until you begin to tune it. These strings are nylon
and won't put too much strain on it."

He led me inside and to the harp. I sat down and got out the
strings and my tools.

"Ye dinna mind gien I watch ye?"

"Not at all."

I took out the old strings one at a time and replaced each with
a new one before going on to the next. "You probably don't still
have the tuning key?" I asked.

"There's naethin' but the harp that I ken o'."

"I might have one that will fit. Otherwise I will have to tune it
carefully with a small wrench."

Ranald Bain watched in fascination as I progressed. After about
an hour I was ready to begin tightening the strings, although keeping them several steps below pitch. The harp seemed to do fine.
After getting it in approximate tune with itself, though the strings
felt loose to my touch, I played a couple of simple tunes.

Ranald's face lit up at the sound. I thought he was going to cry!

"Lassie, lassie," he sighed, "sich soun's haena been heard in this
cottage for sae mony a year I forgot fit a lovely soun' it is. I haena
words tae thank ye."

I continued to play lightly some simple arpeggios. Quickly the
strings began to stretch and drop in pitch. From what I had seen
and felt, I was confident the harp would be able to stay in tune.

"Why don't you get your fiddle, Mr. Bain," I said, "while I retune? Could you tune your strings down a bit to match the harp? I don't want to tune it all the way up just yet."

He rose, then paused. "Gien we're tae make music together," he said, "which is one o' the most intimate o' joinin' o' the souls o' men, ye maun call me Ranald. I dinna care muckle for the *Mister*. Gie me yer A."

I smiled and nodded.

Twenty minutes later, with a lovely old threadbare and thumb-worn book of old Scottish tunes leaning on a chair between us, Ranald Bain on his fiddle and I on his grandfather's harp were playing through one old Scottish ballad after another. It was the most wonderful thing!

"The *auld wife* an' the *auld mither* still ken one anither a' these lang years syne!" he said.

Most of the tunes I had never heard of. But after Ranald ran through the tune once I could usually either add arpeggios to his melody, or I would play the melody and he would wander all over up and down with harmonies and counter melodies. We stopped every so often while I retuned and he would match the tuning with his own strings.

He was a *very* accomplished violinist, or fiddler if you prefer. Every melody he played had that same unique Scottish flavor that so distinguishes the folk music of the Celts—melancholy and minor keys, a strange, repetitive, wild irregularity of rhythm that calls to mind the desolate, treeless, windy peaks and empty moors of the Highlands. Something about every tune was similar, yet so different from most other music.

You can instantly recognize a Scottish folk song from a hymn, a classical piece, or a folk song from another country. What is that unique sound? I don't even know. Perhaps it is the unique Scottish "snap" in the rhythm. Or is it that centuries ago they originated on the basis of different scales, or *modes*, altogether distinct from the classic western European music?

It was haunting, sometimes almost primitive in its simplicity. Was it that most were originally sung in Gaelic to accompany various tasks in the fields or around the family home? I could never quite lay my finger on the basis of the uniqueness. But it was a music that moved me on a deeper level than any other. I suppose that is why I began playing the harp in the first place—the *music* of the harp drew me. Then the *instrument* drew me in its turn.

So Ranald Bain and I played and played, and indeed it was, just as he said, as if the two instruments were being reunited after a long silence. They seemed to play themselves.

Neither of us spoke. The music spoke for us. Words would have been a distraction, an interruption. Ranald turned page after page, played a portion of the tune until I began to pick it out on the strings of his auld mither, and then we played together until each song or ballad somehow came to a close of its own accord and we went on to the next. I remember playing "Charlie Is My Darling," "Farewell to Lochaber," "Far O'er Yon Hills," "Hush Ye, My Bairnie," "Robin Adair," "My Ain Fireside," "McGregor's Gathering," "Lochnagar," "Wi' a Hundred Pipers," and so many others.

How long we went on, I didn't even know. When finally both instruments stilled and somehow we knew that the day's music was at an end, I realized there were tears in my eyes. I drew in a deep breath.

"It is a lovely instrument," I said, looking at Ranald with a smile. "It has a wonderful sound."

"I had nae idea ye were sich a harpist, lassie."

"Nor I that you were such a violinist!"

"I canna think fan I hae had sich a time! I haena played wi' a harp in my life."

"The two instruments go together like they were made for one another."

"Ye'll hae tae come again. Noo I'm anxious tae try my ain hand at the wee strings."

"Would you like to try it now?" I asked.

"I dinna like tae spoil the memory o' the music in the air," replied Ranald. "But my fingers is itchin' tae try. Maybe jist a wee pluck or twa."

I stood up and showed Ranald how to sit and where to place his hands. He didn't pick it up as quickly as Gwendolyn had. But his knowledge of music was enough that he could distinguish the notes and could pick out a melody. Since his harp was now strung, I had the feeling the next time I saw him he would be playing tunes with ease.

When I returned down the hill to Port Scarnose, I felt good, as if I had accomplished something worthwhile that day. Yet by the middle of that night, the emotional upheaval from Saturday and Sunday had returned. Even making such wonderful music with white-bearded Ranald Bain couldn't keep the swirl of conflicting thoughts at bay.

Chapter Twenty-four

Along the Headlands

The waves are dancing merrily, merrily,
Ho ro Mhairi dhu, turn ye to me.
The sea birds are wailing, wearily, wearily,
Ho ro Mhairi dhu, turn ye to me.
Hushed be thy moaning, lone bird of the sea,
Thy home on the rocks is a shelter to thee.
Thy home is the angry wave, mine but the lonely grave,
Ho ro Mhairi dhu, turn ye to me.

—"Turn Ye to Me"

For the first time I began to question my decision to postpone my flight and rent the cottage in Port Scarnose. My life was suddenly getting a little too complicated. I hadn't counted on a spiritual crisis and crisis of the heart at the same time.

Actually I hadn't officially admitted to either.

But the warning clouds were on the horizon. There was no mistaking them.

When you can't go to sleep, when you wake up in the middle of the night thinking about...well, *things*...a *man*...*God*...that's when life is getting too complicated!

After the day in Aberdeen and "the look," and my flurry of thoughts during Iain's sermon on Sunday, and with lying awake until after midnight that night, the music in Ranald Bain's cottage and Iain's words from the pulpit intermingling like some other-worldly Scottish tune, by Monday I was beginning to think that maybe another road trip was in order.

There were still dozens of places in Scotland I hadn't seen. It would be good to get away and clear my head. Everybody talked about Edinburgh and Princes Street and the Royal Mile, maybe a visit to the Scottish capital, the jewel of Scotland, wasn't such a bad idea.

Before I had the chance to crystallize my plans, on Tuesday afternoon about one o'clock, I heard the doorbell. I knew it had to be either Iain or Mrs. Gauld. I wasn't especially eager to see either of them. But I couldn't pretend I wasn't home. They both knew my rented car and could see well enough that it was next to the house.

Slowly I went to the door and opened it. A gasp of astonishment escaped my lips. There sat the black BMW on the street. In front of me was *neither* Iain nor Mrs. Gauld.

It was the duke himself . . . in person!

"Mr., uh . . . Mr. Reidhaven!" I stammered. "I mean . . . Mr. Duke . . . that is, uh, I mean . . . Duke Reidhaven!"

"Hello, Ms. Buchan," he said, a slight smile on his lips at my discomposure. "I apologize for calling unexpectedly. I found my-self thinking of the sea, and I realized it had been years since I walked along the headland. I wondered if you might like to ac-company me."

Overwhelmed and still gaping, I babbled something I've forgot-ten, then went back inside to get my jacket and key and rejoined him. He led me away from the house and down the street in the direction of the Scar Nose. Among my babblings must have been something that we both construed as a *yes* to his invitation. As we passed the BMW I saw Nicholls sitting inside.

Gradually I caught my breath and began to relax. Actually I felt a sense of relief. *Okay,* I thought, *here it is out in the open. Every-body look! I don't mind.*

I *knew* everyone was watching by now anyway. I had half a mind to lead the duke by Mrs. Gauld's on our way.

Let the rumors fly!

It felt good to not hide it and to not think about Iain and church and God and "the look." There was a certain safety being out with a duke. I felt no pressure or expectations. It was like walking, I don't know, with my father or something. It had been that way at first with Iain. I'd felt safe because he was a minister. But then it had begun to get more complicated than I had anticipated.

But *this* wasn't complicated. Well...except for the fact that he was a duke, and a recluse who owned half the town and was the subject of a hundred weird rumors, and that I had been to the castle twice, and that I was teaching his daughter the harp and—

All right, it was a *little* complicated!

But not *personally* complicated in the same way things had suddenly become with Iain.

We walked about halfway to the next street in silence. Again I was aware of the duke's seeming uneasiness. For someone who had gone to the trouble to invite a comparative stranger out for a walk, he didn't seem to be enjoying himself much.

"Did you, uh, used to come to the sea a lot?" I finally asked.

"Oh, yes," he replied, almost eagerly. "As a boy, you couldn't keep me from it. I grew up in the castle, you know. I loved the sea."

"Did you sail?"

"Not much when I was young. My friend and I had a little dinghy. We used to take it out in the bay."

"That sounds fun."

"We pretended to be sailors. But whenever we capsized we were not so far out that we couldn't swim ashore. My father wouldn't let us take it out among the rocks or off the Scar Nose. I do have a boat now, though I rarely go out. What about you—did you grow up near the sea?"

"Oh, no," I said. "I'm from Alberta—prairies, lots of high mountains...the Canadian Rockies, you know."

"Ah, right."

"I think that's why I fell in love with it here—the rugged seacoast, it's so different. I walked along the trail above the cliff between Port Scarnose and Findectifeld even before I had booked myself into Mrs. Gauld's bed-and-breakfast. I was just driving along, stopping wherever I felt like it. When I stopped here and went for a walk on the trail, something drew me. That's where I first played my harp in Scotland. After that, I knew I wanted to stay for a while."

We reached the end of the village and the road that wound along the promontory. We began walking in the direction where, about a hundred yards away, a trail led out of town along the headland.

"Have you seen the dolphins?" asked the duke.

I shook my head. "Everyone talks about them, but I've seen nothing."

"You have to be lucky. It's unpredictable. I've lived my whole life here but have only seen them three times."

"Maybe today will be my day." I said.

"Where is it you played your harp?"

"Up there, on the trail along the cliff. It's still my favorite place. Do you want to see it?"

"I would."

We continued to chat. The duke seemed to be feeling more at ease, as was I. This was so much better than touring the castle and looking at old paintings of his dead ancestors! Ten minutes later we reached the bench. I still thought of it as mine.

"There it is," I said. "That's where I first brought my harp to play."

"Why here?"

"I don't know. I liked the view. It just seemed right. And I think a seagull told me this was the right place."

He glanced at me with a curious expression. But he did not ask, and I did not explain.

We sat down. The duke was breathing heavily. The climb out from the village, while not steep, had been steady. We sat for several minutes staring out at the expanse of blue ocean in front of us. With the sea to look at, with its ever-changing motion and colors and the rhythms of the waves and tide, you didn't need to say anything. Just being there was enough.

Then I heard the last sound I would have expected. I glanced next to me and saw that the duke was chuckling.

"What is it?" I said, smiling.

"I was just thinking of something that happened a long time ago," he said.

I waited, gazing at him, hoping he would explain. The look on his face caught me off guard. It was one I would hardly have thought him capable of—an expression of boyish delight.

"There are caves down there," he said after a bit. "All along this coast there are dozens—hundreds of caves. Large, small, of every shape you can imagine, some harmless and some quite dangerous. Stories and legends about them abound, from pirates to the blind piper escaping from Culloden and hiding out in the caves with an infant son. But what happened to my friend and me, a couple of young scamps who couldn't have been more than ten at the time, was enough to keep us out of the caves for a good long while."

"What happened?"

"Do you really want to hear it?" he said, beginning to retreat back into his shell of seriousness.

"Yes, please!"

He smiled, kind of a sad and faraway smile, and drew in a deep breath as if thinking about many things. I was afraid the moment had passed and would not return. But then he spoke again.

"There was one cave in particular—just down there," he said, pointing down over the edge. "We discovered it one day at very low tide. We used to roam all along the coast for miles. What adventures we had. On that particular day we found a cave we had never noticed before because when the tide is in it is impossible to get to. We did not even know it was accessible. On this day the tide was out and we walked around the rocks and inside on dry sand. We found a huge room in the cave that went farther back than we dared go. We ran to my friend's house and got a torch and hurried back. Once we were able to see we explored as far back as we could go, so far inside we were out of sight of the mouth. It wound back in and made its way deep into the cliff, right here beneath us," he said, looking about and gesturing with his hand.

"But as always happens with young nickums," he went on, "the time got away from us. As we were looking about, we began to hear water sloshing behind us and we realized it was sloshing about *inside* against the walls of the cave! We scampered out through the tunnel, but already the mouth of the cave was under-water and we could not get anywhere near it. We didn't know what to do. Had we just gone ahead immediately and forged out into it, it would not have come higher than our waists. We could have got-ten out of the cave and easily have swum around to the shore where we had come from. But once the tide turns, it comes in rap-idly. And we waited . . . and waited, not knowing what to do.

"Before another twenty minutes went by we knew that we had waited too long. The mouth was filling up and the waves were coming in harder and faster. To try to swim for it now could mean getting dashed against the rocks. We might easily have been knocked unconscious. It wasn't a stormy sea, but neither was it a calm summer's day. The water was rough and we knew we were in serious trouble. All we could do was back up farther in, and keep backing up inside the cave as the water crept higher and higher. The day was getting late, too. It was teatime and darkness was descending and we knew our parents would be frantic if we were not home by dark.

"The water came on, and we crept farther and farther back in-side until we were all the way back in the tunnel we had explored earlier. Finally we could go back no farther. Had the tide come up another foot or two, we would have drowned right there. But though it was a high tide we managed to wait it out, terrified and freezing. Gradually darkness closed in and we knew we would have to spend the night where we were. We entertained ourselves by seeing who could think up the scariest ghost and pirate stories.

A silly thing to do! We were already frightened out of our wits, so we did everything we could to add to our terror. I suppose that's the way boys are."

I laughed, and the duke began chuckling again.

"The wind came up and moaned through the rocks and into the cave," he went on. "I knew we were going to die right there. At least Reddy had the sense to conserve the batteries of his torch. By the time we finally realized the tide had begun to turn again, and checked the water level with the torch, it was well on toward eleven o'clock at night. I suppose we dozed a little on and off, though we were wet and numb from the cold. Low tide didn't come till four or five in the morning. It wasn't light yet by then, but the instant the water was low enough that we could get out, we ran out and home. At first our parents were relieved, then furious. But we had learned our lesson."

"That must have been terrifying!" I said. "Who told the scariest story, you or your friend?"

"Oh, Reddy, hands down! He always had a spirited imagination. He could spin a tale."

He let out a long sigh as the memory faded and with it the happy expression that had prompted it. In its place, a look of pain, or it might have been anger, passed quickly across his features.

"Then I wouldn't want to meet *him* along here on a dark night!" I said, laughing. "Actually, I'm not sure I would want to meet him anywhere if ghost stories and pirates were his stock in trade."

"They aren't anymore," rejoined the duke. "He spins a different kind of tale now. Besides, it's too late for you to wish for that."

"What do you mean?" I asked, confused.

"You already know him."

"Huh?"

"It's Reddy . . . Reddy Barclay, the curate."

Chapter Twenty-five

Warnings

Cold, alter'd friendship's cruel part,
To poison fortune's ruthless dart –
Let me not break thy faithful heaert,
And say that fate is mine, love.

—Robert Burns, "Forlorn, My Love, No Comfort Near"

I did my best to hide my shock to find out that Iain and the duke had been boyhood friends. Wheels within wheels, just like Iain said!

The duke rose and walked to the edge of the cliff and peered down toward the water, as if looking for the exact spot he had been telling me about. When he returned to the bench a minute later, I rose to meet him and we began walking slowly back down the trail toward the village.

"Tell me about some of your other adventures," I said.

"I doubt they are anything that would interest you," he replied.

"What about the pirate stories? Were there really pirates around here?"

"That was a long time ago. To be honest, I've completely forgotten."

He had retreated back into his subdued mode. Something strange was going on.

We passed several people walking their dogs. A few did double takes when they recognized the duke, but no one spoke to us other than a "Hi, ya" or a "Fine day." A biker sped by in blue-and-yellow biking clothes, but seemed too absorbed in his ride to notice us.

"Would you like to come in for a cup of tea and a scone?"

I asked as we approached my cottage ten minutes later. Nicholls was still sitting there just as we had left him.

The question seemed to throw the duke.

"I don't have maids and butlers to wait on us," I said with a laugh, "but I am able to boil water. Who *are* all the people I see at your, uh, your house—the castle. They don't all live there, do they?"

"Oh no, only four."

"That man who served us lunch—he looked like something from an old movie. I didn't know people still had butlers nowadays."

The duke smiled. "That's Campbell, Jean's husband...Jean, my cook. He doubles as part-time butler and valet for me—a stuffed shirt, I'll admit—never smiles, never shows the slightest expression, just *Yes, sir...no, sir.* But between he and his wife, and Alicia and Nicholls, the place is kept in tolerable order, and I am able to conduct my affairs unencumbered by the details of managing a house, much less a castle."

"Do the Campbells live at the castle?"

He nodded. "Nicholls, Alicia, and Jean and Campbell, all have rooms and apartments on the grounds."

"So, what do you say—would you like to come in?" I asked as we stopped on the walk in front of my house.

"I, uh...that is very kind of you," he said hesitantly. "But I think I need to be getting back. Thank you for the walk."

"Thank you," I said. "I enjoyed it."

He got in the car, Nicholls drove off, and that was that. An interesting encounter.

I went back inside and my thoughts drifted back into the channels they had been in before the duke's unexpected visit.

I *would* go to Edinburgh.

I needed to get away and figure out some things, mainly what I felt about Iain. Also what to do with regard to Gwendolyn and the duke. I couldn't keep seeing both of them without knowing what the situation was. It didn't seem altogether honest. If the duke was

Gwendolyn's father, then I still had some pretty serious issues with that. But to be fair to him, I hadn't heard his side of the story.

What about Gwendolyn's mother? There were things I didn't know. Who was she?

After meeting the duke, I had a hard time believing he was as bad as Mrs. Gauld said. But was I being duped? Maybe he was casting a spell over me. Somehow I doubted it. He was inward, withdrawn, I suppose you might even say a troubled man. He didn't seem at ease with people or himself. But I sensed no *dark powers* emanating from him. He struck me as a man who was hurting.

There were certainly no dark powers in Gwendolyn!

She was a sweetheart. Who would spread such things about a child?

I decided to leave the next morning. I told Gwendolyn and Mrs. Urquhart that afternoon that I would be gone for a few days but would let them know the moment I got back. Gwendolyn started to cry and it broke my heart. I put my arms around her, the sweet thing, and stroked her hair.

"I will be back before you know it, Gwendolyn," I said. "I will come visit you with my harp the moment I return. And do you know what will happen?"

"What?" she said, sniffling.

"After two or three days of *not* playing, you will enjoy the harp even more. You will be amazed at the music you will be able to make. Sometimes your fingers need a little rest. We will make some wonderful recordings when I get back."

"But why do you have to go, Marie?"

"I just do, Gwendolyn. I'm sorry. Why don't we promise to think about each other while I am gone? Would you like to do that? We will think good and happy thoughts about one another. It will make the time pass quickly."

"All right, Marie. I will try. Will you think about me, too?"

"Of course I will, Gwendolyn."

I said good-bye to Mrs. Urquhart, who seemed genuinely sorry that I wouldn't be coming for a while. It surprised me, but I was glad.

On the way back to my cottage I went by to see Mrs. Gauld. She had invited me to visit her, after all, and we had been friendly when I had been with her. I had imagined so much ill will on account of the duke. Maybe I *was* just imagining it. She was the first friend I had made in Port Scarnose. I didn't want to lose that.

She was surprised to see me, and invited me in with a friendly smile.

"Hoo are ye, dear?" she said.

"I am well, Mrs. Gauld," I said. "And you? Have you been busy with guests?"

"An English family left this mornin'. I had a family o' Americans for three days afore them. But I've no one tonight, least no yet."

"Well, I have decided to drive down to Edinburgh for a day or two, perhaps even three. I wanted to tell you so you wouldn't worry if you didn't see me around."

"'Tis very thoughtful o' ye, dear. But I—"

She paused.

"You *have* been worried about me?" I said in a questioning tone. "Because of the duke?" I added.

"I canna weel help it, dear."

"He asked me to play my harp for him," I said in as kindly a tone as I could manage. "How could I turn down a chance to play in a Scottish castle? I wanted to do it. Everything was fine."

"Ye dinna ken fit I ken, dear. Gien ye did, ye wad ken why I hae been worried for ye."

"Then tell me what you know," I said. "If there are reasons for me to avoid him, tell me what they are."

Mrs. Gauld thought a minute.

"It all started wi' the auld duke's father," she began after a long pause. "That's the yoong duke wha's there noo—his gran'father. He was forever travelin' aboot, a' roun' the world, an' whene'er he

came back tae Port Scarnose he might hae wi' him a Turk or a
Chinese or a red Indian fae America. He was always bringin' some
strange ane or anither wi' him, an' women, too. He consorted wi'
strange fowk o' all races. That's hoo they say the place came tae be
possessed o' dark powers an' secrets—fae the strange folk an' their
strange ways. An' he was always havin' tae do wi' Gypsies an'
fortune-tellers an' the like. He was aye drawn tae the dark side o'
things, bein' a Celt like he was. An' ane year he gaed off in the
summer tae Skye whaur there was some gatherin' o' druids an' the
like—the summer solstice, it was. An' fan he came back, he had wi'
him a woman fae the islands fit he'd married there. She was aye a
Celt as well as he, wi' powers o' the second sicht, they said, an'
worse. That was the end o' the comin' an' goin' o' fowk fae ither
lands, but no the end o' strange goin's on at the castle."

Footsteps sounded coming down the stairs behind us. It was
Tavia Maccallum who had been cleaning upstairs.

"No athegither the end o' it, Isobel," she said. "Dinna forgit the
young doctor fae Germany wi' his strange potions an' the like."

"He wasna sae lang there, Tavia."

"Aye, but lang enough 'tis said he brought the madness wi' him,
an' it stayed ahind after he gaed awa'. Ye mind hoo auld Struana
Grant fae the Seaton said Olivia hersel' had insanity in her blude
fae him, though he was gane lang afore she was born."

"'Twas auld Struana that was insane," rejoined Mrs. Gauld
authoritatively. "It was jist on account o' the curse Olivia said
against her cat, ye mind."

"Aye, an' the cat was foun' deid twa days later."

"Oh, aye, an' after that, auld Struana spread tales aboot Olivia
bein' mad tae git her revenge. But the way she deid hersel', I'm
thinkin' she had the worst o' that battle, as maist did wha crossed
Olivia till her face."

Tavia nodded, but said nothing more and returned upstairs with
a load of fresh linens in her arms.

"How does everyone know so much about the castle?" I asked.

"Abody kens the goin's-on at the castle," Mrs. Gauld answered. "My husband, God rest his soul, worked as a lad for the gardener on the grounds, Farquharson, ye ken, whan he had jist begun an' was a young man himsel'. An' he heard things, my man said, strange chants an' moanin' an' the like, comin' fae the tower on the east side. He knew 'twas the duke's wife, though he ne'er once laid eyes on the woman. She ne'er once set foot in the village. No one laid eyes on her. Then came word that she was wi' child. An' fan the auld duke was born, the duke's father, ye ken, she didna last long after. Some say the life began tae go oot o' her the day the auld duke's father brought her fae Skye, an' I dinna ken aboot that. But the auld duke was born, an' a year or twa after that she was gone. Some say she went back tae Skye. Some say her ghost still roams the place dressed in green, seekin' some kind o' revenge on her husband for takin' her fae Skye, but no one kens for what or why she deid. But mair nor ane's heard strange noises, an' moanin' jist like my man heard fan she was alive. Ever syne there's been a curse on the place. 'Course some say the green lady's the auld coontess, nae the witch woman fae Skye. Ane thing's for certain— 'tis madness in the family an' that's God's trowth, sae fan the auld Struana Grant laid sich a chairge at Olivia's door, sma' wunner Olivia put ane o' her hexes on her."

"What happened to her husband, the woman from Skye, I mean," I asked, "—the duke's grandfather?"

"He lived a lang life, but went mad in later years. They say once he began seein' her ghost he was ne'er the same. He was found deid one day in his bed. The present duke's father was away in the south at the time as a yoong man. Some say the auld man took his own life wi' poison, but I dinna ken. But the curse has been on the place ever syne. The duke's father was aye a strange ane, too, as was his wife, and they had but ane son, too, that's the duke fit's the duke now, an' his sister—"

By now I was shaking my head with confusion, trying to keep three generations of dukes straight!

"—an' his marriage was as ill-fated as the ithers. His wife, puir thing, died wi' oot e'er layin' eyes on wee Gwendolyn. 'Tis the curse o' the druid folk fa came fae Skye, an' 'tis been in that castle e'er syne, an' all wha hae tae do wi' it an' wi' any o' the dukes, they all come tae ill."

She took in a deep breath and let it out, as if punctuating her final words with an emphasis that ought to tell me all I needed to know.

"Well, no harm came to me, Mrs. Gauld," I said. "I heard no strange noises and the duke treated me with courtesy. I think he enjoyed my harp. And now I am going to Edinburgh, so you have nothing to worry about."

"I am glad t' hear it. But they say he has been callin' on ye, lass."

"Only once. And, my goodness, that was only two hours ago. Do you mean to tell me you heard about it already?"

"Word spreads fast in a wee village the likes o' Port Scarnose."

"But in two hours!"

"There's eyes everywhere, lass."

"Do people really care so much what the duke does that they watch his every move?"

"Nae one cares aboot the duke, dear. 'Tis yersel' they're curious aboot. Fan the duke comes callin' on a lass fa's new tae toon, folk tak notice."

"He didn't come calling on me, Mrs. Gauld." I laughed. "We just went for a walk. It was perfectly harmless. He is a lonely man, there in the castle by himself. I saw no harm in it."

"An' Gwendolyn's a lonely lass."

Her words stopped me in my tracks. I had no reply.

"Jist watch yersel', lass," she said after a moment. "Jist watch yersel'. Things arena always fit they seem."

"I will, Mrs. Gauld," I said.

"I also took a walk up the Bin," I said. "I met an old shepherd who lives in a stone cottage and tends sheep. I thought I had stepped back into the nineteenth century!"

Mrs. Gauld nodded. "Aye—Ranald Bain."

"You know him?"

"All Port Scarnose kens Ranald Bain, puir man."

"Why do you say that?"

"He lost his puir wife six years syne. She was oot walkin' tae
Findlater, they say. 'Twas a fine day, but cauld, wi' wet on the rocks
an' in the shadows. When she wasna back by afternoon, Ranald
came doon fae the Bin an' went searchin' for her. He foun' her at
the base o' Findlater, sae he said. Slipped on the bank is what folk
said an' we've nae reason tae doobt it. 'Tis nae way tae lose a loved
one—the puir man. The children o' the village tell dreadfu' tales
aboot him, the way they do when they're feared o' someone fa
luiks different than the rest, an' there's folk fa winna gae near him.
There's stories aboot him like aboot the duke an' Gwendolyn. But
in his case, they're naethin' but auld wives' gossip, naethin' mair."

"He told me he had a daughter who also died."

"Aye," said Mrs. Gauld, nodding once again. She grew quiet and
thoughtful. I had obviously asked about something involving more
than met the eye. "She went oot walkin' alang the sea an' wasna
seen agin. A dreadfu' thing it was. But that was many lang years
syne, when we was all yoong. I was achteen at the time."

"Did you know her—Mr. Bain's daughter, I mean?"

"Aye, lassie," she replied, again looking away. For a moment I
wondered if she was going to start crying.

"Were you and she friends?" I asked slowly.

"Aye, but I was a wee bit older, ye ken." She brushed at her eye,
then looked back at me and forced a smile. "Winifred was aye
everyone's frien'. All Port Dochy lo'ed Winny Bain, comin' doon fae
her father's croft ilka day tae the school, wi' her straw-blond hair
blawin' in the wind, an' her happy smile. Wasna a lad in a' Port
Scarnose that wasna in luv wi' her. An' she was as kind an' thoughtful as she was bonnie."

Again Mrs. Gauld looked away. Now the tears were flowing from
her eyes in earnest.

I reached out and placed my hand on her arm.

"Mrs. Gauld, I am sorry," I said.

She drew in a deep breath and again wiped at her eyes. "Thank ye, dear," she said. "'Twas a lang time syne. But whiles it a' comes back like 'twas yesterday, an' I maun hae a wee greet."

"It must have been awful for you, to lose someone you were so close to."

"Aye. Wasna an easy thing. But losin' a frien's no the same as losin' a dochter. Puir Maggie...puir Maggie Bain—she ne'er got ower it."

It was quiet again for a minute and I tried to change the subject. When I stood to leave a few minutes later, Mrs. Gauld again warned me about the duke and reminded me that people noticed everything I did. I glanced up and saw Tavia watching me. I left feeling more self-conscious than I had been before.

Was everybody in the village really watching me so close?

Chapter Twenty-six

The Curate and the Latitudinarian

Oh, Charlie is my darling,
My darling, my darling.
Oh, Charlie is my darling,
The young Chevalier.

—"Charlie Is My Darling"

I left Mrs. Gauld's and went to see Iain.

"Hi, Marie!" he said enthusiastically when he answered the door. "I was just going to go over and see if I could find you. I thought you might like to come over for supper tomorrow night."

"Oh, I would," I said, "except that I'm leaving in the morning. I'll have to take a rain check."

"Leaving...what!"

"Only for a couple of days," I said. I couldn't help laughing at his expression, like my leaving was the end of the world. "I decided to take a drive down to Edinburgh."

"I thought you didn't like cities," said Iain, inviting me in.

"I don't usually," I replied. "But if I'm going to do the tourist thing, it seems I ought to see it."

"Your Scottish excursion hardly seems to qualify as doing the tourist thing." Iain laughed. "Most tourists don't cancel their flights and rent cottages for indefinite periods of time."

"I suppose you're right. Okay, then let me rephrase it—if I'm going to pretend to be a Scot, it seems I ought to visit Edinburgh."

"That makes sense. Then don't miss the zoo and the penguin parade—every day at two in the afternoon."

"That sounds fun. How long does it take to drive down there?"

"Do you drive fast or slow?"

"Slow."

"Are you going through Aberdeen, straight down through Huntly, or along the Spey?"

"I don't know. Which is best?"

"None, they're just different. Driving conservatively, all three will take you about four hours or slightly more. The nicest route for scenery," he added, "in *my* opinion at least, is the direct route south through the Cairngorms—to Huntly, then to Ballater and south to Perth. You'd be on smaller roads, but it's beautiful."

"I'll look at my maps. That sounds good."

It was quiet a minute. There was so much I wanted to tell Iain. But how could I bring up Sunday's church service without Saturday's drive into Aberdeen coming into it, and how that day had ended? As if reading my mind, it was Iain who brought it up instead of me.

"You know, I've been wanting to tell you," he said, "how much I enjoyed our drive into Aberdeen on Saturday."

"I did, too," I said. "Thank you for taking me."

"Oh, thank *you*. It is so nice to get out and away and just have the chance to talk with someone who is..."

He sighed as if struggling for the right words.

"Not from around here," I suggested.

"Yes—exactly!" rejoined Iain. "Don't get me wrong, I love the people here. I love my parish. But when you're locked into the life of a church, the perspective cannot help but tend inward. You see everything through churchy eyes, so to speak, and that's not necessarily always good. Sometimes you need to break out of that to get a larger view, a wider outlook. It's true of churches, of communities, of spiritual philosophies and points of view. You need a more expansive vantage point to keep you from getting ingrown.—Hey, this is pretty good! I ought to be writing this down...potential sermon material."

I laughed again. Sometimes Iain's down-to-earth manner caught me off guard.

"What I was trying to say," he went on, "is that talking with you helps break me out of all that."

Now it was my turn to be thoughtful. His look from Saturday returned to my mind.

"You really don't mind, do you," I said at length, "that I'm not a Christian?"

"*Mind*—of course not!" he replied. "I find it *more* invigorating that way. You challenge and mentally stimulate my mind. I love the dialogue. Besides, whether you're a Christian or not, you are still God's child."

"You don't think of them as the same?"

"Being a Christian and being God's child?"

I nodded.

"Not at all."

"What's the difference, then?"

"A Christian is a follower or a disciple of Jesus Christ. Making yourself his follower is something you do by choice. It is a decision you make at some point when you say, 'Jesus Christ is my master and I intend to make myself his disciple. From this point on my life is not my own. My goal henceforth is to do what he says, to follow his example, to see life as he saw it, to treat people as he treated them, to think as he thought.' That's what it means to be *anyone's* follower."

"But you say I am God's child whether I'm a Christian or not."

"Who else could possibly be your Father but God? Your earthly father, of course, but I mean, who is the Father of all mankind?"

"God, you mean?"

"Of course. Who gave mankind life? We are all God's children. He is our Father. He sired us, brought us into being."

"What about people who don't believe in him?"

"Even atheists are God's children, though they don't acknowledge the relationship. Many earthly sons and daughters don't lovingly acknowledge their parents either. They are their parents nonetheless."

"What about the elect and, and all that? I thought Christians believed only the elect were God's children."

"That view is a relic left over from a Calvinism that ought to have been tossed on the scrap heap of failed belief systems long ago. I know millions of people still believe in Calvinism's false portrayal of God, but I am not one of them. I hate the very term *the elect*. It conveys such dreadful wrong about the nature and character of God. Not just wrong, it implies *evil* at the heart of the Godhead. I loathe the very thought of it."

"You continue to surprise me!" I laughed. "For a minister, the things you say seem scandalous."

"I am certain many would agree. I would not speak so strongly from the pulpit. For one in my position, I have to walk carefully and allow people to grow slowly. Casting aside the constraints and false doctrines of long-held traditions is fearful. It takes time for religiously trained people to get used to the idea of a larger God. Especially here."

"Why here?"

"In Scotland, I mean. Many vestiges of Calvinism remain in the Scottish church. This is where Calvinism first took root outside Geneva. I always try to gently open eyes to the fact that the God of Calvin and Knox and the Father of Jesus Christ are two *very* different portrayals. As for me, I cast my lot and my future with the Father of Jesus Christ."

I did not reply. I was starting to get that overwhelmed feeling again. I decided to change the subject.

"Where did all these ideas come from?" I said. "I mean, how did you come to hold such, uh…unconventional perspectives? I mean—don't get me wrong, I like what you say. But even you say that they are unusual views, especially in Scotland."

Iain laughed to hear me talk about him so.

"There is a man who took me under his wing," he answered. "I really was a scamp when I was young. Though much of it was harmless fun, by the time I was fifteen, the boyish mischief was gradually becoming more serious. I could have gotten into some pretty serious trouble had I continued along that road."

"But you didn't."

"No, and I have the man I told you about to thank for that. For reasons I still don't completely understand, he saw something in me, even though he hardly knew me. He saw where I was headed. He grabbed me and stopped me in my tracks and set me on another road. I owe him everything, literally. I owe him my life, my faith, my ministry."

"But was he the one, like I asked before, was it because of him that you came to hold such unconventional views?"

"Indirectly. He taught me to *think*, to think for myself, to look at things from many vantage points and consider implications and consequences. The first thing he forced me to think about was myself—who I was and where I was headed. I was just a kid, but he got my attention. I listened, and gradually I began to change. After that, he helped me learn to think about many things—spiritual things, where I was going in life and what I wanted to make of myself. He constantly turned my eyes toward the bigger picture. Eventually he led me into faith. It was in his stone cottage, with him and his wife, that I prayed to give my heart to the Lord. It was there, a few years later, where I reached the decision to go into the ministry. And the dear man and woman—they substantially financed my education. I would not be where I am today without them. How well I remember that night," he added with a smile. "It was in the middle of winter and the wind was howling through the trees. I had spent the afternoon helping him round up his sheep and get them safely into the pens because snow was in the air. Then about dusk we went in. His dear Maggie had just taken a batch of fresh oatcakes out of the oven—"

"His *Maggie*!" I interrupted in surprise. "You don't mean, the man you've been talking about—it's not Ranald Bain?"

"Yes!" exclaimed Iain. "Don't tell me you've met him?"

"Yes!" I laughed. "I've been to his cottage twice. He and I spent an hour or two just yesterday playing together—he on his fiddle while I played his grandfather's harp."

"That's brilliant! I can't believe you actually met him. But the old harp, its strings are broken."

"I restrung it."

Iain laughed again and shook his head. "I can't wait to hear the two of you together."

"But I am a little puzzled," I said. "In both my visits to Mr. Bain's house, he hasn't said a spiritual word. Well, I think he may have mentioned God. But other than that, I would never have guessed him to be such a man as you describe."

"He is not pushy about faith. He was a little pushy with me, I will admit, but that was because I needed it. Generally, however, he is not evangelistic about his views. He trusts God to see to all things in the proper time."

"Is he as unconventional as you in his beliefs? Is that where *you* come by it?"

"Not at all. It may surprise you to learn that Ranald Bain is about as conventional in his doctrine as you could imagine. Theologically, he is actually a thorough Calvinist."

"Now I am really confused," I said.

"Let me take that back—Ranald *is* totally unconventional in this: He does not feel that everyone has to believe exactly as he does. He values individual prayer and thought and scriptural study over doctrine. Maybe I should say he values each individual's quest for truth above his *own* particular viewpoints. In that sense he is unconventional and certainly *un*-Calvinistic. So he taught me to think, to ask questions. He taught me how to pray, how to take every uncertainty to God in prayer, and how to dig in the Bible to discover truth. He taught me by his own example, but never pushed me to adopt *his* doctrinal conclusion on every matter."

"What an unusual thing."

"Unusual, and wonderful. It led to some of the most invigorating discussions. He sharpened my mind, my intellect, my whole spiritual being. In the end I came to many conclusions different from his. Yet he is not bothered by that. Do you remember what I said earlier about God being the Father of all mankind?"

I nodded.

"Ranald disagrees with that view completely. I'm not sure whether he fully believes in a predestined elect, but he does believe that God is the true Father only of those who are saved. He and I have spent hours discussing this one issue. Yet we both find the difference stimulating because neither of us is so arrogant as to think we possess the full truth. Likewise, he still adheres to the traditional Calvinist doctrine of the total depravity of man, while I do not. I believe that good exists in all humanity, whether saved or not. Yet we rejoice in the unity of our faith in spite of those differences."

"That is so interesting, and unusual."

"It is," Iain nodded. "Ranald is what I would call a latitudinarian. His acceptance of people is broader and wider than his doctrine, which is one of the reasons I respect him so highly."

"It's too bad more aren't like that."

"I agree. But back to your question—yes, I suppose I believe as I do because of him, because he taught me how to be a *thinking* Christian. He did not tell me *what* to believe. He taught me to go to God for myself. He taught me *how* to believe. Wisdom, to a man like Ranald Bain, is not based in specific beliefs or doctrines, but in one's *approach* to truth. He is the humblest man I have ever met. I think in the end that accounts for his huge impact in my life. Even though there is a great disparity in our ages, I consider Ranald my closest and dearest friend."

"How did he, as you say, turn you around when you were young?" I asked.

Iain smiled a nostalgic and far-off happy smile. "I think," he said, "if you are truly interested to know, I will let you hear that story from Ranald."

It was silent for a minute or two. We were both lost in thought.

"Do you mind if I ask you another question?" I said.

"After all this time, and you don't know the answer to that yet! Of course I don't mind."

"All right—I will ask it then. I was talking with Mrs. Gauld earlier. She said some spooky things about the castle and the duke, about the ghost of the duke's grandmother haunting the place, and that there has been a curse because of his grandfather and druids and all sorts of things. Is any of that true?"

Iain shook his head.

"I've heard it all, too, since I was a boy."

"But you don't believe it?"

"I'm not the superstitious type. If you ask me, there is far too much superstition in both Scottish theology *and* Scottish legends. No, I don't believe it. I have no doubt that Alasdair's—that is, the duke's grandfather, was something of a strange bird. So was his father. But that doesn't imply hauntings and ghosts and curses and all that sort of mumbo jumbo."

"I, uh…I understand you and the duke were boyhood friends?"

The question obviously took Iain by surprise. He looked at me with an odd expression, then nodded.

"Yes—yes, we were," he said. "How did you hear that?"

"Actually, he told me."

"Alasdair…the duke?"

I nodded. "You remember his invitation for me to play for him at the castle?"

Iain nodded thoughtfully. "What did you think of the castle?" he asked.

"It is quite a place. I thought I was in a fairy tale."

"That's when he told you, when you were there?"

"No, actually I saw him again and he told me about you and him exploring the caves along the shore and about the time you were trapped inside one when the tide came in."

A nostalgic smile came to Iain's lips. I could tell he was reliving the incident.

"Well, that is interesting," he said at length, nodding slowly. "Yes, we used to have a lot of fun together back in those days."

"But not anymore, I take it?"

"No, not for a good many years."

Chapter Twenty-seven

Brief Good-Bye

Flow gently, sweet Afton, amang thy green braes,
Flow gently, I'll sing thee a song in thy praise;
My Mary's asleep by thy murmuring stream,
Flow gently, sweet Afton, disturb not her dream.
—"Flow Gently, Sweet Afton"

The following morning, I got ready to go, then locked my little cottage and left.

I had a stop to make on my way out of town. I needed to let the duke know that I would be away for a while. I wasn't even sure I could find my way to the castle, but I had to try. What if the gates were closed? How do you call on someone in a castle, just walk up and knock on the door?

It seems odd that I felt obligated to tell the duke I was leaving town. I hardly knew the man. I had only seen him twice in my life. But there was something peculiar going on with him. I almost felt—it was strange to think it—because of those two encounters that he had almost come in a way to depend on me, that I might be one of his few friends.

What a presumptuous idea!

Especially about an important man, and me a nobody, a stranger. I was just "passing through," as the old westerns used to say.

Yet the duke's demeanor when he had come to the cottage some-how gave the impression right then that he...well, almost that he needed me in some way I could not understand.

· The music of the harp had obviously drawn him. I hoped that maybe the music, and my being a friend to him...that maybe those things might somehow bring him and Gwendolyn back together, if indeed the situation was as Mrs. Gauld had said.

What I said a moment ago about feeling *obligated*...that is probably the wrong word. I just felt he ought to know I was leaving, that it was the considerate thing to let him know. I didn't want him coming to call at the cottage again and find it empty. How embarrassing that would be for him, with the whole town watching.

I found my way, with only one wrong turn. The gates were open. I drove in and continued all the way to the castle and parked in front. People probably weren't supposed to just drive in like that, but I did. I knew they wouldn't throw me out.

Miss Forbes answered the door. She was obviously surprised to see me.

"Oh, it's you, Ms. Buchan," she said. "Just...wait, please—I will tell the duke you are here."

The look on the duke's face a minute later when he saw me took my breath away. His expression positively lit up. He was genuinely *glad* to see me! It was so unexpected. To have that kind of an effect on another individual, it is a humbling thing. I was simply overwhelmed.

"Now it is my turn to apologize for calling unexpectedly!" I said, laughing as I nervously tried to recover myself.

"Oh, no, Ms. Buchan," said the duke. "I am so happy to see you."

"Please, I feel awkward enough coming here, without adding to it with the *Ms.* Couldn't you just call me Marie?"

"I, well, yes, of course. But I hope you don't feel too awkward... please, come in!—Alicia, would you please bring us tea...in the library, I think."

"I really only came for a minute," I said, following as the duke led the way inside. "I wanted to tell you that I am leaving for a few days. I'm taking a drive down to Edinburgh."

His face now fell as suddenly as the light had broken into his eyes a moment before. The news seemed to shatter him.

"Oh, of course," he said as we walked up the stairs. "Well, I hope you have a good time."

We arrived at the first floor, which I recognized from before. He opened a different door for me this time and I walked into what was obviously the library. My eyes opened wide at the sight. Books lined every wall. Bookcases were arranged in rows along the floor, with old Persian rugs running between them. I stood gaping at the sight.

"But...you will be back?" said the duke.

"Oh yes," I said. "I just want to visit the city. I haven't seen it yet."

Miss Forbes came in a side door with a tray of tea things, which she set down on a small table across the room. She left and we sat down.

"You will like it. Edinburgh is a lovely city," said the duke. "But—"

He hesitated. The look of uncertainty and embarrassment I had seen before came over him again.

"I really want to hear...no, I *need* to hear your harp again," he said. "You won't leave, to return home, I mean, without...I mean, I *will* have another chance to hear you play?"

I smiled. "I will be back in a few days. I'm sure we can arrange something. Maybe you will let me return your hospitality and you can come have tea at my little rented cottage."

"Perhaps I shall at that."

Unexpectedly he now smiled.

"What is it?" I said.

"Oh, I was just thinking of the villagers," he said. "They love to gossip about me. I was thinking what they would say to my having tea in a little fisherman's cottage instead of my big fine castle."

"Is the place I am staying a fisherman's cottage?" I asked.

"It used to be. Most of the houses in the village were at one time. Everyone thinks I am too proud, too high and mighty for that. I might surprise them yet. Yes, I will do it! I accept your invitation. And I will not back out the next time as I did yesterday. I apologize for that."

"Think nothing of it. Do you know Ranald Bain?" I asked, surprised at my own question. I had not intended to ask it.

"Ranald Bain!" he repeated, almost fondly. "I haven't seen him in years. Of course—everyone knows Ranald Bain." He glanced away thoughtfully, an expression coming to his face that I could not altogether understand. "I should probably have visited him, after Margaret's death," he said slowly. "He is one of my tenants, after all. Thank you for reminding me. I have been remiss. I will attend to it soon. He is a good man, despite what some people say of him. I am certainly one who can understand *that*," he added sardonically. "Why do you ask about him? Have you made his acquaintance?"

"I was out walking, up to the Bin, last week, and I ran into him. He invited me to his cottage for tea."

"Is that so!"

"I found him delightful. Then I went back and restrung an old harp he has that has been in his family for years."

"That's right. Now that you mention it, I recall stories of his grandfather—the Bard, they called him."

"Did you ever hear him play?"

"No, that was long before my time."

"I heard about his daughter's death, too," I said. "He didn't tell me himself. I heard about her later. It must have been a terrible tragedy."

Expressionless, the duke gazed back at me as if my words had suddenly caused a trance to come over him. The look on his face had gone blank. He seemed to be staring straight through me.

What followed of my brief visit was strained. The duke hardly said a word after that, and I soon left to be on my way south.

Chapter Twenty-eight

Right There Beside Me

I heard the voice of Jesus say, "I am this dark world's Light;
Look unto Me, thy morn shall rise, and all thy day be bright!"
I looked to Jesus, and I found in Him my Star, my Sun;
And in that light of life I'll walk, till trav'ling days are done.
—Horatius Bonar, "I Heard the Voice of Jesus Say"

When I drove out of Port Scarnose, how different were my feelings than when I had first driven into it. I was now leaving a part of me behind. There were people here I truly considered friends, people I would think about and miss. I had hardly missed anyone from Canada in all the time I had been in Scotland.

What was happening to me here?

The drive south, as Iain had suggested, through the Cairngorms, was lovely. As I left Braemar, the traffic thinned and the way became more desolate and lonely. The heather was beginning to bloom—gradually more vibrant the farther south I went. But as I looked at the hillsides rising on either side of me, there were times I couldn't quite tell the gray from the purple. The blossoms of the heather produced a color too subtle to detect with ease. Close beside the road, the color appeared vibrant. But on the hillsides in the distance, its hues blended more mysteriously with the surrounding terrain. This was no straightforward flower, this *heather* of the north, but a blossom of curious mystery.

What tales did it have to tell?

As often happens when I am driving, my thoughts drifted inward. How could I not reflect on the past few weeks and the changes that had taken place within me? I found myself thinking about things I had not thought of in years, perhaps that I had never thought of at all.

Being around Iain Barclay forced a person to *think*. He was having the same effect on me that he said Ranald Bain had had on him.

Spiritual things were real to Iain, so present, so daily, so much a part of *life*, that they came out as naturally as breathing. In all the years I had been in the church, religion and faith had never been like that—so much a part of life.

Iain *lived* it.

He *thought* about everything. He didn't just accept ideas because he was supposed to believe them. He tried to make *sense* of what he believed. That was new to me. You couldn't be around him for long without his commonsense logic rubbing off on you. At least that's the effect he was having on me. I was *thinking* in new ways.

I smiled as I remembered the first moment I had laid eyes on him, his red-topped head popping up below the cliff from out of nowhere! *Reddy*, the duke had called him. And that happy, child-like exuberant smile, full of the joy of life.

Almost immediately, the vision of Iain's face—whenever I thought of him he was either smiling or laughing—began to speak in my mind. Words he had said began drifting back into my brain.

God's Spirit resides in all men and women . . . we are beings created in God's image.

His words challenged both my present *unbelief* and my former lethargic *belief.*

I was beginning to wonder about both. What was the difference between belief and unbelief? Did it have more to do with how you lived than doctrine?

Did I really *disbelieve* as much as I thought? If so, why was I thinking about God and Iain Barclay and church so much? And if the "beliefs" I once held were so superficial, what *had* I believed during all those years?

Had I *really* been a Christian at all? According to Iain's definition,
I mean—one who had made oneself a follower of Jesus.

That was not something I had ever thought about!

Even so, Iain said he could see God in me. *Whether you're a*
Christian or not, you are still God's child.

He had been talking about my harp playing. But I had the feeling he meant more, too. I knew he valued me as a person. I had
the distinct idea that he felt God valued me, too.

That was another pretty heavy idea! God *valuing* me, some part
of God living inside me.

I remembered Iain speaking of his desire to preach the true essence of Christianity. What was that *essence*, I wondered.

Again words out of Iain's mouth came back to answer my own
question: *A Christian is a follower or disciple of Jesus Christ. That's*
something you do by choice, a decision you make. "From this point
on my life is not my own."

He had spoken of life being a journey, a quest for truth and understanding. *We are all on individual journeys,* he said. *Growth is*
individual. It has no straight paths. But I'm sure you will get there in
the end.

Was that what he meant when I asked him where "there" was,
and he had smiled a knowing smile, and simply answered, *"Where*
you are going."

Had he been thinking of that moment of choice?

I had so many questions. Whatever I might have believed, whatever it was that I had once called my faith, it hadn't been a very
thoughtful faith. If I had been a Christian at all, one thing was for
sure, I had been a lazy one.

Suddenly everything was more involved than just going to
church and sitting absently listening to a sermon and then going
home. If what Iain said was true, these were matters that encom-
passed every aspect of life.

And yet there was something exciting about it. How could the
happy enthusiasm of a man like Iain Barclay not be infectious? If

what he said about Christianity was true, who *wouldn't* want to be part of it? What else could possibly matter but discovering truth and trying to live by it?

As I drove I also now remembered the meal in Aberdeen.

Across the table Iain's sensitive, caring, green, earnest eyes stared straight into mine. I could see his eyes as vividly as if he were right in the car beside me. *The look*...a look of love.

With a replay of "the look," came Iain's words I had heard him speak in church when he hadn't known I was there:

When he looks you deep in the eye.

I knew he was talking about Jesus.

Gradually, in my mind's eye, Iain's face began to change. I cannot say what face it was that I saw, whether from some painting or image from my childhood. But I knew that *Jesus* was looking at me, not Iain, and that *his* eyes were staring straight into mine.

I could hardly concentrate enough to keep my eyes on the road. What do you do when you suddenly realize that *Jesus* is looking deep into your soul?

His look was exactly as Iain's had been, a look of knowing, a look of understanding, a look of love.

He was probing deep into the most hidden places inside me, just as he had the rich young ruler.

And I knew, as Iain had said, that he *loved* me.

I was overwhelmed. My eyes were watering and my vision blurry. I had to stop.

I began looking for a place to pull the car to the side of the road.

The eyes of Jesus continued to bore into mine. Then I saw tears begin to gather in his eyes. Gradually the tears fell down his cheeks. I knew they were tears of love, tears that wept for me because, like the rich young ruler, I, too, had turned away and had *not* followed him. I knew that the pain from his love for me was breaking his heart.

I pulled off the road, stopped the car, and burst into tears.

Chapter Twenty-nine

Mystery of the Heather

Thus bold, independent, unconquer'd, and free,
Her bright course of glory for ever shall run,
For brave Caledonia immortal must be.
—Robert Burns, "Caledonia"

It took me the rest of the day to recover from what had happened.

I cried for a long time. There was such grief in my heart to realize that I had drifted from Jesus but that he had continued loving me all these years, even after I said I no longer believed.

How could that be? How *could* he love me with those eyes of love, even though I had turned away?

I began looking for a B and B not long after that. I did not want to drive. I needed to walk and rest and think.

The next day I continued on into Edinburgh, where I spent three days. At last I was ready to respond in a complete way to everything Scotland was, to all it meant, to all it was *supposed* to mean. My "adventure" had turned inward. The adventure had become a quest, a journey, a pilgrimage. I walked the Royal Mile and went to museums and toured Edinburgh Castle and Holyrood. It really is a fabulous city. I enjoyed myself immensely.

I remembered Ranald's words about the history of Scotland being the history of its religion. I had always known that Scotland's music was special and unique. More than anything it was Celtic music that had drawn me here in the first place. But it wasn't only the music that had gotten inside me. It was the history, the culture, the people, the language, the lore, the literature, the hopes, the disappointments, the triumphs, the poetry, and the pervading *spiritual* atmosphere that overspread them all. God had used the land of Scotland to awaken me spiritually. Surely that was no accident. Scotland's multidimensioned magic knit together *many* factors into a unique tapestry, melancholy perhaps, woven in subdued shades and minor chords of mystery and undefinable meaning. Subdued shades, exactly like the heather. At last I was ready to discover what that interweaving of music, history, and religion signified. I wanted to take in the full scope of the subtle heathery tapestry and perceive the tale it told.

No longer were the tourist sites mere "tourist" sites—suddenly they had become intricate and important threads of the vast tapestry that was Scotland.

I toured the Museum of Antiquities in Edinburgh with heightened interest, even excitement. To see the ancient Queen Mary harp and Lamont harp and Pictish stones sent thrills through me. Everything was newly alive with meaning. The harmonies of my own harp were now more than mere music—they were alive with harmonies of the spirit resonating with the deep longings of my soul. I think it was perhaps while touring Edinburgh Castle that the history at last began to organize itself and give its particular nuances to the three-dimensional tapestry. The stark, rugged majesty of the castle itself, seen from across the valley, so perfectly typified the land and its personality—it appeared to grow literally *out of* the stones themselves, exactly like so many of Scotland's ancient castles. Out of a foundation of granite had emerged a people, a culture, a nation—hard, determined, rugged, enduring, like the stones of their homes and castles and buildings and bridges. But they were likewise a people of passion and vigor and creativity, for they also derived much of their national character from the peat that overlaid the granite substrata, peat that had not only warmed their cottages but whose warmth fueled the fires of their hearts with vitality and energy and pride. Granite and peat *together*. Both defined the national character.

When I gazed upon Bonnie Prince Charlie's red cape and trousers in their display at the castle, my heart *felt* something, a connection with the reality of Scotland's history that plunged yet deeper at the sight of the bust of Mary Queen of Scots. These heroes of Scottish legend and song were *real* people! With wonder I beheld the crown jewels, then the Stone of Scone, upon which had been crowned British kings and queens for centuries. The awe deepened as I stood in Queen Margaret's tiny chapel and recalled my own epiphany of the spirit on the drive south.

I left the castle in a daze, overwhelmed by the emotional experience of being in the midst of a history that suddenly seemed so much a part of my own inner story. I walked back to the hotel where I was staying, in no hurry as I made my way through the streets. All about me was modernity and bustle and noise. But my mind and heart, all my senses, were engrossed in events and people of centuries past. I felt as if I were walking in a dream, where busyness swirled about me but wasn't really there.

I went back to my hotel room and sat down to read a fifty-page book outlining Scotland's history I'd bought at the castle gift shop. I read it straight through, two hours without a break. I read slowly, almost methodically, trying to absorb not merely the details but the overview of two thousand years of history. The minute I was finished, I was on my way back to the castle.

I don't know how many people tour Edinburgh Castle twice in the same day, but I did. I spent the whole rest of the afternoon, more slowly this time, visiting every room and listening in detail to every segment of the tour-guide CD. In Margaret's Chapel for the second time that day, I read selections out of another book from the gift shop, *Prayers of Mary Queen of Scots*. I felt such a spiritual bond with these two women, both queens of Scotland separated by almost five hundred years, Queen Margaret and Queen Mary. As many terrible things as had happened in the name of religion, there was yet an undercurrent of true faith throughout the history of this land that could not be denied. They lived so long ago, yet what incredible women of deep and abiding faith they both were! That faith was now real to me, too, as it had been to Margaret and Mary.

Changes were taking place inside me—*deep* inside me. I left the chapel in cleansing tears.

It was late by the time I made my way back down the Royal Mile from Castle Hill, sometime after six o'clock. I realized I was hungry. I'd had no lunch. I hadn't even thought of it. But I didn't want to waste time in a restaurant. There was too much to read, too much to learn. I knew there was a third movie I needed to see, one that would add a *spiritual* component to *Local Hero* and *Braveheart*. I had seen it years before. But as it came back to my mind I realized that I needed to see it *here*, in Edinburgh. More than the mere story, I was ready to absorb the full message of Eric Liddell's life. Therefore, on the way down the hill I bought a sandwich, a bottle of wine, a package of oatcakes, then went into a video store I remembered seeing and bought a used copy of *Chariots of Fire* to watch on the DVD player in my room.

I don't know when I've spent such an enjoyable evening! After *Chariots* I read till after eleven from various of the other books I had with me.

From Edinburgh I drove to St. Andrews. Most people probably go to St. Andrews for golf. I went for its connections to the Scottish Reformation, to touch one more facet of the spiritual roots of the nation that had become so newly meaningful. Many of the events that had taken place at St. Andrews reminded me how horrible and ugly and ungodly much of that history was—burnings and beheadings and excommunications. But the evil that existed in man toward his brother could not invalidate God's truths. That was a fallacy of logic to which secular intellectualism was prone that I had no intention of falling into. Though it had been turned toward both good and evil, there could be no denying that a spiritual passion existed in this land that was part and parcel of its history, and perhaps part and parcel of my own spiritual journey as well. *It was a passion to know God.* It was a passion that had been wrongly directed and entirely misplaced in the hearts of many through the years of Scotland's bloody past. But it was a passion that reached its flowering fulfillment in men like Iain Barclay and Ranald Bain and others like them, who connected the dots of history and spirituality into the unified personal story they were *meant* to tell. History is supposed to tell the story of increasing truth. That it didn't always tell that story in the life of every observer of history meant nothing to me. I wanted to make certain that *my* reading of history produced increasing truth in *my* life. I was hungry to know the story history was *supposed* to tell.

I had already decided to visit Stirling and Bannockburn again, though I had seen them cursorily during the drive of my first week. It was there that Scottish history had reached its zenith in 1314 with Robert Bruce's triumphant defeat of the English. I wanted to drink it all in again, this time with a more complete understanding of the events of that pivotal time.

As I had in Edinburgh, I took my time, savored each new tidbit of history I could fit into the historic drama. After watching the video and perusing the books at the visitors center at Bannockburn, I left the crowd of people and walked out through the tree-lined avenue across to the battle monument. I made my way slowly, gazing over the gently sloping plain, allowing the quiet sense of history to speak its faint words. I wanted to feel the legend.

I had been to so many of Scotland's historic places. I had just left Edinburgh and St. Andrews. I had walked Scotland's coasts, driven its Highlands, toured castles of magnificence, and had tea and oatcakes in a humble crofter's cottage. But in the center of it all, where geography itself seemed to demand a climax...*here* at Bannockburn did the history of this nation converge into an inevitable pinnacle of drama.

In the distance, singularly situated at the very heart of the country, Stirling's castle rose out of the valley floor itself, as if the ground had burst apart one day and exploded upward with granite—exactly as I had observed at Edinburgh—growing of itself the mighty gray fortress-flower that now sat proudly atop it.

No site in all Scotland was fuller or richer, no place contained more symbolism, than right here. It was the site of the greatest battle in all Scottish history—where independence had been won. I walked the rest of the way to the Bannockburn battle monument. Slowly I made my way around it, reading the posted information with historic reverence.

Leaving the circle, I continued on toward the giant bronze statue of Robert Bruce himself. In the same way that Stirling Castle emerged from the rocks of the valley, the silent, massive sentinel from the past seemed to grow up from the surrounding terrain.

I stared upward at the majestic figure. The expression of fearlessness on Bruce's face, looking down from out of his helmet of mail, was so lifelike as to compel obedience, commanding all to behold the mighty hand that subdued this land and vanquished its enemies. The wide eyes and flared nostrils of the mighty beast he was seated upon likewise compelled, not hushed submission like its master, but terror, lest any stand in its path and be crushed beneath its powerful hooves. Truly were horse and rider one, fit symbol of that independent spirit of a proud nation who would not forever remain under the rule of another.

Were any of *my* Buchan ancestors here on that fateful day? I wondered.

Several minutes later, feeling full with the sense of history, I made my way back to my car. I was ready to point it again toward the north.

As I drove away from Stirling, I was overflowing with a thousand sensations...music, spirituality, and history all blending as one. Everywhere about me the heather was in bloom. Yet it still seemed to hide its most vibrant color from view. The tapestry of its colors remained obscure. Like Scotland's history, it would not divulge its secrets easily.

As I went, with images of the triumphant Robert the Bruce still so fresh, it occurred to me how different were Scotland's other heroes—William Wallace, Mary Queen of Scots, her son King James VI, even MacDonald of Glencoe whose clan had been massacred in 1692, and especially that epitome of the Scot's hero, Bonnie Prince Charlie. None had triumphed like the Bruce. Actually, in a sense they had all *failed*—even King James, who, though he had not personally failed in his reign as king, had certainly failed the land of his Stewart roots by abandoning her at what could have been her singular moment of greatest triumph, helping set in motion the series of events that ended at Glencoe and Culloden, and eventually doomed Scotland's nationhood.

Why, I wondered, did Scotland so immortalize in ballad and song what could only be viewed as the *failures* of its great figures?

There were so many *could-haves*, things that didn't go their way that could have, and maybe that *should have,* so many *what-ifs* that turned against them. And in the great irony of Scotland, the Scots even turned against themselves. James VI abandoned Scotland for the lure of London as the seat of his crown. If the Bonnie Prince had chosen his ground more carefully, as I had learned at one of the historic visitors centers, and attacked Cumberland's troops the night before, *he* might have occupied the throne of Great Britain rather than the Hanoverian George I. The Stewart dynasty might still be in power today, ruling all of Britain from Edinburgh rather than a line of German ancestry ruling from London. But the greatest irony of all was that, in the end, no battlefield defeat at the hands of the English in 1707 cost Scotland its independence. It was the Scottish Parliament *itself* that voted to end nationhood and allowed Scotland to be swallowed up in Britain. Many of Scotland's ironic *what-ifs* of history were self-inflicted.

North of Pitlochry I stopped at the Hermitage of Dunkeld. There

I spent several hours thinking and praying and walking about, this time with a volume of Burns's poetry, trying to answer some of these very questions. From there I returned over the desolate moors again to Glencoe, where I spent the night at a B and B. The next day was bright and warm. Most of the morning and well into the afternoon I hiked on the high trails surrounding Glencoe. Though Lord Byron's immortal poem had been penned about another mountain peak farther east, it was while walking the lonely mountains surrounding Glencoe, as I read them over again and again until they were burned into my brain, that the solemn splendor of Byron's words entered my soul:

Away ye gay landscapes, ye gardens of roses—
In you let the minions of luxury rove;
But restore me the rocks where the snowflake reposes,
If still they are sacred to freedom and love.
Yet, Caledonia, dear are thy mountains,
Round their white summits tho' elements war,
Though cataracts foam 'stead of smooth flowing fountains—
I sigh for the valley of Dark Lochnagar.

Ah, there my young footsteps in infancy wandered,
My cap was the bonnet, my cloak was the plaid;
On chieftains departed my memory pondered
As daily I strayed through the pine covered glade.
I sought not my home till the day's dying glory
Gave place to the rays of the bright Polar star;
For fancy was cheered by traditional story,
Disclosed by the natives of Dark Lochnagar.

Shades of the dead, have I not heard your voices
Rise on the night rolling breath of the Gael;
Surely the soul of the hero rejoices,
And rides on the wind o'er his own Highland vale.
Round Lochnagar while the stormy mist gathers,
Winter presides in his cold icy car;
Clouds therein circle the forms of my fathers:
They dwell midst the tempests of Dark Lochnagar.

Years have rolled on, Lochnagar, since I left you,
And years must elapse e'er I see you again;
Though nature of verdure and flower has bereft you,
Yet still you are dearer than Albion's plain.
England, thy beauties are tame and domestic
To one who has roved o'er the mountains afar;
Over the crags that are wild and majestic,
The steep frowning glories of Dark Lochnagar.

And there, at historic Glencoe, the heather finally began to unfold its mystery.

I saw what it signified, and why Scotland's history burned so bright and alive in the heart of the Scot's soul. It was because of a new kind of Scottish hero that emerged out of the ashes of defeat following Culloden—a *literary* hero. In Robert Burns and Sir Walter Scott and Robert Louis Stevenson and George MacDonald and many others, the Scots truly did "conquer" the literary worlds of their day. Their battlefield predecessors may have failed, but their literary warriors triumphed! What the prince's Highlanders had not accomplished at Culloden with the *sword*, these new men of letters achieved in the century that followed by the might of the *pen*.

In so doing, they recast the history of their land and imbued it with immortality. Out of the mists of the past arose new heroes like Rob Roy MacGregor and Flora MacDonald and so many more, to take their place beside the Bruce, the Queen, and the Prince. The very defeats of martyr-heroes like Mary and Charlie were turned into the legends by which Scottish history derived a new identity and yet greater power.

Scotland's heroes thus became larger in death than they were in life, greater in defeat than they perhaps could ever have been in victory. Burns's nostalgic lamentations invoked a pride that was palpable, imbuing the past with heroic overtones more significant than the events themselves, giving the history of the past a seductive mystery capable of firing the imaginations of future generations.

Nor was this a mere imaginary mythology born of failed hopes and dreams. It was far more. The great Bard immortalized a *true* reality existing in the tales of his homeland's lore. He discovered what the history *meant*. No revisionism this, but a history that had been awaiting the eyes of the insightful poet-Bard to pull from between the lines of history's unfolding panorama.

Burns's verses and Scott's tales and MacDonald's wisdom thus elevated those whose names might otherwise have faded into the mists of the past with new stature.

I recalled to mind the great statue I had just seen of King Robert on his enormous bronze mount. But as I saw him now, the Bruce was not alone.

There was Bonnie Prince Charlie beside him to the right on his own mighty steed of valor. Mary Queen of Scots sat to his left astride a magnificent white horse. The Bonnie Prince raised the sword of freedom in his hand high overhead. Her head high with queenly dignity, Mary quietly held the Bible and prayer book as weapons of faith that her cousin Elizabeth could never vanquish. Marching out proudly in front of them I envisioned a ten-foot-high statue of bearded, kilt-clad MacDonald of Glencoe, bearing a great claymore in his muscular arm. "Let the Campbells of the Dutch king's legions do their worst," I could hear his silent cry, "the free spirit of the Highlands will never die!"

What a vision of four hundred triumphant years of history!

King Robert Bruce did not reign over the now silent expanse of Bannockburn alone. All Scotland's great men and women rode with him. Behind MacDonald of Glencoe and the Bruce and the Queen and the Prince spread out a great gallery of witnesses— Dundee and Montrose and Flora MacDonald and Rob Roy...old Columba and Saint Ninean and Kenneth MacAlpin, King Malcolm and Queen Margaret...yes, and there were Burns the Bard and Sir Walter and George MacDonald trailing their forebears with proud and vigorous step and the light of truth radiating from their eyes.

No defeat at Culloden could silence such a band of warriors!

All had fought worthily and nobly for the right of Scots to call themselves free *Scots*. In the hearts and minds of their descendants, they were fighting still. Nothing could silence the collective majesty of that eternal freedom-song.

What all these had fought for, what some of them had given their lives for, it lived on!

Of course, things *could* have been different, perhaps *should* have been different, and may yet be different again. Scotland may not have presently been an independent political entity. But the Scots knew themselves as a *people*, proud and strong and, yes, independent. No one could rule their *hearts*. They lived in no mere northern extension of England, they dwelt in Scotland!

I could hear their voices from the field of Bannockburn echoing silently north and west across the Highlands, in all directions to the sea—to the Atlantic of the Western Isles, to the Orkneys, to the Moray Firth, to the North Sea off Aberdeen and Dundee: *This is proud Caledonia!*

Along with Byron's "Lochnagar," I read Burns's "Caledonia" again and again as the *type* of this heroic outlook of history, climaxing triumphantly with the words read throughout Scotland by every Scottish boy and girl: *"Thus bold, independent, unconquer'd, and free, Her bright course of glory forever shall run, For brave Caledonia immortal must be."*

As I walked, with the valley of the Coe below, the heather's nuanced colors had nearly reached their glory, a subtle robe of Caledonia's regal majesty spreading over otherwise barren slopes.

I stooped to pluck a tiny sprig, then sat down and gazed at the blending of purples and whites.

In one of life's many mysteries, it is death that brings life, winter that leads to spring. As quickly as the bloom of heather comes, it fades and gives way to the harsh realities of its own death. In flower it serves no useful function. Only in after years, as decaying blooms pile upon one another, layer upon layer, century upon century, millennium upon millennium, does the heather, like the tiny blossoms in my hand, gradually solidify into that miraculous substance known as peat, which contains within its bosom the invisible fire of life, the heart of the Scot. The dying purple bloom of ages past thus yields up its life for a more useful end, that its long-dead blossoms might warm the homes of the Scottish Highlands for a thousand cruel northern winters yet to come.

In the same way, with the fading blooms of their gallant reigns, short-lived in Mary's case, and fired but briefly in the imagination of the Bonnie Prince, was born a lasting vision of national pride and freedom for the country they loved. It was a vision like the heather-symbol of their homeland—everlasting and glowing bright through ongoing centuries.

What a fit token was this tiny plant, I thought, for the young queen and the boy prince whose rules were so poignantly brief. The purple garment of their royalty burst into glory but for a moment, quickly to be extinguished by the sword of Elizabeth's executioner and the sword of Cumberland's cruelty. As short-lived as were those their radiant hours, however, out of the fading bloom of the Stewart dynasty in the years following Culloden was born a hope that gave new meaning to the very land that neither could conquer, and infused a yet deeper life into Caledonia's consciousness.

The Queen and the Prince were reborn every year in the heather—their royal robes flowering afresh, though, as in their lives, always but for a fleeting remembrance. Yet it was a memory that would always return. For as long as time existed, the Scots would forever sing, "Will ye no come back again?" Neither sword nor winter could kill the legend.

As I left Glencoe midway through the afternoon, playing the CDs of my expanding collection, the music of pipers, accordians, fiddles, and tin whistles wove a magical spell, now with a ballad, now with a dance tune, now with sad lament of poignant historic Burns's verse, infecting me with a full sense of pride, contentment, and significance. Never, I thought, was the folk music of a nation so perfectly one with the evocative sensations caused by the land itself. If these Highlands, these streams, these forests, these bare and rocky mountains, these jutting and jagged seascapes...if they could produce music *of themselves*...if out of their very essence the sounds of symphony could arise from the places where hidden melodies haunted the ground and rocks, and lift their strains to the heavens—surely that glorious symphony would be a combination of the melodies, rhythms, instrumental combinations, ballads, and harmonies the musicians of Scotland had given her people through the years in song.

Chapter Thirty

"Home" Again

Hail! To the mountains with summits of blue;
To the glens with their meadows of sunshine and dew;
To the women and men ever constant and true,
Ever ready to welcome one home.

—John Cameron, "The Mist Covered Mountains of Home"

When I returned to Port Scarnose on Monday, I felt almost as if I were a different person than the woman who had left five days before. I arrived late in the day, about seven-thirty in the evening. It was so much like coming home it was almost frightening.

How could I feel so at home in a place I had never heard of less than a month before?

On the floor lay two envelopes that had been put through the door while I was gone. Without even opening them I knew who they were from.

I opened the first, a blank envelope. *Marie,* read the sheet inside. *I hope you had a wonderful visit to Edinburgh. Things here were dull, dull, dull without you! I hope you will come by and let me know when you are back, and I can take you up on that rain check for dinner. Iain.*

Then I opened the second, the monogrammed envelope. The message was similar. *Dear Marie, I hope you still want me to call you by name. Please come by and let me know when you are back. I very much want to see you. Alasdair Reidhaven.*

It was the first time the duke had used his name with me. It was going to be hard to think of him as Mr. Reidhaven rather than "the duke," even harder to think of him as *Alasdair.*

207

Could you ever really call a duke by his first name?

I put on water for tea, and ate oatcakes and jam and read awhile and then went to bed, glad that I had gone, but happy and content to be back.

As I drifted to sleep, the last thought I remember was the question of which of the two I would go visit first the next day.

The question answered itself the following morning.

The first person I knew I had to see was Gwendolyn.

About ten-thirty I packed up my harp and the tape recorder and set out for the Urquharts. Dear little Gwendolyn, she nearly knocked me over with a hug when she saw me at the door. Even her ordinarily subdued aunt smiled.

"Did you bring your harp, Marie?" asked Gwendolyn.

"I did. It's in the car. Would you like to play?"

"Yes, please!"

Five minutes later Gwendolyn was at my harp lost to the world, oblivious to the tape recorder beside her, making some of the most beautiful and haunting music I had yet heard from her fingers. It brought tears to my eyes as I listened. I knew I was participating in the expression of a musical gift I might never see again.

I went to see Iain that afternoon. I wanted to tell him about my drive to Edinburgh. It was hard knowing how to begin.

"I went the way you suggested," I said as we sat in his kitchen with a pot of tea and oatcakes and biscuits on a plate between us.

"Some of that scenery is so stark and desolate. Didn't you find it so?" he said. "Yet beautiful in its own way."

"I stopped somewhere south of Braemar, where the road turns south and winds through those lonely hills. I found myself thinking about many of the things you've said to me."

I paused. I smiled a little nervously. I didn't know what to say.

"I hope I haven't—" began Iain. I heard the concern in his voice and saw a look on his face I hadn't before. I realized he might have misunderstood.

"No, it was nothing like that," I said. "Don't worry—you haven't offended me. They were good thoughts, or perhaps I should say, necessary thoughts. I thought about Jesus and the rich young ruler."

Iain glanced up at me with a questioning expression.

I smiled. "Sorry," I said. "I suppose I have a confession to make. I snuck into church last week and hid in the back where you wouldn't see me. I heard your sermon about Jesus and the rich young ruler."

Iain was stunned. In one of the rare times since I'd met him, he was at a loss for words.

"And what you said then," I went on, "and other things you've told me...everything just culminated, I guess you would say, as I was driving."

Iain listened patiently.

"I came to no resolutions," I said. "All I would say, I suppose, is that God has my attention. I'm not sure what it all means."

"Well," he said at last, "it is always good when we are thinking, even if we can't see where the path is leading. My only word of encouragement would be not to rush whatever is going on inside you. In our personal journeys of growth, time is an important ingredient. Things take time to resolve themselves."

"Thank you," I said. "I will remember that. But what about the rich young ruler? He didn't have time. Jesus put a life-changing decision before him and he had to decide right then. His delay meant that he turned and walked away. So how does what you just said apply to him?"

Iain nodded thoughtfully.

"That is a very good question," he said after a moment. "Honestly, I have never thought about it in the context of the rich young ruler. I don't have an answer. I'll have to think about that."

"Fair enough," I said.

"So tell me about Edinburgh. Did you enjoy yourself?"

"Oh, like you wouldn't belive. It was a trip of revelations—historical, spiritual, in so many ways. I finally read Burns with meaning. I see clearly how his poetry lies at the root of the great Scottish pride that is so evident everywhere and is responsible for the legendary and heroic perspective Scots have of their history. It is all beginning to fit together for me at last."

"Fit together...what?"

"*Everything*...the history, the music, the spirituality...the magic. It's a grand tapestry! It's all about the heather, by the way."

"The heather—how so?"

"Scotland's history—it's all about the heather, and Mary Queen of Scots, and Bonnie Prince Charlie. It's what the heather *means*."

"This I simply must hear!" Iain laughed.

I recounted all my touristy and revelatory activities and we visited for another hour.

As I was leaving, Iain asked me about the rain check. We made arrangements for a second dinner date on Friday evening. He said there was a place he wanted to take me in Banff, about fifteen miles away, with a spectacular view of the seacoast. He said he would pick me up at five-thirty.

Chapter Thirty-one

Rose Garden

Oh, there's meal and there's ale whaur the Gadie rins,
Wi' the yellow broom and the bonnie whins,
There's meal and there's ale whaur the Gadie rins,
At the back o' Bennachie.

—"The Back o' Bennachie"

After more than an hour with Gwendolyn, and an hour and a half with Iain, I was nearly visited out for the day. I went back to my cottage and lay down for a while, then spent the rest of the day reading and taking a long walk along the shore to Crannoch and back.

The next morning I drove to the castle and left a brief note for the duke with Miss Forbes at the front door. All it said was, *Duke Reidhaven, I wanted to let you know that I am back in Port Scarnose. Marie Buchan.*

I wasn't even back to my car yet across the parking area when I heard the door open again behind me and footsteps come crunching across the gravel toward me.

I stopped and looked back.

It was the duke. He wasn't exactly running, but he was *hurrying*. He held my note in his hand.

"Marie...Marie, please!" he called after me. "Do you have to go?"

I waited. He slowed and came toward me, breathing heavily. Whatever had been the cause of his sudden change of mood the last time I had seen him, it was gone now.

"Could you come in for a while?" he said. His face wore an expression of such boyish eagerness, I truly thought he would crumble if I said no.

211

"I suppose," I said, smiling. "I didn't want to presume."

"Presume!" he said, almost in disbelief. "I have been waiting days to see you again. Please, won't you stay for a visit?"

"Of course," I replied, turning away from the car. "I have nothing urgent on my schedule," I added, laughing.

"Oh, good! Come—have you had breakfast?" he asked, leading me back toward the castle.

"Just tea and a few oatcakes, but—"

"Good! I'll have Alicia prepare us something."

"Something light," I said. "I'm not a big morning eater."

"Of course, something light! Tea and scones and butteries."

He led me inside, had a few words with Miss Forbes, then took me along a corridor, still on the ground floor, and a few minutes later we emerged outside again at the back of the castle.

"I want to show you the gardens," said the duke. "They're not visible from the front. I'm very proud of them."

He led me from the door over a stone path across a mown lawn, and through a "doorway" through a giant thick hedge that must have been seven feet tall. We emerged into an extensive rose garden, with paths winding through it in several directions. Invisible from the other side of the hedge, it was like walking into another world. There were so many hundreds of blooms that the air itself hung heavy with fragrance.

"Oh, it's spectacular!" I exclaimed. "From the other side of the hedge I would never know this was here. It's lovely. Who tends all this for you?"

"Actually I do most of it myself," replied the duke. "I love gardening. Roses especially. Keeping up this rose garden is one of my most enjoyable pastimes."

"What else do you do?" I asked as we slowly wound through the garden's paths. "I've never met anyone from the aristocracy before—what *do* dukes do?"

He laughed. It was a good laugh, a gentle laugh, a nice laugh. He was changing, relaxing, becoming more comfortable and at ease right before my eyes. I tended to think of myself as timid. But compared with the duke, I was the belle of the ball! He was *really* inward and withdrawn. To have hidden from me, not even showing his face, at our first meeting...now that was being a serious introvert.

Yet now he was opening up, slowly, like a flower blossoming.

Was it because of *me*, was it the harp, was it the music, was it simply because *someone*—it could have been anyone—was showing an interest in him and was drawing him out of his lonely existence?

"What do dukes do?" he repeated, still smiling. "Probably not as much as they should."

"Do you travel?" I asked.

"Not much. You have to have someone to travel with, and I don't. Mostly I see to my business interests."

"What are they?"

"Property. The estate has vast holdings that have been in my family for generations. Managing them is on my shoulders now, like it was on my father's and my grandfather's before me. Of course, it is different than it used to be, but still there are hundreds of individual properties, a great deal of forest acreage, several home farms that cultivate hundreds of acres of barley and oats and raise cattle and sheep. It is an extensive operation."

"I had no idea. I just thought...I guess I just thought that you had this castle and lived here and...well, I didn't know what you did. And you manage all that yourself?"

"There are dozens of people who work for me. I have a business manager who oversees it all from the Buchan Estate offices in town. But I am involved at the decision and administrative level in most of what goes on. I have offices both here at the castle and in town, though I do most of my work from here."

"And you have no other family?"

"A few distant cousins scattered through England and Scotland, but they are very obscure relations, not even considered legally such in the line of succession, so to speak. I was the only son of an only son. I do, however, have one sister. She and I are the only ones left.—And, by the way, your name, Buchan...are you a long-lost relative come back to trace your lineage or something, to discover your roots? *Do* you have family in Scotland?"

"Maybe, but I know nothing of it. It is purely coincidental. I didn't even know that this region of Scotland was associated with the Buchan name."

"That is quite a coincidence."

"What about you—I heard that you were married, but—"

The words just popped out before I realized it.

"Oh—good heavens!" I said, glancing over at the duke. "I'm sorry. I didn't mean to say that." There was a look of pain on his face. But just as quickly, he tried to put my embarrassment to rest.

"It's all right," he said. "Think nothing of it. You are right—it was a brief marriage. My wife died in childbirth."

"Oh, I am sorry," I said.

He nodded in acknowledgment.

"And...the child? The child died as well?"

I felt cheap and dishonest asking that after what I'd been told about Gwendolyn. But I had to know.

He winced slightly at the question. "There was a daughter," he said vaguely, leaving me to wonder how he meant the words to answer my question. Knowing how the villagers talked, he probably knew that I knew. But we didn't talk about it further.

We walked on in silence awhile. I regretted having taken the conversation down that path just when the duke had been relaxing and talking more freely.

"This is a beautiful rose," I said, pausing to bend down to a bush full of yellow blossoms tinged at the edges with red. I put my nose to one and inhaled. "And so deliciously fragrant!" I exclaimed. "What is it called?"

"It is one of my favorites," answered the duke. "It is a hybrid tea rose called Broadway. It is very hard to find. I had to order it from the States, then I propagated several additional plants from it. The combination of color and fragrance, and the perfection of the shape of the blossom—it is truly a stunning rose."

We reached the far end of the rose garden where another opening appeared in the hedge.

"Come through here," said the duke, leading the way.

Again, the tall hedge obscured sight of what lay on the other side. Now I suddenly found myself walking toward a small pond with a stream running into it from the far end. All around it were rocks and ornamental trees of various kinds. Fish swam in the pond and paths led out from it toward several smaller gardens bordered on all sides by tall hedges.

"It's beautiful!" I exclaimed. "Wherever you turn, there are new mysteries to discover. Did you plan it this way? You see just a little at a time, then you go through an opening in the hedge and find yourself in a new little world all its own."

"You are very perceptive, Marie. That is it exactly—the secret of a good garden is gradually revealed mysteries."

"Well, you have certainly succeeded. I have never seen anything like it. This is stunning!"

"I am glad. It pleases me that you enjoy it."

I had been prepared to be angry with the duke for abandoning his daughter. But there had to be more to the story. This could not possibly be an evil man.

"I don't see how you have any time for your business," I said. "This garden must take an enormous amount of work."

"It does. But I have help. I do not do *all* the maintenance of the grounds myself. I have a man on my staff who doubles as a gardener and a gamekeeper—Farquharson is his name. The estate also employs many maintenance people if I need them.—What about you?" he asked abruptly. "Were you never married?"

The question surprised me, though I don't know why. People are curious about such things. If I was curious, why shouldn't he be?

"Actually I was married, too," I said. "For seven years, in fact. It was a good marriage. My husband was a fine man and I loved him. But he died suddenly and I have been alone now for six years. We had no children."

"I am sorry," said the duke.

"Thank you." I nodded. "It has been hard, I admit that. I have been alone, and sometimes...I don't even know what I was going to say. Sometimes it is just hard being alone."

"I understand. Of course, it is exactly the same for me. Here I am in this huge castle, one of the wealthiest men in the north of Scotland, but I am alone, too."

At mention of the castle, I glanced back. From the vantage point of where we were walking, with the sun coming through the trees and falling on the light gray of its stones, it was a sight that could have been taken straight out of a fairy tale.

"It's so beautiful," I said. "But it must also be spooky living in such a huge old place, at night I mean, during a winter storm. Although men probably don't get afraid of ghosts and goblins like women do."

"Don't be too sure!" The duke laughed. "There are enough stories and legends and tales about this old place to fill a book, and to keep anyone—even a man—lying awake in the middle of the night listening to every little noise and thinking the worst. There are secret passageways even I don't know about."

"I would think you would have explored them all as a boy."

"Many—but not all. My sister, however, was fearless. She boasted that she could get from any room to any other room in the castle completely unseen, that no lock could keep her from wherever she wanted to go."

"Is that true?"

"I don't know. Knowing her, it might have been!"

"Why do you say that?"

"Let's just say she was very skilled at terrorizing me."

"She was older?"

"Actually no, she was a year younger. But she had, I don't know, a spiritual, perhaps an occultish power that could strike terror in a young boy like me."

"How? What did she do?"

"She was an amateur poet," he replied with a little laugh. "Not really a poet. But she loved to speak in little ditties that she turned into hexes and curses. Just phrasing them as rhymes added to their terror—I'm not sure why. Perhaps because that made them lodge in my mind where they would work on me."

"It sounds awful. What kinds of things did she say?"

"She loved to frighten me. There was said to be an underground passageway that leads over to the church. In ancient times, when the church was Roman Catholic, its crypt was connected by this passage to a monastic school located at the castle. But when bones were discovered in the passage, thought to be those of monks from centuries past, the passage was closed up. So the story goes. I was terrified of the stories and stayed well away from the spookier parts of the castle—the attics of the various wings, the basement rooms beneath the east wing, even musty old storage rooms could be terrifying, and there are dozens of such rooms. But Olivia claimed to have explored everywhere, from roof to basement. She told me she had seen the bones and had even picked up a skull in her hands. I was horrified at the thought, but she just laughed at me. She was always trying to frighten me. I'm afraid I wasn't very brave as a boy. I never knew whether to believe her or not.—Do you like to sail?" he asked abruptly.

"*Sail?*" I repeated, taken by surprise at the sudden shift in the conversation. "I don't know. What do you mean...like in sailboats?"

The duke laughed again, like he had before. "Yes, sailboats!" he said.

"No," I answered. "I mean, I have never been on a sailboat in my life."

"Oh, then you must! There is nothing like it."

His face came alive with animation, like I had not seen it before that moment.

"Can you…are you free? Come out with me—we'll go out and have lunch amid the wind and waves! Say you will, Marie. I haven't had anyone to take sailing in years. Maybe we will see the dolphins."

I was so surprised by this sudden turn in the conversation, all I could do was stare back at him with my mouth open.

"You mean…actually go sailing—out on the North Sea?" I said, beginning to laugh. "You're not joking?"

"No, of course not! It will be great fun."

"You didn't exactly inspire my confidence with your tales of you and Iain capsizing!" I laughed.

His expression clouded at the mention of Iain's name, but only for a moment.

"I have learned how to sail properly since then," he said.

"And you have a boat?"

"The most beautiful fifty-two feet you have ever seen in your life!"

He grabbed my hand and pulled me back through the hedge. Releasing it, he led me, hurrying almost frantically and talking all the way, back toward the castle. Within minutes the arrangements with Miss Forbes for breakfast had been changed to orders for a complete lunch basket to be packed.

Nicholls was summoned from somewhere.

Twenty minutes later we were in the BMW, my car still parked where I had left it, and on our way to the harbor.

Chapter Thirty-two

On the Firth

The sailor's cheerings aloud in the bay,
Yo-ho, my lads, heave-ho!
Away! O'er the rolling brine, away!
Where the winds their bugles blow.

Let the weakling crouch by the hearth,
Let the worldling gloat o're his gold,
O'er the wave let me bound with a ship that is sound,
And a crew that is staunch and bold.

Up to the breeze with the shivering sail!
Yo-ho, my lads, heave-ho!
Let the straining shroud ring loud in the gale,
Where the breaker curls in snow.

—"The Rover"

When I thought of a "sail," I had not imagined a yacht! But that's what I found myself boarding—a beautiful white pleasure yacht outfitted for use with either sails or engine. I had seen it in the harbor before but had taken no notice. Today it would be a *sailing* vessel.

The moment we were out of the harbor and sailing toward open water, the duke changed even more than I had noticed that morning. He was animated, excited, full of boyish enthusiasm for the adventure.

And so confident and in command. He knew everything to do. Before long he had me holding ropes as he adjusted sails, shouting orders and laughing at my ineptitude. Suddenly he had become the captain of an ancient sailing ship, and the two of us were setting out for lands and seas unknown.

I had the time of my life. I didn't even get seasick.

He took us straight out from the harbor. It was remarkable how quickly the shoreline faded behind us. Then he dropped the sails and we began floating gently with the water lapping against the sides. He got out Miss Forbes's basket and, the perfect host, set out tea and sandwiches.

It was so quiet, so peaceful. I had heard people who loved the sea talk about what it was like being all alone out on the water. After experiencing it I knew what they were talking about. It was one of the most peaceful settings I had ever been in.

Except for the mystery about Gwendolyn, I couldn't understand why the people in the village thought so ill of Duke Reidhaven, or, as I suppose his proper title would be, the Duke of Buchan. I was still a little uncertain what to call him. Names and titles were so confusing! I still wasn't quite sure if that was the proper term of address. But whatever I was supposed to call him, I liked him. He was pleasant and courteous. Now that we were talking more freely about things, I found him an interesting and engaging man. Maybe he wasn't that way toward the locals. I didn't know.

I lost track of time. After lunch we were sitting on the deck on two chaise lounges chatting and laughing about nothing important. The sun was warm and the fragrant sea breeze so intoxicating.

I began to doze. Vaguely I knew that Gwendolyn would be expecting me before long. But I couldn't bring myself to call an end to such a wonderful afternoon. I was happy. I would let it run its course and go see Gwendolyn when I got back.

Then I woke up, still lying on the deck. The duke's chair was empty. I sat up and glanced around. He was at the wheel. One of the sails was up again and we were moving gently through the water.

I stood up and stretched and walked toward him. He smiled.

"You went to sleep," he said.

"I did," I said, drawing in a deep, contented sigh. It was so peaceful and quiet and warm, I couldn't help it. "Where are we bound, Captain?"

He laughed with delight. "Back toward the harbor," he said. "I didn't want to take advantage of you and keep you to myself for the whole day. I remembered what you said before about the girl you are teaching to play the harp. I thought maybe I should get you back."

"That was considerate of you—thank you," I said. "What time is it?"

"A little after three."

"I'm already late!" I laughed. "But it's not set in stone. I'll go see her when I get back."

We stood there beside each other for several minutes in silence, gazing out in the distance where the shoreline was gradually coming into view.

Suddenly I saw a great splashing and movement in the water only twenty or thirty yards off the side.

"Dolphins!" I exclaimed. "Look... look, Alasdair—there must be ten or more! Look, they're jumping in and out—oh, wow!"

He laughed at my enthusiasm. I hadn't even realized that I had called him by name.

"They love to lead a boat like this," he said. "I don't know what it is, but it's quite common."

I continued to watch in wonder.

"How long will they follow us?" I asked.

"Until we reach shallow water."

"How do you know where to go?" I asked as we continued to approach the shore. "Or maybe I should ask, how do you know where we are?"

"I have a GPS on board if I need it. But for a short excursion like this, I just follow the coastline. There in the distance," he said, pointing, "the outline of Crannoch Bin is just coming into view. I use that as our landmark and simply set our course toward it. If we were going into Inverness or up to John O'Groats, or around the point to Aberdeen, I would do the same, use visual landmarks. If we were bound for Shetland or Orkney or the European mainland, that would be different. Then we would have to use GPS."

"Do you really sail that far?"

"I've taken her all the way into the Mediterranean, to Italy, Greece, Malta, but not for a very long time."

"My goodness—I had no idea."

"Perhaps you would like to join me for an extended excursion later in the summer."

"To the Mediterranean—that sounds like an indecent proposal!"

"Oh, I'm sorry," said the duke, obviously flustered. "I meant nothing like that."

"I was only joking!" I laughed.

Again we slapped along in the waves for a while in silence.

"Tell me about your daughter," I said at length. "Never having been a parent, I don't know what it's like."

If the duke took offense at my question, he didn't show it. He didn't answer immediately.

"To answer your question from earlier," he said after a bit, "no, she did not die. She lives with her aunt, my sister."

"Why is that?" I asked.

"It seemed best," answered the duke vaguely. "I was in no position to care for an infant."

"And now?"

"She is still with her."

"Do you see her?" Again I felt a little deceptive for asking.

The duke glanced away. Slowly he shook his head. "No," he said softly. "No, I don't."

He sighed deeply, still looking away. The emotions my question had stirred obviously ran deep. I waited a minute or two. But it was clear he was not going to say more.

I reached up, hesitated a moment, and laid my hand on his shoulder briefly.

"I'm sorry, Mr. Reid—uh...*Alasdair*," I said. "I didn't mean to stir up anything. I know it's none of my business—I am just interested."

He nodded. I withdrew my hand and walked away to the bow and stood watching as we sliced through the blue water. I stood for twenty or thirty minutes until we began to draw close again to the little harbor of Port Scarnose. By then the dolphins were gone. I turned and walked back to the duke where he still stood at the wheel. I went to his side and slipped my hand through one of his arms.

"This has been a lovely day," I said. "Thank you."

"Thank *you*, Marie," he said, looking toward me with a quiet smile. "You've wakened me from a long sleep."

"I'm sorry if I—"

"Say no more," he said. "I understand. It is just that your appearing from out of nowhere like this, it has stirred up many things inside me that I thought were dead. So you mustn't mind if I occasionally grow quiet or withdraw into my shell. I am still learning many things."

Now it was my turn to smile and nod with what I hoped was understanding.

"What is that?" I said, pointing to a tiny little domed structure perched on a knoll a little inland toward the castle.

"It's called the Temple. It's an abandoned summerhouse the inhabitants of the castle used years ago when they were going to the beach.—But we are approaching the harbor. All right, then, First Mate," he said. "Man your post. We must bring in the sail and swing her around before we run aground!"

I had no idea what I was doing, and I don't think it was really all that dangerous. Actually I doubt he really needed my help at all. But he pretended to. Working together we brought down the sails, then he started up the engine. Five minutes later we were gliding into the harbor as gracefully as a white swan over a placid lake.

We tied off the yacht, then walked along the dock back to shore and to the BMW.

"About the harp," said the duke as we drove up the steep hill from the harbor into the village. "I told you I hoped to be able to hear you again. When do you think that might be possible?"

"And I invited you for tea, if I recall," I said. "You said you might accept next time."

"Touché! That I did."

"Then let me extend the invitation anew. Would you like to come to my little rented cottage for tea, and harp music?"

"I would indeed. I accept."

"Tomorrow, noonish?"

"I will be there."

"What about Nicholls? I will feel bad for him just sitting outside in the car."

"I'll come without him. I *can* drive, you know."

We both laughed.

Chapter Thirty-three

Tea with the Duke

Last Hogmanay, in Glesca' Fair, me an' mesel' and several mair,
All gaed off to hae a wee tair, to spend the nicht in Rothesay, O.
We started off frae the Broomielaw, baith hail and sleet
and rain and snaw,
Forty minutes after twa, we got the length of Rothesay, O.
—"Rothesay, O"

The next day promptly at noon, the duke drove up behind the wheel of the BMW. It was hard to think of him as *Alasdair*, not "the duke." But he was just a man, a person, like everyone else.

I was watching for him. As he got out and came up to the house, his step was almost jaunty. He had been that way the day before at the castle too. Though out on the boat there had been some emotional moments, it still seemed, I don't know, that he was coming to life somehow, coming out of his shell. His expression was more animated. He was dressed in blue slacks, with a light tan pullover sweater over dress shirt and red tie. I suppose it would be called casual, even with the tie. The men here wore ties to work in their gardens!

I opened the door and he greeted me with a warm smile.

"Hello, Marie," he said. "Here I am. No backing out this time."

"I am impressed! Come in. Welcome to my humble abode."

My harp was standing to one side of the room. His eyes went immediately to it and he began walking in that direction.

"Would you like to try it?" I asked.

"What—are you kidding? I came to listen to you."

"That doesn't mean you couldn't try it, too. I am a harp teacher, after all. I can teach anyone to play the harp."

"I could never do it."

"You can't make a harp sound bad. Just try it."

He sat down and probed the strings with his fingers. It reminded me of Gwendolyn's first attempt.

"Here," I said, "let me show you how to play a chord."

Just as I had with Gwendolyn, I placed the fingers of his two hands on the strings. He plucked them, a little awkwardly, but the sound of the chord came through.

"Try some more," I said. "Experiment with it. See what your fingers do."

It was obvious that Gwendolyn had not inherited her talent from him. Without my actually placing his fingers on the strings, he could do nothing but make random sounds.

"I told you I couldn't do it!" He laughed. "This sounds dreadful. It *is* possible to make a harp sound bad—I just proved it."

I laughed. "All right, you win! But after a few lessons, I would have you playing 'Twinkle Twinkle Little Star' like nobody's business."

"I would rather listen to you," he said, standing and stepping away.

I sat down and quickly strummed several glissandi. He laughed with delight, then backed up and sat down in the overstuffed chair by the window. I began to play and went through several of my favorite Scottish ballads. Every time I glanced over at him he was staring at me as if in a trance.

"You were so right in what you said to me before," he said as I brought my hands to rest. "The harp is a very visual instrument. It is as mesmerizing to watch your fingers as to listen to the music itself. It is a total experience. I see why you love the harp."

"What about you?" I asked. "Why do *you* like the harp so much? Are you that way with all music?"

"I've never been musical. I'm sure you can tell that from my attempts."

"I'm not through trying to teach you."

"It's no use."

"Then what is it that draws you?"

"I don't know that I can put it into words," Alasdair replied. "From the moment I first heard you, that day in the churchyard, something sparked to life inside me. It wakened a little more when you came to play at the castle. I feel, I don't know, different than I have in years. The music *does* something to me. I feel like I have been asleep, in a dream, for so long, and now I am suddenly coming awake. Whatever that place inside me is, or wherever it is, I feel like it is waking up a little more every time I hear the music."

"That's beautiful," I said. "I've never heard anyone say something like that about my music."

"It's true."

I could not help thinking that what he had described was exactly what I was feeling, too, though for spiritual reasons. I was waking up spiritually. What my music was waking in him though, I wasn't sure.

"Then let me continue with the awakening!" I said. "Or on second thought, maybe I should put on the tea and get lunch started."

"No, please," said Alasdair. "There is plenty of time. Play a little more first."

Again I set my hands to the strings. I played for perhaps fifteen minutes. Neither of us spoke as I moved from one song to the next.

All of a sudden, in the middle of "Yesterday," the doorbell rang. I stopped and looked toward it.

"Who could that be?" I said, rising. Inwardly, even as I said it, my stomach began wandering up toward my throat. There were only two people it could possibly be—Iain or Mrs. Gauld—and I didn't want either of them to be paying me a visit with the duke here. I wondered if I could keep the door from opening all the way. But who was I trying to fool—there was his BMW sitting on the street in front of the house.

I drew in a breath of air as I got up and walked slowly toward the door. To my surprise, there stood Gwendolyn's aunt.

"Mrs. Urquhart!" I exclaimed.

Whether she had recognized the car or not, she did not at first seem to know I had a guest.

"Hello, Marie," she said. "I came by to tell you—"

A movement inside the house caught her eye and she saw that I was not alone. Apparently she still did not recognize who was with me. She hesitated briefly, then went on.

"I wanted to tell you that Gwendolyn has taken sick today. I think it would be best if you did not bring your harp to her today. The doctor says she needs to rest and not—"

At the sound of her voice the duke had turned. Now Mrs. Urquhart saw his face in the room behind me. A gasp escaped her lips and her face went pale.

The two stared at each other for a moment.

"Hello, Olivia," said the duke, speaking first.

"Alasdair," she said, then turned back to me. "I will let you know when Gwendolyn is better," she said, then turned and began walking away from the house.

"Would you mind if I came to visit her?" I said after her. "Without my harp, I mean."

She paused and glanced back with the strangest look on her face. She began to reply, but then turned again without a word and continued to the street and up the pavement.

I turned back into the house and closed the door. Alasdair was quiet, but I asked no questions. I went back to my harp and played for another five or ten minutes. But my music mood was gone. There was obvious tension in the air. Was there some sort of feud between this brother and sister who hadn't seen each other in ages? The atmosphere had been so thick you could have cut it with a *sgian dubh.*

When I finally got up and went to the kitchen to fix tea and prepare lunch a few minutes later, Alasdair was himself again.

Chapter Thirty-four

Angel in the Making

Fair and lovely as thou art, thou has stown my very heart;
I can die, but cannot part, my bonnie dearie.
Ca' the yowes to the knows, ca' them whaur the heather grows.
Ca' them whaur the burnie rows, my bonnie dearie.

—"Ca' the Yowes"

The duke and I had an enjoyable lunch together. By now we were able to visit and talk freely. The stiffness and awkwardness of our first few meetings was completely gone. I played for him again. Alasdair left about two-thirty.

I would have to talk to Alasdair eventually about what was going on with him and Gwendolyn and Mrs. Urquhart. I had to know. There must be more to the story than the bits and pieces I had heard.

Now that my initial prejudices against the duke, that is, Mr. Reidhaven...that is, *Alasdair*, were fading, I could not help wondering if *all* the blame really lay with him as Mrs. Gauld had implied. Relationships are rarely one-dimensional. Now that I knew Alasdair Reidhaven, two things were plain to me—one, he was probably the kind of man people could easily misunderstand, and two, beneath an exterior that might be a little difficult to penetrate beat the heart of a sensitive human being.

After Alasdair's departure, I went out for a walk. On my way back I stopped by the Urquharts'.

Mrs. Urquhart was noticeably cool. I knew it was because of Alasdair. Slowly but surely, things Mrs. Gauld had told me were being confirmed.

"Hello, Mrs. Urquhart," I said. "How is Gwendolyn?"

"About the same," she replied without smiling.

"May I see her?"

"I will see if she is awake."

She left me standing on the porch. She returned a minute later and nodded for me to come in. She led me to Gwendolyn's bedroom and left me there. Gwendolyn lay in bed looking very pale.

"Hi, Gwendolyn," I said, walking toward the bed. Her face, encircled by her bright red hair, was as pale as the pillow behind it. But her eyes brightened when she saw me.

"Marie!" she said. "I can't play today. I'm sick."

"That's what I hear," I said, sitting down beside her and taking her hand. "What happened?"

"I don't know. I got sick."

"Are you very miserable?"

"I sleep when I get sick. Mummy sometimes reads me stories."

"Do you get sick often?"

"Sometimes. Mummy says it is the way my body is. She says I have to go to bed and wait till it is gone. But I want to play on your harp. I hear songs that I want to make on it."

"Where do you hear them, Gwendolyn?"

"I don't know. Somewhere inside me. I don't know where the songs come from."

"I am sure you will be out of bed and making music again very soon."

She looked away and stared up at the ceiling for several long seconds. She seemed to be thinking. I said nothing. I hoped she might say something more about where the music inside her came from, and how she heard it. I was fascinated. Her next words, however, were not what I expected.

"Do angels play harps, Marie?" she asked.

"I don't know, Gwendolyn," I answered. "They might. Some people think so."

"Sometimes I think about dying and being an angel. Especially when I get sick. That's when I think about dying, when I am in bed. Mummy doesn't say anything, but I know she thinks I am going to die. I've heard her talking to other people."

The simple words stung my heart. The poor thing, to have to carry such a burden alone in the midst of a lonely life because other children were afraid of her.

"I am sorry, Gwendolyn," I said. "You are not afraid, are you?"

"I think I used to be afraid. But I am not afraid now. Because when I die I will become an angel. That's what happens when people die—they turn into angels. I used to think I might die and they wouldn't let me be an angel and that I would have to go to the other place, where there aren't any angels." Then her face brightened. "But now I can be an angel because I can play the harp."

I was so moved by her words. I had used my harp to help ease suffering before—in care homes and hospitals. I had seen its music bring peace. I had seen Alzheimer's patients start to sing old folk songs. But never had I seen the music of my harp remove the fear of death.

My eyes filled with tears and I glanced away. I wiped at them hurriedly and looked back with a smile. Gwendolyn was looking straight into my eyes.

"Don't be sad, Marie," she said. "I want you to be happy."

"I am," I said, taking in a deep breath. "Knowing you makes me happy."

"You taught me to be an angel, Marie. You taught me to play the harp. I don't have to be afraid anymore."

"Would you like to hear some of the music *you* made?" I asked.

"Oh, yes, please! Did you bring your machine?"

"I have it right here."

I set the recorder on the bed. The tape was inside. I rewound it to the beginning and turned it on. The sound of my harp, even out of a little plastic box, had a magical, soothing effect on her.

Whether her brain made the connection that this was her *own* music, I have no idea. But wherever it had come from, it wove a spell on us both. Slowly she closed her eyes, a smile on her lips, and we listened in peaceful silence. After about ten minutes, her breathing became deeper. Within moments I saw that she was drifting to sleep to the sounds of her own music, the smile of contentment still on her face.

I sat awhile longer, listening and gazing into her dear white innocent face. When I knew she was sound asleep, I turned off the tape and left the house. I walked back to my cottage and dropped off the recorder, then went walking through the village thinking of many things.

Mostly of Gwendolyn.

Chapter Thirty-five

The Old Story

Tell me the old, old story,
tell me the old, old story,
tell me the old, old story,
of Jesus and his love.

—Catherine Hankey, "Tell Me the Old, Old Story"

The next morning I set out for a walk along the headlands.

I looked inland, however, and saw Crannoch Bin standing guard silently over the coastline. My thoughts turned again to Ranald Bain. With a pang I realized that I ought to be sharing with him the progress and insights of my spiritual journey.

Alasdair talked about my harp music waking something inside him. New awakenings were taking place in me, too. If Ranald Bain was the wise man Iain said he was, perhaps he could add to the new perspectives coming to life within me.

Five minutes later I was walking away from the coast in the direction of the Bin.

I found the old shepherd outside with his dogs and sheep.

"Lassie!" he called with a wave and smile. "Ye're back, an' welcome tae ye!"

"How goes the harp playing?" I asked as I walked toward him.

"Middlin'," he replied. "The brain is willin', but the fingers is stiff an' slow."

"I thought today might be a good day for your second lesson."

"Aye! Jist gie me a minute tae see tae these lads an' lassies an' clean up a mite. Gae ben the hoose gien ye like—put the water on for tea...ye ken whaur I keep the pot?"

233

I nodded. "I'll find it."

I was seated at the harp, retuning it as best I could by ear when Ranald came in five minutes later.

"It has kept its pitch remarkably well," I said. "Sit down and show me what you can do."

I stood. Ranald took off his hat and sat down, pulled the harp toward him and placed it on his left shoulder. I smiled as slowly he began to play.

"That's very good!" I said. "I would know that tune anywhere."

"All right, then, lassie, fit hae ye tae show me?"

"The first thing you might try is to lean the harp on your other shoulder."

We both laughed.

I brought another chair over from his kitchen table and sat down beside him. After a few pointers, and help with his fingers, within thirty minutes he had already improved his tone. We read through a few tunes from the same book we had used before. After that I was confident he would be able to continue improving steadily on his own.

"It would be fun if I had my harp here, too," I said. "Two harps together make a lovely sound. But is there a road up here? How do you go down to the village? Do you have a car?"

"Oh, aye—'tis in the garage oot back. The road winds doon ahint the hoose an' comes oot on one o' the Home Farm's roads. I'll take ye doon gien ye like, sae ye'll ken the way gien ye want tae drive up noo an' then."

"Thank you for the offer. Perhaps I shall. But the walk is part of the magic of coming up here—the woods, the meadow, coming upon the sheep, then encountering a wild old mysterious shepherd appearing out of nowhere."

Ranald laughed at my description.

After tea we began to talk of more serious things. I shared with Ranald about my trip, and both my spiritual and historical revelations, if that's what they would be called.

Even as I was telling about it, as if he sensed what was coming about the heather, he rose and added several chunks of dried peat to the wood burning in his hearth. Within ten minutes it began to glow red and orange. He added more, until the fire was fully aglow with peat, and the faint aroma from a few errant puffs of smoke had invaded Ranald's cottage with its unique fragrance, as subtle as the heather's color, so beloved in the Highlands as a sure sign that the warmth of a peat fire was not far away.

As I concluded my story, he grew quiet and reflective. "Ye've aye touched some ancient threads, lassie," he said. "The heather an' the peat's the slowest growin' o' nearly all things in makin' the heat they give. Peat's ane o' the ancient wonders o' life. 'Tis one o' the mysteries the Creator put in the good earth he gave us."

He paused briefly, a faraway look crossing his face. "Wud ye like me tae tell ye what the colors o' the heather put me intil the mind o'?" he asked after a moment.

"Yes, I would love to hear it," I answered.

"'Tis a reminder o' the auld times," said Ranald. "The auld men an' women fa spoke the Gaelic tongue—'twas peat that kept them alive . . . the heather abune, the peat belaw . . . an' the hue o' its blossom tells the story but only few een can see. But ye've learned tae see it, haen't ye, lass?"

"I think I am beginning to." I smiled.

"'Tis jist what ye were tellin' me—the shades o' Caledonia's royalty . . . no a royalty weel kent by earthly rule, but a royalty o' the hert that all Scots treasure in their ain way."

We sat staring into the fireplace, where heat now emanated in earnest from the hot-glowing sides and corners of the ancient black bricks whose legendary warmth was not merely physical, but emotional and cultural as well, symbolizing a heritage now kept alive only by those few who did not allow the flow of modernity to rob from their sight the capacity to look back . . . and remember.

"The auld story's what makes a Scot a Scot," said Ranald. "'Tis what ye discovered walkin' its hills and moors. 'Tis nae place it's sae alive as Glencoe, whaur the spirit of the clan o' Donald cries oot fae the mountains: *Dinna forgit . . . dinna forgit!*"

We stared into the fire a long time, sipping at our tea. "Iain said you might like to tell me a story about you and him," I said at length, "—from when he was a young scamp. He credits you with turning his life around."

The smile on Ranald's face gradually changed to a thoughtful and nostalgic one. The question obviously sent his mind back many years.

"'Twas a hot summer in Scotland," he began. "The local nickums were oot an' aboot ilka nicht wi' their mischief. 'Twas jist afore the school was tae start up again an' the hairst was weel under way, an' though maist o' the apples on the trees roun' aboot werena ripe yet, they were a sair temptation. The nickums, ye ken, hae a tradition o' strippin the apples aff the trees o' someone or anither's. Seems a simple enouch thing noo, but 'twas a time when puir fowk depended on their apples for food. Folks love their apples, ye ken.

"Weel, a nicht came an' I was oot late wi' somethin', I hae forgotten what. My Maggie was in her bed. I heard sounds comin', an' whisperin' an' footsteps in the wood, an' I suspected the nickums wi' their mischief. They mostly didna bother us, we were so far up the hill an' most were mair than half feart o' me. But they must hae got their courage up because here they came. But I heard them an' I crept roun' wide up the slope o' the Bin an' by the time they had sneekit o'er the two stane dikes an' had begun tae strip oor three apple trees an' were throwin' the apples at my sheep an' their wee lambies, I had got roun' nearly ahint them. The poor sheep were fleggit oot o' their wits an' runnin' an' bleetin' in a' directions.

"So I came oot o' the woods an' walked toward the nickums wi'oot a word. Some o' them saw me an' the sight must hae been fearsom an' they turned an' fled o'er the dry stane dike, not quite so brave meetin' the auld man they'd heard aboot a' their lives noo that they saw me face-tae-face. They were shoutin' an' runnin' awa' in terror like they were in mortal danger."

Ranald chuckled at the memory.

"As gien I would hae hurt a hair on any o' their heids—the foolish yoong scamps! But there was ane fa was farther up toward the hoose, chasin' after the sheep wi' his handful o' apples. I took him for the leader. He was a mite taller than the rest, an' fan they a' began runnin' awa, he didna ken I was there. I walked up ahint him, an' jist as he was aboot tae throw the last apple in his hand, I reached oot an' laid my hand on his arm an' stopped him. He spun aroun' an' fan he saw my face so close, instead o' anger I saw fear in his eyes. Imagine it—he was feart o' me, wha wadna hurt a dog, still mair ane o' God's wee sons. My hert smote me wi' pain, an' a' I can say is that I loved him as gien he were my ain son.

"An' as I luiked intil his een, I kennt that the moment had come fan the mischief o' childhood was aboot tae gie way tae somethin' mair evil—the sin o' manhood. I saw him standin' atween twa roads, an' saw that the next step he took wud set him on the way he might gang a' the way till he was a man. Fit I saw in his een was that here was a lad that God loved wi' a' the love o' a Father, but that the puir lad didna ken't. An' wi' the sheep runnin' awa' ahint him, he looked jist like ane o' them—a poor lost sheep o' a boy fa needed a shepherd. An' my eyes luiked intil his, an' his luiked intil mine, an' he said nae a word.

"'Ah, laddie,' I said after a bit, 'why div ye want tae be fearin' the wee lambies like that? They've no dun ye no hairm, hae they? Luik at them—they're so fleggit they dinna ken what tae de. Ye wadna want me doin' sich like tae yersel', would ye noo?'

"'No, sir,' he answered.

"'They're God's wee anes, laddie. They hae a special place in his hert, jist like ye do yersel'. We're God's wee lambies, jist like those there are mine. Div ye ken fit I'm sayin', laddie?'

"'I think so, sir.'

"'Then gang hame wi' ye. An' next time, stop an' gie a wee thoucht tae mind fit ye're doin' feels tae the one ye're doin' it til. Noo, off wi ye, laddie,' I said, an' I gae him a smile.

"He ran off doon the hill after his frien's. But the biggest surprise o' all was when the bell o' the cottage rang one evenin' twa week later in the gloamin'. An' there stood the same lad, wi' his red shock o' hair. An' fan he saw me, in his een was a different luik than afore. An' I kennt some change had come upo' him, that he had begun tae think aboot fit life should be. I saw that his conscience had been speakin' till him, an' most important o' all, that he had been listenin' till it.

"'I'm sorry I frightened yer sheep, mister,' he said. 'I winna do it again.'

"'Thank ye, laddie,' I said. 'I'm aye glad tae hear it. Will ye no come in for a drap o' tea an' fresh scones?' An' in he came."

"And that, I take it, was Iain?" I said.

"That was aye the lad Iain Barclay. An' fae that day on, we were the best o' frien's. He listened tae the speakin' o' his conscience, an' he listened tae the truth fan he heard it, an' he took the path o' right rather than the path o' wrong."

It was quiet as I reflected on the story of Iain's youth.

"Why did he think ye needed tae hear aboot when he was a lad, Marie, lass?" asked Ranald after a moment.

"I don't know exactly," I answered slowly. "I don't know if he thought I *needed* to hear it. I asked what had happened to turn him around. He said I should ask you. I think because of the changes I have been going through myself. I suppose everyone encounters a time in their life when they have to make some decisions about who they want to be. That was such a time in Iain's life."

I paused and smiled thoughtfully. "Maybe now is mine," I added.

He let my words settle a moment.

"What kin' o' decisions, lass?" he asked after a few seconds.

"About life, and God—you know...what everything means, what life is supposed to be about."

"Are ye strugglin' yersel' wi' what it's a' aboot?"

"I don't know if I am *struggling* exactly," I replied. "But the moment I met Iain, everything began to change."

"Change...hoo?"

"In my outlook about life, I suppose I would say."

This time Ranald simply waited.

"I told Iain that first day I met him," I went on, "that I wasn't a *church person*. He laughed at my description. And even as I told him how I had drifted away from my beliefs, he took it so in stride. He wasn't bothered in any way by it. Gradually we began talking about spiritual things, I guess you would say. I began to think about what I believed. I realized I had never really thought about spirituality in much depth before. And, well, here I am."

"Still thinkin', are ye?"

"I think so."

"An' prayin' as ye do, askin' God tae gie ye light?"

"I'm trying, though it is new."

"Then ye'll fin' the truth ye're luikin' for."

"That's just what Iain told me. But he says you and he don't always see eye to eye."

Ranald smiled fondly. "Only on wee matters o' theology that winna coont for muckle in the end. On the ae thing that *will* remain fan a' the wood, hay, an' stubble's burned awa' in the great furnace o' God's reckonin', on *that* ae thing—oor twa herts is joined as ane. 'Tis why we dinna worry muckle aboot the rest. I call them the *wee* things—though they've split kirks an' caused murders an' hangin's an' burnin's, in the end they'll add up tae nae mair than a puff o' passin' wind. 'Tis the wood, hay, an' stubble o' doctrine, an' I winna contest wi' my brithers an' sisters ower the likes o' ony o' it. But I would lay doon my verra life for the *ae* thing."

"And what is that one thing?" I asked.

"In answer tae yer question, lass," he said, "I'll play ye a sma' tune. 'Tis but a wee simple tune, but it's got a' the answers tae a' the questions o' life. 'Tis the melody yoong Iain heard fan I spoke till him fan he was a lad. 'Tis the melody we a' got tae heed by an' by. 'Tis the sang that tells o' the ane thing."

Without another word, Ranald rose, walked across the room, returned with his violin, tightened his bow, and began to play. As I listened I recognized the tune, but could not remember from where.

It wasn't Scottish, but from somewhere further back in my memory.

It was a far-off strain that seized my heart and sent undefined chills of longing through me. I felt the strangely familiar melody probing and penetrating the deepest corners of my being. But why?

Where was the song from?

Why did it touch me so?

After several minutes, Ranald's violin went silent. The tune had evoked such deep feelings within me, from some deep memory that I could not lay hold of with my conscious mind. Unaccountably I found that I was crying.

"I know that song," I said softly. "But I cannot remember its words or what it is called."

"All men ken it, lassie," said Ranald. "Some remember it fae whan they were bairns. Some come tae ken it later, like Iain. But a' o' us ken its meanin' in oor herts. 'Tis the sang that answers ilka question—gien we're willin' tae listen."

"But why is it so familiar?"

Ranald smiled. "Ye'll ken it when I tell ye, lassie," he said. "It gangs, *'Tell me the auld, auld story . . .'*"

The instant I heard him speak the words, my heart stung me.

"Tell me the auld, auld story o' unseen things above," Ranald continued, *"o' Jesus an' his glory, o' Jesus an' his love. Tell me the story simply, as tae a little chil', for I am weak an' weary, an' helpless an' defiled . . ."*

I knew every word from years long gone by.

Now Ranald began to croon softly, his voice eerily resembling the sound of his own fiddle.

"Tell me the auld, auld story, tell me the auld, auld story, tell me the auld, auld story o' Jesus an' his love."

I was crying in earnest now. Ranald continued to sing in a voice that seemed as ancient as the old story itself.

"Tell me the story slowly, that I may take it in,—that wonderful redemption, God's remedy for sin. Tell me the story often, for I forget so soon, the early dew o' mornin' has passed away at noon.

"Tell me the auld, auld story, tell me the auld, auld story, tell me the auld, auld story . . . o' Jesus an' his love."

I heard Ranald get up and leave the cottage. I sat for several more minutes. Finally I wiped my eyes and followed him outside. Ranald was nowhere to be seen. He was not one to add words if they were not necessary.

He knew the old song, and the story it told, had gotten inside me. He would let it do its work.

In spite of what he had said about driving me down to town, I turned into the meadow that led to the path by which I had come.

Chapter Thirty-six

Banff Springs Hotel

How pleasant thy banks and green valleys below,
Where, wild in the woodlands, the primroses blow:
There oft, as mild ev'ning weeps over the lea,
The sweet-scented birk shades my Mary and me.
—"Flow Gently, Sweet Afton"

As I walked back down the hill, I made a decision.

After what the duke had told me earlier about the harp music waking something inside him, and Ranald Bain's simple old story of Jesus and his love, and with Gwendolyn's words about no longer being afraid still in my thoughts, I realized that it was time I played in church again. If the music could do what it was doing inside Duke Alasdair Reidhaven, and inside the heart of his daughter, as I was now certain was the case, perhaps there might be others it would affect the same way.

Most important, maybe I needed to do it for me.

Things had changed since the first time I had played at Iain's church. I was thinking about God and the church and what they meant in new ways.

I was ready to play again.

I *wanted* to play again. I was ready to go to church openly and say to Iain, to God, and to myself, "I am here for whatever there is for me to receive. I am ready to discover what Jesus' love means for *me*, here and now. And if I can *receive*, perhaps I can *give* something to others as well."

I walked straight to Iain's. I was so disappointed to find him not

242

at home. I had made my decision. I didn't want to chicken out and change my mind.

I hurried back to the cottage and drove to the church, hoping to find him there. But he wasn't there either. So I wrote him a note saying that if he still wanted me to play again for church, this Sunday or whenever he wanted me, I would like to. I put it through the letter slot of his door and then returned home.

I didn't hear from Iain all that day. I didn't see him again, in fact, until he came to pick me up for dinner the next evening.

He was so excited as we drove out of town toward Banff.

"I'm sorry I wasn't home yesterday when you came," he said. "I had a funeral to do in Inverness and stayed over for the night—dear friends of my parents from years ago. The husband, who just lost his wife, is eighty-six and asked me to stay. I only got back into town three hours ago. I cannot tell you how pleased I am that you want to play for services!"

"If you will have me," I said.

"Are you kidding? I'm delighted. Many people have asked when you would be back. I haven't mentioned it to you because I didn't want to put pressure on you. I sensed that you were going through struggles of your own that you needed to resolve."

"Very perceptive."

"And have you resolved them?"

"Not entirely. But like you once told me, life's journeys are not always straight. Still, I feel like I am moving forward—and am on some new paths."

"I am glad to hear it."

"Where are we going?" I asked.

"The Banff Springs Hotel. It's about fifteen miles. Banff used to be the county seat of Banffshire. Then they reorganized all the counties and regions in Scotland, and we are now in Moray. Banff is one of Scotland's oldest towns, in the heart of Buchan country."

"They must have named Canada's Banff after it."

"I'm sure they did. Many Scots from here immigrated to Canada. The hotel sits high up on the edge of town with a wonderful view of the sea, and serves great food besides."

We arrived. During dinner we talked about many things. I told Iain about my drive through the hills again, and this time about my stop. This led to my telling him about my most recent visit with Ranald Bain.

Iain listened quietly and smiled every once in a while as I spoke. I was so at ease. I think it was on this evening that I realized, whatever else he was, that he had truly become a *friend*.

"Ranald speaks very highly of you," I said. "I asked about when you were young."

"Did he tell you the story?"

"He did. He told me several *old stories*," I added, smiling. "One he told with his violin—a very old story. It made me cry."

"What story was that?" Iain asked.

"One that you know well," I said. "One that I am beginning to learn for myself."

Iain looked at me with a puzzled expression. I laughed lightly. "It's the same story you tell every Sunday in church," I said, "the story he told you when you were fifteen."

"Ah, right. And he told it to you, with his *violin*?"

I nodded. "But it was enough. I told you—it made me cry."

The next day I drove to the castle. I had written a note for the duke. *I don't know if you would want to know,* I said in it, *but I thought I would tell you that I will be playing my harp at the Deskmill Parish Church for the service this Sunday morning at ten-thirty.*

For some reason, after having such an enjoyable dinner with Iain the previous evening, I was shy about seeing Alasdair. I gave the envelope to Miss Forbes, asked her to give it to him, and left. I had nothing to hide, from him or anyone. Indeed, you couldn't hide much around here! But I knew I would feel funny seeing him right then.

I hurried back to my car, half expecting to hear him calling my name behind me as he had last time. But no voices stopped me and I drove away with no more words with anyone.

Chapter Thirty-seven

Doorway to Oneness

Oh the roses in their bloom
Shed a brightness through the gloom
Which envelops all this weary field of strife,
Brother wipe away your tears,
And forget your little fears,
Looking thankfully to Him who gives us life.
—"Where the Roses Blush and Bloom"

Sunday came. Iain asked me if I wanted a ride to church. I said I would drive myself. I arrived about ten o'clock, half an hour early, and got my harp ready and tuned up. I began playing at ten-fifteen. By then people were coming in pretty steadily, visiting with one another and milling around.

About ten twenty-five the church was mostly full and nearly everyone was in their seats. There was still a general hubbub of noise and talk and commotion. I saw Mrs. Urquhart take her customary seat, respected elder of the kirk that she was. She never glanced my way or made an attempt to greet me.

I had my eyes on the music on my stand and was absorbed in what I was doing. I vaguely heard a creaking of wooden stairs but thought nothing of it. Then a sudden hush swept through the church. I heard several exclamations and whispered words of astonishment.

"Look...it's *him*..."

"What's he doing here?"

"...the duke..."

I glanced up.

246

There was Alasdair!

He was walking up the old, long-unused steps into his private little balcony that everyone said hadn't felt feet on them in more years than most people could remember. Every eye in the place was on him.

I tried to keep playing, but I'm afraid I flubbed a few notes! I was dying to look again, but was afraid to at the same time. I knew I would lose my concentration. If I knew Alasdair, he would probably be looking straight at me.

I played one more hymn and glanced toward the clock on the wall. Ten-thirty sharp.

I heard the door open where Iain came out. The church was dead silent except for my playing. Iain walked up the steps to the pulpit and I brought the hymn to an end. Then I rose and took a seat in the first row.

I didn't dare look up. Either toward the pulpit *or* the duke's box!

"Good morning!" said Iain exuberantly.

"Good morning," the congregation repeated back to him.

Whether Iain was immediately aware of Alasdair's presence, I couldn't tell. Nothing in the sound of his voice gave away his thoughts. But from the direction the pulpit faced, it was possible he hadn't seen him.

Iain went through the announcements, thanked me for being with them again. We sang two hymns. Iain prayed. Then I got up for the first of my special numbers. I tried to put the distractions out of my mind while I played "This Is My Father's World," which I had wanted to play in church ever since that day I had played it in the churchyard.

It went fine. I went back to my seat and the service progressed. I played again for the offering. Then Iain got up for the sermon. I had by now been watching him enough to be sure he was aware of Alasdair's presence. Still he gave no indication of it and hadn't looked directly at him.

When he began to speak, however, I thought I knew Iain well enough to recognize that, whatever he had been intending to say, he was now thinking on his feet. He was obviously very thoughtful, even occasionally hesitant, as he spoke.

"My friends," he began, "I would like to speak to you this morning about reconciliation. It is what the Bible calls *unity*."

He paused to allow the word to sink in. He may have also been trying to settle his own thoughts.

"I believe," he went on, "that unity is what God cares about more than anything in all the world. The Jews still repeat the prayer called the Shema. I am sure you are familiar with the words. They are taken from the words of Moses in Deuteronomy. The Shema begins, *Hear O Israel, the Lord our God, the Lord is one.*

"Think about that carefully. God is *one*. God's very nature is singleness, oneness...unity. For things to be one as God intends, for relationships within God's creation to reflect their Creator, all apartness, all disconnection, all discord, all separation, all disharmony...these must be reconciled, brought together, made *one*. Everything in life, everything in the world, must be made one, because God is one. That is why Jesus prayed, *That they might be one as we are one.*

"Reconciliation is the great goal and purpose of God's heart. He would have his created beings reconciled with his Father-heart. That is the ultimate oneness, the ultimate unity, the ultimate reconciliation. God would have his prodigal children brought home to that great Heart of the universe. Until this reconciliation is perfected between God and his created universe, all creation is in strife. There can be no peace until we as a race rise and return to our Father, until we are again *one* with him, until unity is fulfilled within us."

Iain paused and drew in a deep breath. His eyes closed briefly. He seemed to be thinking—or praying—about what he was about to say.

"But this unity is not a reconciliation that can take place in some grand and sweeping way between *mankind* and God. It is a reconciliation that takes place individually—one man, one woman at a time. It takes place in *my* heart, not mankind's heart. And it takes place in *your* heart, not the whole world's heart.

"That is where unity originates—in my heart, and yours. The words of the prodigal are the universal words of the reconciliation of the universe, the words by which we acknowledge and repent of our disconnection, and return to oneness in relationship with God our Father. They are beautiful words that Jesus gave in this extraordinary parable that is the story of mankind's entire history. Every time I read them I think of the father waiting to receive the prodigal with a smile and outstretched hand, waiting to receive his son home. And the first step in that homecoming is the son's humble acknowledgment. *I will arise and go to my father. I will say to him, 'Father, I have sinned against heaven and before you. I am no longer worthy to be called your son.'*

"What wonderful, beautiful, touching words of reconciliation!

"Then the Lord's next words tell us God's response. They are more beautiful even than the son's humble repentance. They are among the most important words in the whole Bible, for they tell us what God is like. Can you imagine it—we here have a personality description of God himself! *While he was still far off, his father saw him and was filled with love. He ran to him and threw his arms around him and kissed him.*

"This image makes my heart swell. God is waiting for us! He sees us coming even while we are yet far off!

"He runs *to* us, filled with love. Can you grasp it—God running to us, waiting to throw his arms around us and kiss us in loving welcome!

"How different this is from the austere image of God presented by the old theologians. Does this sound to you like the God of the hellfire evangelists who rant and rave about sinners in the hands of an angry God, about sinners being dangled over the flames of hell?

"Of course not. The Father of Jesus Christ does not demand that we repent in sackcloth and ashes before he will deign to look down upon us from his almighty throne, wielding thunderbolts of retribution if we do not. He is a *loving* Father, a *patient* Father, a *good* Father, a *forgiving* Father.

"Of course there are consequences if we refuse this reconciliation. But they are consequences we bring upon ourselves, consequences that he watches with tears in his loving eyes. They are not the consequences of vengeance, retribution, and wrath. They are consequences of our own stubbornness.

"Oh, my friends, if we could but grasp the reality of who and what God really is, how it would change our lives!

"He is waiting to run to us and throw his arms around us and kiss us! His heart is full of the love of reconciliation. God is nothing more nor less, than our *Father*."

Iain paused again and drew in a deep breath and closed his eyes briefly. This time I *knew* he was praying.

"But there is another kind of reconciliation," he went on after a moment. His tone was softer, gentler, and, I sensed, full of compassion. "I believe this other kind of reconciliation is just as dear to God's heart as that his children are reconciled to him. He also longs for them to be reconciled with one another.

"When division exists within humanity, *any* division—between man and man, between man and woman, between father or mother and son or daughter, division between friends—that division pierces to the very heart of God. It is a pain only God, as the Father of all, can possibly know. This reconciliation, too, is made in the same way as the prodigal made reconciliation with his father. The father of the prodigal was not unaware that the return of his son would in some measure remain incomplete until his two sons were reconciled to each other. And he would wait patiently and prayerfully for them to mature into that reunion.

"It takes humility, great humility, to seek reconciliation. Yet *humility* is the doorway into reconciliation. The prodigal son whose story Jesus told looked around and realized he was eating with pigs. He had had such dreams! He had been so eager to claim his inheritance and to live life, as we of this modern age say, *on his own*. But where had it brought him in the end? What did he have?

"Only loneliness. He was eating with pigs!

"When he realized it, and admitted it, there was born in him the *humility* that leads to reconciliation. That humility, that swallowing of pride, that recognition that he had sunk to the level of the pigs, led him home to his father. It is humility that leads us home. It is *humility* that leads to *unity*.

"It is that same humility that leads us to be reconciled with our brothers, with our fathers, with our daughters, with our mothers, with our sons, with our friends and acquaintances.

"Humility, my friends. The humility to say, *I do not want to be alone and disconnected any longer. I do not want to be apart from this other whom I once loved. I am ready to swallow my pride and say, 'I will arise and go to my brother.' I will say, 'I am no longer worthy to be called your brother, but with all my heart I desire again to be your brother. And thus, I will be your brother again.'*

"Humility, my friends. Substitute whatever words are appropriate. The humility to admit, *I no longer want to be apart from this one whom I once loved. I am ready in humbleness of heart to say, 'I will arise and go to my sister...my mother...my daughter...my father...my son.' I will say, 'I am no longer worthy to be called your loved one, but with all my heart I desire again to be in relationship with you. I am sorry to have failed in loving you, but I will try to love you again.'*

"The humility to acknowledge, *I do not want to be estranged one day more. I will arise and go to my friend. I will say, 'I am no longer worthy to be called your friend, but with all my heart I desire again to be your friend. And thus, I will do my best to be a friend to you again.'*

"Humility, my friends. Humility to recognize that life is not what we had hoped. Humility to re-extend the hand of fellowship and friendship. Humility to recognize that life is full of mistakes, that we have made our own share of them, that we have hurt others. Humility to apologize. Humility to arise and go to the one we have hurt.

"Humility is the doorway, my friends. It is the door to reconciliation, the door that leads to our brethren, the door that leads to our
sons and daughters and mothers and fathers and our friends, the
door that leads to the heart of God."

Iain stopped. He glanced around for a moment, exhaled deeply,
then sat down with his head bowed. It was obvious he was spent. The
church was silent. Iain sat for probably thirty seconds in silent prayer.
Finally he stood again, and asked the congregation to stand with him
as the organist played the introduction to the closing hymn.

As we sang, I saw Alasdair descend the steps from the duke's
balcony, the eyes of half the church upon him, and walk to the
door at the back and outside. I knew what he was feeling, the same
thing I had felt last time I was here. But I stayed where I was. This
time I would not be afraid to face Iain as I left.

When the hymn was over and Iain left the pulpit, he glanced at
me with a smile as he passed down the aisle.

Chapter Thirty-eight

I Will Arise and Go to My Father

Oh, the Gallowa' hills are covered wi' broom,
Wi' heather bells, in bonnie bloom.
Wi' heather bells an' rivers a',
An' I'll gang oot ower the hills tae Gallowa'.

—"The Gallowa' Hills"

Whether Iain's sermon had stirred up a hundred thoughts and feelings in anyone else, I didn't know. But it had in me.

I was an emotional wreck!

I tried to hide it, but not very successfully.

People came up to me after the service and thanked me. I tried to smile and return their words. Mostly I was anxious to get out of there so I could be alone. Gradually the little cluster dissipated and followed the rest toward the door. I put my harp and music away as the last of the congregation filed out of the church. I was just getting up to walk out as Iain, the last of the handshakes behind him, came back inside.

"It was beautiful, Marie," he said. "Thank you again."

"Of course," I replied, forcing a smile. "I should probably also thank you...I mean, for your sermon—"

It was useless. I couldn't continue. I didn't know what to say. I felt myself starting to cry.

I gave Iain a quick hug, then grabbed my harp case as my eyes filled with tears. I ran from the church.

I got home, still struggling with my tears, took my harp inside, changed my clothes, and immediately left the cottage and set out for the headlands.

I had never been that much of a walker before coming here. Now I sometimes walked for several hours a day. It was so peaceful and so beautiful, the scenery and coastline so infinitely varied and changeable. I never tired of it. Whether I was up on the cliff a hundred feet above the water, or walking down along the sandy beach, or picking my way among the rocks and tide pools of one or another of the coves, the ocean was mesmerizing. The sea had become my solace, my companion, my friend.

Now I sought this friend to try to figure out what to do with everything Iain had said, and where it fit with the tune from Ranald's violin and its old, old story, and with my teary drive down through the Cairngorms.

I walked and walked. I walked along the sand, up to the top of the promontory, scrambled down one or two steep paths to the rocky shore, and back up again. The emotion I had felt at the end of the service waned. But its impact remained with me. Something had happened as I listened. It was a culmination of everything that had been building since the day I first met Iain by the bench along the path.

In the churches I had been part of in my life, Jesus had always been the sole focus, the basis for salvation. Everything was Jesus, Jesus, Jesus.

Suddenly for the first time in my life I wondered what it was Jesus *saved* us from. I knew the stock answer ought to be, from *sin*. But now it dawned on me that what I had actually thought down inside, without saying it, maybe without even actually thinking it, was that Jesus saved us from *God*—from God's wrath and punishment.

All at once—how could I have never seen it before!—I saw how little sense that made. How could there be a division between Jesus and God? How could *one* save us from the *other* when they were supposed to be one?

It was very confusing. Today's sermon had set my brain spinning with possibilities that blew my mind.

Suddenly I heard Jesus' words, *Come, follow me,* being spoken in the midst of the prodigal son parable. Suddenly the picture came into my mind of Jesus going to that prodigal as he sat with the pigs, stooping down and taking his hand, and saying, *Come, follow me...I will lead you home. I will take you back to your father. He is waiting for you.*

It was a completely new image. It wasn't Jesus as *protector from wrath*, it was Jesus leading us home!

It was Jesus leading us to the *Father's* open arms, to the *Father's* love.

He came to lead us home to God...home to his Father!

It was our home, too. *That* was the old story, of Jesus and his love...and his *Father's* love, too.

All this raced through my brain as I listened to Iain talk about the prodigal, and what it meant to be reconciled to God. It was a completely new image of what Christianity meant!

In the middle of the afternoon I found myself sitting on a large rock, my shoes off, my feet dangling over the edge, listening to the sounds of the waves ebbing and flowing about me. The sun was warm. Nobody was nearby. I felt like I was all alone in the world.

Everything Iain had said from the first day I had met him, along with the sound of Ranald's violin, and my recent trip...Bannockburn...Glencoe...everything, the whole tapestry was stirring in my brain.

Suddenly a wave came in, splashed against the rock and up onto my feet and ankles. The cold momentarily took my breath away. It felt invigorating. I looked about and realized the tide was coming in. The wave that had splashed me continued onto the sand behind me. I glanced back over my shoulder.

The rock I was sitting on had briefly become an island.

It lasted but a few seconds. Then the water retreated back down the gentle slope of the shoreline. Within two hours, this rock would probably be underwater.

I sat for another thirty minutes. By then my feet were being splashed and inundated by every incoming wave. The water was reaching a point where any minute a larger wave might knock me off my perch.

It was time to move.

I put on my sandals and climbed to my feet. As I stood, Iain's voice came back to me as vividly as if he had been right beside me.

I will arise and go to my father.

I stood on the top of the rock for a moment, pondering the words. I had been thinking about them all day. Yet suddenly it was like hearing them for the first time.

Waiting for the water to retreat from around the base of the rock, I leaped across to the sand and ran up the shore.

I had never thought of myself as a "prodigal." Why did those words from the parable suddenly hit home so hard? I hadn't squandered my life on riotous living. I'd married as a virgin and had always been faithful to the one man who was my husband. Actually, I had been the kind of girl people called a Goody Two-shoes. I remember going through a phase when I was in church when I wondered if there was something wrong with me because I hadn't had a dramatic conversion out of the depths of "sin." I had no flamboyant testimony. I had grown up in the church and had been generally a pretty good person.

And yet, here I was identifying with the prodigal son.

Gradually, because of Iain Barclay, I knew why.

I had never known God as my own personal, intimate *Father*...as a Father in the way Iain seemed to know him, as a Father in the way Jesus talked about him and knew him.

Then again came Jesus' words to the rich young ruler: *Come, follow me.*

No, they *weren't* his words to the rich young ruler.

They were Jesus' words to *me.*

Come, Angel Dawn Marie...follow me. I have someone to introduce you to, someone who has been waiting for you. He knows your name. He knows all about you and he loves you. He is your Father, and he wants you at last to become his daughter.

A chill swept through me. My eyes began to fill with tears.

Jesus was speaking *to me.*

I knew it. I felt it. I could almost hear the words. I was hearing them in my heart.

I started walking along the sand. In my mind I held out my hand as if for Jesus to take it. I walked slowly, conscious that he was leading me and that I was following. For the first time in my life I was really *following* Jesus, doing what he had asked me to do.

I had read the Footprints poem. I looked down at my feet, almost as if expecting to see a second set of indentations in the sand beside my own, from Jesus walking beside me.

After a few seconds I looked up. There was no blinding flash of light, no vision, only a solitary beach on the coast of northern Scotland. But I knew what was ahead of me, waiting for me, though my physical eyes could not see him. My *heart* saw him, and that was enough.

Jesus' Father was waiting to receive me into his embrace!

Jesus let go of my hand and stood back. He had brought me to where he had wanted to follow.

I fell on my knees in the sand and burst into sobs.

"Oh, God," I said, "I am sorry for waiting so long. I want to be your daughter! Help me, my *Father.* Help me be all you want me to be!"

I wept for several minutes with my head buried in my hands and lap. I was almost afraid to look up. I was so aware that Jesus and his Father were with me, I could almost feel the Father's arms encircling me in his loving embrace as the prodigal's earthly father had embraced him.

After another minute, suddenly the final remnants of an incoming wave gently surged past me, soaking my legs and feet and sandals and jeans and jolting me out of my reverie.

I smiled and stood, wiping my eyes with a dry part of my shirt. Then slowly I began to laugh. I felt so good...clean...free...happy.

I was awake!

Chapter Thirty-nine

Looking Ahead

Far frae my hame I wander, but still my thoughts return,
To my ain folk ower yonder, in the sheiling by the burn.
I see the cosy ingle, and the mist abune the brae:
And joy and sadness mingle, as I list some auld-warld lay.

—"My Ain Folk"

With the changes taking place inside me, so many things began to fit into a perspective that had been missing before. What could represent a more massive reorientation than turning your whole view of religion and everything else in life upside down, recognizing God as a good and loving Father, and saying to him that you want to be his daughter!

Of course I was filled with questions. I felt like I was starting life all over again at forty-one!

Maybe I was. But along with the questions, I was deeply at peace.

That's what I felt—simply *at peace.*

I knew I had turned a corner. I knew it was a turning point I would look back on as a major one. I was ready to engage with God, ready to discover what being a Christian really meant, ready to live it twenty-four/seven.

Or at least *try* to live it! I had a lot of catching up to do.

Along with the spiritual changes that were blossoming within me like a new birth, there were practical changes, too.

For one thing I began to wonder how much longer I was supposed to stay in Scotland. I wasn't overly concerned about the financial aspect of it. But paying what amounted to more than $300 a week for a cottage and another $150 a week for a car, along with food and gas, added up.

Obviously I couldn't stay forever.

I began to wonder if perhaps the reason I had been meant to come here was accomplished. Was my time here gradually coming to a close?

Had God been leading me without my knowing it, leading me to this place even after I no longer thought I believed in him? Was he now ready to lead me back home?

The thought of it filled me with sadness. I loved it here!

I was excited about what lay ahead. There were worlds of new discovery awaiting me. But how could I not be sad that this change in spiritual outlook might bring with it a close to my Scottish adventure?

The minute I started thinking about leaving, other thoughts began to fill my mind, too.

How could I separate the change inside me from Iain Barclay? He was such an intrinsic part of it. He was the one God had used to get my attention, to open me to new realities I had never considered before.

I was changing. And Iain Barclay was at the center of it.

The Aberdeen *look* filled my mind's eye.

Was I in love with him? It was a question I had not wanted to face. The idea of falling for a minister so weirded me out at first that I couldn't deal with it.

The main thing was simply that Iain had become a good friend. I would miss him. That's what I had to focus on. I couldn't let myself daydream beyond that.

Those weren't my only thoughts. Alasdair was also there in the thick of them...simpler than thoughts of Iain in one way perhaps, but more complex in another.

A *minister*...and a *duke*. Whew, what a turn my life had taken!

The idea of leaving also filled me with thoughts of Gwendolyn, and Ranald Bain. God had used Iain and Ranald to awaken me to his Fatherhood, but he also seemed to be using me to alleviate both Alasdair's and Gwendolyn's loneliness.

What was to become of Gwendolyn?

I had already decided to leave *Journey* with her rather than take it home. I loved that harp. But it had a new purpose—to bring joy to a dying girl's heart. She was another of the reasons I knew I had come here, or perhaps been sent here. I hoped the music I had introduced into her life would make her last years on this earth happier.

How special a young innocent like her must be to the Father's heart!

I also decided to make a CD of her playing. Gwendolyn had been so at peace when listening to the music she had made. I wanted her to be able to hear it anytime she wanted. I had enough recorded for probably half an hour of music. I wanted to tape more. I might even leave the recorder with Mrs. Urquhart and have her send tapes to me periodically so that I could make two or three CDs.

Chapter Forty

Unexpected Blow

I'm wearin' awa', John, like snaw-wreaths in thaw, John,
I'm wearin' awa', to the land o' the leal.
There's nae sorrow there, John, there's neither cauld nor care, John;
The day is aye fair in the land o' the leal.
—"The Land o' the Leal"*

I was not the only one who had been affected by Iain's words from the pulpit, though I didn't know it at the time. Nor did I realize how much I had been stirring things up. People had been talking about me. As a result, things were about to take a turn.

I went to see Gwendolyn later that day, after my walk and time with God on the beach. I felt so alive, I did not want to keep it all to myself!

I was in for a disappointment.

"Hello, Mrs. Urquhart," I said, unable to keep the smile from breaking out all over my face when she opened the door. "How is Gwendolyn?"

"She is better."

"Oh, good! Is she out of bed? Would you want me to bring my harp over so she could play?"

---

*Every language contains certain words and concepts that are unique to it and that do not translate completely into other languages. *Leal* is such a word in Scots. As used here, the "land of the leal" is obviously a reference to heaven. The word *leal* contains an abundant richness of meaning that draws all the following into it: loyal, faithful, spiritual, faithful to one's duties, constant in friendship and love, honest, true, honorable, just, fair, chaste, pure, trustworthy.

"She is out of bed," replied Gwendolyn's aunt, a serious look on her face, "but I do not think that would be a good idea."

"Oh, all right," I said. "Perhaps tomorrow, then."

"That is not what I meant," said Mrs. Urquhart. "I do not think it would be a good idea for you to come back."

"I don't think I understand," I said.

"I do not want you here. I do not want you visiting Gwendolyn as long as you are seeing *him*. Good day, Ms. Buchan."

Stunned, I suddenly found myself staring at a door that had been closed, gently enough but in no uncertain terms, in my face.

I stood for a moment bewildered. I didn't know what to do. I rang the doorbell again.

With obvious reluctance, Mrs. Urquhart opened it about a foot. This time the look on her face was unmistakable. There was no hint of a smile. Behind her, across the room, Gwendolyn stood staring at me with wide eyes that were red like her hair. It was obvious she had been crying. I could see fear in her expression, too, that she was afraid to speak to me. My heart ached for her.

"Mrs. Urquhart, please," I began. "Surely you can give me some explanation. I mean, have I done something to offend you? If so, I—"

Gwendolyn's aunt opened the door a little wider and took a step forward onto the porch and closed the door behind her.

"I cannot have Gwendolyn's heart broken again. That man has hurt her enough."

"Hurt her?"

"He is an evil man. I will not have you raise Gwendolyn's hopes with dreams of harps and music, only for her to be disappointed and heartbroken in the end. Anything good that comes to her life, he will try to destroy it, just as he is now trying to lure you away from her."

"It is not like that at all," I said. "I assume you are talking about the duke, Mr. Reidhaven. He has never so much as suggested—"

"Nevertheless, I will not have you seeing him and then coming to visit Gwendolyn. I have told her you will not be coming back."

I stood listening with my mouth hanging open.

"But, surely there is some mistake," I said, shaking my head.

"There is no mistake," said Mrs. Urquhart firmly.

"I could tell there were vibes between the two of you the other day at my house," I said. "But he has not tried to make me think ill of Gwendolyn or you or anyone."

"He wouldn't be so obvious as *that*," she replied, almost derisively. "His ways are more subtle. Devious and cunning are the wiles of a fraud...don't believe what you see, it's a mere facade."

She seemed to hesitate a moment, as if surprised herself at what had come out of her mouth. "You do not know what you have become involved in," she added.

"I have no idea what you're talking about," I said, looking at her a little strangely because of the way she had spoken.

"Of course not. How could you?"

"But what is it all about, Mrs. Urquhart?"

"Mrs. Gauld said she told you. He is Gwendolyn's father, at least so most folk believe, though there are still those who think there is more to it. He abandoned her. I took her in to save her life. But the curse came with her—his curse. Ever since he has been doing his best to ruin us. He never forgave me for exposing him. Now the whole village knows what he is. I will not let Gwendolyn near him, or near anyone who has to do with him. I care for her too much to see her hurt like he would hurt her if he could. There is more, but that is all you need be told. Be careful, Ms. Buchan. That is all I will say. Be very careful. Do not be fooled."

"But if he is her father, does he not have the right to see her?"

"She is terrified of him. She does not want to see him."

"She doesn't want to see her own father?"

Mrs. Urquhart shook her head.

"You don't really think he would hurt her?" I said incredulously.

"He has not struck me as cruel. Beneath the shell, he actually seems like a warm and sensitive man."

What I can only describe as a sarcastic snort sounded from Mrs. Urquhart's mouth. "You don't know him like I do," she said. "He puts on his smooth airs for a pretty thing like you. But I am not fooled. No one who *really* knows him is fooled. His talk is smooth to make you believe, but his real intent is to deceive. Stay away from him, Ms. Buchan, is my advice. Go back where you came from and forget this place."

She turned and went back inside. This time she closed the door with even more vigor than before. I was left pondering her strange rhyme, shivering briefly at the sound of it. I knew I could stand on the porch and ring the doorbell all day, but I would not see her face again.

Stunned, I left and walked slowly back to my cottage.

After what had happened at the sea and on the little sandy beach along the cove where I had prayed, I didn't know what to think. This was a blow.

The rest of the day and evening was the most depressing time for me since I had arrived in Scotland. It hardly seemed like the same day of Iain's sermon about the prodigal and my walk at the sea. My happy mood from before was shattered.

Chapter Forty-one

Eleanor Rigby

Since my dear one's gone, all the joy of morning,
All the peace I've known, gone, till her returning;
My own dear one's gone!

Weary and alone I must bear this yearning,
Comfort there is none till my love's returning;
My own dear one's gone!

Spring will soon be here bringing joy and gladness;
But to me no Spring can bring ought but sadness;
My own dear one's gone!

—"My Own Dear One's Gone"

I woke up on Monday morning after a surprisingly sound sleep. With all that was on my mind, I had expected to toss about all night.

As I awoke, my mind turned toward God.

How different were my thoughts on that Monday morning than any thoughts about him I had ever had before. Even as I lay in bed, I felt warm and cozy, strange as it is to say it, knowing that God's fathering arms were still wrapped about me just as they had been on the beach the day before. With a return of that memory, everything Mrs. Urquhart told me no longer seemed quite so overwhelming.

If God loved *me* as a good and loving Father, he must also love Gwendolyn and Mrs. Urquhart and Alasdair Reidhaven. His open arms must be waiting for *them*—though Gwendolyn's aunt was an elder and supposedly one of the spiritual leaders of the church— just as they had been waiting for me.

But what was I to *do*? What should I do now...today?

What was I *supposed* to do?

As far as I could tell, it seemed that I was the only person who had a relationship with all three. Yet they were of the same flesh and blood, and I was an outsider.

Almost the moment the question came to me, two thoughts popped into my head.

After morning tea and some time reading and playing my harp, I set out on the two errands that resulted.

The first was to the Urquharts where I put a note through the door that read:

Dear Mrs. Urquhart,

I will not ring the bell or try to talk to you out of respect for what you said. But if you would agree to one more visit from me, I would like to bring my harp over and set it up so that Gwendolyn can continue playing, even if I am not there. I think it is good for her. You know where I am staying. I will await your reply.

Marie Buchan

Then I set out for the castle. I needed to find out from Alasdair what was going on.

He almost seemed to be expecting me. He opened the door himself, nodded, almost without a smile yet with an expression that said without words, "Come in, we've got things to talk about."

He led me upstairs and along the main corridor of the first floor, but continuing on to the end of it, then turning right for a short distance along a narrower hallway. He stopped and opened a door and I found myself on the other side of the tapestry wall where he had been sitting when I had first played my harp for him. An end of one of the screens had been folded back so that the larger room was visible beyond it. We sat down in the sitting area that I had not seen before now. It was furnished much like the rest of the room. From this side the large tapestries on the walls were spectacular.

We had hardly taken seats before Miss Forbes followed with a tray of tea things, which she set on a low coffee table in front of the couch where I sat down. Then she left us and we were alone.

"I am glad you came," said Alasdair. "I half expected you. If you hadn't come, I would have gone to you."

"You wanted to talk to me?" I said.

"I felt I needed to explain about yesterday."

"You owe me no explanations."

"But I do. I owe you *everything.*"

"I don't understand. For what?" I asked.

"Don't you know?"

"No."

"For bringing me out of my shell, for waking life in me again," he said.

"What did I do?" I laughed.

"Your music sparked something in me that I had not felt for many years, maybe that I had never felt. It began that first day when you played in the churchyard. Then when you were here, at the other end of this same room, when I was sitting here, I thought I had never heard anything so lovely, so peaceful, so haunting. I could not see your face, but I knew that whoever was capable of making such music must have a soul that somehow understood, not just the music... but that somehow understood me... that must *know* me. The music of your harp was like a surgeon's knife. It probed deep into me as only music can. It made me both sad and happy at once. I wanted to jump up and shout for joy. I wanted to weep in despair for a life wasted and squandered."

I could hardly believe that *my* music could have evoked such a deep response. Especially when I hadn't even known him at the time.

"When you were almost through, that first day," Alasdair went on, "when you began playing 'Eleanor Rigby'—I felt, not the surgeon's knife, but a dagger of loneliness stabbing straight into my heart. The song came rushing back upon me out of my memory. Poor Eleanor Rigby, alone in a church where nobody hears...'all the lonely people'...'where do they all belong?'"

I sat listening in silence as he continued to share deeply from his heart.

"All these thoughts rushed through me in an instant," Alasdair went on. "The stunning realization hit me with almost heart-sickening force...I myself had become Eleanor Rigby. You were playing my song. *I was Eleanor Rigby.* I was alone and lonely, only a stone's throw from the church, over which, technically you might say, I am titular head as laird of the parish. But I never darkened its doors. Eleanor Rigby, or make it Alasdair Reidhaven, near the church where nobody hears his lonely heart.

"I sometimes used to open my window on a Sunday and listen to the sounds from the church across the wall, listen to them singing the hymns. I could even hear Reddy's voice, though I couldn't make out what he said. But I could never actually show my face there. It would cause too much talk, and stir up too many old wounds."

"But surely *you* could go to church. You would be as welcome as anyone."

"Welcome, perhaps. But it would stir up too much. So I chose to listen in my Eleanor Rigby loneliness from the other side of the wall, separated from that church and all it represents by only a few yards, but separated by a gulf too great to cross. The irony of hearing you play that song about loneliness in the church, as such a picture of my own life...it finally overcame me as I listened to you that first day. Tears stung my eyes. I am sorry, but that is when I rose and left, through that door there. Even though you were not finished, I was too overcome. I have wanted to apologize to you ever since. I had not wept since I was a boy, but I wept on that day. Your music woke tears in me. I could not face what they meant. I don't know that I have yet faced what those tears meant. But...I am sorry."

I shook my head and tried to smile. I was too choked up to speak.

"Your music forced me to confront myself," Alasdair continued. "What I found I did not like. I found bitterness and ugliness inside. Yet, in my aloneness, at the same time something fluttered to life within me. I knew that I had to know the maker of the music. I know it was awkward for you at first. I am sorry. I'm afraid I was not very personable. I didn't know what to do, what to say. It had been so long since I was with people, especially a beautiful woman. I was nervous, shy, embarrassed even to ask you to see me. I was so afraid for what you might have heard about me. But I had to know you. I had to find out who was the creator of this music that stirred me so."

He paused and drew in a deep breath.

"When I did at last meet you," he went on, "I discovered that it had not been about the music at all. It was about *you*. You were the reason all this had happened, not so that I could hear 'Eleanor Rigby,' but so that I could meet you. The music began the waking, but you continued it. *You* watered the tender plant that was my soul and helped it continue to blossom."

"But, but what have I done?" I said.

"You accepted me, you talked to me, you went on walks with me, sailed with me, you laughed with me...you treated me like a human being. I even flattered myself that you might have enjoyed the few times we spent together."

"I did, of course, Alasdair," I said. "I *have* enjoyed our time together."

"I know it doesn't sound like much," he said, looking down at the floor with an almost boyishly timid smile. "But for one who has been alone for so long, who has had to enjoy roses alone, with no one to share them with, for one who knows the dreadful things they think about me in the village, your simple kindness meant more to me than I can tell you."

"I still do not understand why people think ill of you," I said. "Why not show them they are wrong?"

"They would never believe it. Their minds are made up."

"But why?"

"From things that happened a long time ago. There is much about me you do not know, Marie."

I pondered his words.

"If what you say is true," I asked, "why did you go to church yesterday?"

"I had to hear you play," Alasdair replied. "I have to hear your music every chance I get. I knew they would gawk the moment I walked in. Probably the whole town is talking about it, wondering what an old hermit and sinner like me is doing in church. But let them talk. I no longer care."

"Why do you and Iain no longer see one another?" I asked. The words came out more bluntly than I had intended them.

The question obviously caught Alasdair off guard. My words seemed almost like a blast of cold water in his face.

"It is a long story," he sighed at length.

"I have all day, if you want to tell me about it."

He stared down at the floor, thinking.

"I don't think I do," he said at length. "I'm not sure I am up to it. It is water under the bridge. We had a parting of the ways—let's just leave it at that."

"Maybe it shouldn't be left at that," I said. "You heard what Iain said yesterday, about reconciliation between people as well as between people and God."

"I heard. But some things go deep and are too entrenched in the past. They are long past healing."

"Do you really think that is true?" I asked.

"Honestly, I don't know. I leave the religion to Reddy. That's a world I don't know much about."

"I don't mean religion," I said. "What about simple human relationships? I can't imagine that any relationship is beyond healing,
if the people involved want it. I suppose it all depends on that."

"I haven't thought much about it," said Alasdair. "But I doubt
there's hope of changing things now, after so long."

"I hope that's not true."

Alasdair nodded thoughtfully.

"If I didn't know better," he said with a sigh after a moment, "I'd
have thought Iain knew I was coming yesterday and had planned
that sermon just for me. You didn't tell him you invited me, did
you?"

I shook my head. "Funny," I said. "I thought he was speaking
to me."

"In what way?" asked Alasdair.

"I've been I suppose what you might call estranged from God for
a long time," I replied.

"You!" said Alasdair in surprise.

"Why do you say it like that?" I laughed. "You sound surprised."

"I am. I took you for…I don't know, a religious person, a Christian."

"Why?"

"I don't know. I suppose because you played for church, and,"
he added with a sheepish smile, "because you've been spending a
lot of time with Reddy."

"Before coming here, I hadn't been in a church in years."

"I would never have known," said Alasdair slowly. "Why are you
playing in church then?"

"The first time it was just because Iain asked me to."

"It sounds as though yesterday was different."

I nodded. "It was," I said.

"How?"

"Since coming here, I've been changing," I replied. "Yesterday I
wanted to play for myself."

"Whatever is going on seems to be catching," said Alasdair.

"Maybe it's something in the air!" I laughed. The sound of my voice seemed out of place. I grew serious again. "All I know is that I am seeing many things in a new light," I said. "After church yesterday I went for a walk along the shore. I realized that I had never recognized God as a good and loving Father. Once I started thinking of him in that light, my perspective about everything began to change."

"Why was that?"

"Because, I don't know, if God is like that, then everything about life, the entire universe... everything takes on a different meaning."

"Do you think God *is* like that?"

"That's what Iain says."

Alasdair smiled a little sardonically but said nothing.

"I *do* believe it," I added. "It has taken me some time to get used to the idea of God being different than I have always thought. But I do believe it. I am feeling his love more than ever. Maybe I am, like you say, a more religious person than I had realized. I never thought of myself that way. But I realize that I *want* to know God. I want to know what he is like. Before now I never tried. I ignored him, which is maybe the worst thing to do. That's why I felt that Iain's sermon was for me. I realized that I was the prodigal, or *like* the prodigal. I needed to go home to God."

"How could someone like *you* be a prodigal?"

"Don't you think we are all prodigals in our own way?"

"I never thought of it like that."

Alasdair paused briefly.

"Do you think I am like the prodigal?" he added.

His question caught me by surprise. "I don't know," I answered. "You and I have never talked about spiritual things."

"But you think I should be reconciled with Iain?"

"Because of what I said a minute ago?"

Alasdair nodded.

"I don't know that either," I said. "I was just asking. For two men who were such good friends, and who live and work within two hundred meters of each other, never to speak, somehow it doesn't seem right."

"It is a complicated situation."

"What about Gwendolyn?" I said. "Did you have a parting of the ways with her, too, like with Iain?"

If my question about Iain had taken him by surprise, this one hit Alasdair between the eyes like a shotgun. His head almost visibly jerked back as if the words themselves had landed with a physical force.

"Oh—I'm sorry," I said. "I shouldn't have said that."

"You *know*, I take it?" he asked after a moment.

"Mrs. Gauld told me you are her father."

He nodded. "I am. Yes, it is true."

"And Mrs. Urquhart?"

"She is my sister, Gwendolyn's aunt. I am afraid she harbors great animosity toward me. Olivia is determined to keep Gwendolyn from me. As I said, complicated."

"She told me this morning that the separation is because of you—that you abandoned Gwendolyn."

Alasdair smiled so sadly I thought I had never seen such a for- lorn expression.

"Yes," he said softly. "I am aware of that. It is the story she has spread for years."

"But it is not true?"

"If the last twelve years have taught me anything, it is that truth is not so easy to define as I once thought. People have to decide what to believe about things, don't they?"

"Then what about what she said?"

"I suppose one might place such an interpretation on the events. It is how Olivia chose to see it and that is the story she spread. Her slant on things is now taken as fact. No one has cared to inquire about my point of view. People rarely do. They eagerly believe the worst."

"But you do not see it that way?"

"I do not," answered Alasdair softly.

"Would you like to tell me what happened?" I asked. "I don't mean to pry, honestly. I am only interested because I care for both of you. If you don't want to tell me—"

"No, of course . . . I do," said Alasdair. "You have to know eventually. I *want* you to know."

A long silence followed.

Chapter Forty-two

Fateful Night

Mak' my grave baith lang and deep,
Put a bunch of roses at my head and feet,
And in the middle put a turtle dove,
Let people know I died of love.

—"Will Ye Gang Love?"

At length Alasdair let out a deep sigh.

"Gwendolyn's mother died in childbirth," he began. "I don't even know why Olivia was there. I certainly did not send for her. But she seems invariably to be present at most of the births in the village. Maybe the doctor sends for her, I don't know. I have my suspicions, but they are best kept to myself. I had not been well, and my wife's death shattered me. Olivia took the child...*Gwendolyn*, home with her. The doctor was on hand, of course, and sent for the undertaker. I was exhausted from having been up most of two nights. A funeral was quickly arranged, and the next day I collapsed and took to bed. I have never had a robust constitution and was, in fact, quite sickly as a boy. Even as a young man I suffered from long bouts of fatigue and exhaustion. It all came rushing back and I simply fell apart—physically, emotionally, psychologically. I have no defense to offer—I fell apart."

"What happened?"

"I lay in bed for almost three weeks. How much stress and depression contributed to my physical condition, who can say. Olivia already had concocted a reason to prevent my seeing the child. I should say, what she took as reason for it. To this she added the charge that I was shirking my duty, that I had turned my back on

275

the child in its time of need, that she had whisked her away to her own house for the child's own good."

"Why would she think such a thing if you had collapsed physically?"

"There had been tensions between us for years. There was always tension between us. The child's birth increased the conflict all the more. I'm afraid I said and did some dreadful things that only made matters worse. I had a temper back then. When I was able, I went to Olivia to bring the child home. She refused to give her to me, telling me I could never care for a child, saying that I was the cause of my wife's death. I flew into a rage and went away. I'm afraid I left the country in anger and confusion and frustration. I had lost my wife and took it out on everyone around me. My leaving made matters far worse and I have only myself to blame. I fell sick again when traveling. I did not return to Port Scarnose for a year. By then Olivia had spread the story that I had flown into a rage both that a girl had been born rather than a boy, as well as that something seemed to be wrong with the child, which, as she grew, became more and more apparent. Probably I did say something about her being a girl as Olivia and I argued. I don't remember—Olivia has always had a way of twisting the truth around, distorting it to something very different from the reality. By then my being gone so long had deepened the apparent truthfulness of her story. In its simplest form that story amounted to my abandoning the child and that I had gone away to another woman on the Continent, and that Olivia, out of compassion for her niece, had taken Gwendolyn in. There was a more sinister element to the story, too, which I did not even know about. I only knew that when I returned people were different toward me. I did not know why at first. But I learned the rest of the story soon enough."

"What was it?" I asked, almost timidly.

"When I returned from the Continent, having been thinking all the while I was gone about what to do, I went to Olivia, assuming that I would at last retrieve my daughter. By then I had reconciled myself to the fact that I was a single father. But I thought, with the help of nurses, and Olivia as well, that I would raise Gwendolyn at the castle. I assumed that Olivia would be agreeable and would come to the castle to help me, and perhaps even that the child would continue to stay with Olivia some of the time. I suppose I did not think of all the implications of caring for a child. But I hoped with the help of others that it would be possible for her to live a somewhat normal life.

"I was stunned to find people looking at me almost with fear in their eyes, others with loathing, turning the other way, mothers hurrying their children across the street when they saw me coming. The looks, terrible looks on people's faces. Olivia, too, was changed. She was more cold and hard and haughty than ever before. She looked at me as if she actually believed the stories she had spread. Whether she encouraged people to believe the falsehoods directly or merely by innuendo, allowing conclusions to be drawn, I cannot say. But to my amazement I later learned that Olivia had allowed it to be circulated about that I raped my wife prior to our marriage and forced myself upon her in order to coerce her to marry me when she was actually in love with someone else. Then, discovering that she had given me a girl instead of a boy, the consensus was that moments after the birth of the child I had flown into a rage and hit her violently and was myself responsible for her death. If people actually believed such horrible things of me, they could hardly be blamed for not wanting their children around me. It was thought that my flight to the Continent, as it was viewed, was as much for the purpose of putting myself beyond the reach of the law as from fury at finding myself father to a sickly girl."

"Surely the attending doctor would tell what really happened," I said.

Alasdair smiled a bitter smile and sighed as he shook his head.

"If only it were so simple," he said. "People believe what they want to believe. Truth is often gray. Even the doctor's story, to one who *wanted* to believe the worst, seemed to corroborate the rumors Olivia had allowed to run wild during my absense."

"How could that be?" I asked. "What did he say?"

"That he left the room briefly a few minutes after the birth, that he heard a bloodcurdling scream from the open door behind him, that he ran back to find my wife unconscious, a welt swelling on her cheek obviously from a blow that had just occurred, and that he saw me bent over her bed. He said he *saw* nothing conclusive. But his way of recounting the story was so full of uncertainty that everyone took his story as confirming the worst. Olivia was in attendance but was also out of the room at the moment. She also heard the scream, though she said she heard my wife cry out twice. The two stories together came to be regarded with the veracity of multiple eyewitness accounts. Along with knowing looks and glances and my sister's persuasive manner, I was damned by public opinion from the start. All the while these and other dreadful rumors were taking root in the community, I was away and unable to counter them."

"What really did happen?" I asked.

Alasdair drew in a long, deep sigh and exhaled slowly. I was almost afraid to hear what might come next.

"It is difficult to relive those terrible events in my mind," he said. "My whole life changed that night. My world crumbled, my fate as an outcast and pariah was sealed. If only I could forget it altogether. Yet it is always with me. In my loneliest moments I even despise myself."

I waited, still fearful of what might be coming.

Alasdair drew in another breath. "The labor was long and hard," he said. "My poor wife spent what remained of her life getting little Gwendolyn into this world safely. She cried out all through it. What the doctor heard was but one of a hundred cries of an excruciating labor. It was probably ten minutes after the birth. Everyone in the room was resting after the ordeal. Olivia had taken the baby to clean it up and get fresh linens and towels. I thought my wife had dozed off. Suddenly a horrific cry sounded from the bed. My eyes shot open and I jumped to my feet. Her face was contorted in pain. She seemed trying to speak but was obviously suffering too much to get anything out. Her hand was on the side of her stomach. Suddenly she lurched up in the bed in yet greater agony, pushed herself up, shrieked out again, twisted her body halfway round, then collapsed back. As she did, the side of her face slammed hard against the bedpost. By then I was at the bedside as Olivia and the doctor rushed back into the room. The doctor saw immediately that she was unconscious and set about trying to revive her. Within thirty minutes he pronounced her dead."

I could not prevent a sharp breath of astonishment escaping my lips. I felt such agony for Alasdair. His eyes were full of tears and pain.

"I was in such a stupor that I hardly thought to question what was going on. I had no idea that I would later, if not actually be accused of murder, at least by implication find the blame for her death laid at my doorstep. It was not until I tried desperately to piece together in my mind what had actually taken place that I became aware of what Dr. Mair and Olivia were permitting to fester through the community in my year's absence. By then, of course, my reputation was in tatters and Olivia was spreading tales about me that have persisted until this day. Eventually a family curse came into it, and much from our past—things I had done as a child that confirmed my sadistic tendencies. Olivia has a method of communication that is measured and calm—mesmerizing in its own way."

"What about those weird rhymes she makes?"

Alasdair sighed and nodded. "Yes, there is that, too," he said. "Her voice almost casts a spell. No one questions that she is other than a paragon of virtue and truth. She can direct a conversation with such subtlety and cunning that people believe whatever Olivia wants them to believe."

"Alasdair, I am so sorry. I had no idea."

"In any event," Alasdair went on, "I had to know and understand for myself. The conclusion I finally reached, as I recall the look and what it seemed she was trying to say, and where she had placed her hand, was that the cause of death could well have been a burst appendix. She had been complaining of stomach pains for weeks. We thought it was from the pregnancy. But now I wonder if those were the warning signs. By then it was too late for an autopsy. The doctor was unresponsive to the idea. Nothing conclusive was ever known. The complaints of abdominal pain are in Dr. Mair's records. But he dismissed my theory. He, too, had fallen under Olivia's spell and began to alter his interpretation of events against me. It was said that I had been a troubled youth and that now the true nature of my dark character had resulted in murder. Olivia can weave a story such that facts take whatever shape she wants them to. When she was a girl, I marveled at her ability to bend people to her will. It was more than mere persuasiveness—it had a dark side, too, those rhymes were often in the form of curses and hexes. She was but a girl, but people all through the village were afraid of her. She was always getting *me* into trouble for things *she* had done. I honestly do not know if she is herself aware of what her powers of control have made of her."

"Why would she do this to you?" I asked. "It sounds like she has a vendetta against you."

"It was not that way at first. But that is what it has become. I am not exactly sure how to answer you. Eventually it became her mission to destroy me in the eyes of everyone in the community."

"But why? You are her own brother."

He smiled sadly. "I think the root of it is that I was the one person in the world she could not manipulate with her cunning. I know some of her secrets and she hates me for it. Once I was old enough to begin standing up to her, when I saw her using her wiles to manipulate events or twist facts to get her friends to do her bidding, I just laughed."

He became silent for a moment and a faraway look came into his eyes.

"Until…" he added, then shook his head. "Until a day came when I could no longer laugh. I knew the games she played with people. She was the same with our parents. They never knew when she was lying through her teeth. But I knew her better than anyone. I think I knew her better even than she knew herself. I was the one person she could not con. She hated me for it. Deep inside where she lets no one see, she is not only cunning, she is utterly unforgiving. She despised me because she knew I was the one person who could expose her for what she was. The only way to keep that from happening was to destroy my credibility. The events surrounding Gwendolyn's birth at last gave her the chance she had been waiting for for years. And for reasons of her own, she also hated my wife."

"What reasons?"

"Olivia was jealous of us, jealous of me that I had inherited the castle and the title, jealous of my wife for being able to bear children. Taking Gwendolyn away from us both was Olivia's revenge. Olivia is barren, you see. She could never have a child of her own. Taking Gwendolyn gave her a daughter to raise as her own. She was looked upon by others as the perfect adoptive mother, sacrificial, compassionate, rescuing the poor child from a dreadful fate. She was able to spread enough lies to prevent me from seeing the child again. She even used the court system."

"How so?" I asked.

"She had an injunction filed against me. I would have had to break the law to see my own daughter. Can you imagine the humiliation of such a thing?"

"Goodness! I had no idea."

"I was not even allowed the privilege to name my own child."

"*You* didn't give her the name Gwendolyn…you or your wife?"

Alasdair shook his head. "I discovered that Olivia had already named her," he said, "and witnessed the birth certificate with the doctor while I lay in bed ill after the birth. No one consulted me concerning the name. That is probably one of the reasons even now that it is difficult for me to say the name. Gwendolyn is a lovely name. But it is not *my* name for my daughter. And though her name is technically Gwendolyn Reidhaven, she is known to everyone, and to herself, as Gwendolyn *Urquhart*. My role in her life has been carefully, almost surgically, excised. To poor little Gwendolyn, I do not exist. But that is not the worst indignity of all."

"I do not understand. What is?"

Alasdair drew in a long breath. As he let it out, the pain was palpable.

"That she calls Olivia's husband *Daddy*, and calls Olivia *Mummy*. I have not heard it with my own ears. If I were to hear it, I cannot tell what I might do. But I have heard that it is true. Max is not around much. He works on the oil rigs offshore. I have heard that he takes on extra duty."

I didn't say that I *had* heard Gwendolyn call Olivia *Mummy*.

"That's awful," I said.

"I have been relegated to a nonperson in Gwendolyn's life. She does not even know her real name. She fears me, as all the children in the village fear me. Can you blame me for isolating myself away and becoming a hermit? When I go out, wherever I go, knowing what people think of me, knowing that I am despised, that people think I am a rapist and murderer, that they think some diabolical curse of the devil is on me. Good heavens—what people think of me is sometimes more than I can bear. It is an indignity that destroys a man's manhood, his sense of worth, his sense of who he is."

"What did you do?"

"What could I do? I gradually isolated myself more and more, until..."

He paused and tried to take a steadying breath.

"Can you imagine—"

His voice broke and a cry that was almost an involuntary sob of anguish came from his lips.

Alasdair turned away. I could tell he was fighting tears, sniffling and breathing heavily. My heart was breaking!

I rose and walked slowly to him and placed a hand on his shoulder. At my touch, his body heaved. Still looking away, he grasped my hand and squeezed it as if it were a lifeline. He sat, looking away, and I stood beside him for a long time in silence.

"Alasdair," I said softly at length, "would you like me to go? Would you rather be alone?"

Again it was silent.

Slowly his head began to nod. Still he had not turned back to face me.

"Yes...yes, perhaps that is best," he said, his voice quavering and so soft I could but barely hear it.

I waited a moment longer, then gave his hand a squeeze and turned and left the room by the door through which we had come in. As I closed it, my heart nearly broke to hear behind me one of the most terrible sounds in the world—the sound of a man crying in grief for his child.

It took me awhile to find my way through the maze of corridors. I was glad I knew my way around enough to get to one of the outside doors without encountering Miss Forbes or any of the other staff. Long before I felt the fresh air on my face I was crying, too.

I ran across the gravel entry to my car. A minute later I was on my way driving back through the woods away from the castle.

Chapter Forty-three

Sobering Question

Before we heaved our anchor,
Their evil speech began,
That you no more should see me,
The false and faithless man;
Droop not thy head my darling,
My heart is all thine own;
No power on earth can part us
But cruel death alone.

—Hector MacKenzie, "Health and Joy Be with You"

I was crushed by what Alasdair had told me.

I wept all the way back to the cottage. I ran inside and fell on the bed and sobbed and sobbed. It was all so terribly sad!

There was so much pain everywhere, so many hurts and misunderstandings. I had no idea what the full truth even was. All I knew was that I ached for them all because I had learned to love them. I had even learned in a way to care for Olivia Urquhart. I was dreadfully confused.

And there was poor little Gwendolyn right in the middle of it.

How right Iain had been. People needed to be reconciled—fathers and daughters and brothers and sisters. There was too much heartache in the world for people not to forgive!

Without realizing it, I began talking as I lay there crying, hardly realizing at first that I had begun to pray, praying from the depths of my heart, praying to God as a *Father* not as a religious image or caricature—as the Father of a family of which I was part, a family of humanity, a family of brothers and sisters, a family in which there was too much pain.

"God," I said through my tears, *"please bring healing and reconciliation between Alasdair and Olivia and Gwendolyn! If there is any way you can use me, I am willing, even eager."*

The moment the words were out of my mouth my tears began to subside and my spirit calmed. I began to breathe more steadily. Within five minutes I was sound asleep.

When I woke up it was midafternoon. I thought I had heard something. As I came to myself, I wondered if it had been a knock on the door.

I rose from the bed and went out to the lounge. Through the window I saw Olivia Urquhart walking away from the house along the pavement.

I hurried out and ran after her.

"Mrs. Urquhart!" I called.

She stopped and turned.

"I'm sorry. I was asleep," I said as I approached. "I didn't hear you."

"I just came by to say that you may bring the harp if you like," she said in a businesslike tone. "Gwendolyn is pining away for it. I have not changed my mind about what I said before, but I have no objection to Gwendolyn playing your harp."

"Oh, thank you," I said. "I will bring it over later today and leave it for Gwendolyn to play!"

I went back inside, dashed my face with cold water to wash away the remnants of tears and sleep, then sat down and played my harp for perhaps an hour. It was different playing this time, knowing that in a sense I was saying good-bye to my longtime friend for a while.

Perhaps for a long time.

Finally I was ready to send it on, I hoped, to the greater work of bringing joy to a young girl's heart. Somehow I hoped, though I could not yet see how, that either I or my harp, or even the mysterious music from inside her, might be a bridge between Gwendolyn and her father. But how to achieve reconciliation and healing with

Mrs. Urquhart standing in the way determined to prevent it, that I didn't know.

Then it occurred to me what Alasdair had said, about no one asking his point of view. I didn't want to be guilty of that. I needed to be open to the truth, whatever it was, wherever it led. That meant I needed to hear her point of view, too.

Suddenly from deep out of the past, my father's words returned to me:

Don't charge off condemning someone, or defending someone, unless you know the whole story. You may find yourself defending someone you wish you hadn't and who isn't as innocent as you first thought, or condemning another who isn't as guilty of wrong as you assumed. Drawing conclusions too soon, and without full informa-tion, will only result in your getting egg on your face. Nothing in human relationships is as clear as it seems.

Perhaps it was time I told Olivia Urquhart what I knew, and what I didn't, and let her tell me *her* perspective of the events surround-ing Gwendolyn's birth.

Who was I to have coincidentally developed a relationship with all three people in this sad family?

And why?

Yet, was that one of the reasons I had come to Scotland? Per-haps, like Ranald had said when we were talking about Scotland's music, the harp as well as the music had invisible qualities that worked for peace and healing, and perhaps even reconciliation, by touching the deepest longings of those who heard it.

If I was ever to know the full truth, I had to hear both sides.

What if Alasdair was putting a spin on what he told me, just as he said his sister did with her interpretation of events?

Wherever this led me, I had to find out more.

Chapter Forty-four

The Other Side

Her beauty's skin deep, an' that's a',
It's the velvet that covers the claw,
She's a honeyless floo'r, she's as light as the stoor,
Ye may trust her an hour, an' that's a'.
—"She's Bonnie an' Braw an' That's A'"

I took the harp over to Mrs. Urquhart's in the early evening.

Gwendolyn was nowhere to be seen. Mrs. Urquhart asked me to set up the harp, which I did. She thanked me dispassionately and I left. I thought about trying to talk to her right then, but decided not to.

I needed more time to think.

By the following morning I was convinced that talking to Olivia was the right thing to do. Now that thoughts of leaving this place had begun to stir within me, I had to get to the bottom of the situation...for them...for *me*.

All night, on and off, I thought about it. By morning I was determined to know the truth, if *truth* was even possible in a relational dispute as complicated and as emotionally charged as this one. Confrontation was not my style, but I was determined to not let Mrs. Urquhart close the door in my face again without getting some answers.

I walked over to her house about ten-thirty in the morning. All the way I kept reminding myself of what to do, drumming up my courage so I wouldn't turn around. Olivia Urquhart was intimidating. I was not looking forward to this.

I got to the house, drew in a deep breath, and walked up to the door and rang the bell.

When Mrs. Urquhart opened it and saw me, her eyes narrowed imperceptibly. She did not smile.

"Mrs. Urquhart," I said, "I want to talk to you."

"I told you, Ms. Buchan, that I do not—"

"I *want* to talk to you, Mrs. Urquhart," I interrupted. "You told me things about Alasdair...Mr. Reidhaven...the duke...I don't even know what I'm supposed to call him—but I have to know if those things are true."

"Are you doubting my word?" she asked slowly.

"I don't know what to believe. He has told me some things. You have told me other things. All I know is that it cannot be right to keep a girl from knowing her father. He tells me that is your doing, not his. He says that whatever his mistakes of the past, he has wanted to know Gwendolyn but that *you* have prevented it. If it is true, that seems a cruel thing to do, Mrs. Urquhart. You tell me he has abandoned her. He tells me you have prevented all contact. Both perspectives cannot be true. So I want to hear your side of it. I am willing to listen to whatever you want to tell me. If it is true, I want to know *why* you have kept Gwendolyn from her father. You probably think this is none of my business, but I have come to care about both of them very much."

Mrs. Urquhart's eyes flashed, though the rest of her features remained calm. I could tell she was furious. She glanced back into the house, her mind obviously working quickly.

"All right," she said. "I will come round to your cottage in an hour."

With that she closed the door. Again I was left alone on her porch.

I walked back, breathing more easily now that the tense exchange was behind me. I put on water for tea and waited.

Punctual as fate, exactly one hour later Mrs. Urquhart's knock came on my door. I opened it expecting to see her breathing fire. I was astonished as she greeted me with a kindly smile.

"Come in," I said.

She followed me inside.

"Would you like some tea?" I asked, leading her into the lounge. "I have water just boiling."

"That is very kind of you, uh...Marie. *May* I call you Marie?"

"Of course," I replied as I brought in the tea things. The sudden friendliness of her tone caught me utterly off guard.

"You said you had some questions," said Mrs. Urquhart in a soft voice as she sat down. "Ask whatever you like and I will try to set your mind at ease."

"Thank you," I said. "Mostly I just want to know about Gwendolyn and Alasdair. Is it true that you have kept him from being involved in her life?"

"Not in the least, dear," she replied. "I long for the day that Gwendolyn can know him again. But Alasdair is a troubled man. Surely you can see that. He is much better now, thank God. But he is still not able to care for a young girl. I have only taken Gwendolyn in temporarily because she needs the stable influence of a home and family."

"But did you get the courts to prevent his even visiting her? He said you filed an injunction against him."

"That was a long time ago. I only did it for Gwendolyn's safety. Alasdair forced me to use the court. I would never have done so otherwise."

"Have you removed the injunction?"

"Not in a technical sense. But whenever Gwendolyn wants to see him, now that she is twelve, she may do so."

"But does she even know about him? How would she ever ask to see him if you do not encourage her to? She is just a child. It seems that she will do whatever you want her to."

"There is much you do not understand, Marie," said Mrs. Urquhart, her voice growing yet softer. She smiled, almost a sickly sweet smile, and stared straight into my eyes. I could feel myself growing sleepy, almost as if I were under a spell. "I did all for Gwendolyn's best," she said. "I did all in love, Marie. Only in love. I know what is best for her. She has suffered much at her father's hand. There are things you cannot understand. You do not know Alasdair as I do."

My eyelids grew heavy as I listened. I had to shake myself almost physically to keep my wits about me.

"How was Alasdair troubled?" I forced myself to ask.

"He was disturbed—emotionally, if you know what I mean," replied Mrs. Urquhart. "And he had a violent temper. I lived in terror of him as a young girl. And he—"

She broke off. The look on her face said that something she had not intended had about slipped out. A long silence followed. She seemed to be recalling something horrid.

"There is also the matter of his wife's death," she went on after a moment. "He probably did not tell you about it?"

"He said she died in childbirth."

Mrs. Urquhart smiled a knowing smile and nodded, a little sadly it seemed. "Poor Alasdair," she said. "He never could face the truth of what happened."

Again her voice softened. Once more I felt myself growing drowsy.

"He even invented a story about appendicitis," she went on, "so as not to have to face his own guilt. The poor man. He is so desperate not to face the truth of what he has done. I feel so badly for him."

"What did happen, then?" I asked.

"You don't know, Marie?"

"I would like to hear it from you."

"He hit his poor wife, Marie."

She said the words as if expecting me to be shocked, as if it pained her to have to say it.

"She was already weak from the birth," she went on. "When he saw that she had given him a daughter instead of a son, and when he saw the child's red hair, it brought back all the jealousy of his suspicions, and he flew into a rage."

"What suspicions?" I asked.

"Of an affair she had been involved in before they were married. The doctor left the room and I grabbed the child to hurry it to safety before he could strangle it. I only returned in time to hear the poor woman screaming for her life and to see Alasdair deliver a dreadful blow to the side of her head."

"You saw him hit her?"

"Oh yes, dear."

"You are saying that he actually killed his wife?"

"Those are not my words, dear. I would not accuse my brother of murder. But it came to be widely believed. When the authorities sought to question him as a result of the doctor's testimony, he fled to the Continent. Since nothing was ever proven, no actual charges were filed."

"What about your testimony, if you were the one who actually saw it?"

"I would never testify against my own brother. What kind of woman do you think I am? Even so, I knew I had to get the child out of the castle as soon as possible. I feared for her life. In his state at the time, there was no imagining what Alasdair might do. I was terrified. That night of the birth brought back all the fears of my own childhood. But now it was for the child I feared rather than myself. I could not allow him to harm her."

"But later, after all that, he says he wanted to raise Gwendolyn himself, but that you refused to allow it."

"I have already explained that, dear. Oh, Marie, it is impossible for you to understand. Alasdair was in no position to give Gwendolyn a proper home. I did what was best for the poor girl. There were still so many legal complexities surrounding his wife's death."

"He says that you had yourself named the legal guardian for Gwendolyn to prevent him from having any contact with her."

"I had to, dear. It was the only means to protect dear Gwendolyn. Believe me, I harbor not the slightest ill will. Whatever Alasdair has done to me, I bear him no malice."

"And you and your husband never had children of your own?"

"That is true. That was our decision. When all this took place we decided to take Gwendolyn in, even though it would be a great sacrifice for us. We did so out of love. That is another story Alasdair has allowed himself to believe, that we could not have children and that I was motivated by some twisted desire to possess other people's children. Poor Alasdair, he is so bitter against me. It has blinded him to the truth. This vendetta keeps him from being able to look at things realistically. I feel sorry for him. He needs to forgive, as I have done. But I see little hope of it as long as such bitterness is in his heart."

"Are you saying that *you* have forgiven *him*?"

"Certainly, dear."

"But you will not let Gwendolyn see him?"

"It would be too stressful for her. You know she is not well. She is happy with us. She thinks of my husband as her daddy. It would be too disrupting to her fragile constitution, especially now. It is best to let things remain as they are. The court authorities agreed, saying that it would be too difficult for her to be taken back and forth between different homes, and that it was best that she remain with me."

"But is it right?" I asked. "It is not the truth."

"The *truth*, dear...according to whom?" Again Mrs. Urquhart's voice grew soft and mesmerizing.

"Just the truth," I struggled to say. "He is her father."

"Physically perhaps—though that is not known for certain. As I said, Alasdair himself had suspicions. But for all practical purposes, *if* he is her father, he abandoned that role in her life years ago."

"What do you mean, *if* he is her father?" I said. "Who else would be her father?"

"Why, Iain Barclay, of course."

My jaw dropped three inches and my face went pale.

Mrs. Urquhart saw the look of shock on my face and showed surprise. "Oh, dear," she said, as if she had blundered. "I merely assumed, as you have been seeing both men, that you knew."

My throat was suddenly dry. My head was spinning. Had I not been sitting down, I'm afraid I would have fainted.

"*Iain Barclay,*" I managed to croak. "You cannot be serious. The *curate*?"

"I am sorry, Marie," replied Mrs. Urquhart in a sensitive and sympathetic voice. "I had no idea you did not know. The love triangle involving them is common knowledge in the community, though no one *really* knows the full truth of what happened. Obviously I do not believe the rumors *myself.* People who spread such things should be paid no heed. I love Gwendolyn as my own flesh and blood, as my niece. That is why I have taken her in as I have. I am only telling you what *some* people believe. It no doubt explains why the two men haven't spoken in years."

I sat stunned. Suddenly all my questions about Gwendolyn and Alasdair had evaporated.

Chapter Forty-five

A Third View

We'll meet where we parted in yon shady glen,
On the steep, steep side o' Ben Lomond,
Where in purple hue the Hieland hills we view,
And the moon looks out frae the gloamin.

The wild birdies sing and the wild flowers spring.
An' in the sunshine the waters are sleepin':
But the broken heart it kens, nae second spring,
Tho' the waefu' may cease frae their greetin'!
—"Loch Lomond"

I was worn out emotionally. What had I gotten myself mixed up in!

I wanted to go for a long walk on the beach or along the headlands and forget about it all. I even thought about just packing up my few things, getting in my rented car, and driving away and going back to Canada on the first available flight.

I walked for a while to try to calm down.

I cried a good deal, too. But the next interview I needed to have couldn't wait. If any more hammers were going to drop on my head, I wanted them over with.

Thus it was that about two hours later I found myself walking up the path to Iain's house. I closed my eyes, took a deep breath, and knocked on the door.

"Marie!" said Iain when he opened the door. He always seemed so happy to see me. But I was too full of conflicting thoughts and emotions to return his smile. Part of me wanted to fall into his arms and have him tell me everything was going to be all right, and then talk to me about God's loving Fatherhood.

But suddenly he looked different. I could not help it—Olivia Urquhart had planted seeds of suspicion in my mind. My eyes went to his bright red-orange hair and my heart sank with doubts. For the first time since coming here, I wasn't sure I could trust Iain. Odd words and mysterious looks came back to me from our first conversations whenever Gwendolyn came up.

Every time I brought up Gwendolyn or Alasdair or the past, Iain became quiet and subdued. There were obviously secrets I didn't know. What if everything hinted at by Olivia Urquhart was true?

It would kill me. But I had to know.

I hated thinking such thoughts! But I could not dismiss them from my mind. Once the doubts were there, I couldn't make them go away. She had planted doubts about both Iain and Alasdair.

They were tearing me apart inside.

Iain saw immediately that something was wrong. My eyes were probably still red.

"Marie, what is it?" he asked, leading me gently inside and helping me to a chair.

"I have to talk. I need to ask you...there are some things I've heard," I fumbled. "I have to..."

I didn't know what to say. I glanced away, my eyes filling again.

Iain waited patiently until I had stuttered my way through telling him that I had heard a rumor about him and the duke and his late wife and young Gwendolyn.

He nodded as I finished, then smiled sadly.

"I am sorry, Marie," he said. "I hoped you wouldn't have to hear about all that. I wasn't trying to keep it from you. There was just no need. I hope you can see the wisdom of that statement. It is nothing but the sordid gossip of a soap opera best left to the auld wives that traffic in such wares. I would ask you where you heard it, but I refuse to stoop to their level."

"I just have to know whether it's true. I've heard so many things about the duke, and now about you, I'm just confused. I care about...about everyone. I have to know."

"Do you want to know the *whole* story?" asked Iain. "Everything?"

Feeling the same fear clutch my chest as when I was talking to Alasdair, I swallowed hard and nodded.

Iain drew in a long breath. He was quiet for several minutes. I had never seen him so silent and reflective.

"It is not easy," he began after some time, "when a child of a small town grows into man's estate, as they say. Though he may put away childish things, it is not so simple for those who knew him as a youth to recognize the change. I would not go so far as to speak of prophets being without honor. Yet there is a principle involved that applies to all who find themselves as men walking the same streets and byways that were also the scenes of their boyhood. Those who were his elders during the days of his youthful mischief do not readily relinquish their perceptions.

"In my own case, I was a scamp, a scallywag of the first order, fully deserving of my disorderly red mop of hair. My school chum was the duke's son, who, before he was sent away to private school, attended school in the village. The adventures we had together, and the scrapes we got into, would have filled a book. They kept half the town angry and the other half laughing. Many a time we were hauled before the old duke, young Alasdair's father, for stern reprimands, though his position kept us from serious consequences at the hands of the local magistrate. Most of the locals put the blame on me for instigating the troubles that seemed constantly to surround us. Eventually Alasdair was sent south to Eton, then to Oxford. That the mischief largely ceased after that in no way changed local opinion about me. It got around that my father had given me a whipping and told me that if I didn't mend my ways he would not lift a finger, nor would the duke now that Alasdair was gone, to keep me from the consequences of my foolishness. There wasn't a word of truth in it. I'm not saying that my father didn't whip me when I deserved it—bless him—but such was not the case when Alasdair went away to school.

"—By the way," he added. "Ranald tells me that he thinks very highly of you. I find it remarkable, Marie, how you have managed to work your way into the hearts of so many in our village.

"In any event, the long and the short of it was that I did begin to pay more attention to my studies and gave neither my father, the old duke, nor the townspeople more cause for concern. But the change was due more to Ranald Bain than anyone else—because he cared enough to confront me. I owe him as much as one man can owe another. And because of him I also began to take matters of faith more seriously than most young men. I nearly shocked my poor father into dropping the whisky glass in his hand several years later when I announced that I had decided to pursue a university education and a career in the church. In the years since the apples, Ranald had mentored me in faith, teaching me to think and pray and begin walking as a disciple of Jesus Christ and his Father. Attending university was no easy thing to do coming from a poor background as I did, even with Ranald's and Margaret's help. But, as you can see well enough, I managed it, though that is getting ahead of the story.

"Alasdair and I both returned to Port Scarnose, having seen nothing of one another in nearly six years. We tried to rekindle the former friendship, or perhaps I should say I did. But we were by then much too different. He was a sophisticated Oxford graduate and had grown into manhood steeped in the class distinction, which, in spite of what anyone may tell you, is far from dead in this country. That I had pulled myself out of my humble beginnings to gain an education *almost* the equivalent of his in no way changed the low station of my birth. My new status was rendered meaningless in his eyes by the fact that I was using my education in the church. He would himself be the duke one day, and I could tell he looked down on me for the religious turn I had taken.

I think it embarrassed him that he and I had once been closer than the brothers neither of us had.

"We had but one thing in common after our return."

Iain paused. A nostalgic wave seemed to pass briefly across his face.

"That," he added, "was a young lady by the name of Fiona."

Again he paused, this time for longer. I could tell that his thoughts had drifted back and that he was reliving events from years before.

"Fiona came to Crannoch while we were both away at university," Iain resumed at length. "Her pedigree was humble enough. She was neither aristocrat nor peasant, but the daughter of a local antiques dealer recently arrived from Edinburgh, a man of both means and some stature in the community for he was also the author of several books. Fiona was stunningly beautiful. Her family had not been in the area a week before she was the chief subject of conversation from Findectifeld to Banff, turning heads and breaking hearts wherever she went, not unlike Winny Bain years before.

"Alasdair returned from Oxford and of course heard of her instantly. Alasdair was different then...thin, muscular, dashing—an aristocratic young man in the classic mold. They were already seeing one another when I returned from England. In my initial attempts to rekindle my friendship with Alasdair, Fiona and I inevitably crossed paths, and...well, I am embarrassed to admit that I was smitten with her along with everyone else. I had studied for the ministry, and was serious about my faith, but I was a young man susceptible to the same influences that have moved young men to both bravery and foolishness throughout all time. I did not actually pursue her as I suppose you might say because she and Alasdair were fast becoming what is called *an item*. But as we both lived in Port Scarnose we could not help running into each other, and a friendship began to develop."

I was getting a very weird feeling, like I had been here before,

that a story was being told that I was part of, or an old story that
I had once been part of, and maybe was destined to be part of
again. Shudders went through me. I didn't like the sound of it—two
men…the same woman. But I did my best to hide what I was
thinking.

"As you might imagine," Iain went on, "it did not enhance my
relationship with Alasdair. He was furious whenever he saw us
talking or walking together. But he needn't have been. I liked
Fiona. We had some wonderful times together. We became good
friends. And I think there was a hunger, a *spiritual* hunger within
her. It seemed she was longing for something I might be able to
give her, not as a man but spiritually. Yet it was a place within her
I never seemed entirely able to connect with. There was a mystery
about Fiona, too, that seemed to prevent her from being able to
enter into life's spiritual dimension, though I think part of her
wanted to. It was a puzzle.

"In any event, I was convinced in my own mind that she loved
Alasdair. So I gradually distanced myself from the whole situation.
The upshot was that their engagement was announced about a
year later, and they were married a year after that. I was not curate
at the time. I was still in training and was reading and filling in
for churches throughout the northeast of Scotland. I was invited,
however, and did attend their wedding, which was held at the
castle.

"I saw little of either Alasdair or Fiona after that, only if we happened to pass in town. I was filling in regularly at the church here
by then. The Deskmill Parish minister, old Reverend Cowie, was
aging and in ill health. The older people of the parish were not
altogether in favor of the young scamp Reddy Barclay, as I had
been called as a boy, occupying their pulpit. But the younger
people seemed to respond to my youthfulness and energy. When
Reverend Cowie retired, there happened to be a shortage of potential candidates—the church goes through ebbs and flows in that
regard. It being a small and out-of-the-way parish that had always

struggled financially made it a difficult vacancy to fill. The long and the short of it is that I was fortunate to be named curate.

"Then came word that Fiona, now the Duchess of Buchan, was pregnant. All the auld wives of the village followed the times and seasons in minutest detail. Every visit Dr. Mair made to the castle was duly noted, and as the time drew near, expectation mounted. It wasn't exactly like Charles and Diana, but something similar to it. The duke and duchess were our *own* local royalty, and Fiona was every bit Diana's equal in beauty. People loved her and every eye was on them.

"For some reason Alasdair went into Aberdeen one day. I think it had some connection to his offshore oil investments. A messenger came to me from the castle while he was away. He handed me a brief letter. I recognized Fiona's hand instantly. She said she had to see me...urgently. At the time I did not know that Alasdair had gone into the city. I dropped everything and hurried to the castle.

"I was led upstairs, surprised to be shown into Fiona's bedroom. She was in bed with Dr. Mair at her side. Her face was pale. She dismissed the doctor, then told me why she had sent for me. Her labor had begun. She was afraid and in pain for more reasons she thought than the pregnancy. She was afraid of dying. I tried to reassure her that such fears were normal during childbirth. She had called me there as a friend, but mostly as a minister. She wanted me to assure her that she would go to heaven. Finally the spiritual uncertainties and questions from before all spilled out. We talked for a good while, though she was interrupted periodically by labor pains. At one point she reached out and took my hand. 'You were one of the best friends I ever had, Iain,' she said. 'I always admired you for what you did. But I am afraid, Iain. You will pray for me, won't you?'

"Before I had the chance to reply, suddenly the door flew open and Alasdair burst in. His face was red with rage to see me at the bedside with his wife's hand in mine. I stood, obviously mortified to have him find me in what looked like such a compromising position. He roared in fury, and I'm afraid used language that did not become him in the presence of a woman, not to mention his wife. I wish I did not have to tell you such things," he said, letting out a long sigh.

"But you asked for the whole story. Alasdair was full of threats. His whole demeanor portended violence. Had it not been that Dr. Mair had followed him into the room, I would have been afraid to leave Fiona alone. But the doctor hurried to Fiona's side and, assured that she was safe, I hurried from the room and left the castle. Now I had more reason than ever to pray for Fiona.

"The next morning I learned that a girl had been born but that Fiona was dead, that Alasdair was weak and under the doctor's care, and that the child was safely with Alasdair's sister, Olivia. My position was precarious so I did not visit the castle that day, but sent condolences to Alasdair by letter. The situation remained extremely awkward. I was not asked to preside at the funeral. A few days later I heard that Alasdair had suffered a collapse and had taken to bed.

"Rumors almost immediately began to circulate both about the child's parentage and Fiona's death, which involved both Alasdair and me. I tried to ignore them. Alasdair left, they say for the Continent, some time later and was gone a year. During that time, certain legal allegations were made which resulted in Olivia's being named Gwendolyn's legal guardian. So the situation has remained until now.

"I am sorry to say that Alasdair and I have only seen one another two or three times since then, and have not spoken a word. I know he still harbors bad feelings toward me for what happened. Every time I set foot in the church I am aware that just over the fence not a quarter mile away lives a man I once loved as a brother whom I have not spoken to in years."

Iain let out a long sigh with an expression I can only describe as mingling embarrassment, confusion, and heartache.

We sat for a long time in silence.

"I have heard so many conflicting things," I said finally. "What is the truth in all this? Can one ever really know?"

Iain shook his head. "I don't know," he sighed. "That is the most difficult question in all human relationships—how to resolve differences and conflict and bring healing, when there are so many versions of truth. I am afraid there are some things that no one will ever know until God reveals it all."

"But from your sermon, you believe healing and reconciliation are still possible?"

"I do. I absolutely do. Being of one mind concerning conflicts of the past is no prerequisite for healing, only a mutual desire to forgive and move forward. Complex and selfish emotional creatures that we humans are, *resolution* is not so important as *reconciliation*. Healing can take place even where scars remain. The body uses scars to heal over wounds, and perhaps there is a spiritual principle involved, too. In the end, character must surely be the most reliable validation of truth we have to go on."

Chapter Forty-six

Character

Gone are now those blissful days—
Too ecstatic while they lasted,
All the flowers that gemmed my ways
By misfortune's breath are blasted.
  —"Maiden by the Silver Dee"

I scarcely slept that night.

I could not stop my brain from spinning like a merry-go-round. Weird dreams flitted in and out of my consciousness as I dozed on and off, images of Alasdair and Iain and Gwendolyn and red-haired circus clowns and the three of them spinning around on a carousel of horses, and Olivia Urquhart's mesmerizing voice hanging like a thick stupefying fog over everything...soft, calm, soothing like an antiseptic drug...speaking in otherworldly chanting rhymes. *There is much you do not understand,* floated the voice of reason through my dreams...*much you do not understand. I know all. You cannot understand...her father's hand. Only I understand. You cannot know of Alasdair's youth...only I can tell you the truth.*

Several times I awoke with the words, *You cannot understand... only I understand,* in my ears. I could not remember whether Olivia had said she was the *only* one who understood. Yet somehow, after my dreams, I knew that it was what she had meant.

It was all so confusing!

How was one to get to the bottom of such a dispute where truth was so nebulous and vague?

I finally could lie there no longer. I got up, took a shower, and fixed myself tea. It was only six o'clock but the sun was up.

303

I went out for a walk. I had not been out so early before. It was gray, drizzly, but not too cold. The thick, misty air suited my mood. Again I sought the cliff paths, where the constant ebb and flow of the waves against the rocky shore never ceased to soothe my spirit.

As I walked, I found myself praying. It felt good. Somehow I knew I was not alone. But the only thing I could pray was simply, *God, help me understand what is going on.*

I walked for some time. Slowly, as I gazed out over the sea, a tiny hole of blue became visible through the gray clouds of the morning sky. I stared at it and knew that beyond it the sun was shining clear and bright. That little patch of blue was like a doorway through the gray mist into the light beyond.

Suddenly a light burst in my brain. In the same way, perhaps there was also a doorway through the clouds of doubts and uncertainties that seemed so overpowering right then, a doorway into the light of truth. Almost instantly the answer came.

The doorway through the mists of doubt was individual *character.*

It was exactly what Iain had said. *Character must surely be the most reliable validation of truth.* You have to discern individual *character*, and let it lead you to truth.

I walked along trying to absorb what this answer meant. I saw that perhaps I would never understand *everything* that was going on around me. Iain was right about that, too. Relationships were too complicated. Who but God himself could fully understand all the complexities of the human condition? But I could still follow that little pathway of blue into the light, by looking for true character in people, and by letting character lead to truth.

With such thoughts, the face of Iain Barclay filled my mind. I could not help smiling. The image I saw was smiling, energetic, animated, occasionally laughing, yet it was a thoughtful face, too, and serious when the occasion demanded it. Iain's was a countenance that was looking *up*, trying to follow God in all he did. In an instant I knew that he was not a man who would or even *could* lie to me.

I believed him, because I believed *in* him. He was a man of character. I *trusted* him.

I trusted Ranald Bain, too. His eyes shone with the same light—the light of character and truthfulness and humility.

Slowly the images of the two faces faded from my mind's eye.

Into my thoughts came the face of Alasdair Reidhaven. The *duke*...now my friend...perhaps even more than a friend. It was not a smiling, happy, laughing image like Iain's had been. Alasdair wore a complex expression, thoughtful but in a different way...pained...yes, perhaps in a way even troubled. But as I continued to watch his face in my imagination, almost as if I were with him and we were talking and he was struggling to find expression, I sensed something in him I had not realized before.

I saw *humility*.

Was it an odd thing to say of a duke? Perhaps. But it was true. He was growing, changing, trying to better himself. Alasdair was far from perfect. He had made many mistakes and blunders. But he knew it. He admitted it. He was trying to *grow* from them and put them behind him.

What could be more important than that?

We all are incomplete. There are flaws in our personalities. We make mistakes. Some mistakes are more serious than others. Perhaps Alasdair had made big mistakes in his life. Maybe he was more flawed as a person than Iain Barclay. But now he was trying to grow. And I respected him for it. It takes humility to admit one's flaws and try to grow out of them.

This I sensed in Alasdair. *Humility*...the humility of character.

Humility was a virtue that could be trusted. Yes, I believed Alasdair, too. Because I believed, with all his flaws and mistakes, that he had come to possess that indefinable quality called humility. He was a *growing* man of gradually deepening character.

Then Alasdair's face, too, faded from my mind.

Into it came the face of Olivia Urquhart, whose expression was different from that of the three men. Enigmatic, mysterious, hiding more than it revealed. There were no smiles on her face. Try as I might, I perceived no humility, no humor, no growth. I saw calculation and cunning. I didn't know what to make of who she was inside.

Doubt and confusion filled me again. What was I to think? I saw her speaking in that calm, measured, smooth, mesmerizing voice that had become so familiar. I heard nothing, only saw her lips moving. I *felt* rather than heard the hypnotic power of her voice trying to lure and persuade me to believe what she said.

My chest began to tighten. My eyelids grew heavy. The doubts increased...doubts about Alasdair...he was evil, a murderer, he was trying to get his clutches into me by pretending to be what he wasn't. Iain Barclay wasn't what he seemed. He went about pretending to be—

No! I said to myself. I couldn't let myself believe such things.

Desperately I tried to shake myself awake, to cast off the spell.

Even as I did so, another face came into my mind's eye—the wonderful, innocent face of a young girl, a girl who did not know her father.

I knew something about not knowing one's Father. I was forty-one years old. Yet it had taken coming to Scotland and all the circumstances of the past weeks to wake me to the fact that God was a Father who loved me and wanted me to be his daughter. But maybe the same thing could be said of Gwendolyn. She had a father who loved her, too, and she didn't know him, maybe didn't even know he existed at all.

It wasn't right. She *had* to know her father, because he was a man growing into character, and he wanted to know and love her.

Now the image in my imagination changed again, this time into a wonderful one.

I saw Alasdair and Gwendolyn together, hand in hand...
Gwendolyn chattering away in delight to be with the man who had
given her life...Alasdair smiling down upon her with the love of a
father, maybe even with a reflection of God's love for all humanity.

I continued on my way. The images of faces now fading and the
sea and the cliffs, the rocky shoreline and the gulls, all came back
into focus. As I went, the words of Iain's sermon returned to me.

*When division exists within humanity, any division—between
man and man, between man and woman, between father or
mother and son or daughter, division between friends—that division pierces to the very heart of God.*

I realized that perhaps reconciliation was possible without resolving every detail of the past. People could still be reconciled.
Healing could still take place. Just as Iain had said, humility was
the key.

*It takes humility, great humility to seek reconciliation. Yet humil-
ity is the doorway into reconciliation.*

If that was true, and if, mistakes and flaws and all, Alasdair possessed humility, why could not he and Gwendolyn be reconciled?
I saw only one thing standing in the way, one *person* standing in
the way.

Olivia Urquhart.

How poignant Iain's words suddenly became.

*It is humility that leads us to be reconciled with our brothers, with
our fathers, with our daughters...Humility, my friends. Humility to
admit wrong, to recognize that life is not what we had hoped...
Humility to apologize. Humility to arise and go to the one we have
hurt. Humility is the doorway, my friends. It is the door to reconciliation...the door that leads to our sons and daughters...the door
that leads to the heart of God.*

Even as the words from the sermon were still echoing through
my head, I knew that before this morning was out, I needed to see
the man who had spoken them.

I felt the familiar injustice and anger starting to rise up within me. I knew the feeling. It was exactly as it had been with the bully on the playground and when I had angrily confronted Clarissa about the prom.

I began to tremble just thinking about it. Was I about to do something stupid again, something I might regret? Or was *truth* at stake, and did I have to take a stand, come of it what may?

Chapter Forty-seven

Decision at the Bench

If your heart should faint or fail you,
Striving sore and toiling long,
If the wasps of care assail you,
Clear the way with dance and song.
—"Hark! How the Skinner's Fiddle Rings"

Iain seemed surprised to see me standing at his open door.

"I need to talk to you, Iain," I said.

It was obvious from his expression that he realized some change had taken place within me.

"I would like to go for a walk, if you don't mind," I said. "To my favorite bench, you know."

"Sure," he replied. "Just give me a minute."

Twenty minutes later we were walking together on the path out of town thirty meters above the sea.

"I am sorry for being abrupt when I came to see you yesterday," I said. "Asking you all those questions. It probably wasn't fair of me, but I had to know."

"Think nothing of it," said Iain.

"There is something I have to tell *you,* too," I went on. "It has to do with your sermon last Sunday."

I went on to tell him of my realizations about God's Fatherhood, and my thoughts and prayers and my walk on the beach. He smiled a quiet, happy smile and said he was proud of me.

"Even more than all that," I went on, "I want to see Gwendolyn and Alasdair together again, reconciled, just like you talked about. I know I am just a visitor here. I have no business being involved.

But I can't help thinking that perhaps I came for a reason, and that this is part of it. But I don't know what to do. Mrs. Urquhart seems to hate Alasdair. Once she found out that I knew him, she told me not to come visit Gwendolyn again."

"She said that?" said Iain, glancing toward me, his forehead clouding.

"Yes," I answered. "She was more than insistent about it, she seemed angry at me. I know *hate* is a strong word. But she seems absolutely determined to keep Alasdair from seeing Gwendolyn, and now me, too. It makes no sense."

"It might make more sense than you realize."

"But it isn't right. Surely something can be done."

Iain was quiet a long time. We reached the bench and sat down. Whatever he was thinking, I had never seen him like this. At last he drew in a long sigh.

"You are right." He nodded with a serious expression. "It makes no sense. Or it *seems* to make no sense. As much as she has told you, and as much as I told you, there is even more involved, things from long ago, things that may never come to light. I have tried many times to talk to Olivia. But she is adamant that she will not allow Alasdair near Gwendolyn. It has become an obsession with her. Her feelings toward me are almost as hateful, though for the sake of propriety she behaves civilly toward me. Down inside, however, she despises me, too."

"Does it have to do with the night of Gwendolyn's birth?"

"Somewhat, perhaps, though that is but the tip of the iceberg."

"What really did happen that night?" I asked.

Iain sighed. "Honestly, I don't fully know," he replied. "Knowing both Olivia and Alasdair as I think I do, and knowing Olivia's predisposition to twist and spin facts to manipulate opinion to serve her purpose, I am inclined not to give her account of events much credibility. But, too, it must be acknowledged that Alasdair was different back then. I am not one to pretend faults and weaknesses do not exist. At the same time, for all his human flaws, I never knew Alasdair to lie."

"And Mrs. Urquhart?" I said. "Would she lie?"

Iain thought a long while.

"That is a terrible charge to bring against any man or woman," he replied at length. "But if it suit her purpose, I have little doubt that Olivia would lie. What takes place in her conscience between herself and God, I have no idea. When I became curate I was not happy about her as one of the elders. An elder, in my view, is one who possesses the twin Christlike characteristics of *humility* and *wisdom,* and is thus capable of living as an example to the church of discipleship and obedience. I certainly saw neither trait in Olivia Urquhart. But because she possessed enough clout, to put it bluntly, in the local community, and my own standing was at that time a little less secure, I did not feel I could do anything about it."

"Why would she spread stories about Gwendolyn?"

"Control. And indirectly, to cast suspicion on Alasdair. And also to divert attention from herself, to keep herself from being looked at too closely. I know Olivia thought of me as a simpleton ever since I turned my life around and decided to study for the ministry. She thought she could do whatever she liked and I would look the other way. But though a minister is not privy to everything that takes place in his parish, at the same time, not all ministers are the dunces some people take them for. I think I know more about Olivia and her secrets than she has any idea. Maybe I have looked the other way too long."

I shook my head. It was all too much to take in. I let out a long sigh.

"Everything you have told me is all the more reason why I should talk to her," I said, "why I feel that I am *supposed* to talk to her. I know it's probably stupid, I know I'm a newcomer and newcomers shouldn't go around butting into other people's affairs. I know it's impulsive. I got angry with one of my friends in high school and couldn't keep my mouth shut. My father said I overreacted and he was right. But I can't help it. It just rises up within me and I *have* to speak out. It's a compulsion. My father also said to get both sides, and I think I have, and he said that if you're sure you're right, then go ahead. So I have to talk to her. But I don't want to go alone. Would you go with me?"

Iain exhaled and glanced away. If I didn't know better I would have thought he was about to cry. I had never seen him look so sad, so disconsolate, so heartbroken. I think I knew him well enough by now to know that he wasn't heartbroken for himself. I think he was feeling a little of what maybe God feels for his children who refuse to be reconciled—to him, and to one another.

We sat for a long time staring out over the North Sea. Probably fifteen or twenty minutes went by. As anxious as some people are to fill up every relational gap with words, it felt good just to sit beside Iain in silence. I simply waited. I sensed that he was struggling with a decision. I wasn't anxious to hurry him.

"You're right," he said finally. "It is time." His tone was decisive and final.

I glanced to my right. Iain returned my questioning glance by simply nodding. "I have waited long enough...*too* long. It is time."

He climbed to his feet. "Let's go," he said.

I stood and joined him as we began walking back toward Port Scarnose.

"Where are we going?"

"To see Olivia Urquhart," he replied.

Chapter Forty-eight

Authority's Demand

Let the learned wig and mitre
Wrangle over right and wrong;
Would you make life's burden lighter;
Clear the way with dance and song.
—"Hark! How the Skinner's Fiddle Rings"

When Mrs. Urquhart opened her door and saw Iain Barclay and me standing there, the expression on her face did not register pleasure.

She said nothing, neither greeted us nor invited us inside. She obviously sensed some impending doom. Though she masked it well, it was clear her defenses immediately went up.

"I want to talk to you, Mrs. Urquhart," I said. "I asked Mr. Barclay to come with me."

"I have already told you everything I have to say, Ms. Buchan," she said.

"I have something to say to *you*, Mrs. Urquhart," I said. "I will not leave until I say it."

She stood staring at me, obviously surprised at my determination.

"Very well, then," she said. "I am listening."

"May we come in?" I said.

"Why can't you just tell me what you want to say and leave?"

"I would rather not do so standing here like this."

She stared at me a moment longer.

"Let me close the door to Gwendolyn's room," she said, then turned back into the house. The door closed behind her. We waited. About a minute later it opened again.

"All right," said Mrs. Urquhart in a chilly tone. "Come in."

We walked inside and sat down.

"I want to talk to you about Gwendolyn," I said. "I do not feel it is right that she has no contact with her father. I would like to ask you to allow me to take her to visit him."

"That is out of the question," replied Mrs. Urquhart. Her face filled with silent fury. "I explained everything to you before."

"I know you did. But I would like to take her regardless."

"What business is this of yours? Who do you think you—"

She paused abruptly. Her face changed. Her voice softened and became cold and hard.

"I could not possibly allow it," she said. "I would be too afraid for Gwendolyn."

"*Afraid*...of what?"

"Of what he might do to her. I know him, Marie. You do not."

"I will take care of her, Mrs. Urquhart. No harm will come to her, I will personally see to that."

She smiled with condescension. "If you will excuse my saying so," she said, "that is hardly a guarantee that engenders confidence."

"You do not consider me capable of protecting her?"

"You know nothing about my brother."

"That is not true. The years of pain have done more than you know."

She stiffened but kept her composure. "I told you before," she went on, "there is much you do not understand."

"Perhaps. But this is the present, and the past is no reason to deny my request."

"You do not know Alasdair like I do."

"I am sorry, Mrs. Urquhart, but I think it is you who do not know him. You have not been willing to see that he has grown and changed."

For the briefest instant her eyes flashed. Quickly she recovered herself and smiled. Then came the voice.

"I think I know how you feel, Marie," she said soothingly. "You simply must believe that this is for the best."

"For Gwendolyn to not know her father? No—I *don't* think it best."

"But it is, dear. I know."

"I know what you told me, Mrs. Urquhart," I went on. "Perhaps it is all true. I don't really know. But it doesn't matter now."

"How can you say that? Of course it matters."

"People can change. I believe Alasdair has grown. Maybe it no longer matters what happened a long time ago."

"You don't know what he was like. I will never forget."

"Healing and forgiveness are still possible. People can move on from the past without resolving every issue. Why can't you give him that chance?"

"Because of what he is."

"Maybe he is becoming something better."

"Then let him become it and prove it." She spat out the words. "Then maybe a visit with Gwendolyn might be possible."

"What if by then it is too late?"

My question hung in the air and put a temporary stop to the conversation.

"You are very persuasive, Marie," said Mrs. Urquhart after a moment. "Nevertheless, I will not allow it. I cannot allow it. And I have the legal means to prevent it if you—"

Suddenly Iain spoke. His voice was unlike anything I had heard from his mouth before—forceful, determined. What surprised me most of all was his obvious anger.

"Olivia!" he said. The commanding sound of her name silenced her.

I was familiar with the term *righteous indignation*. But I had never seen it like I saw it now in Iain's face.

"This lady has made a request of you that is not only reasonable but that is true. I believe God has sent her here to try to set right a wrong that has been allowed to fester in this community far too long. I have spoken to you about it before, always attempting to appeal to your better nature, to reason with your humanity. I have tried to be patient, to wait for you to grow into readiness. But I begin to doubt that even a germ of human compassion exists in your heart. I realize that I have waited too long. I have waited in vain, and I repent of my indecision in this matter. I will wait no longer. Right must prevail, and now is the time."

Mrs. Urquhart shot him a glance of indignation that was *not* of the righteous variety.

"Don't try to intimidate me with all your religious talk!" she shot back at him. "You may be able to fool everyone else. But I know who you are, Reddy Barclay. You don't frighten me," she almost snarled.

The two of them locked eyes. I was stunned to witness such a tense exchange. I had never seen either of them so uninhibited and bold. For two or three highly charged seconds neither said a word. Then Iain turned to me.

"Marie," he said, "would you mind waiting for me outside? I would like to have a few words with Olivia alone. I will be no more than one or two minutes."

I rose and left the house. I had no idea what might be going on behind the closed door. But I was dying of curiosity.

I heard the door open a short time later. I turned and saw Iain on the porch. He motioned to me. I hurried back up the walk and followed him inside.

Mrs. Urquhart still sat in the chair where I had last seen her. Her countenance was dramatically altered. She sat like a statue of stone, her face pale, her body trembling.

"Olivia has agreed to let you take Gwendolyn for a drive," Iain said to me, "to show her the castle, and to introduce her to her father."

He turned to Mrs. Urquhart.

"Have Gwendolyn ready," he said forcefully. "Marie will be back for her in an hour."

Mrs. Urquhart turned on him a look of seething wrath such as I had never seen on a human face. Iain led me away, and we left the house together. Despite my persistent questions, he would tell me nothing of what had taken place. He told me only to come back for Gwendolyn, to have a talk with her, that I should expect her to be fearful but to tell her that she could trust me, that I knew her father, and that I knew that her father loved her. He told me to remember what he had told me about God at first, and that I had had a difficult time believing it, too, and to put myself in Gwendolyn's place.

Then he left me, obviously spent from the interview with Olivia.

Chapter Forty-nine

The Prodigal's Loving Father

There I shall visit the place of my birth;
And they'll give me a welcome, the warmest on earth;
All so loving and kind, full of music and mirth,
In the sweet sounding language of home.
—"The Mist Covered Mountains of Home"

I knew poor little Gwendolyn was nervous and frightened as we walked up to the imposing castle where she was born twelve years before.

I felt her little hand trembling in mine. I hated to put her through it. But I knew all would be well soon enough, when she discovered how full of love her father's heart was for her. Even good change can be fearsome at first.

She had been so overjoyed and excited to see me again, it brought tears to my eyes. I had taken her first for a walk above the sea. We sat down on the bench and I reminded her of the first day when she and I had met. We talked for a while, mostly about the harp. Then I told her that I wanted to take her to meet her father, her real father.

Her mood immediately changed. She was clearly frightened. What she had been told in the last hour I could only imagine.

"But he is mean," she said. "I am afraid. I don't want to see him. Mummy says I don't have to see him, that you can't make me see him, that I should tell you to take me home."

"But you don't think I am mean, do you?"

"Oh, no, Marie! You are the nicest person in the whole world."

"You can trust me, can't you?"

"Oh, yes!"

"Well, I know your father, Gwendolyn. I know him very well. I have seen him and spoken with him. He is not so very different from me. And I know that he loves you very much."

"Mummy said you would tell me that, but not to believe you."

"Have I ever not told you the truth, Gwendolyn?"

"I don't think so."

"I promise you, I haven't. I will *always* tell you the truth. Do you believe me?"

She nodded.

"Your father wants you to know him just like I know him," I said. "So I have come to take you to him."

"But I have heard terrible things about him, that he is mean and will be angry with me."

"He only seems that way to those who don't know him. But I do know him, Gwendolyn. You will soon know him, too, if you can just trust me. Can you trust me, Gwendolyn? Can you trust me to take your hand and lead you to your father?"

"I will try, Marie."

"You know that I love you?"

"Yes, Marie."

"Then trust me that your father loves you, too."

In spite of our talk, however, twenty minutes later, I could tell that Gwendolyn was still frightened as we approached the castle. We stopped in front of the great oak door. I looked down at her and gave her a smile of reassurance.

"Would you like to ring the bell or use the knocker?" I said.

She stretched up on her toes and turned the bell-knob. Then we waited.

When Miss Forbes opened the door, her eyes nearly fell out.

"Hello, Miss Forbes," I said. "Would you please tell the duke that he has a very special guest who would like to see him."

She turned and disappeared inside the castle, leaving the door open with us standing there. As she looked inside, even though there was not much to see in the entryway, Gwendolyn's eyes took in the splendor with wide-eyed astonishment. How could she fathom that everything we could see—the grounds and this enormous and ancient edifice—was her true home.

After several minutes we heard heavy steps approaching. I don't know what Miss Forbes had told him, but when Alasdair appeared he was hurrying toward us from the other end of the corridor. The look of eager anticipation on his face was of such childlike joy that after one look at him no one could possibly be afraid.

It was the expression of a father's boundless love! His look brought tears of joy to my eyes.

He slowed, glancing back and forth at the two of us with wonder and disbelief. He looked for a second or two into my eyes, apparently trying to speak though no words came out. Finally his gaze settled on the red-haired girl beside me. His eyes were misty. He stooped down and smiled.

"Gwendolyn," I said, "this is your father."

"Hello, Gwendolyn," said Alasdair in a soft, husky voice.

"How do you know my name, sir?" said Gwendolyn timidly.

"Because I am your father," replied Alasdair, smiling and blinking hard. "I have known you all your life, though I have not seen you for many years. You do not remember, but you have been here before."

"In this castle?"

"Yes."

"When?"

"You were born here."

"I was?"

"Would you like to see where?"

"I think I would. You won't hurt me, will you?"

"Of course not, Gwendolyn. I love you very much. I have been waiting many years to see you again. You have made me very happy by coming here today."

"Gwendolyn," I said, "you would not mind going with your father, would you? I will wait for you outside."

She looked at him, then back to me.

"I don't think I will mind," she answered. "But I am still a little afraid."

"Just remember what I told you, that you can trust him, because he loves you just like I do."

"I will try to remember."

"I will be in the rose garden," I said.

Gwendolyn turned back to Alasdair.

"What should I call you?" she asked.

"Call me Daddy," he said, standing and holding out his hand.

Gwendolyn glanced up one more time at me, as if to reassure herself. I nodded and smiled. Then she reached out, still a little timidly, and allowed Alasdair's huge palm to clasp her tiny white hand and close gently around it.

Father and daughter walked away into the castle, and I turned and walked into the grounds crying my eyes out.

About forty-five minutes later, as I sat on a bench in the garden, I heard a happy shout followed by running footsteps. I looked up to see Gwendolyn running in her awkward gait toward me, followed by Alasdair walking and trying to keep up with her. I stood and waited. In her eyes was a look of radiance such as I had not seen on her face before. She ran straight into my arms.

"Daddy is nothing like what Mummy said," she said excitedly. "He is as nice as you, Marie. I sat in his lap and he told me stories. He told me one story about you and him. He told me stories about when he was a little boy. He said I could come back anytime. He told me about my real mother. He said Mummy was really my auntie but I could keep calling her Mummy if I liked. I think my real mummy must have been nice. I saw her picture. It is too bad she died. May I call you Mummy now, too?"

The question took me so by surprise that I was speechless.

Luckily I was rescued by Alasdair's arrival a moment later. I was glad he hadn't heard her question.

"Alicia is preparing us tea and some sandwiches, Marie," he said. "Gwendolyn and I came out to ask you to join us."

Gwendolyn took my hand and pulled me up from the bench.

"Come, Daddy," she said, now taking Alasdair's hand as well. We walked back toward the castle, hand in hand with Gwendolyn between us.

"I don't know how to thank you, Marie," said Alasdair as we walked. "I think you know what this means to me. There are no words to adequately express it."

I looked over at him and smiled.

Gwendolyn, meanwhile, continued to chatter away.

Chapter Fifty

Strange Castle Among the Cliffs

O weel may the boatie row,
And better may she speed;
O weel may the boatie row
That wins the bairnie's breid.
The boatie rows, the boatie rows,
The boatie rows fu' weel;
And muckle luck attend the boat,
The murlain, and the creel.

—"The Boatie Rows"

I decided to try to drive instead of walk up to Ranald Bain's croft. The Ordinance Survey maps of Scotland's and England's various regions were so detailed that every trail was shown. I even found a map that had "Bain Croft" on it, with a dotted line winding down to one of the Home Farm roads. So I determined to try it.

Now that Gwendolyn had my harp, I needed to play! Ranald's was the only other harp I knew of for miles.

I had not gone into great detail with Ranald about the situation with Alasdair, Gwendolyn, and Olivia. His looks and expressions, however, and occasional questions and remarks convinced me that he knew more about it all than he let on.

How could he not?

He had lived here all his life. He was closer to Iain than a brother. He had been Iain's confidant and mentor during Iain's youth. He had to know about the stories, about Iain's and Alasdair's friendship, then their estrangement. Likewise, he had to know about Gwendolyn.

When I told him about her reunion with her father, I sensed a deeper response than he allowed himself to show. He was clearly pleased. He nodded knowingly, with the hint of a smile on his aging lips, though it was mostly obscured by his white beard.

Whenever Olivia came up in conversation, his countenance clouded—again, subtly, imperceptibly hidden by his beard. More than once I knew I had not imagined his eyes narrowing slightly. Whether it was talk about Gwendolyn, or the mention of Olivia's name, I sensed that he was thinking about his own daughter, and what she might have been had she lived.

Iain had once let slip that Margaret Bain had despised Olivia Urquhart until her dying day. It was hard to imagine Ranald's wife not being as loving and forgiving as he.

How Ranald and his wife and daughter were connected to the hostility between Olivia and Alasdair, I couldn't begin to conjecture.

Most of Ranald's interest seemed to be about me. That I was involved, that I had been part of taking Gwendolyn, against Olivia's wishes, to the castle, something about that concerned him, and concerned him deeply. Again his eyes narrowed, but he said nothing except cautioning me to be very careful, especially when I went out walking, as the weather was beginning to change and the shoreline could be windy, slippery, and unpredictable. I assured him that I never went near the edge anyway. He nodded, though he did not seem altogether relieved.

He repeated his warnings.

When we played together on the harp and violin after tea, his mood was different—solitary and more melancholy than I had ever seen him. More than once he lapsed into doleful wailing tunes of lament and sorrow that I knew came from deep within his heart.

Over the following days, there were more visits between Gwendolyn and Alasdair. Before long they became a daily routine. Either Nicholls or I now went for Gwendolyn every morning about eleven, according to Alasdair's instructions and schedule, and took her to him at the castle. Sometimes the three of us did things together, sometimes she spent the time alone with Alasdair for most of the day.

Mrs. Urquhart went along with everything with silent compliance, though it was obvious she hated it. She spoke not another word to me, shooting daggers into my eyes every time I appeared at the house.

"I asked Gwendolyn if she would like to take a trip on my yacht," said Alasdair one day when I returned in the afternoon to take her back into the village.

"That sounds wonderful," I said.

"Can Marie come with us, Daddy?" exclaimed Gwendolyn, glancing back and forth between Alasdair and me.

"Perhaps we shall have to ask her," replied Alasdair.

"Will you, Marie, will you come?" pleaded Gwendolyn.

"I don't know." I laughed. "Something tells me that perhaps this is a trip meant for a father and daughter to share together."

"I have never been on a ship!" said Gwendolyn excitedly.

"Will you go, then, Gwendolyn?" I asked.

"I hope so. But I do not think Auntie will want me to."

"You let me take care of Auntie," said Alasdair. Despite his confident expression, he glanced over Gwendolyn's head toward me with an expression that silently said, *Though I'm not sure how!*

Gwendolyn hardly spoke of anything else after that. I knew it was best I not accompany them, as did Alasdair. But we did go out on the yacht one lovely day, just for the afternoon, to Buckie then to Sandend and back, to test Gwendolyn's sea legs, Alasdair said. This time, so he would not have to worry about all the details of the boat as when he and I had gone out together, Alasdair's captain was at the helm.

It was a perfect day. Gwendolyn was positively exuberant with delight about everything, running about the yacht like an excited little red-haired Shirley Temple. When we saw a half dozen dolphins swimming and jumping as we passed off the Scar Nose on our way east, I didn't think she would be able to contain herself.

"That is the first time I have seen the dolphins, Marie!" she exclaimed as we stood at the rail. "Everyone talks about them, but I have never seen them, not so close like that. I thought I saw them once, but Mummy said it was only waves. But I see them now, I really see them! Look, they're jumping and playing! Do you think it's fun to be a dolphin, Marie?"

I couldn't help laughing. It was indeed an exciting sight.

We turned around off Sandend and made again for Port Scarnose. As we glided westward, closer to shore, I thought I saw something along the cliff as we were approaching Logie Head. The yacht was well equipped with binoculars and I had a set hanging around my neck for watching for dolphins. Quickly I placed them up to my eyes and peered through.

"Alasdair," I called. "What's that, there on the shore? It looks like ruins of some kind."

He walked toward me, though he did not need to look through binoculars to answer me.

"Those are the ruins of Findlater Castle," he said.

"But what is it? Why have I never heard of it? It's built right on the rock face, like it's growing out of the stone itself. I want to know about it!"

"There's not much to tell."

"It's spooky-looking. Some of the openings... it almost looks like two eyes, and a slit like a mouth below. It must have a history."

"I suppose."

"Alasdair!" I laughed.

"All right," he said, almost with a sigh.

I couldn't understand his reluctance to tell me about it.

"Findlater was the original castle here, long before Castle Buchan," he began. "There may have been a castle here as early as the thirteenth or fourteenth century. But the certain date of construction by the Sinclairs was in the early 1400s. It remained the home of the Ogilvies, my own ancestors and related by marriage to the Sinclairs, for two hundred years, and was one of the great strongholds in the north of Scotland. Castle Buchan was built in 1600 and the Ogilvies moved inland and Findlater was abandoned. By the eighteenth century it had become a ruin and has disintegrated all the more ever since. There, you see—not much to tell."

"I think it is fascinating," I said, again raising the binoculars and scanning the cliff face. "I want to see it up close."

"Don't even think it, Marie."

"But why?"

"It is far too dangerous," replied Alasdair, then paused briefly. "I do not want you to go there," he added. "The place is treacherous."

I brought the binoculars down and looked at Alasdair, puzzled by his expression. He had never pulled rank on me like that before. I had never heard his voice sound as it did at that moment.

We were moving past the ruins by then. My curiosity was greater than ever. Again I lifted the binoculars, adjusting the lenses and trying to sharpen the focus.

"All right, I agree. I won't go exploring," I said, still squinting through the binoculars. "But can you just answer one more question? It looks like...I can't be sure from this far away, but it looks like there is an opening, there at the top...does that go down into—"

"Marie!" Alasdair interrupted. "Drop it. Please, no more about Findlater!"

He turned and walked away. I stared after him, more confused than hurt. I was glad Gwendolyn hadn't heard the exchange. She was excitedly searching for more dolphins.

I found Alasdair on the other side, staring out over the waters of the firth toward the Orkneys.

"I am sorry," I said, joining him at the starboard rail. "I didn't realize you felt so strongly about it."

He nodded in acknowledgment but said nothing further. The subject of Findlater Castle did not come up again.

Chapter Fifty-one

Inside Castle Buchan

In yon garden fine and gay,
Picking lilies a' the day,
Gath'ring flw'rs o' ilka hue,
I wistna then what love could do.

Where love is planted there it grows,
It buds and blooms like any rose;
It has a sweet and pleasant smell,
No flower on earth can it excel.
—"In Yon Garden"

With Gwendolyn coming to visit her father regularly, the entire spirit at the castle changed. *Life* suddenly blossomed within its walls.

I don't know if it was only because of Gwendolyn, though she was certainly part of it. Everyone was more cheery and friendly. Stoic Harvey Nicholls, whom I had known only as the uniformed chauffeur with all the personality of a stuffed mannequin, now smiled and tipped his hat at me whenever he saw me, and even came out with an occasional, "Fine day," or "Morning to you, Ms. Buchan." He was tall and lanky, pure blond and fair, and actually very dashing and handsome, with a smile to die for. It's just that he hardly ever *did* smile! I began to take it as a personal challenge whenever I saw him to get a word or two out of him, followed by that smile. Gradually, after Gwendolyn began visiting, it became easier. My heart was touched one day to see the two of them, Nicholls and Gwendolyn, alone beside the door of the open garage, I assumed waiting for Alasdair, Gwendolyn babbling away with childlike abandon, while Nicholls kept his half of the exchange going with free-flowing questions and replies and laughter like I didn't imagine him capable of. An observer would have taken him for her father, or perhaps uncle. I had no idea what his personal situation was, but I couldn't imagine why such an eligible catch in a small village like Port Scarnose hadn't been scooped up long ago.

The gardener-gamekeeper Farquharson was a tougher nut to crack. I saw not so much of him. He didn't live at the castle as did Alicia Forbes and Harvey Nicholls, as well as the cook and her husband. His work for the duke, I assumed, was part-time and my opportunities to draw him out of his shell were more limited. Whenever I saw him in the rose garden or trimming one of the hedges, I took a few minutes and tried to engage him in conversation. But he wore the gruff exterior of the prototypical curmudgeon. I was able to elicit nothing but the occasional grunt or mumbled reply that I could no more understand than had he been talking in ancient Gaelic or Norse.

Alicia Forbes slowly began to warm to me as well.

I called one day when Alasdair and I had made arrangements to have lunch together. I was met at the door by a girl—a young woman, actually, probably nineteen or twenty—whom I had never seen before.

"Oh...hello," I said in surprise. "I am Marie Buchan. I am here to see the duke."

"He isna here jist the noo, mum," the girl replied.

"I see, hmm—"

As I was debating whether I should ask to see the housekeeper, she came around the corner as if appearing out of my thoughts.

"Marie!" said Alicia in a friendler tone than I was used to. "The duke telephoned a few minutes ago from Fochabers. He was held up at his meeting and will be another thirty or thirty-five minutes. He asked me to entertain you while you're waiting.—Sarah, meet Marie Buchan," she said to the girl who was still standing at the door. "Marie, this is Sarah Duff. She has just started for us here this morning."

"Hello, Sarah," I said, extending my hand.

"Pleased tae meet ye, mum," said Sarah with a pleasant smile and curtsy.

"Sarah works part-time up at the Leith Care Home," said Alicia "She is going to help us here two days a week."

"Well, Sarah," I said, "I am sure you will enjoy it...if you don't get lost!" I added with a laugh.

"Actually," said Alicia, "that brings up exactly what the duke said. He said that he has never given you the grand tour, and suggested I might show you around the castle more than he showed you before."

"I would love it!" I said.

"Good.—Sarah, you may return to Jean in the kitchen," she said to Sarah, who then turned and disappeared.

When she was gone, Alicia led the way to the main wide circular staircase. "Shall we go, then," she said as I followed. "You obviously know your way up to the Music Room, so we might as well start there so that you will have your bearings."

As we walked up the staircase side by side, her uncharacteristically friendly demeanor on this day caused me to take in Alicia Forbes's appearance in a different way than before. She had struck me as distant and melancholy, like someone carrying a secret sorrow. She was always pleasant, but in a manner similar to that in which she dressed, in a white housekeepery uniform, and the aspect with which she bore herself had seemed antiseptic and sterile, without emotion.

Her smile on this day surprised me. It gave her countenance a new warmth. She was a very short woman, no more than about five foot one or two, but well-proportioned, neither too thin, which would have given her a pixie look, or too plump, which would have tended toward the "short and fat" stereotype. She looked strong, healthy, and fit. Her features were a little darker than what you normally saw in Scotland, perhaps with a hint of the Polynesian, her nose small, her cheekbones prominent, and the lines in her forehead expressive though reluctant to reveal the thought behind them. What gene of her ancestry would account for the skin coloration I hadn't an idea, but it contributed to the air of mystery about her. Though redheads in Scotland were a dime a dozen, and though her flesh tones might have led to the expectation of black hair, Alicia's hair was a rich auburn, which was doubly unusual. It looked natural, but sometimes with perfect auburns it is hard to tell. I saw no telltale roots of differing shade, however, as I surely would have since she kept her forehead bare and her hair pulled straight back either into a bun or held in place by twin barrettes above both ears.

"The Music Room of course you know," said Alicia as we reached the first floor and turned left along the wide, familiar corridor. "The duke has only been calling it the Music Room since that first day you played your harp for him."

"What was it called before that?" I asked.

"I don't know if it had an official name, it was just one of many drawing rooms and sitting rooms. Actually, I think we called it the Occasional Room—a nondescript name if ever there was one. Music Room is a great improvement, and we have you to thank. The library is just across the hall—I think it is my favorite room in the whole castle, though Olivia used to tell spooky stories there when we were young. You have been in the library, haven't you?" she asked as we passed its great double-oak doors.

"Yes," I answered.

"No need to detour there now, then." We continued along the corridor. "Even though the Music Room is in the northeast corner of the castle," she said as we went, "all this area is considered the north wing."

"Are all the wings separate?" I asked as we turned right and made our way into what she said began the east wing. "I mean, were they built separately, or are they meant to serve different functions? I don't really know very much about castles—we don't have castles in Canada."

"Every castle in Scotland is unique. Some were built as fortresses, others as homes, others as mere showpieces."

"Which was this?"

"Mostly as a home. But it is old enough that a little of the fortress look remains. Findlater was the original castle here, and it was definitely a fortress. When the Sinclairs and Ogilvies moved inland, that wasn't needed so much. Here at Castle Buchan, the wings all flow together. Different functions were defined more by the different floors rather than the wings—the ground floor for casual entertaining, the Great Room, and the rooms where much of the daily work of the castle took place—the kitchen and garages and maintenance rooms and workshops, those sorts of things. The first floor contained the more extensive entertaining rooms, drawing rooms, the Grand Ballroom, and of course the library and the Music Room. The second floor contained most of the living quarters, as did the third floor, along with storage rooms and the old servants' quarters."

"Did they really occupy and use the entire castle?"

"Two hundred years ago, for a family of six or eight, there might have been thirty or more full-time servants, with the whole castle bustling with activity from morning till night."

"Times have certainly changed."

"All along here it's mostly guest rooms and bedrooms and storage rooms," said Alicia as we went, "one not much different from another. I don't know why they built these castles with *so* many bedrooms."

"How many bedrooms are there in all?" I asked.

"Actually, I don't even know. I've never counted them. But I would guess at least thirty or forty."

"You seem intimately familiar with every nook and cranny," I said. "Though I suppose being the duke's housekeeper you have to be. How long have you worked for Mr. Reidhaven?"

"I've been here, let me see, about twenty-five years, I think. I worked for the old duke before Mr. Reidhaven came into the title."

"No wonder you know the place so well."

"It's not only that. I was also here as a girl. Olivia and I, and Alasdair, of course—the duke—were friends."

"You grew up here? I suppose I assumed otherwise from your speech."

She smiled. "I was not born here, so in that sense I cannot be said to *belong* to Port Scarnose. We moved here when I was eight. That's when I met Olivia . . . and some of the other village girls," she added in what struck me as an odd tone. "Adela Cruickshank, whom you know—she was among them, and Cora who works at the co-op."

We continued to the end of the wing, circling through the south wing, which she said wasn't used for much of anything anymore on any of the upper floors, only the workrooms of the ground floor. From there we took a back circular stairway up to the second floor. Passing all the way again through the south and east wings, past maids' and servants' rooms, the cook's apartment, then through the north wing, past the main staircase again, and up another flight of stairs to the third floor.

"That's the duke's apartment just there," said Alicia as we turned onto the staircase.

I found the third floor the most interesting of all with some of its more private rooms—especially the armory full of swords and shields and guns and coats of mail, even two full sets of body armor. From the walls draped ancient faded tartans.

"Many of these swords were actually used at the Battle of Culloden," said Alicia as we glanced about. "It makes them historic, I suppose, but the thought that some of them may actually have been used to kill people . . . I don't particularly like this room. But the duke loves it here. I suppose it's a man thing."

We continued through the Game Room and several private

sitting rooms that were wonderfully intimate and cozy. There were so many interesting places, but not enough people to enjoy them. The third floor comprised mostly bedrooms, all vacant now.

"There is one large apartment on this floor," said Alicia, "the dowager countess's apartment."

"Who is she?" I asked.

"Who *was* she," corrected Alicia with a smile. "She lived at Castle Buchan about a hundred years ago after her husband died and her son inherited. Some people think she is the green lady who haunts the place, but I don't believe a word of it."

We continued on, then backtracked, still on the third floor, all the way back around to the west wing, finally descending several flights of stairs into the kitchen, where Jean and Sarah were busy—probably with preparing lunch for Alasdair and me. Alasdair returned just as we had completed the circuit. I hadn't exactly seen every room of the castle, but we had walked through most of its corridors and all of its wings, though we hadn't ventured into the garret regions. I now had a much better sense of where everything was.

As glad as I was to see Alasdair, I was sorry for my visit with Alicia to end. For the first time I felt that there had been a true connection between us. I hoped it wouldn't be the last time.

Chapter Fifty-two

A Boy's Terror

Ghaist nor bogle shalt thou fear;
Thou'rt to love and heaven sae dear,
Nocht o' ill may come thee near,
My bonnie dearie.

—"Ca' The Yowes to the Knowes"

As Alasdair and I were eating lunch outside half an hour later, as it often did our conversation turned to Gwendolyn, and then to Olivia Urquhart.

"What is with those strange rhymes of Olivia's?" I asked. "You've mentioned them before, and she's done that once or twice when talking to me. At first I hardly noticed, then I realized she'd said something just as you described. What's it all about?"

"It was Olivia's way when she was young of frightening people—especially me!" Alasdair added with a little laugh.

"Were people actually *frightened* of the rhymes?"

"Yes, I think they were," he replied. "Especially the younger children. There were rumors that if Olivia took a dislike to anyone she would put a curse on them."

"Was there anything to it?" I asked. I suddenly felt cold and strange.

"I don't know, maybe," answered Alasdair. "Children are fascinated with weird occultish things like that. I don't know that there's much difference between Olivia's conjurations and Reddy and me trying to frighten each other with pirate and ghost stories. That's part of growing up, trying to scare your friends. Yet somehow there was more to it with Olivia. It was darker and more sinister. She could frighten me out of my wits even though I was older than she. At least she could until I was old enough to laugh it off. Once she could no longer control me with her hocus-pocus, it didn't bother me. That's when she began to hate me. What she couldn't control, she hated. And what she hated, she tried to destroy. She was a cruel little girl."

"What kind of hocus-pocus?" I asked.

"She was always making up limericks and ditties to frighten the rest of us and pretend she had special powers. That's how the rhyming thing began. How did that one go...she used to say it to me whenever she got angry...let me think, something about her dancing on my grave."

"Alasdair, that's awful!"

"That's how Olivia kept everyone in line," he said. "She was always saying nonsensical things and speaking in rhymes. Sometimes when she and her friends were walking about, she would chant a hex as she went by someone's house she didn't like. All the children were terrified that she would mutter a rhyming incantation or perform some chicanery or another, and they would turn into a toad or fall over dead or get sick. That's what I mean by hocus-pocus. Let me see, now I remember—*Brother of mine, you'd better behave...or the younger will dance on the elder's grave.*'"

I shuddered at the words. "What did you do when she said it?" I asked.

"I tried to laugh. But to some degree she had me under her spell just as she did her friends. Whenever she wanted to bend me to her will, all she had to do was wag her index finger at me in warning and say, 'Remember, brother, behave...don't forget the grave.' Then she would turn away with a wicked smile on her face and in a singsong voice chant the whole ditty again. There were dozens of them. She could make up a ditty on the spot to fit any occasion, every one laced with a threat. Such conjurations were her way of controlling everyone around her. No one could help being silently terrified that the next words out of her mouth would be about them. She *had* to be in control. By pretending she had magical powers she achieved her goal."

"*Was* it only pretend?" I asked.

Alasdair was thoughtful.

"Not entirely," he said slowly. "She truly could bend people to her will. There was no pretend in that. Yet some of her threatening incantations were so inane I can't believe anyone took them seriously. They sound completely silly and childish now."

"Like what?"

"Like, '*Look on the path—a slithering snake . . . tonight Alasdair will tremble and quake.*'"

He laughed as he said it. But I didn't think it was funny.

"Or," Alasdair went on, "'*Cross me not, brother, or aye . . . the next may be the day you die.*'

"And then there were the perennial favorites, '*Spiders, lizards, and black slimy leeches . . . are Alasdair's friends and crawl up his breeches.*'"

"That's terrible!"

"She loved to plant seeds of creepy, scary thoughts. I can still hear her chanting the words—'*Witches, wolves, and a gathering of devils . . . will come to your room and make nightly revels.*'

"She was fascinated with witches—'*Trolls, goblins, kelpies, and witches . . . will gnaw your insides like unscratchable itches.*'"

"Ugh!" I said, shuddering again.

"They did, too . . . they gnawed at you," Alasdair said, laughing. "And to top it off and make sure I lay awake thinking about such horrors, '*Do you think you can keep me out of your dreams . . . I will haunt your sleep, and delight in your screams.*'

"If I clasped my hands to my ears or yelled at her to stop, or worse, if I tried to run away, she had a rhyme to meet that need, too, ensuring that even my trying to escape would only worsen my plight in the end, '*There is no use in trying to hide . . . my words will come back like an incoming tide.*'

"Whatever you tried to do, her words would flow back into your brain and you would repeat them over and over to yourself. You couldn't help it. You were powerless to stop them. Olivia's voice possessed your thoughts. It might have been different had they been nice things—pleasant sayings, proverbs of truth, the golden rule...whatever. But they weren't. They were dark, frightening, and always placed Olivia in control of your thoughts. The way she manipulated those around her was devious, cunning. I don't know what else to call it but evil."

"How do you remember all those horrid ditties?" I asked.

"I don't remember them all. There were hundreds. Such things poured out of her all the time. Once they lodged in your mind, many of them never went away. They still reverberate in my subconscious all these many years later. I *tried* to forget but couldn't."

"What horrible things to say to a child."

"The young are not known for their sensitivity to the feelings and fears of others. Especially those like Olivia. They were childish little sayings," Alasdair went on, "obviously not such as to appear in a collection with Shakespeare. But that she made them up on the spot to suit the occasion always struck me as remarkable."

"What did you do?" I asked.

"What was there to do?" Alasdair laughed. "Try not to anger her. If she said I was going to lie awake at night because a snake had crossed in front of me, I usually did. Or I would lie there trembling, afraid that witches, devils, and wolves were somewhere gathered in the blackness, or imagine spiders in my bed crawling up my legs. I couldn't keep the words away. It was tormenting. They fulfilled themselves simply by lodging in my memory."

"I can't imagine the terror of it."

"It wasn't just the images she put in my head to haunt me either. She haunted me herself, in person."

"What do you mean?"

"She occasionally snuck about the castle at night, and came into my room and moved things around, just to frighten me. More than once I woke up to see her standing over me. There were times I made absolutely certain that my door was locked, yet she still found a way in. Olivia could come and go like a wraith. I actually think she knew the castle even better than our father. She would stand over me in the dark and mutter incantations or throw bits of straw all over my bed while mumbling some old Highland curse."

I shook my head in disbelief. I couldn't think how awful it must have been to grow up with Olivia.

"I wasn't the only one Olivia terrorized with her rhymes," Alasdair went on. "The villagers avoided her. And she did mimic Shakespeare in her own way, too. She loved to recite the scene of the three witches. Maybe that's where the obsession came from. Had she lived in an earlier era, I've often wondered if Olivia would have been branded herself. I cannot but believe that she did in fact possess occultish power."

"Surely no one thought there was anything to it."

"The Scots are a superstitious people. Hexes and curses and the second sight—they are deeply embedded into the national consciousness. Yes, people take that sort of thing *very* seriously."

"Even now?"

Alasdair nodded. "It may not be talked about like a hundred years ago," he said, "but it still lurks beneath the surface."

"But... *was* there anything to it?"

Alasdair sighed and thought a moment. "The power of a curse or a threat can be as much in the eye of the beholder as in the curse itself. To one who believes it true, perhaps it *becomes* true. A curse is self-fulfilling if someone believes it. Look at me—I spent many a terrified night imagining wolves and spiders and demons."

"But none of those things were *really* there. You said it yourself—you imagined them."

"If I thought they were there, isn't that just as bad?"

"No—imagining a spider isn't as bad as a *real* spider."

"What about a demon? Even if you imagine it, the fact that her words made me believe it, meant she was successful in implanting a *real* demon of fear. I was afraid. That demon controlled me. So what began as mere words became very, very real...you might even say factual."

"I see your point. But that is pretty weird."

"Even if half of it was imaginary, Olivia spread great evil around this community because people came to believe that she possessed the second sight and was in league with dark forces. Her words could haunt me for days, even weeks. I remember once we had a terrible row. She had taken something from my room, I can't even remember what. When I found that she had it, I was furious and went after her. We tussled and fought. I wound up with a bloody nose for my trouble. She was uncannily strong for a girl and would strike at me with her legs and feet with abandon. Once she nearly broke one of my ribs with a kick from her foot. After that particular fight, in tears I stormed away full of threats to tell our father. But her voice at my back stopped me in my tracks before I was out of her room. *'If you dare speak a word of this fight...demons will haunt your bed tonight.'*"

I shuddered to hear Alasdair repeat the words.

"What happened?" I asked.

"It was exactly as she said. I lay awake most of the night, trembling in terror. Snakes, wolves, kelpies, vampires...she turned everything into something scary. Fear was her weapon."

"Did you tell your parents?"

"Not a word. I was afraid to."

"But where did it all come from?" I asked after a moment. "Why was she like that? How did she think of such things?"

"I don't know," sighed Alasdair. "She was always...I don't know, *different* in a way. I suppose all children are cruel and selfish. But Olivia was *mean*. She—"

Alasdair paused. A faraway expression came into his eyes.

"There was something," he said after a moment, "an incident I haven't thought of in years. Our parents took us to visit our old Highland grandmother—she was my father's mother and she lived on the far end of Skye. I know little of her history. So many stories circulated back in those days, as a child you had no idea what to believe. I hardly knew my grandfather—on my father's side, my father's father, the old duke. Most of the dark legends that swirled about in our family had something to do with him. He was a great traveler and seafarer and they say he mixed with strange and unsavory people from all over the world."

Suddenly I remembered the stories I had heard from Mrs. Gauld about Alasdair's forebears. I wondered how much of it was true and how much mere village gossip.

"The story goes," Alasdair continued, "that he was on Skye for some druid gathering or other, probably the summer solstice. The druids are great for that sort of thing, but I never put any stock in it. When he returned to Castle Buchan, my father's father, he had a new wife with him, a woman from Skye, a Celt with the second sight and other powers too, some said. The villagers were afraid of her and stories immediately spread that my grandfather had married a druid's daughter, which made her a witch in their eyes. In time my father was born, but not long after the Celtic woman disappeared from the castle—at least that's how the story goes. Some say she died, others that she was poisoned, others that she was pining for her beloved Skye and just went home to the island. Villagers are great for tales, but when I was growing up my father never talked about it. Whether his mother deserted him, I have no way of knowing. For all I know she lived here until he was old enough to be sent off to school. Maybe she and my grandfather divorced—I really do not know. But the story that came to be circulated was that she died or left and that eventually my father's father went mad from some curse she had put on him for taking her from Skye, and that she had been haunting the castle ever since, roaming about the tower on the south side dressed in green, moaning and uttering strange chants and devilish incantations and rhymed curses.

"In any event, I always assumed her to be dead until one day we were informed that we were taking a trip to Skye to see my father's aging mother, whom he had not seen, he said, in a long time. Why my father wanted Olivia and me to visit her, I never knew. If a quarter of the tales were true, I would think he wouldn't have us anywhere near her. But she was his mother, after all, and his father was by then dead. Maybe he wanted us to know of our Highland roots, though they were roots I would have preferred not be stirred up. Maybe the visit had nothing to do with us. Perhaps he was discharging some debt of his own to a mother he hadn't seen in years. I honestly have no idea.

"One thing for certain—she *wasn't* dead. I saw her with my own eyes on Skye...though now that I think about it, yes—actually, she *was* dressed in green. That *is* curious. And she was a strange one, too...spoke only in rhymes, nothing but strange sayings. There were little statuettes and odd things, carvings and peculiar designs on stones, all about both outside the house and in her room. Snakes, I remember—images of snakes everywhere. I have been terrified of snakes ever since. It was altogether a spooky place."

I was getting chills and goose bumps as I listened!

"I was frightened the instant I laid eyes on her," Alasdair went on. "I somehow knew that she was my grandmother, but that made no difference to the terror of the sight. She had things hung around her neck and bracelets around her thin wrists and was dressed more like a Gypsy from Eastern Europe than anything I ever associated with the Highlands of Scotland. I had a vague image in my mind of what a witch was like and she could hardly have fit it more perfectly. Ever after she became that image and haunted my nightmares for years. It is a terrible thing for one's own flesh and blood to make your skin crawl, but she did mine, God forgive me.

"She was ancient beyond years, wrinkled with white hair shooting out from her head. We were five or six at the time. She took to Olivia immediately. She didn't seem to have any use for men or boys. Olivia was the only one she wanted to talk to. She ignored my father, only occasionally casting on him a contemptuous look even though he was a duke and her own son and had come all that way to see her. She completely ignored me. To her I didn't exist, though I was older than Olivia by a year.

"My father sat us in front of her and told her our names. She muttered something about me being an ugly one, then glanced up at my father with a look, as I said, that was not one of respect and that said clearly enough that I had inherited my looks from him. Our father left the room. I stood in front of her trembling in my boots.

"Slowly a smile came over her face. It was a hideous smile, and her old wrinkled lips were mumbling about the beautiful little girl. I was happy enough to keep as far away as I could. I didn't want to get close enough that she might try to touch me. But I needn't have worried—her only thoughts were for my sister. She took Olivia in her arms and asked if she would like to sit in her lap. Olivia didn't seem repulsed by her peculiar ways. Actually, Olivia seemed drawn to her just as Granny was to her. She climbed into her lap and Granny began speaking strange things to her, all the time with that hideous smile on her face. She gave her something, some object, I don't remember, a little carving or one of the statuettes that was nearby, and put it in Olivia's hand and continued her mumbling, almost as if she was praying or chanting some old ritual or some such thing. I could make nothing of it. I think it may have been in Gaelic.

"When we finally left and returned home, my chief emotion was enormous relief to be away from her. But now that I think about it, Olivia was quiet for days after that, and I occasionally heard her mumbling things—they *may* have been little rhyming ditties. It may indeed have begun with the old witch-woman from Skye."

Chapter Fifty-three

Formal Differences

Ye banks and braes o' bonnie Doon, how can ye bloom
sae fresh and fair?
How can ye chant ye little birds, and I sae weary, fu' o' care?
Ye'll break my heart ye warbling birds, that wonton through
the flow'ry thorn,
Ye mind me o' departed joys, departed never to return.

Oft hae I rov'd by bonnie Doon, to see the rose and woodbine twine,
And ilka bird sang o' its love, and fondly sae did I o' mine.
Wi' lightsome heart I pu'd a rose, fu' sweet upon its thorny tree;
And my fause lover stole my rose, but ah, he left the thorn wi' me.
—"Ye Banks and Braes"

Alasdair's plans for a yacht voyage of more than a mere afternoon spread throughout Port Scarnose the way news about the duke probably always did.

How it got out was a mystery. Gwendolyn was still living with Olivia Urquhart and she was certainly not talking.

Olivia, in fact, from all I could tell, was furious and would have stopped the planned excursion if she could. Whatever Iain had said continued to exercise its powerful influence over her. But the expression on her face told me that she hadn't given in. She was merely biding her time.

Once when I came for Gwendolyn a man dressed in an expensive business suit and carrying a briefcase was leaving the Urquhart home.

"What is a solicitor?" asked Gwendolyn as soon as we were alone.

"Why do you ask?" I said.

"That's what that man said he was."

"What did he want?"

"He asked me a lot of questions about Daddy. He said I did not have to go with you if I didn't want to, but I said I did."

In private I reported what she said to Alasdair. He was obviously concerned.

"I had better accelerate our plans for the trip," he said, "before Olivia gets an injunction to prevent Gwendolyn accompanying me."

"Could she do that?" I asked.

"I don't know. But if there is any way she can legally complicate my life, she will not hesitate to do so."

"But why?" I said. "I still do not understand it. Gwendolyn is obviously happy and wants to be with you."

"Some people cannot let go of the past. Hatred is a powerful emotion. Strange to say, people enjoy hanging on to it. What can I say—she hates me. The thought of my being happy or being with Gwendolyn is hateful to her. She does not even mind making Gwendolyn suffer to feed her own hatred."

I shook my head. "When I think of all the years Gwendolyn hasn't been able to know you, when you were right here, so close, it makes me angry. *Why* would she keep a daughter from her father?"

"She would say because of me."

"That is ridiculous. I know you, and you are a good father to Gwendolyn."

"I am trying to be. But in all fairness, perhaps I would not have been ready before now."

"Still, I can hardly stand the thought of the wasted years."

"All we have is what is ahead of us. We must make the best of it. In that light, I think we shall leave next week. Will you help get Gwendolyn packed and ready?"

"Certainly."

Two days before their departure, an invitation arrived for me at my cottage.

The honour of your presence is requested at a special dinner for two at Castle Buchan. Sunday evening, the seventh of September, eight o'clock. Car and driver will collect you at seven forty-five.

Accordingly, the evening before the scheduled father-daughter voyage, I found myself again seated in Alasdair's black BMW behind a silent Nicholls on my way to the castle.

Alicia showed me to the drawing room, where I was left alone. In classic old-world style, at one minute before eight a gong sounded somewhere. At the same instant a door opened and Alasdair appeared. He was dressed in a kilt in formal old-style evening attire, all the way down to a tiny fresh yellow rosebud in the lapel of his jacket.

He looked so stately and magnificent!

Not a hint remained of the hesitation, timidity, or awkwardness that had been so apparent when I first met him. His confidence had returned. His bearing was so regal, for a moment the sight took my breath away.

He walked toward me, tall, poised, self-assured, smiling but saying nothing, then bowed slightly. I returned his nod with a modest curtsy. He offered his arm. I took it, and he led me away.

As we entered the Formal Dining Room, I was astonished at the sight. Three servants, a man and two women whom I had never seen before, stood like statues around a lavishly appointed table. Candles flickered from the middle of the table.

Alasdair led me forward, released my arm, pulled out a chair for me and helped me to the table, then took his place opposite me.

The moment I beheld the formality and elegance of the setting, the thought flitted through my mind that perhaps Alasdair intended something for this evening beyond a mere farewell dinner before his trip with Gwendolyn. Pangs of undefined emotion raced through me, with the looming question of how I would answer him. But as the evening progressed, I detected no hints in that direction and was able to relax and enjoy myself.

Wine was poured, and soon the servants had disappeared and we were enjoying our dinner and talking and laughing freely.

"Do you think Olivia will cause any trouble tomorrow?" I asked.

"I will not rest until we have loosed our moorings and are floating away from the shore," replied Alasdair. "If she can stop Gwendolyn from seeing me again, as I told you before, she will. Apparently she has not been successful yet. She has said nothing to you?"

"Not a word. She stares daggers at me, as if I betrayed her."

"In her mind, you have. She is not thinking of what is best for Gwendolyn, only the injury to her own pride. The worst of it may be yet to come—from *her* perspective."

"What do you mean?" I asked.

"If the trip goes well, and if she wishes it, I intend to bring Gwendolyn here to the castle to live."

"That would be wonderful!" I exclaimed. "I am sure she will want to."

"We shall see."

"But what about your sister...Olivia—isn't she Gwendolyn's legal guardian?"

"If she wants to take me to court over the matter, she will be free to do so. But at this point in her life, with Gwendolyn's health precarious as it is, I think the court will weigh her wishes in the matter more heavily than Olivia's. Unless I misjudge the situation, Gwendolyn will want to come."

"I'm sure you are right. She dearly loves you, Alasdair. I am so happy for you both. Will you keep her from seeing her aunt?"

"Not at all. Whatever her twisted motives, Olivia has been devoted to Gwendolyn. She probably did save her life after her birth. Gwendolyn loves her, too. I have no wish to separate them. She would be free to see Olivia any time she wished, or to return to live with her if that is her choice. But Gwendolyn is actually very sick—more than people realize. For whatever time she has left, I want her to be happy, and to give her as much of myself as I can. I have a great deal to make up for as her father."

He paused. A poignant, melancholy look came over his face.

"The dreadfully ironic thing about it," he said sadly after a moment, "is that Gwendolyn inherited her condition from me, you know. My health is in jeopardy, too. The early teen years are the most critical. I managed to survive them. But I was more hardy than she. The doctors I have spoken with are not sanguine in their prognosis."

By now the meal was over, capped off with a light strawberry trifle. We had just been served coffee and were again alone.

"I don't think I ever told you," I said, "that Gwendolyn spoke to me once about death...her death."

Alasdair nodded thoughtfully. "She is not the fool many in the village take her for, that much is clear. I think she is aware she is different from other children. But to what extent she is aware of her own mortality, I have no idea. You may be right—she may be more aware where it is leading than we know."

We were both silent awhile.

"I so want you to hear her play on my harp," I said at length. "It is the most amazing thing. You will weep when you hear her. And as long as she is where she is, I want to keep it there for her."

"I am content to wait until we return. Then perhaps I will be able to hear you both play to my heart's content on the instrument that brought my soul awake."

I looked across the table, probing Alasdair's face and eyes for a moment.

"You really mean that, don't you?" I said. "It is hard to believe since in my own way I was spiritually lost when I came here. But my harp music really did help wake something in you?"

"Do you even need to ask? I am a completely new man!"

I smiled. "I have changed in many ways, too. It is a wonderful thing to wake up, to come alive...to the world, to God, to nature, to the people around you...and to know *yourself* better than you ever have."

"I owe so much to you, Marie," said Alasdair. "There are no words to tell you all that is in my heart, my gratitude that you gave me a chance just to be a real and normal person with you. I, too, am rethinking my relationship to God. I'm not sure where it is leading, but I am open to anything, and I want to grow. Especially I am more thankful than I can tell you for what you did in bringing Gwendolyn back into my life, that you had the courage to go to Olivia the way you did. It means the world to me. More than that, you and Gwendolyn—you both mean the world to me."

"I really didn't do much," I said. "It was Iain who was responsible. Had it not been for him, she would never have allowed me to bring Gwendolyn to you."

The mention of Iain's name jarred Alasdair visibly. He winced slightly.

"What does he have to do with it?" he asked.

"He is the one who spoke to your sister. I have no idea what he said, but whatever it was, it made her furious. An hour later, Gwendolyn and I were at your door. It is he you ought to be thanking, not me."

"*Me* . . . thank Iain Barclay!" Alasdair rejoined angrily. "What kind of a fool do you take me—"

Suddenly he stopped himself. He gazed a moment at me. I was shocked at his sudden outburst. He realized he had gone too far. He glanced away. A pall descended over us.

"Look, Marie," he said after a minute, "I know it is probably hard for you to understand, but sometimes things come between men that women cannot understand. You think you know Iain. You think you know me. Perhaps you do. But there are things you don't know, too, long-standing things. All I am saying is that you shouldn't interfere."

"I do not mean to interfere," I said. "But if you and Gwendolyn could be reconciled, why cannot the same take place between you and Iain? I don't see the difference."

"*Reconciled* . . . to Iain Barclay?" he said, his voice again growing heated. "It could never happen. It will never happen. I will never speak to that man as long as I live."

"But why, Alasdair? *Why?* What from the past could possibly be worth hanging on to such bitterness and unforgiveness?"

"Are you calling me bitter and unforgiving?"

"I did not say that. But if you refuse to see him, *isn't* that being unforgiving?"

"So what if it is, then? Yes, I have no intention of forgiving him. There, have it your way!"

"Alasdair, what are you saying? That isn't *my* way. It is because I believe in healing that I brought Gwendolyn to you. She opened her little heart to you, and love rushed in. Why cannot you open your heart in the same way to an old friend?"

"It is entirely different."

"I don't see that it is. I think it is just the same. Except that Gwendolyn was willing, and you are not. I think you are being stubborn about it. Can you see that—"

"What gives you the right to preach to me? You've been listening to too many of Iain Barclay's ridiculous sermons! You have no right."

"Love has its rights, my lord," I said, hardly realizing what I had said until the words were out of my mouth.

I'd been reading too many books where people used the old terms of address to the aristocracy!

But now that I'd blurted it out, I couldn't unsay it. I started to cry. I think Alasdair was as shocked to hear what had come out of my mouth as I was.

I stood and ran toward the door.

"Marie . . . please, wait!" Alasdair called behind me.

I stopped. My eyes were stinging. I was trembling from head to foot. I could not turn around. I heard him push back his chair and stand. His footsteps approached behind me.

"Marie," he said softly. I felt a hand on the back of my shoulder. Slowly I turned to face him.

"I shouldn't have said that," he said. "Chalk it up to the dying remnants of the old me. I may be changing, but I'm not there yet. I could never be really angry with you. Please forgive me."

I nodded and tried to smile. "Thank you," I said softly. "I know you weren't angry with me. But that doesn't change anything. You still have to be reconciled with Iain. I won't be able to stand it for two people I care about to be at odds with one another. Thank you for dinner. It was a lovely evening. Good night."

I turned and left the room and walked downstairs and outside.

Then I realized that I hadn't driven here and had no car. I'd made a scene, left the castle, and now suddenly I was standing alone outside without a way to get home!

I would walk, I said to myself, even though it was after ten and dark. There was enough of a moon.

I started off into the darkness.

I hadn't gone more than a quarter mile, however, before I heard a car engine behind me. Nicholls pulled alongside, got out and opened the door for me, and then we drove back into the village in silence.

Chapter Fifty-four

Away with the Tide

And it's oh! but I'm longing for my ain folk.
Tho' they be but lowly, puir, and plain folk.
I am far beyond the sea, but my heart will ever be
At home in dear auld Scotland, wi' my ain folk.

—"My Ain Folk"

The *Fiona* was to sail from Port Scarnose harbor a day later.

The duke's reunion with his daughter, setting more than a decade of rumors and speculation to rest, had caused such a stir throughout the community that several hundred were on hand at the harbor and spread out along the promontory to watch the beautiful white yacht sail with the tide.

By then, along with Gwendolyn's pedigree, the death of the yacht's namesake twelve years before, and the estrangement between Iain and Alasdair, I had myself become an equal topic of conversation and question.

As I walked toward the harbor I noticed the solicitor I had seen at Mrs. Urquhart's, briefcase in hand, hurrying through the crowd. I didn't know what he was doing there, but I quickly made my way to the yacht and told Alasdair what I had seen. A cloud passed over his face.

"Then we need to get under way as soon as possible," he said.

A few minutes later, as I stood on the deck saying my good-byes, I knew the whole village was watching.

"I wish you were coming with us, Marie," said Gwendolyn.

"I know, Gwendolyn," I said, stooping down until my face was even with hers. "But I can't."

"Why, Marie?"

"Because this is a special trip just for you and your daddy, so that you can get to know everything about each other."

"You will be here when we get back?"

"That depends on how long you are gone. If not, I will see you again. I promise."

I stood and turned to Alasdair. "I am sorry about last night," I said. "I had no right to say what I did."

"Marie, you had every right," he replied. "I just don't know if I am strong enough to do what you say. To be honest, I don't know if I even *want* to. Maybe my own words about Olivia, about hate dying hard, maybe they are true of me as well. It is something I have not wanted to face."

He glanced away. When he turned back I saw that he was blinking hard.

I reached out and placed my hand on his arm, and stood for a moment. He took my hand and held it a second or two, then smiled and gave me a profound look of silent gratitude.

Finally I bent down and gave Gwendolyn a hug. At last I turned and walked down the gangway to the stones of the quay.

I knew every eye in town was on me, probably half of those present whispering their speculations about Alasdair and me. But I determined not to think about it. This was a day to rejoice in the healing that had come between a father and his daughter.

I stood alone at the edge of the massive stone-and-concrete harbor facing the sea and the yacht, with the eyes of the village on my back thinking whatever they might be thinking. Slowly the *Fiona* inched away, then gradually moved with the outgoing tide into the firth toward open sea.

I stood until I could no longer see Gwendolyn's bright hair and her hand waving to me. After waving back, I continued to stare after them until, forty minutes later, the white yacht had disappeared from sight.

If Olivia Urquhart had been trying to prevent Gwendolyn's going, it was too late now.

I turned and walked back along the quay to the shore, relieved to see that most of the townspeople who had gathered to watch the sailing were gone.

The two people most conspicuously absent from the morning's memorable event were Olivia Urquhart and Iain Barclay.

Mrs. Urquhart had not spoken to me since my visit to her with Iain. I knew I would not soon, if ever, be forgiven for what I had done. But I had done it, and I was glad.

With the *Fiona* on her way toward Peterhead, my own future suddenly loomed in my thoughts.

Gwendolyn and Alasdair would be gone for what might be as long as three or four weeks, sailing south into the Mediterranean and back. Everything was quiet and empty as I walked back to my place.

What was keeping me here now? If indeed I had done what I had been sent here to do, was it now time for me to return home?

Summer was about gone. Signs of approaching autumn were in the air. Occasional gusts of colder, harder rains fell. Leaves were fluttering earthward more regularly.

As Iain had said, was it time?

But then what about Iain? And what about Alasdair?

I had been so preoccupied with Alasdair and Gwendolyn that I had seen Iain only once since our visit to Olivia Urquhart. That was from the pew in church the previous Sunday. Now all at once questions about my future and Iain Barclay and Alasdair Reidhaven merged together into a single giant looming uncertainty.

The first thing I wanted to do, even as I walked up the hill from the harbor, was to go see Iain. But suddenly I felt shy about doing so.

Why?

I wasn't sure. Somehow something had changed.

The first thing I did instead after returning from the harbor was walk to the Urquharts.

"Hello, Mrs. Urquhart," I said when she appeared. "I would like to pick up my harp."

She opened the door without a word. I went inside. She disappeared somewhere. I removed the legs from my harp, put it in its case, and left.

I saw nothing more of her.

I hadn't played for a couple of weeks and was having withdrawal symptoms. After getting the harp back to my rented cottage, I played for two hours, went out for a walk, came back and played again.

I felt unaccountably lonely. As the day was winding down, I went out once more, this time to the grocery co-op for some fruit, yogurt, and fresh croissants, and I was about out of milk for my tea. As I approached the co-op from about half a block away, standing outside I saw Cora MacKay in her blue co-op smock talking to someone who looked like the lady from Mrs. Gauld's, Tavia Maccallum. I shouldn't be surprised that they knew each other—they were about the same age, and everybody here knew everyone else.

As Cora seemed to see me out of the corner of her eye, she turned so that her back was to me. The two spoke for another few seconds, then parted. Cora went back inside, while Tavia turned and hurried down the pavement. I tried to speak to her as I approached, but she looked at me strangely, as if we had never met, then turned into the computer shop without a word.

When I had collected my things at the store and walked to the counter, I greeted Cora as I had many times before. But she neither smiled nor returned my greeting, nor once met my eye. She rang up my items, put them in a bag, then looked past me saying, "Next, please," and I drifted toward the door feeling as much a stranger as the first day I had come.

Did this town have even more secrets that I knew nothing about?

I saw no one else the rest of the day.

Chapter Fifty-five

Failing

Oh I've heard the liltin' at our ewe-milkin',
Lasses a-liltin', before the dawn o' day.
But now they are moanin', on ilka green loanin',
The flow'ers o' the forest are a' wede away.
—"The Flowers of the Forest"

The next few days went by slowly and drearily. As the time passed, I felt more and more reluctant to appear at Iain's door. I longed to see him. But I wanted him to come to see me. But he did not come. I did not understand why. It was a question I could not ask him.

I visited every other day or so with Ranald Bain. We played together and began to make some decently good music, if I do say so myself. Mostly we talked about spirituality and the Christian life. Now I saw what Iain had said—that Ranald did not care about theological agreement on issues, but rather about the shared unity of seeking truth. I began to look to Ranald as a spiritual mentor just as he had been to Iain—as a spiritual father.

How peculiar it was that when I had come here I knew no one, yet had been so excited. A mere passing smile from a grocer or baker had been enough to lift my spirits for the entire day. Now, after all that had happened, with all the memories, the new friendships, I was feeling lonely.

It made no sense.

I suppose human emotions often don't.

Slowly, through my doubts, the conclusion began to come to me that the reasons for this trip were nearly completed. Perhaps the reason I was feeling at loose ends was because the end had come.

A little sadly I realized that it was probably time for me to go home. Even Iain's silence contributed to it.

About a week after Alasdair and Gwendolyn's departure—much of which I had spent going through the recordings of Gwendolyn's harp playing and trying to pick up some of the haunting melodies myself—I finally reached a decision. I would make a few calls the next day about flights and see what I could arrange.

Usually making a decision is a good feeling—putting uncertainties to rest. But the decision to leave this place was an incredibly sad one.

I woke early the next morning. I might not leave immediately, but this would be the day of transition, the day of decision. If I booked a return flight, I would not change it again.

Today was the day I would decide what to do. This was it.

However, I didn't get around to it that day.

It was a bright sunny morning, though chilly. After tea and an hour of reading, I bundled up and went out. I suppose in a way I was thinking that the time had come to begin saying good-bye to this special place. I intended to walk out along the headland and sit down on my favorite bench, and maybe have a good cry.

I got about halfway to my intended destination. I had been absorbed in my own thoughts and prayers, not paying much attention to my surroundings. I chanced to look up and out to sea, then glanced back toward the town and the harbor below.

There sat a white yacht in the harbor, glistening in the morning sun!

It was the *Fiona*.

I turned and ran back the way I had come. I ran all the way down the steep road to the harbor and out onto the quay.

Everything was silent and still. There was no sign of life. But the gangway was down, and I ran straight up it onto the deck.

"Alasdair...Alasdair!" I called. "Gwendolyn—are you back?"

I hurried toward the cabins and the galley, calling as I went. No reply came from anywhere. Finally I slowed and walked about, remembering that it was early. Maybe everyone was still asleep.

Suddenly a sound startled me. I spun around. There was the captain, a man named Travis whom Alasdair took with him to command the yacht on long trips. He was walking along the deck toward me. From the look of it, I had probably awakened him in his cabin.

"Captain Travis," I said. "When did you get back? Where is everyone?"

"Mornin' tae ye, ma'am," he said, rubbing his stubbly face. "They's up tae the castle, far as I ken. We come in late in the nicht."

"Why did you return so soon?"

"The wee lass took sick, ma'am. We was off the coast o' Spain. The duke gie orders tae turn aboot an' make for home wi' all the speed I could gie him."

Even as the last of his words were out of his mouth I was running back toward the gangway.

By the time I reached my cottage I was panting and sweating. I hurried inside to get the car keys. Moments later I was on my way to the castle.

Alicia answered the door, looking haggard.

"Alicia...is Gwendolyn—" I began.

She nodded and smiled thinly. "The doctor was here," she said. "They took her to hospital in Banff."

"Is she..."

"I cannot say, Marie."

"And the duke?"

"He is asleep. He only just returned from the hospital after Gwendolyn was settled and sleeping."

"Then don't disturb him," I said. "Tell him I was here. I will drive to the hospital. If I am not at home, tell him that's where I will be."

Chapter Fifty-six

Humility to Look Inside

When I look to yon hills and my laddie's nae there,
When I look to yon high hills it makes my hert sair.
When I look to yon high hills and a tear dims my e'e,
For the lad I loo dearly lies a distance fae me.

—"A Peer Rovin' Lassie"

I dozed off in the waiting room of the Banff hospital. When I woke up, Alasdair was sitting beside me.

"Alasdair!" I exclaimed.

"Hello, Marie," he said wearily.

"How long have you been here?"

"Not long, ten or fifteen minutes," he replied.

"Any word on Gwendolyn?" I asked.

"She's better. The doctor says he would like to keep her until tomorrow."

"What happened?"

"At first I thought she was seasick," replied Alasdair. "The first day or two out she was fine. We had the most wonderful time. She was radiant. I could not stop her talking. She wanted to be with me constantly. I never realized how fatiguing fatherhood can be!" he said, laughing. "Then she began to complain of not feeling well. She vomited twice. The sea was calm, but I thought it must be seasickness. But when she fainted and I could not rouse her for an hour, I ordered us about and we made for home. The doctor thinks she probably became dehydrated. He says also that it could be a sign that her condition is advancing."

"Oh, Alasdair!"

"Not to worry. She is recovering. But we have to be realistic about the future. In one way I am heartbroken that it has taken so long. Yet on the other, I am so enormously thankful even for this week I have had with her. It almost makes me begin to forget the years I was by myself. Those were lonely years, my 'Eleanor Rigby' years," he added, looking at me with a sad smile. "Perhaps they were necessary to ready me for this, to purge out of me things that needed to go. I will probably never understand it all. For reasons maybe I cannot know, this was the right time. Perhaps I would not have been ready sooner. Suddenly you came into my life and the sun came out...then Gwendolyn. You and Gwendolyn have brought so much joy into my heart, there are no words to tell you what I feel."

He reached out and took my hand. I smiled.

"And about what you said, before," he went on. "You know, the night before we sailed. I have been thinking long and hard about it. I behaved very badly to you. I am so very sorry. Can you ever forgive me?"

"Of course, Alasdair," I said.

"Perhaps I shall always—"

Alasdair paused. "Shall we go for a walk outside?" he said. "I don't want to talk in here."

We rose, left the hospital, and were soon walking in a residential part of the city.

"As I was saying," Alasdair resumed, "it may be that I shall always have to struggle with my temper. I hope not, but I was shocked at what I said to you. I spent several sleepless nights at sea terrified that you would be gone when we returned and I would not have the chance to apologize."

"As you can see, I am still here."

"I am so glad. And I *do* apologize, a second time. And I think...well, perhaps I am ready to see Iain again."

"Oh, Alasdair!"

"I did some hard soul-searching aboard the *Fiona*," Alasdair went on slowly. "The very name of my yacht brought into focus all my resentments. I realized that I had never been honest with myself. I allowed my irrational anger toward Iain to fester for years. It has been a cancer inside me. I don't even know why. Why do people hold on to resentments against people they once loved? It makes no sense. But that is exactly what I have done. I treated Iain no better than Olivia treated me. I have been filled with the same silent anger and bitterness. How am I any different from her?"

He grew thoughtful a moment.

"I have not been a religious man," he continued, "but I think I remember something in the Bible about people who are like white-washed tombs, clean on the outside, presenting a respectable image, but full of ugly dead things on the inside. I realized I have been telling you things about Olivia, but how am I any better? In the same way that she has not forgiven me, I have not forgiven Iain.

"And for what? What am I holding against him? Being a man of truth, being a friend?

"His only sin was setting me a higher example of character than I was capable of perceiving. In my heart I knew he would never betray me. I knew he and Fiona would never have done that to me. She told me she had asked him to call, and why. But I was too arrogant to believe it. The anger that was in me was just looking for an excuse, something to latch on to to keep from looking inside myself at its root cause.

"All these years I have nursed an animosity over an imaginary offense. What kind of a fool would do that? Who nurses a grudge over something that did not even happen? Especially toward a friend! What kind of man behaves so irrationally?

"And even *had* there been cause, can a man not forgive in spite of it? Even if Iain *had* done everything I accused him of in my mind, what was to prevent my forgiving him anyway? I saw that his sin, or his perceived sin, really had nothing to do with it. The ball of reconciliation was in *my* court no matter what the circumstances."

I could not believe what I was hearing. Suddenly Alasdair...he was almost sounding like Iain himself!

"Does not the reestablishment of relationship," he went on, "outweigh by far *any* cause of grievance a man can harbor against his friend, his brother? Not even the love of a woman should separate men, if they are *true* men. You were right in everything you told me, Marie. And you were right when you said I was being stubborn. God forgive me for not being man enough to admit it then. But I admit it now, and I admit it to you, my dear Marie. I thank you for having the courage to challenge me to my face. Not many people are willing to challenge another with the truth, knowing that it may cost them rejection or an angry retort. But you did, and you received an angry retort for your trouble, which I regret more than I can tell you. It will not happen again. I think I learned my lesson. Or at least I learned one more in what may be an ongoing life of lessons painfully learned. Thank you for speaking to me as you did."

He stopped and drew in a deep breath.

My eyes were filling. I had no words of reply.

"Would you go with me?" asked Alasdair after a moment.

"You mean—"

"Yes, to Iain's," he answered. "I am ready. I would like to go see him this afternoon, once we know that Gwendolyn will be asleep for several hours."

"If you like," I said hesitantly. "But don't you think you need to talk...just the two of you?"

"Perhaps. Then at least take me to him. It is not that I fear I will back out or that I need moral support. I would just like you with me. Actually, though," he added with a sardonic smile, "probably I *do* need moral support—part of me is terrified to face him after all this time."

"You are not *really* afraid, are you?"

"Of course. Eating crow and apologizing—that is not easy for a man."

"But you are not afraid of Iain's reaction? You do not think he will be angry?"

"No. When I am honest with myself—a new sensation—I know exactly what he will do. But still it is hard for men to be open and honest with one another. And *humble*—that is the hardest thing to be of all. Humility does not come naturally to the male ego, you know. You are such a part of all this, I would like you with me."

"Of course," I said. "Nothing could please me more."

Chapter Fifty-seven

Brotherhood

Then let us pray that come it may,
As come it will for a' that,
That sense and worth, o'er a' the earth,
May bear the gree, an' a' that!
For a' that, an' a' that,
It's coming yet, for a' that,
That man to man, the warld o'er,
Shall brithers be for a' that!

—Robert Burns, "A Man's a Man for All That"

We remained at the hospital until Alasdair saw Gwendolyn again. The doctor assured us that she was in no danger, but thought it best that I not see her, to keep her agitation and emotions from getting keyed up.

I drove back to Port Scarnose. Alasdair said he would come for me as soon as Gwendolyn had drifted back to sleep. After his business with Iain, he planned to return to the hospital and spend the night until they released Gwendolyn the following morning.

Alasdair appeared at my door about three o'clock that afternoon. The lack of sleep and anxiety over Gwendolyn were evident on his face. But he wore a determined expression. It was clear he was a man who knew what he had to do. I went with him. We left the village hardly speaking a word.

I wasn't sure where we would find Iain. Alasdair wanted to try the church first. Iain wasn't there, but Alasdair wanted to stay a few minutes. I left him alone. He walked slowly about the churchyard, then all around the building. I knew he was thinking hard about many things.

What goes through the mind of an Eleanor Rigby when he or she begins to see the church in a new light, and realizes that perhaps it contains life after all, more life than was evident during all the lonely years?

At length Alasdair returned to the car, serious, quiet, thoughtful. He simply nodded.

Then we drove to Iain's house.

Alasdair was obviously nervous. I would have been, too. I could hardly imagine how much more difficult this must be for him. It was probably one of the hardest things a man ever did, just as Alasdair had said—facing another man in humility, and admitting wrong.

Probably I could never really understand what such things were like inside a man's brain. But from where I stood, as a woman, that took more courage than the muscle-and-brawn kind of thing that Hollywood portrayed as courage. Any blowhard could pick a fight. More often than not it was stupidity, not bravery, that did so.

To humbly admit wrong takes a greater kind of courage, a deeper strength of character.

I've always thought that under the right circumstances, any man—and maybe any woman, too—can summon bravery from within to boldly face a crisis, even to give his or her life for something if it comes to that. That's probably a good thing, too, when righteous causes and true heroism are involved.

But I'm not sure whether it takes much character to be brave in that way. Maybe such people are brave, I don't know. But the courage of *humility* and *character* is a different thing altogether.

What Alasdair was doing was one of the finest examples of real courage I had ever witnessed. As we drove, I knew he would probably rather be on a battlefield at that moment than on his way to see a man he had resented, to whom he was preparing to say, *I was wrong, please forgive me.* No John Wayne or Clint Eastwood or Arnold Schwarzenegger could match the courage of Alasdair Reidhaven I was seeing unfold before my eyes.

We arrived at Iain's. I knew he was home. His car was in the drive.

Alasdair closed his eyes momentarily, drew in a deep breath, then got out. He bent down and glanced back inside the car window at me.

"Maybe you're right," he said. "I think this is something I need to do alone."

I nodded.

"I will be fine now," he said. "I won't back out. There is too much at stake. I have to do this. I *want* to do it."

A funny look came to his face, sheepish yet very serious.

"You will pray for me, won't you?" he said. "That I will have the strength to do this."

"Of course." I smiled. "And you will, Alasdair. You already have shown that you have the strength. I am so proud of what you are doing. I will pray that your strength will continue."

He nodded and turned toward the house. I remained where I was in the car, but with the tinted window open only an inch. I didn't want Iain distracted by seeing me.

Alasdair walked up to the porch. What the observant neighbors might be thinking I could only imagine.

He stood a moment at the door, then reached out his hand and rang the bell.

My heart was beating hard. I could not tear my eyes away.

After several of the longest seconds of my life, I saw the door open. There stood Iain. His wild mop of red hair would have been visible from two hundred yards.

His face lit up in a great smile.

"Alasdair!" he exclaimed. The joy in his voice plunged to my very depths. My heart nearly burst with relief. Tears gushed from my eyes in a waterfall.

Alasdair extended his hand.

"Hello, Reddy," he said. "I came to . . . it has been far too long, too many years."

Iain took the hand and the other went around Alasdair's back.

"I...I came to apologize," Alasdair continued "—to ask your forgiveness for the resentments I have held, for believing lies about you...and for cutting off a man I once loved as a brother."

The men embraced.

Iain pulled away with Alasdair's hand still in his own, and gazed deep into Alasdair's eyes with the most forgiving expression of love imaginable.

"My *dear* friend," he said in a choking voice, "I have always forgiven you. Come in! Please...come in and let us catch up on—"

His voice had grown soft. My heart was pounding and I was sniffling so badly that I could make out nothing more of what either man said. All I could see, though my vision was blurry, was Iain, his hand on Alasdair's shoulder, leading the way into the house.

When the door closed behind them, I tried to compose myself, no easy task!

Then I got out of Alasdair's car and walked slowly home by way of the Scar Nose.

Chapter Fifty-eight

Baby Me

Our bonnie bairn's there, John, she was baith guid and fair, John.
And, oh, we grudged her sair to the land o' the leal.
But sorrows sel' wears past, John, and joy's a-comin' fast, John,
The joy that's aye to last in the land o' the leal.

—"The Land o' the Leal"

I don't know what I expected next. I did not really think I would hear from either Alasdair or Iain the rest of that day.

Nor did I.

Whatever had taken place, it was between them now.

Of course I was dying to see them both. But you can't intrude on holy things. I knew I might never know all that took place between them. I didn't want to know. Fiona was not part of my story. She was part of their mutual past, just as my husband was of my past. I would not have wanted to talk to them about him either. They had loved her. I had loved him.

But life moved on.

Now was now. Life went forward, not back.

That they were together again was enough for me to know.

I was also anxious to see Gwendolyn. Yet I didn't want to rush that either. I knew her condition was fragile.

Once my tears had subsided and my heart returned to its normal rhythm, the quietest sense of peace and contentment stole over me. Things were *right* again!

Healing and reconciliation between people felt so good.

I didn't know what would become of Olivia Urquhart, and

369

whether the humility of self-examination would ever enter *her* heart. But there was nothing I could do about it.

I felt such gratitude and thankfulness pouring out of me. God had one little part of his family back together. How happy it must make him, too.

I drove the two or three miles to the castle late the following morning, intending simply to inquire about Gwendolyn's condition. But Alicia told me to wait and hurried to find Alasdair. He came bounding down the stairs and rushing toward me a couple of minutes later, his face positively aglow. He led me out into the rose garden.

"Marie, Marie!" he said. "It was wonderful with Iain. He was just like I knew he would be. Why did I wait so long?"

"You did it, that's the important thing."

"Perhaps, but I feel more a fool than ever. The difficulty of apologizing is greatly overrated. It's not really that hard. It's not hard at all. And it feels so good! The burden of estrangement is something you don't even recognize, until suddenly it is lifted. Suddenly you realize how crushing the weight of it was. I feel so light, so full of energy. It is as if I had been wearing a ten-thousand-pound coat of lead. All I had to say was, *I am sorry, will you forgive me,* and . . . poof—it was gone!"

"Alasdair," I said, smiling, "I am so pleased. As I said yesterday, I am proud of you."

"Don't be proud of me, be proud of Iain. Forgiveness was always in his heart. He was so warm, so open, so gracious, not a word about the past, not a hint of recrimination. Just complete acceptance. I have always looked down on him for his profession. If ever there was a testimony for the truth of what the church preaches, that man is Iain Barclay. I had so many things wrong about him. I am not afraid to admit it. He is a man of character and dignity."

I could not help myself. I approached and put my arms around Alasdair and hugged him tightly.

"I am so happy, Alasdair," I said. "I know it was hard to do what you did."

I glanced up into his face. He was gazing deep into my eyes.

"Thank you, Marie," he said softly.

"How is Gwendolyn?" I asked, stepping back. "How soon do you think I can see her?"

"You may see her today. I am actually going to meet Iain for lunch in a bit. But first I want to spend some time with Gwendolyn. She has a song she wants to sing to me. It's 'Daddy's Song,' she says. She thought of it when she was sick. Would you want to come back in a little while, or anytime this afternoon?"

"I would, very much," I said.

We walked back from the garden, Alasdair to the house, me toward my car.

I returned two hours later. Alasdair was still gone. Alicia led me upstairs to the room where they had put Gwendolyn. I knocked lightly on the door. I didn't want to disturb her if she was sleeping. Then I poked my head in.

The moment she saw me, Gwendolyn's face lit up.

"Marie!" she exclaimed. "I was hoping you would come! Isn't my new room wonderful?"

I walked forward. She looked pale and weak. But as she sat up in bed to embrace me, she did not seem lacking in strength or energy. I sat down beside her and she was full of stories of their yacht voyage and her sickness and being at the hospital and now coming here. There was apparently no question of her returning to the Urquharts. She did not even mention it. This room had clearly been done up in readiness for her long before yesterday, I assumed while she and Alasdair were at sea. She acted like it had been her home for years.

"Would you like me to bring my harp for you to have in your room?" I asked.

"Oh, yes, Marie, could I really?"

"I already have it back from your aunt Olivia's. I will bring it today. I told your father about your playing. He can't wait to hear you."

"I made up a new song for him. It is a singing song, not a harp song. Would you like to hear it?"

"Very much. Are you sure you want me to hear it? Is it not just for you and him?"

"He will not mind. And I want you to hear it. I will sing it for you."

She began to sing.

A baby came to Mummy and Daddy.
  I do not remember—I had just begun to be.
Mummy and Daddy loved baby.
  That baby was me.

Her voice was so high and pure I thought the sound must be coming from heaven. The tune was just like those she made up with her fingers—eerily haunting, wild, mystical, almost like the wail of a Highland wind over a barren rocky mountain. It was a voice untamed by convention, free to wander, free to travel up and down the scale without restraint, to wherever it would go.

"Mummy and Daddy loved baby," she repeated. *"That baby was me."*

"Gwendolyn, that was lovely!" I said after a moment. "I am sure your father must like it very much."

"He said he did. But he got something in his eye when I was singing it and had to blink very hard. Will you really bring the harp today?"

"Shall I go get it right now? Would you like to play today? Will the doctor let you get out of bed?"

"I am only here because I was taking a nap. He says I may get up if I do not run about and get too excited."

"Then I shall go now and be back as soon as I can."

When I returned, it was not only with my harp, it was also with the microphone and tape recorder. The first thing on my agenda for the day was to get a recording of Gwendolyn's enchanting voice. All I could think of as I drove back into the village were the magical possibilities of Gwendolyn's high voice drifting in and out of the vibrations of the harp strings.

Her music, if anything, now became all the more expressive.

Chapter Fifty-nine

Peace

Oh! haud ye leal and true, John, your day it's wearin' through, John,
And I'll welcome you to the land o' the leal.
Now fare ye weel, my ain John, this warld's cares are vain, John,
We'll meet, and we'll be fain in the land o' the leal.
—"The Land o' the Leal"

With Gwendolyn at the castle, I was able to see her whenever and as often as I wanted. I went to the castle every day, ostensibly to give her a harp lesson.

Obviously I saw a great deal of Alasdair, too. We grew closer than ever.

Gwendolyn recovered from whatever had been the trouble on board the yacht. But she remained pale and, I thought, not quite as energetic as before.

When I had first come, she and her aunt went out frequently for walks. Now, whenever I suggested a walk about the castle grounds or in the gardens, or driving to the sea and walking along the promontory, she usually said she was too tired and would rather stay inside.

Olivia Urquhart did not come up in conversation with either Gwendolyn or Alasdair. She obviously knew that Alasdair and Gwendolyn were home at the castle together. From everything Alasdair had said, she was on more intimate terms with Dr. Mair than he. As Gwendolyn's legal guardian, it seemed likely that she would have been apprised of Gwendolyn's condition. But if there were repercussions of her having been taken to the castle, with no apparent plans for a return to town, they had not yet surfaced. I wondered, however, if the solicitor I had seen was helping her even now marshal a strategy to get Gwendolyn back.

From the beginning, Gwendolyn's lessons had been a little unusual. I truly believed that she possessed more musical gifting than I did. My collection of recordings of her playing were precious beyond words.

I now had several hours of very special music, including "Daddy's Song." I couldn't wait until I could figure out a way to edit and make a CD of Gwendolyn's music, which, now that she had begun experimenting with singing with the harp, took on yet more intriguing dimensions.

The newness of the harp had worn off. Gwendolyn was now eager to learn all I could teach her. I tried to instruct her in reading music, but it was no use. Nor was it necessary. Her ear was tuned so precisely to the inner music of her soul that she had to hear a thing only once or twice before she could play it from memory.

I took to teaching her a great variety of Scottish dances and ballads and folk songs. I played them through once myself, she tried it on her own, then I played it a second time. Usually by then she had it.

Her repertoire, if such it could be called, expanded rapidly. When it came to her own songs, however, she very rarely repeated herself. I don't know if she even remembered them. They were like sunrises and sunsets, something to be enjoyed for the moment but that never appeared in quite the same way again. I tried to make sure the recorder was always on when she was playing, and kept her freshly supplied with tapes so that she could turn the recorder on herself if she felt a song coming on.

The following weeks were an interlude of great happiness at Castle Buchan.

I had never seen Alasdair so relaxed, so content, so happy, so at peace. He and Iain got together, if not daily, at least every other day. The friendship resumed as if no time had passed. They were now men, however, and had much to talk about. Neither divulged their conversations to me. I presumed spiritual things were a topic of regular interest between them.

Knowing Iain as I did, I would have loved to be a fly on the wall listening to his probing yet pressureless questions!

And again I began to think about returning to Canada.

I no longer felt the urge to be pressing as before. It even began to occur to me that I might like to remain in Scotland through the winter. To do so would require immigration permission to remain longer than six months. And I would probably need to rent some other house or flat on a longer-term—and cheaper!—basis than a self-catering holiday cottage.

When I next saw Iain, he, too, was changed, and so appreciative of my involvement both with Alasdair and Gwendolyn. I had not seen him since Alasdair's visit.

"I'm not sure I really did anything," I said. "I think your sermon about the prodigal stirred up many people. I just happened to be one of them."

"You may be right," rejoined Iain. "But Alasdair told me that you challenged him pretty boldly about his need to talk to me."

"I suppose I did," I admitted a little sheepishly.

"He is very grateful," said Iain. "As am I. I have missed him all these years. Yet I always knew that I could not force a reconciliation until he was ready.—Hey, it's a beautiful day…how about a walk to the Salmon Bothy?"

"It's one of my favorite walking loops," I said, "though it's probably four miles there and back. Don't you have pastoral duties?"

"Today is my sermon preparation day," he said. "I feel the need of inspiration from the sea, the beach, the cliffs, and good company. I guarantee you, by the time we are walking back along the viaduct, something will have sprouted to life. What do you say— would you like to watch next Sunday's sermon germinate before your very eyes?"

"I can't think of anything I'd like better."

We set out a few minutes later.

"Any ideas yet?" I asked.

"You are an impatient one!" laughed Iain. "The creative process cannot be rushed. You can't just reach out and latch on to an idea. It has to develop at its own pace. I am, however, struck with something that might be a follow-up to the prodigal sermon, the notion of the joy of reconciliation between brothers and sisters of the human family."

"You mentioned that briefly, the father waiting for the two sons to become one again."

"I hadn't given it a lot of thought beforehand, it just came out. But I have been reflecting on it ever since. Can you imagine the joy in God's heart when two of his children truly come together?"

"I know the joy I felt when I saw you and Alasdair embrace. God's joy must be much greater. And the change in Alasdair is truly remarkable."

"Healing and reconciliation do that to people. They are freeing, liberating, exuberating!"

"There is no such word as that!" I laughed.

"I know. I just made it up! But really, there is nothing quite so wonderful as walls coming down and people coming together. It is amazing that more people don't seek that joy when it is so easily attainable."

Chapter Sixty

Fall

I must away love, I can no longer tarry,
This morning's tempest I have to cross,
I must be guided without a stumble,
Into the arms I love the most.
—"The Night Visiting Song"

The weeks passed into a month, then six weeks. Gwendolyn turned thirteen, the first birthday Alasdair had celebrated with her.

Even in the increasingly blustery fall weather, Gwendolyn was better. She and I took to walking on the castle grounds and occasionally along the sea. Every time we went into town I asked if she wanted to visit her aunt Olivia, but she never did. She and Alasdair began to speak of another voyage, but Alasdair was concerned for her health. It began to look as if it would have to wait until the following spring.

I had spoken with the lady who owned my cottage and told her I would be moving to a flat in the village. She asked if it was because of money and I said it was. She said that I had been such a good and pleasant tenant, and that since the tourist season was now past I could stay if I wanted for three hundred pounds a month, far less than what I had been paying.

I agreed and so remained where I was. I had till almost the end of the year to get permission to extend my stay beyond six months and planned a trip to the consulate in Edinburgh to investigate the procedure.

Whatever might have become of my plans to stay in Port Scarnose beyond Christmas and into the following year, however, were suddenly preempted during the last week of October when Gwendolyn suffered a sudden relapse.

I was frightened nearly out of my wits with a sudden banging on my door in the middle of the night. My first instinct was to call for help. Then I remembered I had no phone. As I was throwing on some clothes, the banging continued. I thought about crawling out a window at the back of the house and making a run for it. Instead I crept into the kitchen without turning on a light to see what I could see.

With relief I heard a familiar voice from the front porch.

"Marie . . . Marie, wake up. It's Iain!"

I flipped on the light and rushed to the door. There stood Iain, a look of urgency on his face.

"Marie, get on your shoes and a coat—you have to come with me."

"What is—"

"It's Gwendolyn. She's not doing well. They want you at the castle."

I ran outside three minutes later. We hurried to Iain's car.

"What time is it?" I asked.

"About two-thirty," replied Iain. "Alasdair telephoned me and asked me to wake you and for both of us to come."

"The poor girl! She has had to face so much in her young life."

When we arrived at the castle, Alasdair was obviously agitated. The doctor was in Gwendolyn's room. We talked for a few minutes in the adjacent sitting room, Alasdair filling us in on what had happened.

"She got up to go to the toilet," he said, "and collapsed on her way back to bed. Her legs simply gave out. I heard the fall and immediately went to her. Even when I helped her up, she couldn't stand. Her muscles are gradually losing their strength and will eventually atrophy from disuse."

"Alasdair," said Iain, "we need to tell Olivia."

Alasdair nodded. "I hate to ask, but—"

"Don't even think it, my friend," said Iain. "I will be happy to go see her. What is your sense of the thing? Should I go *now*? Wake her in the middle of the night?"

"Dr. Mair does not think anything more serious will happen immediately, certainly not before morning. It can wait until then. But I can tell from his face that he is not optimistic. I don't know if Olivia will come, however, knowing that the three of us are here."

"I will do what I can at first light," said Iain. "A minister's job is not to preach clever sermons but to bring about healing in God's family. If I cannot do so with a member who also is an elder in the church like Olivia, perhaps I ought to seek a new line of work."

"I appreciate it, Iain," said Alasdair. "Assure her that she will be entirely welcome. No, more than that. Assure her that I *want* her to come, and that she is part of the family."

Chapter Sixty-one

Angel Harp

Sae dear's that joy was bought, John, sae free the battle fought, John.
That sinfu' man e'er brought to the land o' the leal.
Oh, dry your glist'nin e'e, John, my saul langs to be free, John,
And angels beckon me to the land o' the leal.

—"The Land o' the Leal"

After further consultation with the doctor, Alasdair chose to leave Gwendolyn at the castle. Dr. Mair said there was nothing that could be done for her at the hospital, even at any of the large hospitals in London. She would be better off where she was happy and comfortable.

Love was the only healing power for her now. What medical science could not do for her body, love would have to do for her spirit.

And never had a thirteen-year-old girl been loved the way little Gwendolyn was loved by her devoted father!

Alasdair had a guest room prepared for me, the room next to Gwendolyn's. He asked me if I would stay at the castle for a while, hopefully until she recovered. If not, for as long as it took.

Mrs. Urquhart was as kind to her niece and as helpful as any of us. She acknowledged Alasdair's invitation through Iain and spent most of that first day at the castle. After two more days, Alasdair persuaded her to take one of the guest rooms down the hall from mine for as long as she liked, and to treat the castle of her childhood as her own. He was more gracious than I would have thought possible. His kindness gradually succeeded in softening her a little.

But only a little. She would not speak to me.

It made matters more difficult since we were both attending to Gwendolyn. She still looked upon me as an intruder, especially since my room was next to Gwendolyn's and I was usually the first one Gwendolyn asked for whenever she awoke. When Mrs. Urquhart came, I offered to leave, but Alasdair wouldn't hear of it. We managed by sort of unspoken consent to alternate our times with Gwendolyn.

I played my harp for two or three hours every day at Gwendolyn's bedside. It began to seem that her own playing might be at an end. One day Alasdair and I managed to get her out of bed and seated on a chair in front of the harp. Even that proved too fatiguing. After a short time, she asked if she could go back to bed.

So I played for her and often played tapes of her own music, which she seemed to enjoy in a mystical way, and sometimes read to her.

Mostly it was Alasdair at her bedside, even when she slept.

I knew this was breaking his heart. But he bore up stoically. I saw from his red eyes that when alone he often wept. When he was with his daughter, however, he revealed nothing but smiles and cheery words of encouragement.

"I know you didn't like it when I asked you before, Marie," Gwendolyn asked one day when I was alone with her in her room, "but may I please call you Mummy?"

"But, dear Gwendolyn, I'm not your mummy," I said.

"My mummy's dead. I want to call someone besides Auntie Mummy again, and to feel her arms around me."

Silent tears gushed from my eyes. I bent down to her bed and scooped her into my embrace and held her tight.

"Yes, you can call me Mummy," I said. "I will be your mummy for just a little while."

"Until I see my own mummy again," she said. "I think I will see her before very long. I can hear her speaking to me sometimes, or almost. I think it is her. Maybe it is an angel, I don't know. But I know I have to wait and be patient a little while longer before she will come for me."

It was all I could do to keep from sobbing. I was glad Mrs. Urquhart hadn't heard the exchange.

A few more days went by. Dr. Mair came and went. All he did was check her pulse and blood pressure and occasionally take a pinprick of blood to test. We all knew he was just going through the motions, probably more for our sake, to make it seem that *something* was being done, than for anything to be gained by it.

Then came a day when he and Alasdair closed the door of Alasdair's study behind them. They were alone for ten or fifteen minutes. When they emerged, Alasdair's face was pale.

After that, he almost never left Gwendolyn's room.

The next day, about midafternoon, I heard Alasdair's step coming from Gwendolyn's room. He poked his face through the open door of mine.

"Come," he said, then turned and disappeared.

I hurried after him. Mrs. Urquhart had gone home for the day.

I entered Gwendolyn's room. Alasdair sat on the side of the bed, one of Gwendolyn's hands in his.

"Here is Marie, Gwendolyn, dear," said Alasdair.

"Will you play for me on the angel harp?" said Gwendolyn. Her voice was so soft I could barely hear it.

"Of course, sweetheart," I replied.

I began playing the song that had been inspired by the very first sounds to come out of her on my harp, which I called "Gwendolyn's Song." How many of the notes were Gwendolyn's and which ones were mine, I no longer had any idea. I played as softly as I could, though the sound seemed to fill the room. The moment Gwendolyn heard the familiar melody, she leaned her head back on the pillow, a smile of peace on her lips.

"One of the angels told me she heard you when you were playing once in the church," she said in a voice so soft I barely was able to make it out. "She said she wants me to play for her, too."

I continued to play for several minutes.

Gradually the tiniest sound came from the bed. My fingers stilled and I listened. She was gazing up out of the pillow into Alasdair's face. Gwendolyn was singing, *"A baby came to Mummy and Daddy. I had just begun to be..."*

She stopped to take a breath. Her voice was so faint.

"Mummy and Daddy," she tried to go on. *"Mummy and Daddy...loved baby. That baby...was me."*

The tiny voice fell silent.

I stood and went to Alasdair's side. As I glanced down upon the bed, Gwendolyn's eyes were closed. The light had faded from her face, though the remnant of a smile lingered on her lips. I knew she was gone.

She had taken her music to share it with the angels.

Chapter Sixty-two

Remembering

We silently stray 'mong the tombstones,
And muse on our friends who are dead,
But alas! Here are only the dry bones—
The souls of the dear ones are fled.

The timid, the bold, the young, and the old
Together lie peacefully here,
And it now matters nought what a cold world thought
Of loved ones we held so dear.

—"Wee Jamie"

The events of the past months had so captivated the entire community, Gwendolyn's sudden death was the only thing anyone could talk about.

The sympathetic among them perceived it in terms of the tragic figure of Duke Alasdair Reidhaven, reunited with his daughter after many years, only to lose her so quickly. The more cynical among them tried to revive dark intimations out of the past with speculations that more was involved than mere illness.

Tales of the family curse and the second sight resurfaced, and worse. While there had been talk of a change in the duke, not many of the villagers had seen it with their own eyes. Many of the small-minded were willing, therefore, if not eager, to believe whatever sinister tales they might hear. But there were enough who had seen him with me or Iain to attest to what unmistakably appeared to be a different spirit about him, a spirit of light not darkness. These were mostly able to counteract the influence of the evil rumors.

Even Olivia Urquhart, as much as her natural inclination was to cast suspicion by subtlety and innuendo, could not credibly imply that her niece's death was from other than natural, if tragic, causes.

The outdoor service, presided over by Iain Barclay at the Deskmill Parish Church, was attended by more people even than had come to witness the sailing of the duke's yacht.

Alasdair arranged a traditional funeral as might have been given one of the laird's family a hundred years before. Accordingly, the little casket bearing Gwendolyn's body was loaded into a black-draped horse-drawn hearse at Buchan Castle, myself and Iain and Gwendolyn's two living relatives in attendance. The hearse then began the long procession of two miles into town and in a wide circle to the church, arriving at length on the other side of the high stone fence from where it had begun its solemn journey.

As we walked behind the little girl who had brought us together, Alasdair and his sister leading, Iain and I behind them, we were silently joined along the way. As the hearse passed through the village, no sound was to be heard but the steady *clomp-clomp* of the single horse along the middle of the paved streets. Gradually the processional gathered hundreds behind us, until we arrived at the church more than four hundred strong.

The groom drew the great draught horse in.

The four of us together, for the coffin was not a heavy one, lifted little Gwendolyn from the back of the open hearse and carried her to the small plot adjacent to the churchyard cemetery where those of the duke's family from centuries past had been laid to rest. The very sight of Iain Barclay and Alasdair Reidhaven together again was enough to set what might have remained of the rumors to rest.

With Alasdair, Olivia Urquhart, and myself standing beside the coffin, Iain took his place on the opposite side facing us. He invited the onlookers to come closer and gather round.

"We are here to celebrate the life of Gwendolyn Reidhaven," he began after the movement and shuffling had subsided. "It was a life, to our earthly sensibilities, far too short, brought abruptly to an end by a tragic illness none of us understand. We cannot fathom why death strikes one such as this at such a tender age. But we believe in faith that in God's eyes things are different than they appear. We believe that the measure of a life's significance is not revealed by longevity but by impact in the kingdom of heaven. Some of the world's most selfish misers live to be ninety. Yet our Savior never saw his thirty-fourth earthly birthday. Quantity of years has never been God's standard of reckoning.

"Therefore, as we consider the life of Gwendolyn Reidhaven..."

As I listened, I realized that it was almost unnecessary for Iain to say anything. The fact that we were all standing there together said all there was to say. Gwendolyn's short life had brought healing and reconciliation to this entire community. It was true that Alasdair and Mrs. Urquhart were still estranged. But the healing that had begun between Alasdair and Gwendolyn, father and daughter, and had spread to Alasdair and Iain, had in a short time spread throughout the entire community.

A new spirit was alive everywhere, a new optimism, a new sense of community and brotherhood and camaraderie. The tears being shed that day—I was crying as Iain spoke, as was Olivia Urquhart beside me, and as were many women of Port Scarnose who realized they had not been as kind to poor little Gwendolyn as they might have been—were like warm, gentle rains coming down from heaven to water new flowers of healing that Gwendolyn's short life had planted.

Hovering over us all, I saw Gwendolyn's bright red hair and white face, now smiling and radiant and alive and happy, free at last from the afflictions of her earthly life, and saying to all who were able to perceive her words in their spirits: *Do not grieve for me. I live, I rejoice, I love. I am singing and playing my own special harp with the angels! Be happy for me, and be one with each other!*

My attention was drawn back to Iain as I heard him begin his concluding remarks.

"And now, my friends," he said, "please give the duke and Mrs. Urquhart and Gwendolyn's Canadian friend the honor of retreating a short distance in silence while they pay their final respects to this child of God whom they loved and will continue to love. They will then be borne back to the castle in the carriage which brought little Gwendolyn from the place of her birth to her final resting place. At that time, if you so desire, you may come forward with your own thoughts and prayers."

I could almost hear Gwendolyn's haunting voice singing her own lullaby to Alasdair.

> *A baby came to Mummy and Daddy.*
>   *I do not remember—I had just begun to be.*
> *Mummy and Daddy loved baby.*
>   *That baby was me.*

The reminder brought fresh tears to my eyes.

"Mr. Reidhaven has asked that I convey to you," Iain went on, "his wish that you will afterward join him along with his sister and friends at Castle Buchan for an afternoon of joyful celebration for the spirit of reconciliation symbolized by his daughter's life. He is desirous of rekindling many old friendships of the past—friendships he regrets having too long forgotten. It is his earnest wish that you will all come and share this day, both its sadness of loss and its joy of healing, with him."

Iain stopped and retreated a short distance from the coffin. He motioned for Alasdair to come forward. As he did, with a quiet shuffling of steps, the villagers stepped back. Alasdair stood beside the ornate wooden casket for a minute, his hand lying upon it. He then walked around it, glanced up at Iain and nodded, and took his place beside him.

My eyes came to rest on the two men, standing side by side. I looked deep into Alasdair's face, his stoic eyes red but dry, then over to Iain, his expression serious and full of tender compassion. My eyes flitted back and forth several times between them.

My heart began to pound with what was a sudden and stunning realization. *Oh, my goodness!* I thought as chills swept through me.

But I had no leisure to think about it. Mrs. Urquhart stepped forward, paused at the casket a moment, and went around it and to Alasdair's side.

Then I did the same.

Oh, Gwendolyn, you dear child of God! I said to myself as I rested my hand briefly on the coffin. Then I took my place beside Iain, who nodded to the sexton and his assistant. They came forward and slowly lowered the casket into the ground. I cried again. Then Iain and Alasdair led us to the waiting hearse. We stepped up and the four of us sat on the bench seats that ran lengthwise on either side, flanking the open space between where the coffin had lain.

The carriage jerked into motion. As we began making our way through the crowd and away from the church, the villagers slowly inched forward and began passing the open grave in a long, silent processional, each one as he or she passed tossing in a rose or whatever autumn blossom they had been able to find for the occasion. By the time the last of the mourners passed by, the coffin was covered with fragrant and colorful tokens of a community's belated expressions of love.

Chapter Sixty-three

The Great Tide of Love

Oh, the summertime is coming, and the trees are sweetly blooming.
And the wild mountain thyme, grows around the blooming heather,
Will ye go, lassie, go?
And we'll all go together, to pluck wild mountain thyme.
All around the blooming heather, will ye go, lassie, go?

—"Wild Mountain Thyme"

The ride in the carriage back to the castle grounds, behind the steady clomping of the horse's shod hooves, was mostly silent, as befitted the occasion. Alasdair spoke softly to Iain, thanking him for his handling of everything and his words at Gwendolyn's graveside. I was feeling very uncomfortable, however...for reasons other than Gwendolyn.

Something incredible was happening inside me!

I know I should have been thinking of poor Gwendolyn. And of course I was.

But whenever I glanced up and saw Alasdair and Iain sitting side by side so close opposite me, two men brought together by the death of the little girl who was the daughter of a woman both had loved, I could not help goose bumps rising up the back of my neck.

This had suddenly become intolerable. I had to be alone. I had to think!

We arrived back at the castle, where tables were being set throughout the grounds and gardens with meats and cheeses and breads and cakes and fruits, along with more tea and coffee and ale than would be possible for an entire community to consume in a week. After helping with a few final preparations and as the townspeople began to arrive, I found Alasdair and told him I needed to leave for a while. The surprise on his face was evident.

"You will be back?" he said hesitantly.

"I don't know, Alasdair," I replied. "This is, you know, an emotional time. I need to be alone for a while. I hope you don't mind."

"But I had hoped—I need you here with me."

"I will come back as soon as I am up to it," I replied.

I went to find Mrs. Urquhart.

"Mrs. Ur—Olivia," I said. "I am leaving. I just wanted to say . . . that is, I want you to know how sorry I am about Gwendolyn, and—"

I felt myself beginning to cry again.

Unexpectedly, I stepped forward and hugged her. I was as surprised as she was.

She stood stiffly unresponsive. Then I turned and walked to where I had parked my car.

I cast one final glance around me. Already Alasdair was surrounded by people as they arrived, giving everyone warm handshakes and friendly greetings. Dozens of people I didn't recognize were clustered about him offering their condolences and renewing old friendships.

I needn't worry about Alasdair, I thought. He would be fine without me. The people of the community were anxious to love him. All they had needed was for him to open the door.

Twenty minutes later, a swirl of turbulent emotions racing through me, I was on my way out of Port Scarnose walking along the headland trail. The town was virtually empty. No walkers were out. Everyone was at the castle.

As I went, I was thinking of Gwendolyn. I realized that despite all the other attachments I had formed, *she* had been the main thing keeping me here during the last two months. Without her, I would have found myself in this predicament long before now. At least I might have recognized it before this!

Now what? It was sure to become awkward. Gwendolyn had diverted the focus from what had been in front of my nose for weeks.

I had somehow rationalized everything that was going on with the thought that I had just been developing two very close and interesting *friendships*. But suddenly an explosion had gone off in my brain. They weren't mere "friendships" at all! The fact had jolted me with stunning force when sitting in the carriage, it could no longer be ignored:

I was in love with two men.

There—I said it!

As I reached my favorite bench and sat down, I had to say it out loud before it really sank in. First I *thought* the words. Then I *whispered* them. At last I *said* them out loud.

"*I am in love with two men.*"

And with the realization in all its clarity, I knew I had a problem.

I stared down at the water from the same place where my odyssey here had begun, watching the waves flowing in and out on the tide. The coast along here was so rocky. I never tired of watching the waves come in, crashing now against maybe a small rock and then against one as tall as a house, and go splashing up against it or completely obliterating it in white spray and foam, and then flow out again, leaving the rock exposed until the next wave came crashing in.

When I came to my bench at low tide, the entire look was different than at high tide. Different rocks were more noticeable wherever the tide was, and the waves did different things. It was like watching the tide rise and fall over Florimel's Rock at the western end of Crannoch Bay just off the Bore Crag. Sometimes the rock was invisible, completely submerged by high tide. But at low tide you could walk right out to it and climb on it.

On this day, with so much on my mind, one particular rock about twenty feet out from the shore caught my eye. The tide was about halfway between high and low. Some two feet of this rock was visible above the waterline. Slowly a wave came in and submerged it for a second or two. Then slowly the mussel-encrusted surface reappeared as the wave continued on to shore.

Something about that rock, watching the waves approach it, cover it, then go on by, reminded me of me. I had come here spiritually empty. I didn't know it. But now I realized that's exactly what I was.

Then I met Iain Barclay. Meeting him had been like a wave of *life* coming in and crashing over *me* in the same way that waves were spilling over that rock out there. Life had come awake within me because of him. I had been filled, covered with the incoming water of *life*.

Maybe it was a stupid analogy—the waves and rocks, and my spiritual emptiness and then my waking. But as I sat there on that day, such was the progression my thoughts took. Spiritual *waking*, it struck me, was a moving and flowing thing, like the waves and the tide. Wakefulness had flowed *into* me and *over* me through Iain Barclay.

But then the water continued on from that rock out there. The flow didn't stop. It came in, kept going, and moved on. And remarkably, after I had begun to come awake myself, somehow something within *me*—the music of my harp at first—began to awaken new things within Alasdair. As he had come awake, his relationship with Gwendolyn had come back to life, then his friendship with Iain.

The incoming tide of wakefulness had swept in and covered us all!

As my eyes gazed out over the water, I realized that we were all like the rocks out there, and that the great love of God's Fatherhood was the whole sea, slowly sweeping in as a great tide to cover us. Some, like Iain, felt that tide sweep over them sooner in life than others. Then the tide had overtaken me. After me, life had come to Alasdair. It was a moving, swelling tide surrounding and inundating us all, each in our own way and our own time.

Timings were different, circumstances were different. But the water of life rose and fell, surging in, flowing out, splashing, covering, and laying bare what had been hidden before.

Many awakenings were taking place!

And with them, love, too, had come alive and blossomed.

For what is love but the flowering of God's life? What can be more lovely in all the world than a mind and a heart coming awake to life, to the people nearby, to the goodness of the Father who is waiting for us to arise and return to him?

Nothing is quite so wonderful in all the world as an individual waking.

I felt more alive than I had ever been.

I loved Iain. The life within him had sparked life within me. I had been asleep and had come awake. How could I not love him for helping me wake up? And I loved being with him. He was fun, like a best friend.

But Alasdair's waking, the tearful look in his eyes as he took Gwendolyn in his arms and kissed her and she kissed him and said, "I love you, Daddy,"...it, too, had smitten my heart. It felt right to stand beside him. In that moment weeks before, I realized now that I had begun to *love* the man, love him with all the love that was in me.

As unlikely as it seemed when I thought back to the first moment I had laid eyes on him...I had grown to *love* Alasdair with a woman's love.

I also loved Alasdair for his courage to grow, for the humility that had lately blossomed in his character. I had witnessed something within me spark life awake in him! And I *loved* him.

Iain had helped awaken life in me. I had helped awaken life in Alasdair.

Both were responses of love. Love flowing into me *from* another, love flowing out of me *into* another. Like the tide—inflowing and outflowing, but the same water moved by the same tide of love. How could I not love them both? And presumptuous as it was to think it—I realized that they both loved me.

With the realization of what was happening in my heart, I knew a decision had been reached. It was a decision I did not even realize I was facing until the decision was made.

With Gwendolyn gone, I was not about to put Iain and Alasdair in the same predicament that had torn them apart so many years before.

I could stay in Scotland no longer.

I would *not* allow Iain and Alasdair to again be pitted against each other by either loving or being loved by the same woman. After the healing that had taken place between them, I would not allow myself to come between them. I loved both too much to become a second Fiona.

It would be better never to see either of them again than to disrupt the precious flowering of their friendship. If it took my leaving to preserve the healing, it would be a price I must pay.

My loves would have to remain in my heart, known only to God and myself.

It was time for me to go.

Chapter Sixty-four

Diamond Necklace

Can ye lo'e me weel, lassie, to this heart then swiftly flee;
There ye aye shall dwell, lassie, mair than a' this world to me.
When the moon-beams shine sae clear, at that hour by levers blest;
At the gloaming, lassie, dear, haste to meet this faithful breast.

—"Can Ye Lo'e Me Weel, Lassie"

Love always brings complications.

The divine ecstasy of loving cannot be separated from the pain that is its inevitable counterpart. My agony was now to diplomatically get out of Port Scarnose without divulging the full extent of my reasons for leaving.

Saying good-bye to both men, knowing how much I loved them, and at last knowing the nature of the love in my heart, but knowing I could say nothing, would be the hardest thing I had ever done in my life.

In the days following the funeral, though I saw Alasdair daily, I was able to hide my thoughts and deepest feelings behind the quiet melancholy that was natural after Gwendolyn's death. I made my flight arrangements, and notified Mrs. Mair that I would be leaving her cottage at the end of the week. It tore me up inside knowing that I would be leaving Alasdair in the midst of his grief.

A quagmire of relational complications was sure to result if I stayed longer. I could not tell Alasdair the why of my decision. Yet the anticipation of it was killing me. He had become such a tender man. I feared for the pain my leaving would cause him. I did not want to hurt him.

But it had to be done. He was now strong enough to weather it. A clean, quick break, though painful, would be best.

With Iain it would be easier. He would never say, but I knew he would understand my motives.

He could not be unaware of the terrible irony that once again a woman had entered both his life and Alasdair's. I knew that was why I had seen less of him in recent weeks.

One thing I knew Iain Barclay would never do was vie for a woman's affections. Even if he loved me, he would not fight for me. It was not his way. He believed too much in allowing God to unfold his will to grasp for something he might want for himself.

My leaving would not crush Iain. His life would go on. He would still have his church, his ministry, and his faith. He had not become dependent on me as Alasdair had. Nor had he just lost a daughter.

I waited until two days before I planned to drive from Port Scarnose to Inverness where I would catch the train south. I told Alasdair I needed to talk to him about something important. He asked if I would come for dinner the next evening. I agreed.

When I arrived at the castle the following afternoon about five-thirty, it was already nearly dusk. The hours of daylight changed so rapidly in Scotland.

Alasdair was dressed casually, in tan corduroy trousers and a bluish Shetland pullover sweater. He and I walked awhile in the gardens, then went inside. I didn't have the heart to tell him that I had spent the day packing and cleaning up the cottage and saying good-bye to all my favorite local walks and haunts.

How would I summon the courage to tell him that by this time tomorrow, I would be gone?

We talked informally, though quietly, through dinner. Gwendolyn had been with her other Father almost two weeks. Occasionally a smile returned to Alasdair's face.

"I have wanted to talk to you, too," said Alasdair when dinner was over. "These last couple of weeks, I know it's been difficult for all of us. But I want to thank you again for everything, and for being here with me during this time. It means the world to me, Marie. Gwendolyn loved you so much, and...I—"

He stopped and drew in a deep breath. My heart was pounding. If I didn't get said what *I* had to say pretty soon, it would be too late! What if *he* said something that went further than I wanted this to go?

He reached into the pocket of his trousers and pulled out a small oblong black box.

"This necklace belonged to my mother," he said. "I have been saving it all this time for Gwendolyn, hoping that...well, she will not be able to wear it now, and I would like you to have it, Marie."

He opened the box, then reached out and set it across the table in front of me. It must have contained twenty diamonds!

I gulped, struggling to find my voice.

"Alasdair, it's...I've never seen anything so lovely," I said, fumbling for words. "It's so kind of...I mean, you needn't...but...how could I possibly...I can't accept it, not a family heirloom."

"It would mean more than I can say for you to take it."

"I...I just can't."

Alasdair looked away. The open box with the necklace sparkling on a black velvet bed sat on the table between us. A heavy silence fell.

"It's Iain, isn't it?" said Alasdair softly after a minute.

The words jolted me.

"I've seen it all along," he continued, smiling a little sadly. "I knew you loved him. And I...you need have no worry about me. He is a fine man. You could not do better. Even so, even if you wear it as Iain's wife, I would like you to have this necklace...as a reminder of happy times, times you once spent with a man who cared for you very much, and—"

He drew in a deep breath and smiled again. "And to remember Gwendolyn," he added.

Again it was silent.

"It is not because of Iain," I said softly. My voice was husky.

This was much harder than I had anticipated.

"What then? Please," implored Alasdair. "Say you will accept the necklace, as a token of my—"

"Oh, Alasdair," I said, at last bursting into tears. "I am leaving tomorrow!"

I glanced away, tears falling from my eyes in earnest now. I couldn't look at him.

For a moment all was dead silence. I stared down at my lap.

After a minute I heard his chair slide across the floor. He got up and I heard him walking around the table to where I sat. I stood, and the next moment I was swallowed in his embrace and sobbing uncontrollably.

Alasdair's great hand stroked my hair as he spoke softly.

"I knew this day would come," he said. "It had to come eventually."

"I'm sorry I didn't tell you sooner," I whispered.

"No, no, it's not your fault," he said. "I know you were just thinking of me. I tried to pretend there would not have to be a day of farewell. But inside I knew I was just fooling myself. This will be one of the most painful partings of my life. But you needn't worry. I will be fine. Things are different now. I am a changed man. I have known you and loved you and I will never forget you. I have just one final request to make."

I nodded through my tears.

"Please," he said, "if you can, don't forget me. And, when you remember, perhaps you might occasionally say a prayer for me."

I burst into sobs again, mingled with laughter as I pulled back and gazed deeply into his eyes.

"Oh, Alasdair!" I cried. "How could you even think I would forget you? Some of the most wonderful memories of my life will be of this place. I will treasure them."

"And the necklace?"

Blinking hard, I forced a smile, but slowly shook my head.

I embraced him again, tight and long, then let go and stepped back.

"I will walk you down to your car," said Alasdair, trying to encourage me with a smile. But it was a sad smile and nearly broke my heart.

I took his arm and we walked downstairs and outside without a word.

How I managed to drive to my cottage, I don't know. I hurried inside, fell onto the bed, and cried myself to sleep. It was not how I had envisioned my last night in Port Scarnose.

Chapter Sixty-five

Angel

Angel voices, ever singing, round Thy throne of light.
Angel harps, for ever ringing, rest not day nor night;
Thousands only live to bless Thee, and confess Thee, Lord of might.

Yea, we know that Thou rejoicest o'er each work of Thine;
Thou didst ears and hands and voices, for Thy praise design;
Craftsman's art and music's measure, for Thy pleasure all combine.

Honour, glory, might, and merit, Thine shall ever be,
Father, Son, and Holy Spirit, Blessed Trinity.
Of the best that Thou has given, earth and heaven render Thee.

—Francis Pott, "Angel Voices"

The following morning I went to see Iain. The instant I saw his face I knew that he knew.

I sometimes thought he *always* knew what I was thinking.

"So is this farewell between friends?" he said with a halfway sad and knowing smile.

I stood shaking my head, my mouth open in bewilderment, my eyes filling again. I was doing a lot of crying these days. I had used up a ten-year allotment of tears!

"How did you know?" I said slowly.

"I had a feeling," he replied. "I've seen it coming. But the day of Gwendolyn's funeral...I think I knew what was on your mind."

I hoped he didn't know *all* of what was on my mind that day. Though maybe he did. Iain was like nobody I had ever met in his ability to read people, or, as they say in Britain, to suss them out. He certainly had the reason for my visit on this day sussed.

"I am sorry I didn't tell you sooner," I said. "I just didn't know how to tell you."

"I understand," he said, smiling. "It is a complicated and emotional time, what with Gwendolyn's death, and everything. I know you have had a lot on your mind."

"I suppose you're right."

I paused briefly.

"There is something I have wanted to tell you—something else, I mean," I said after a moment. "You asked me a question once—the day we met, in fact. I didn't exactly give you the whole answer that day. Maybe I should have. I mean, I didn't say anything that wasn't true. But I didn't tell you the *full* truth. I've been uncomfortable with your not knowing. But it was a little embarrassing, I just never got around to telling you. Now that I'm leaving, I want you to know."

Iain looked at me puzzled, but waited.

"It's about my name," I said.

"What?" he laughed. "Your name isn't Marie?"

"No, it *is* . . . well, sort of. My parents actually gave me three names. My full name is actually . . . it's Angel Dawn Marie."

Iain's eyes lit up and a smile spread over his face. "*Angel!*" he repeated.

"I'm sorry I didn't tell you. I should have. But it has always been hard for me, playing the harp, you know. I was self-conscious."

"I don't know why. It's a wonderful name—Angel Dawn Marie!" Iain repeated again.

"There is also my married name. My husband's name was Lorcini."

"Angel Dawn Marie Buchan Lorcini—that's a mouthful! I can see why you would shorten it when you meet a stranger."

I laughed. Iain could always make me laugh!

Even in the midst of this difficult parting, he never lost his sense of humor. I think one day he will be lying on his deathbed and still making wry comments or joking to put those around him at ease.

"I'm not sure why I started using the *Buchan* when I came here," I said, "certainly not out of disrespect for my husband. When you first asked me my name, it just popped out. The *Marie* and the *Buchan* had always been next to each other. I grew up saying them in that order Angel-Dawn-Marie-Buchan, so when I said *Marie*, out came the *Buchan* with it, and nothing else. And after I'd said it, it felt right, and I needed a change in my life, so I just kept using it. My legal name is still Lorcini. I suppose Buchan seemed more Scottish than Lorcini."

I paused and smiled a little awkwardly.

"So, now you know—not exactly everything about me, but at least you know who I am," I said. "And, now I am leaving Port Scarnose.—Iain," I added, "there are no adequate words. I don't know how to thank you for everything. I know God now. I wonder if I ever would have without you. There is nothing more precious one person can give another than a deeper knowledge of God, and you gave it to me. Thank you!"

He nodded, gazing upon me and smiling such a smile of love that I nearly melted right then and there. Then an odd smile crept over his lips.

"What is it?"

"Actually I was just reminded of something—not a secret of my own, exactly, though I'm not sure I ever have told anyone about it. I never mentioned it before, I'm not really sure why, maybe because I didn't want to trivialize your harp playing with the angel stereotype. Especially now that you have told me your name, and that that stereotype was one of your reasons for keeping it secret, I suppose it's a good thing I didn't mention it. But believe it or not, one of my favorite hymns is called "Angel Voices." It is about the music of angel harps."

"No...really! I had no idea there was such a hymn."

"Absolutely—incredibly majestic. *'Angel voices, ever singing round Thy throne of light. Angel harps, for ever ringing, rest not day nor night; Thousands only live to bless Thee, and confess Thee, Lord of might.'*"

"I can't wait to look it up. It will be the first song I learn when I get home."

We both grew quiet once more.

"Again, I am sorry I didn't tell you about my plans sooner," I said. "I should have talked to you, I *wanted* to talk to you, but—"

I looked away and tried to steady myself. I was finally crying in earnest.

I felt a gentle hand on one shoulder, then on the other. I looked up. Iain's face was six inches from mine, his eyes misty, his lips parted as if he was about to speak. But then he closed them and continued to gaze deeply into my eyes.

It was "the look" revisited. This time there was no mistaking its meaning.

Slowly he pulled me toward him. I felt my arms going around his waist as he pulled me into his embrace. We stood a minute in silence. There was too much to say. So we said nothing. I wept.

"Good-bye, Angel," Iain whispered. "You have indeed been a messenger of God to this place, and you will never be forgotten."

"Good-bye, Iain," I said through my tears. "I will always...thank you. Good-bye."

I stepped back. For another moment our eyes met.

Then I turned and walked to my car.

Chapter Sixty-six

Everywhere Is God's Home

Fareweel, fareweel, my native hame,
Thy lonely glens an' heath-clad mountains,
Fareweel, thy fields o' storied fame,
Thy leafy shaws an' sparklin' fountains.
Nae mair I'll climb the Pentlands steep,
Nor wander by the Esk's clear river:
I seek a hame far o'er the deep,
My native land, fareweel forever.

—"The Scottish Emigrant's Farewell"

I had been thinking on and off about returning to Canada for so long, that it was with a deep sense of relief and finality that at last I settled into my seat aboard the British Airways 747 bound for Toronto. It was not really a sigh of *relief* because part of me didn't want to be going home at all.

But I had to. I knew that. I was in too much emotional turmoil to stay. The potential complications were too great.

What would I have done, kept living in my little rented cottage until either Iain or Alasdair proposed to me, and then try to decide what to do?

That was not a decision I wanted to face!

Who did I think I was, anyway? Most women worry about whether *one* man will ever propose, not two! Maybe I was in love with both of them, but what if I had misread the whole thing? What if neither of them was in love with me?

I had never really considered myself a romantic. I was aware of the old saying that a woman always knows when a man is in love with her. Though I hadn't had all that much experience in that department, I now knew what the saying meant. I was pretty certain of what both men *hadn't* said. It seemed...that is—

Forget it! I wasn't going to probe that question too deeply. Weepy farewells and looks did not *necessarily* mean that either of them loved me.

My drab, uneventful life had certainly changed. I'd gone to Scotland and had fallen in love twice!

When I arrived back in Calgary, I was drained on so many levels that for once in my life the exhaustion of jet lag was a blessing. I didn't want to think, just sleep.

By the time I began to recover, the cliffs of Port Scarnose seemed very, very far away.

I did not exactly resume my activities from the previous spring, but I visited a few friends, went to the school where I had worked to inquire about returning, and began contacting my former harp students.

I was melancholy. I didn't know what else to do but resume my former life. I had left so much of me behind.

Would Canada ever really be "home" again?

In spite of such questions, however, part of me was glad to be back on the North American continent. I knew that behind me I had left two men who would be friends for the rest of their lives. It had been a wonderful experience, a fairy tale, a dream come true. Now it was time to put it behind me.

That was easier said than done, however. Less than a week after my return, a letter arrived from Iain. I grabbed it and tore feverishly at the envelope.

Dear Marie,

I have been thinking about what you told me about your name. What a wonderful name it is! I can hardly believe it—Angel, God's messenger. Yet I will always think of you as Marie, no less godly and precious a name. I know you came here as a visitor who did not even know if you believed in God. Not only did you find a relationship with your heavenly Father and his Son, he used you. He used you to bring healing and

reconciliation to an entire community. Everything is changed here. A
new spirit of openness and optimism pervades the very air. I notice it in
church and when walking in town. Everyone asks about you. Of course,
people are sad about Gwendolyn. Yet somehow in her death, life has
blossomed anew. No one here will ever forget you. I will never forget
you. Thank you for being open to God's work in your life, and thus for
being a vessel for his life to flow out to so many others. Alasdair and I
had lunch together yesterday. He asked if I had heard from you. I said
no but that I intended to write. He asked me to include greetings from
him, which I do. Actually, you were nearly all we talked about. Have
no worries—it was all good. It almost goes without saying that we both
miss you.

I think he is doing well. He is often seen in the village now, walking
and visiting. He has lowered the rents for most of his tenants and has
committed whatever funds are needed for the upkeep and maintenance
of the church. He walks along the headlands frequently. I know he is
thinking of Gwendolyn, and you. I pray that in time he begins to absorb
the love of God that is all around him. And he will. Everyone will. They
cannot help it.

May the blessings of the Father fill you, my dear angel-friend!

Iain

The letter fell from my hand and I closed my eyes. Again I wept.
The memories were not ones I would ever forget. I didn't want to
forget them. Maybe I had to. I didn't know.

Walking with the Canadian hills looming nearby, beautiful and
majestic as they were, was not the same as in Port Scarnose. There
was no sea. There were no headlands, beaches, or tides.

But the whole world is God's home. Wherever you are, he is with
you. Gradually I found new retreats, whether on high hills, beside
a lake or river, or in secluded woods, where I could walk and think
and pray to the God I had not known when I was here before. In
that sense, Canada was new. It felt changed. God was now part of
everything.

Or rather, the other way round—I was now part of everything
with God. He had always been there. I just hadn't been aware of

it. I had come awake to what had been around me and inside me all my life—the love of a good and giving and forgiving and compassionate and tender Father.

Was I now saved, I wondered. Had I *not* been saved before? I didn't care about the theology of it. I was *with* God for the first time in my life. That was what mattered.

A smile came to my lips as I tried to imagine what Iain or Ranald would say to such questions. Oh, how dearly I longed to hear what either of them might say in person!

Maybe that's why I wasn't particularly anxious to go to church after my return to Canada. Maybe in time I would try to find a church with a minister who understood God the way Iain Barclay and Ranald Bain did. But I saw little point in hearing things preached and taught that did not resonate with the new image I had of Jesus and his Father.

I had the feeling that the people I had known in church before would probably still wonder about me. They would want to define my new faith, categorize it, ascertain whether Iain had the proper credentials and whether *he* was saved or not. They would want to know if I had prayed the right kind of prayer to guarantee saving faith. They would be concerned that I was trusting more in God the Father for my salvation than in the Atonement alone. They would probably go so far as to think that I spoke *too* much about the Fatherhood of God, and not enough about Jesus and the Cross. They would raise all kinds of concerns based on their own doubts rather than upon my faith.

None of such things mattered to me. I knew only that I had discovered a Father I had never known before.

Chapter Sixty-seven

Facing Destiny

Ae fond kiss and then we sever, ae farewell, alas for ever,
Deep in heart-wrung tears I'll pledge thee, warring sighs
and groans I'll wage thee.
Had we never lov'd sae kindly, had we never lov'd sae blindly,
Never met—or never parted—we had ne'er been broken hearted.
—Robert Burns, "Ae Fond Kiss"

The weather came on.

Winters in Alberta are fierce. I wondered if Port Scarnose was likewise buried in snow. From all I had heard about the Gulf Stream and its effect on western and northern Scotland, probably not.

But it was for other reasons than the mild climate that I wished I was there.

Christmas came and was dreary and sad. I suppose it always is for single people. A Christmas card from my dad in Portland depressed me all the more. He alluded to a few health problems, though he was keeping up his usual sixty-hour workweeks. The card was a reminder that there were unreconciled relationships in my life, too. Yet in this particular case I was not eager to do anything about it. I sent him a card in return but only signed my name. *Someday* I needed to resolve my inner conflicts and questions about my dad, but I didn't know how. I think down deep I knew that there was something blatantly inconsistent with thinking so glowingly about *God's* Fatherhood, when my relationship with my earthly father wasn't right. But I didn't know what to do, except possibly go see him. And personally, I just wasn't ready for that. So I continued to put off thinking about it.

The new year arrived. After another two months, winter began gradually to loosen its grip on the frozen North.

Sporadic letters went back and forth between Alberta and Scotland.

Cordial. Friendly. Impersonal.

Most of Iain's letters told good things about Alasdair's growth. Most of Alasdair's letters told of Iain's help in that growth. Iain mentioned Ranald every once in a while and continued to visit up the hill.

Suddenly in early March I had a realization.

I had relived my good-byes to Iain and Alasdair a thousand times in my mind. I often woke up in the middle of the night thinking about them. I dreamed about them.

I realized that, had it not been for the other, either one of them might well have proposed to me then and there.

I was not the only one being protective of the feelings of others.

They were both doing the same! They were both sacrificing what love they might feel for me for the sake of the other. Their letters were continuing that sacrifice.

As things stood, neither would ever make an advance, however much they might love me. After what had happened years before, and the recent healing, each would be too mindful of the feelings of the *other* to step forward *himself.*

Iain would not allow me to come between Alasdair and him.

But Alasdair was changed now, too. He would do the same thing.

This time around, he would sacrifice *his* love for *Iain's* sake. As I replayed our last conversation in the castle the night before my departure, everything was suddenly obvious.

Was he trying to nudge me in Iain's direction?

Was it perhaps to make up for what had happened before, figuring that this time, to make it sound like a Gene Kelly movie, he would let Iain "get the girl"?

This was too weird!

Both men were subtly encouraging me toward the *other*, loving me so selflessly that they would do nothing to stand in the other's way. Both of their letters were devoted more to talking about the other than themselves.

I had heard of love triangles, but this took the cake.

It was a stalemate!

Most love triangles were fueled by self-centered love. But here was a case where everyone was so concerned for the others, *no one* would make a move.

All three of the loves were so strong, and so based in selflessness, that we were all willing to give up the love we felt for the good of the other two. In the same way that I would not willingly hurt either of them, neither Alasdair nor Iain was willing to hurt each other for love of me.

Suddenly everything fell into perspective. It explained why the letters of the past months had been so newsy but impersonal, why, with *so much* on all three of our hearts to say, *nothing* was being said!

It explained the looks. It explained the silences.

We were all thinking it, but no one was saying anything!

Now that I understood what had been going on—or thought I did—what of the future? Were Alasdair and Iain destined to live out the rest of their lives as a couple of Trappist monks, and I as a nun?

I wasn't sure I liked the prospect.

What else could the future possibly hold? How was such an impasse to be broken?

The question jolted me. Suddenly I realized the implications. What did I mean by breaking the impasse? Didn't it imply that at some point a decision *would* be made, that one of the "loves" *would* emerge from the uncertainty?

That, too, was an astounding thought. It also had huge implications.

Suddenly I saw them clearly.

I couldn't just live in Canada as if nothing had happened. My life had changed.

A destiny, a future, lay ahead of me.

I needed to find out what it was.

In the same way that all this had begun with my realization that I didn't want my dreams to die, neither did I want my destiny— whatever it was—to just fade away. Whatever future I might have, whatever future I was *meant* to have, I didn't want it to die either.

If it was a terrible thing when dreams died, was it also a terrible thing when you allowed your destiny to die?

One thing was obvious: If anything was going to happen, I was the one to decide what it was!

If there was to be a decision about which man declared his love for me, it would be *mine* to make, not theirs. The choice was up to *me*, because neither of them would ever say a word.

I had to decide which man *I* really loved...loved enough to spend the rest of my life with.

I could not run from it nor escape it. I had to face my destiny, and the love in my heart. I had to discover what these loves meant, and toward what future they were meant to lead.

If there was indeed a stalemate, I was the one who had to break it.

Chapter Sixty-eight

Presumptuous Return

Gae bring my guid auld harp ance mair,
Gae bring it free and fast,
For I maun sing anither sang,
Ere a' my glee be past.
And trow ye, as I sing, my lads,
The burden o't shall be,
Auld Scotland's howes and Scotland's knows,
And Scotland's hills for me!
I'll drink a cup to Scotland yet
Wi' a' the honours three.

—"Scotland Yet"

I flew into the Aberdeen airport on KLM via Amsterdam. No Heathrow, no long train ride.

This time I did not come as a tourist. I had only one destination—Port Scarnose. I did not rent a car. I would take the bus. I wanted no encumbrances, no possessions, nothing to tie me down. No one knew I was coming. I had a mission, and I determined not to let anything distract me from it. If this went badly, or I made a complete fool of myself, I wanted to be able to beat a hasty retreat back to the airport. I did not even bring a harp.

I brought nothing with me but my heart.

And that was hidden safely away.

Well...hidden, perhaps, but not so safely.

It was the second week of April. I had been away for half a year, but it seemed like it had been half my life. And I suppose it *was* half my Scotland life.

I took the Bluebird bus from the airport to Fochabers, and there

413

caught the westbound bus to Port Scarnose. I decided to walk to my destination from the hotel where I had booked a room. Wherever my fate led me, I knew this was a decision that would affect me for the rest of my life.

It was unbelievably presumptuous to think that the looks and silences and misty eyes of six months ago might still mean what I thought they meant. Ever since I had begun making plans for a return visit, my initial determination changed to terrible doubts. Doubts assailed me from every side, telling me how stupid this was.

The whole plan was unbelievably stupid!

The closer the moment of truth got, the more persistent became the doubts. Once the bus began to slow down and I saw the Port Scarnose town center ahead, with all the flurry of emotions the sight brought with it, the doubts became so overpowering that I almost decided to stay in my seat and just keep going. Maybe I had hoped there would be yellow ribbons tied all over either the church or the castle, and that music would start playing and I would suddenly find myself in the middle of a country love song.

What was I doing?

No woman in her right mind walks up to a man and says, "Hi. I know you didn't propose, but I'm ready to marry you anyway because I think you might have wanted to if the circumstances had been different."

The bus stopped.

Timidly I stepped down onto the pavement, my heart beating like a drum. What if someone like Mrs. Gauld or Olivia Urquhart saw me getting off the bus? Word would fly through town in less than an hour!

Or worse—what if Iain himself happened to be walking by?

I glanced around in the dusk as the bus left the town. Everything looked so wonderfully but strangely and nostalgically familiar.

Yet I felt like a stranger again. I had no cottage, no "home." I had booked myself by phone into the Buchan Arms, the town's only hotel, for one night.

I looked hastily about again, drew in a deep breath, and set out. It was cold, bitterly cold and windy—like nothing I had felt here before. The wind blasted against my face, accentuating all the more the folly of my coming. A depressing wave of loneliness swept over me.

I made it to the hotel, less than a two-minute walk, without seeing any familiar faces. No one was outside, anyway. It was freezing! I walked through the doors with a great sigh of relief.

I was all the more glad not to see Iain inside. I knew he liked the hotel's restaurant. He and I had eaten here together two or three times, but I didn't think anyone in the hotel would recognize me.

Thirty minutes after my arrival I was seated on an uncomfortable bed in a small, chilly room, wondering all over again what preposterous presumption had led me here.

It was late in the day, just before six o'clock. By now it was dark. I was exhausted from the flight. I went downstairs to the dining room, ordered a salad and a bowl of soup, which I ate in silence, keeping an eye on the window and the pavement outside. No one I recognized walked by or came in. The place was nearly deserted.

I went back upstairs to my room, took a shower, and was sound asleep by seven-thirty.

I slept hard. I needed it. I never get over jet lag in a single night. Previously it took me a week. But a good first night certainly helps your brain and senses recover, even if your body clock remains out of whack a while longer.

I awoke to an even drearier day than before—gray, cold, windy. If I'd hoped a change in the weather might inject some optimism into my spirits, I was in for a disappointment.

My indecision was the worst of it.

Had I known what I was going to do, maybe it wouldn't have been so depressing. Never had I prayed so hard. Yet the only answer was silence. I had somehow assumed that during the plane flight and bus ride, coming ever closer and closer, my final decision would become clear and obvious. But if anything, the long hours of travel only increased my uncertainty.

I began to get seriously cold feet. What if, in the end, fear of hurting one man prevented me loving the other?

What if...?

I could hardly deal with it!

I *couldn't* let myself come between them. Maybe this had all been a huge mistake!

Throughout my growing doubts and fears and cold feet, the unbelievable presumption weighed ever more heavily upon me. What if I made an appearance at one place or the other, only to find out that both men had married since my visit?

That would put me in my place.

The very thought nearly made me get on the Bluebird and leave Port Scarnose for good. What if there now *was* a Mrs. Iain Barclay, just as I had wondered during my first visit to his home?

But an inner compulsion kept urging me to do what I came here to do.

I had to see it through.

That afternoon I finally mustered up the courage to go out. I bundled up tightly in my warmest coat and wrapped a scarf about my head so thoroughly no one could possibly recognize me. If I saw someone I knew, I would turn away or hide my face long before they could recognize me. Just so long as I didn't see Iain walking along the street.

He would know. He always knew.

I went out and walked through the village. I walked past the cottage that had been my former home. It was dark and uninhabited.

I walked past the Urquharts', once the home of such wonderful, happy music, then past Mrs. Gauld's B and B.

I made my way along the Scar Nose, where the sea was gray and stormy and wild. I began walking out on the headland path, but did not go far. It was too cold and windy. Ranald's warnings about the danger of the cliffs floated through my mind, and with them, for some unexplained reason the image of Olivia's face. I didn't want to think about her right then.

"God, help me know my heart!" I cried aloud in the wind.

But there were no revelations.

I walked back into the village and again toward the hotel. As I went I could not help myself, my steps led me onto the street where Iain lived. I was so cold by now, frozen to the bone, but I slowed and continued on.

There was his house a block ahead. The windows were lit. The familiar car sat in the drive.

I stopped. My heart was beating.

I stood for a minute, maybe two, the wind whistling about my face. I couldn't do it. Doubts, presumptions, and *what-ifs* rushed back upon me like a flood.

I found the words of my prayer quietly filling my brain and heart—*God, help me know my heart.* Then slowly a peace began to come.

I turned around and walked away, then veered up a side street and hastened on. Ten minutes later I walked back into the Buchan Arms, booked another night, and hurried quickly up to my room where I threw myself on my bed.

Chapter Sixty-nine

Decision

I think of thee when some sweet song is breathing,
Awak'ning thoughts of early happy days;
When fairy hope its brightest flowers was wreathing,
And seem'd the future one unclouded blaze.

Oft does some song, some olden song, thus sounding,
Thrill o'er the mind like music o're the sea,
Fond mem'ry wakes our life with bliss surrounding,
And as I feel the spell I think of thee.
—"I Think of Thee"

I did not go out again that day.

The following morning showed signs that perhaps the sun might break through. After a downpour about eleven, suddenly the sun came out. The storm obviously wasn't entirely gone, but it warmed a little. It appeared that the next downpour might hold off for several hours, maybe for the whole afternoon.

Somehow the moment I got up, I knew this was the day. It was the day I would face my destiny and decide on my future. If I could not, then I would leave town, go back to Aberdeen, and await my return flight a week later.

Throughout the morning my resolve increased. The peace that had begun the previous afternoon increased.

I prayed. I thought. Gradually I determined that when I next left my room, I would not return until the decision had been made.

I summoned the final measure of courage a little after noon. I left the hotel and walked out along the promontory and up to my favorite familiar bench. It was wet from the rain, but I sat down on the back of my coat and gazed out at the turbulent sea.

I drew in a deep breath and exhaled slowly. "God," I whispered, "I don't know what to do. I have never needed your help as much as I need it now. I know that you guided me all through the years, even when I wasn't aware of it. Now that I am aware of it, I need your help. What you have given me is so wonderful, so overpowering. I have before me two loving men of character and worth..."

My prayers stopped briefly as I gazed out to sea. Slowly, as if borne on the gentle sea breeze itself, Gwendolyn's sweet voice came back to me:

May I call you Mummy?

The words brought a smile to my lips. Dear Gwendolyn! *"Mummy and Daddy loved baby... that baby was me."*

I waited. Slowly I sensed clarity dawning through the mental mist. The peace deepened.

Calm settled upon me. I stared down upon the rocks, the waves moving in and out splashing up and over them, the gulls flying about on the windy currents, the great sea of God's love, moving and flowing and spreading out to fill all men and women as it had filled me.

I continued to sit. I waited... until finally I *knew*.

I smiled to myself and drew the cold sea air into my lungs. Now that the answer had come, I knew that it felt right. It was what I had felt the afternoon before. God had shown me what was in my heart.

I waited a few minutes more just to be sure, then rose and made my way back down the slope just as I had the first day I had come here last summer. No rain chased me today, and I walked slowly. Again I made my way through the streets of the village I had grown to love.

I walked and walked and walked. Now that I had made my fateful decision, I was in no hurry to make the long walk. I was at peace.

When at last I reached my destination and saw the familiar door in front of me, I paused, drew in a deep breath of final resolve, then continued the last several steps. I reached out my hand and lifted the knocker.

A minute later footsteps came from inside. Slowly the door opened.

"Hello, Alicia," I said as she opened the door. "Would you please tell Mr. Reidhaven that he has a visitor who has come to inquire about a certain diamond necklace?"

Chapter Seventy

Unusual Script for Love

Ye ken whar yon wee burnie, love, rins roarin' to the sea,
  And tumbles o'er its rocky bed, like spirit wild and free.

Come when the sun in robes of gold, sinks o'er yon hills to rest,
An' fragrance floating in the breeze, comes frae the dewy west.

And I will pu' a garland gay, to deck thy brow sae fair;
For many a woodbine cover'd glade, an' sweet wild flower is there.

There's a' of nature and of art, that moistly weel could be,
An' O! my love, when thou art there, there's bliss in store for me!
—"Morag's Faery Glen"

When Alasdair saw me a minute later, he stopped and his face
went pale.

He gasped in disbelief.

The look of joy flooding his eyes was so childlike, so happy,
almost in a way so *innocent*—if such can be said of one who was
a man of the world like Alasdair Reidhaven, Duke of Buchan, but
who was now, late in his life, becoming a man of a very different
kind—that it took my breath away.

Chills swept through me and my eyes blurred with liquid.

"*Marie!*" he said in wonder, almost as if he thought I was a ghost
or a specter out of his imagination.

At the sound of his voice, all my doubts and fears vanished and
I hurried toward him. He received me with open arms. We stood
for what seemed like forever—trembling, crying, laughing,
disbelieving.

"I think perhaps I am now ready," I whispered at last. "That is, if you still want me to wear the diamond necklace you wanted to give me."

"Oh, Marie!" he said "There is nothing I want more. But what about...I mean, have you seen—"

"Alasdair," I said, stopping him before he could say it. "I have seen no one else. I came back to *you*."

Needless to say, again I had to change my flight plans. My return ticket to Canada was now one I didn't know if I would ever use!

It was agony to walk up to Iain's door later that same day. But Iain had to hear it from me. I had been there before almost twenty-four hours earlier. It was then that I had begun to know that my destiny for now lay behind a different door than his.

The moment he saw me standing in front of him on his porch, a hint of "the look" flashed like a beam of light from his face, but then I saw him pull it back. His eyes swam, but he did not allow whatever he might be feeling to spill over. He saw the expression on my face, and I knew he knew.

I told him that I had come from the castle, where Alasdair had proposed to me and that I had accepted him.

Only then did he approach and hug me warmly, as a brother now, and with congratulations for us both. I knew his words were utterly genuine. He was an extraordinary man.

The day after my visit, Iain called on Alasdair to personally congratulate him and to offer his services, if Alasdair and I so desired, for the ceremony. Because of the history between the two men, and the similar circumstances fifteen years earlier, I'm sure Iain knew that Alasdair and I would shrink from asking him to participate.

He preempted our concerns by making the offer himself. I knew it was from his heart. He was sincerely and honestly happy for us—I think for Alasdair most of all. Never had I so clearly witnessed an example of one man truly placing another man ahead of himself. However much he may have loved me himself, I also knew that Iain Barclay was genuinely *pleased* that I would be marrying Alasdair instead.

It fit no Hollywood script where men compete for a woman's affections. In its own way it was even more wonderful. Iain *loved* Alasdair in the full sense of brother loving brother. Alasdair's happiness meant more to him than his own. To see Alasdair happy made *him* happy!

Whenever Iain looked at me after that, his eyes were full of unspoken worlds of feeling. I knew what he was saying with his eyes—that he respected me, even honored me, for being able to see in Alasdair what no one else had been able to see, and for loving his longtime friend and drawing the true man out of him.

I remained one more night at the Buchan Arms, then moved back into Mrs. Gauld's bed-and-breakfast. Every morning Mrs. Gauld sat down with me for tea. While I ate, she talked nonstop about the village and the changes in the duke and how he had been at church a time or two—though she felt sorry for him having to sit up there all alone with everyone staring at him.

Alasdair had to go to Edinburgh for a few days. He had several matters to attend to, one of which was to arrange for an agent to fly to Calgary to have my harps, as well as my clothes and what other things I wanted immediately, shipped to Scotland. I could have gone back myself, but I really didn't want to and Alasdair said he would take care of everything.

While he was gone, I invited Alicia Forbes to stay with me at Mrs. Gauld's so the three of us could plan the wedding. Alicia went with me into Elgin several times, and also to Aberdeen, to look at dresses and fabric and tartans.

After being so formal with each other all this time, suddenly we began to become very good friends.

Chapter Seventy-one

Girls' Night Out

A lassie was milkin' her father's kye,
When a gentleman on horseback he cam' ridin' by,
A gentleman on horseback, he ca' ridin' by:
He was the Laird o' the Dainty Dounby.

—"Laird o' the Dainty Dounby"

Alicia wanted to do something special for me before the wedding. I didn't really know very many people in the community so well that I could socialize with them. So she decided to throw a women-only party to give me the chance to become better acquainted with some of the ladies of the village before the big day.

What she eventually settled on was a dinner party at the Crannoch Bay Hotel, which sat on the main road between Port Scarnose and Crannoch.

"We'll have all the ladies from the castle," she said, "and then you know, let's see, Adela and Isobel Gauld, and there's Jean and Moira and Pamela from Crannoch, and of course Tavia and Cora and—"

"They've been a little distant recently," I said. "I'm not sure they will want to come."

"Distant...what do you mean?"

"Something changed with both of them. Neither Tavia nor Cora had spoken to me for weeks before I left. Not that I saw them that often. But when I went into the co-op, Cora acted as though she didn't even know me."

"I have a feeling I know why," said Alicia with a look of annoyance. "I'll talk to them."

"What is it?" I asked.

"You don't need to know," replied Alicia. "But I have a feeling it is because of your run-in with Olivia."

"Are they friends of hers?"

"Olivia knows everyone. People are afraid of offending her. Old superstitions die hard. I've heard talk—not that Olivia would confide in me anymore."

"Did she once?"

Alicia nodded. "I was part of her inner circle, too, along with the others. But I fell out of favor."

"Why?"

"Because I worked for her brother."

"What did she expect you to do, quit your job just because she had differences with him?"

"Olivia's perspectives aren't always completely rational. Loyalty to her is everything. I don't mean loyalty as such, but loyalty *to her*, and *only* her."

"What kind of talk have you heard?" I asked.

"Nothing specific. Just little hints. Olivia has a subtle way of influencing opinion without anyone knowing what she's doing. She is very canny."

"*Opinion*...about what?"

Alicia looked away and hesitated. By then I knew for certain that she was talking about me.

"Has she been spreading rumors about me?" I said.

"In a manner of speaking," replied Alicia hesitantly. "Not rumors exactly, just suspicions. Nothing different from what she has always done with the duke. Now that you and he are engaged, you are coming in for your share."

I shuddered at the thought. "You're right," I said. "I don't need to know—I shouldn't have asked! What I wouldn't have known wouldn't have hurt me, right?"

"Just don't worry about Tavia and Cora," said Alicia. "Generally, they like you. It's just that Olivia can create confusion in people's minds. But I'll talk to them and sort them out. And speaking of

Olivia, do you want me to invite her, and make sure everyone knows she was invited?"

"She will soon be my sister-in-law," I replied. "I suppose we should."

"She won't come, I'm sure of it. But to make sure we don't give her any additional grounds for complaint, I will invite her."

On the night of the dinner, twenty or twenty-five women came whom Alicia had invited, acquaintances and friends of hers she wanted me to know, most of whom I had never met before that night. The place had been decorated with wonderful flower arrangements courtesy of Morag and Awlwyn Mair.

Afterward everyone spoke to me with friendly smiles when I happened to see them, and a number of intimate friendships developed. In addition to her co-workers at the castle, Sarah Duff and Jean Campbell and the other day-maids, I met Catharine, Brenda, and Rosanna from Port Scarnose, and Ann, Ena, Janet, Christine, and Joan from Crannoch, and so many others whose names I can't even recall. And Tavia and Cora were both there, too, which pleased me. Things seemed normal with both of them. There were no strange looks or whispered asides. One lady who was missing, however, was Adela Cruickshank. I didn't know why she hadn't come. We never heard a word from Olivia, and she did not come either, which was a relief.

Alicia passed out brightly colored paper hats for everyone to wear. Then one by one I opened the silly gifts they had all brought, to much laughter and applause. By the end of it we were all giggling and laughing like schoolgirls. Marian, Dorré, and Fiona brought little squares of fabric for everyone to write their names on. They said they would sew them into a memory quilt for me.

When the waiter asked if we would like a round of *aperitifs*, Alicia answered, "Goodness, no, my good man. We are all proper Presbyterian teetotalers! What would we say if the minister walked in?"

A few snickers went around the room, evidence that faithful Scots Presbyterians were not necessarily *all* teetotalers.

Alicia's comment did not keep her from ordering champagne, which she kept flowing through numerous toasts to my happiness, which may have had something to do with the giggling from a few of the women that seemed to increase as the evening advanced.

"Tell me about the temple," I said as we ate, looking through the hotel's window to the domed structure on the hill about a quarter mile away. "It is so unusual perched there overlooking the bay."

"It's called the Temple of Fame," replied Fiona Simpson, whom I later learned was the resident historian of the group. "It was a summer house for the residents of Castle Buchan. It had a room beneath for changing clothes and even at one time was enclosed and contained bookshelves and chairs as a waystation and summerhouse between the castle and the beach. Originally there was a tunnel from the temple under where the road is now leading to the beach, giving the castle residents their own private beach access. It used to have a statue of the trumpeting *Fame*, which was really its *main* claim to fame, as it were, but it has been gone for sixty years. It was a stunning sight as people rode by on the railroad, at least that's what I've heard. That was long before my time."

"What happened to it?"

"Nobody kens," replied Brenda Mair in a mysterious tone. "Some say it was taken awa' for cleanin', but maist think it wis pinched."

"Does the tunnel still exist?" I asked.

"I dinna ken that edder," she replied. "I think parts o' it murlt fan the railway went in an' the excavation wis deen for the road an' viaduct. It hasna been eest in half a century. E'en the temple itsel' is in disrepair an' a' grown ower wi' brambles an' the like."

"That's too bad," I said. "It ought to be restored."

"Well, you will soon be in a position to do something about it," said Alicia.

"You're right. Maybe I will. I'll talk to Alasdair—oops, I mean...*the duke*—about that. What *am* I supposed to call him, anyway?"

The room erupted in laughter.

"I believe, Marie," said Alicia, "that once you are his wife, you may call him anything you like."

In spite of the champagne, Alicia stood up after the main dinner was completed, before they brought us dessert, which turned out to be sticky toffee pudding, and gave a short speech.

"We all want to say, Marie," she began, "that we are so glad that you came here a year ago, and that we are privileged to call you our friend."

I smiled up at her as she spoke, and mouthed a silent *Thank you.*

"We are not losing a duke, are we, ladies?" she went on. "We are gaining a duchess!"

I felt a twinge of guilt at her statement, knowing that none of them knew about my discussions with Alasdair, and the prenup I had requested. But this did not seem the time to say anything about it. Besides, that was between Alasdair and me for the present. We had decided not to make it public until after the wedding.

"And we are very proud that our new duchess will be you, Marie," Alicia continued. "You have brought new life to the castle, to our villages, to the whole community, and especially into the duke's life. From the first day you came to the castle with your harp, and left more confused than ever," she said, laughing, "I knew change was coming to Castle Buchan. I was right. And the changes have all been good!"

She paused a moment. The room was quiet and more serious than it had been all evening.

"We wish you every happiness and joy, Marie," Alicia added. "May your life as the duke's wife, and as our friend, be richer and more blessed than you can even hope for."

Chapter Seventy-two

Gwendolyn in the Gloamin'

Could I but sojourn with thee only
In some green glen, secure and lonely,
Then neither glory, fame, nor treasure,
Could ever bring me half such pleasure.

—"My Pretty Mary"

Alasdair and I were married in the gardens of Castle Buchan in the third week of May, just as the rosebuds were starting to come on.

Tulips were in profusion, and rhododendrons. The earth was everywhere alive and bursting forth with the renewal of spring. I wore a dress of light tan wool the color of a fawn, with the Buchan tartan knotted at my right shoulder and coming round the back to my left hip. From there it fell the length of my long dress. Alasdair was in full kilted regalia. His mother's diamond necklace hung around my neck.

Iain performed the ceremony. A few of the village auld wives might have had something to say about that in the privacy of their own kitchens. But Iain's unbounded sincerity and joy in our union brought the entire community together in embracing us all as true friends.

Everyone within Deskmill Parish was invited to the wedding, and indeed, so many came that the grounds were overflowing. Ranald Bain, in the full Highland costume of his clan, and having been recently appointed official Bard to the Duke of Buchan, added the haunting strains of ballad after ballad to the afternoon from the annals of Scottish legend and lore with his fiddle.

Midway through the afternoon, Alasdair made a speech and

toasted the good health of his friends one and all. He announced certain changes that would be undertaken in the area to continue those he had already begun, a renovation of the harbor and the church being the most important. He also announced that from that day forward, the gates to Castle Buchan, both north gate and east gate, would be open to the community. Visitors would be welcome to quietly and respectfully walk the grounds on all days of the week but Monday and Tuesday. He also proposed, with Curate Barclay's approval, to install a gate through the stone wall separating the castle from the church, adding another route of access to both, and inviting any from the village who so desired to help with the project, which he would supervise and help with himself. Thenceforth he hoped as many as so desired would use the town gate and entryway through the castle grounds to walk to and from church on Sunday mornings.

He announced, too, that, thanks to the efforts and loving labors of his new wife, three CDs were now available of his daughter's enchanting harp music. They were for sale at the church shop. All proceeds would go to the Deskmill Parish Church.

Finally, he invited the community to the harbor that same evening to send him and his bride on the newly christened yacht *Gwendolyn* off into the gloaming on the tide.

They came.

If anything, more people turned out for our departure about eight-thirty that evening than were at the wedding itself. As the *Gwendolyn* slowly slipped out of the harbor, Alasdair and I stood on the deck, returning the waves and shouts of at least a thousand well-wishers covering every inch of the harbor and up the hillside to the village. From somewhere in their midst a bagpipe was playing.

As we cleared the thick cement harbor walls, slowly a familiar tune began to blend in with the pipes. The high, clear tone came unmistakably from Ranald Bain's violin—the fiddle and the pipes intermingling with such mysterious harmony as they can do only in Scotland. Within seconds, hundreds of voices joined in unison. The words of the Scottish anthem of memories and hopes drifted across the evening waters toward us:

Should auld acquaintance be forgot,
  And ne'er brought to mind.
Should auld acquaintance be forgot,
  In days of auld lang syne.

Alasdair looked at me, smiled, and stretched his arm around me. We stood at the rail, gazing back at the harbor and crowd, as both slowly faded into the distance.

Over and over the strains repeated themselves, the sounds growing ever fainter—

...auld acquaintance...to mind...forgot...in days of auld lang syne...
  ...days of auld lang syne...
    ...auld lang syne...

—until we could hear them no longer.

Gradually Ranald's violin, too, faded from hearing.

Finally only the skirl of the pipes remained, and that for but another few moments. At last the pipes, too, were gone, and we were left alone.

Still we stood, gazing back over the *Gwendolyn*'s wake, until land and sea and sky faded into purply haze behind us, and we were left surrounded by the reds and oranges of a slowly dying gloaming sunset over the widening Moray Firth of the North Sea.

Appendix

Scots Glossary

a': all
abody: everyone
aboot: about
abune: above
ahint: behind
ain: own
ane: one
anither: another
athegither: altogether
aye: yes
bairn: child
bin: hill/summit
bleed/blude: blood
bonnie: pretty
buirdly: strong
burn: creek/stream
caw canny: be careful
dee: die/death
deid: dead
de'il: devil
dinna: don't
disna: doesn't
div/du/de: do
dochter: daughter
doon: down
du: do

dune: done
een: eyes
eese: use
fa/wha: who
fae/frae: from
fan: when
feow/fyow: few
fit: what
fitiver: whatever
fleggit: frightened
fleyt: afraid
gae: go
gang/gaed: went
gar: make
gie: give
gien: if
greet: cry
gude/guid: good
hae: have
hame: home
heid: head
hert: heart
ilka: every
intae: into
isna: isn't
ken: know

kennt: knew
lang: long
lauch: laugh
luik: look
mair: more
maun: must
mirk: dark
mony: many
muckle: much/big
murlt: crumbled
naethin': nothing
nor: than
o': of
ocht: ought
oor: our
oot out
ower: over
po'er/pooer: power
puir: poor
richt: right
roon: round
sae: so
sanna: shall not
sicht: sight
siller: money

sneekit: snuck/sneaked
spier: ask
sud: should
sudna: shouldn't
syne: since/since then/ago
tae/till: to
thocht: thought
toon: town
trowth: truth
twa: two
unco: great/much/a lot
upo': upon
verra: very
wad: would
wadna: wouldn't
wark: work
warna: weren't
weel: well
whan: when
whaur: where
whiles: sometimes
wi': with
winna: won't
wis: was

Afterword

Ideas and What We Do with Them

I was scheduled to speak recently at a church in Arizona for a ladies' banquet. As we were chatting beforehand, the pastor asked me, "Where do your ideas come from?" Later, during a Q & A discussion after I had concluded my talk, a woman asked, "How do you get the ideas for your books?"

It is probably the question *most* frequently asked of writers. I cannot speak for other authors and novelists, but in my own case the ideas usually come of their own accord, in their own time, each idea unique, every circumstance unique. One cannot predict or anticipate, perhaps in a sudden flash of "inspiration" or maybe in a slow-growing "what-if" that rises out of the subconscious, what will grow into a full-fledged book. When the germ of an idea begins to grow and send down roots—whether suddenly or subtly— who can tell where it will lead. Some go nowhere and are forgotten within twenty-four hours. Others send roots so deep that the resulting plants indeed grow into living organisms, which we water and nourish and which bear fruit in their due season.

The germinal idea, for example, for my book series, The Secret of the Rose, came unexpectedly one winter's day when my wife, Judy, found a new rose blossom on a neglected plant in our alley in the midst of a January storm. She picked it and brought it inside. As it sat in its vase over the next several days, that blossom seemed to speak unknown mysteries to us, beckoning us to ask what story it had to reveal.

I have recounted elsewhere that the idea for the Shenandoah Sisters series bubbled up inside my brain with a startling "what-if"—What if two girls, one white, one black, were suddenly orphaned and found themselves together as the Civil War opened. How would a black slave girl and a white plantation girl survive alone in the midst of that dreadful war? It was a mere "idea" birthed by my brain, but in the end eight books resulted.

The spark for the book *Rift in Time* was ignited by an even more astonishing "what-if"—Is it possible, I wondered, that evidence for the location of the original Garden of Eden still exists? And if so, what would be the worldwide impact if an archaeologist discovered it? What would opposing forces do to discredit his discoveries?

I believe that ideas are *living* things, to be tended and nurtured and loved in much the same way we care for the plants in our gardens and greenhouses and homes. Not all ideas are good ideas. There are good *and* bad ideas, true and false ideas. There are idea-weeds that are to be gotten rid of. But there are also idea-trees of large truth, though they start as small grains of mustard seed that grow to become trees to give shade, beauty, and substance to the entire garden of our growing intellectual and spiritual souls. I love *ideas* far more than I love the roses of my rose garden or the varietals of heather in my heather garden. I treat the nurturing of ideas with the greatest care and respect, both within myself and within others.

Ideas are precious and important. That we are thinking, creative, intellectual beings is a wonderful gift from God. I spend more energy reflecting and praying and hypothesizing on the ideas of my faith than I do the plot ideas for my novels. Those are the most significant kinds of ideas of all. I remember the day I walked into the house after a long run and announced to Judy, "I think I have just figured out the Atonement!"

Now that is more exciting than getting an idea for a new novel!

As my brain is engaged in wrestling through some deep theological conundrum on one level, a new story idea might be germinating on another level. Often the two will cross paths somewhere within the pages of a story. Ideas are like that—unpredictable ... you never know where they are going to take you.

One of the aspects of ideas I find most intriguing, and which finds its way into every book I write, is simply the question—

How do people respond when confronted with truth, with change, with the demands of the gospel, with relational complexities, with unfamiliar ideas that have not been part of their outlook and perspective?

Whatever else I may be doing in a book, that theme is always present. No matter the character or historical or geographical setting, it is a constant thread: *How do people respond to ideas?*

What do men and women do when the ideas of truth intersect their lives? How do people respond to the new, the unfamiliar, the uncomfortable, the challenging, the humbling?

How you and I respond to ideas says a great deal about the kind of people we are.

In the case of *this* particular story, the book in your hand began with *nothing*, with the absence of an idea.

I had concluded all my existing writing commitments and for the first time in twenty-five years was facing a clean slate as a writer. I had assumed, without the pressure of commitments and deadlines, that a rush of creativity would flow forth from within me.

How wrong that turned out to be!

Clean slates are not all they're cracked up to be. I felt as if my brain had been wiped clean, too. Or, to be contemporary about it, as if my hard drive had been erased. Suddenly there were *no* ideas!

Up till that time my problem had always been *too* many ideas—two or three new book ideas every week, and how to sift from among a hundred ideas to discern those I should pursue. Suddenly during this crossroads period with all commitments behind me, I found my brain empty. I began to seriously wonder, *Is it over—will I never write another book?*

I was convinced that my brain had run out of gas.

In the spring of 2007, I happened to be alone at our home in Scotland. I hadn't been very good company for a few months. Judy was probably glad to be rid of me for a while!

Returning from a long bike ride, I stopped a couple of miles from home and sat down on a bench high on an outlook over the Moray Firth of the North Sea. It was a spectacular day, breezy but pleasant, the ocean a deep blue. As I sat at the edge of the promontory, a seagull flew past in front of me, drifting on the winds blown upward from the ocean against the cliff face at about the height where I sat. Slowly, as it glided by a few feet in front of me, wings outstretched, the gull's head turned and glanced briefly toward me.

It was one of those magical moments of connection between man and the animal kingdom that brings a joy to the heart. Obviously the gull was not thinking about me as he flew by, but the turn of his head stabbed my senses with undefined pleasure. I imagined him saying, "There is a story waiting to be told about that bench you are sitting on, about this coastline, about that village just there along the path. Mysteries are about to be revealed. I know of them, and you will know of them soon."

Just as quickly he was gone.

As I sat staring out to sea, the awe deepened. I was left to ponder the moment of that fleeting eye contact, and what it might mean. "The look" of the seagull haunted me. Gradually one of those creative what-ifs began to coalesce in my brain—

What if someone, a visitor perhaps, came to this part of Scotland as a tourist and actually came to this very spot, this village...and walked this path along the sea and sat upon *this* very bench? What if such a person came here knowing nothing, expecting nothing...and slowly found himself or herself drawn into the life of the community? And what if such a person discovered the story the seagull had to tell?

That was it.

A village in Scotland...a path along a high overlook...a bench above the sea...and the momentary glance of a Scottish seagull.

As I continued on my ride toward our home in Cullen a few minutes later, a sentence came to me. I don't know why, or where it came from. I had no idea what it meant, what it might refer to. I had no idea who was speaking it.

The sentence was—

It is a terrible thing when dreams die.

A curious sentence. What did it mean?

With nothing more than that, I began to write, just to explore what the mysterious look of the gull might have to say. I would write down that one sentence, and hope that perhaps a second might follow.

As I mentioned, Judy was not yet with me in Scotland, but would be joining me in a few weeks. I was obviously thinking of her. I thought, *I will make the unknown visitor to this village a woman, a harpist, like my Judy, maybe who has always dreamed of playing Celtic music on her harp in Scotland...perhaps on a high wind-swept mountain or a cliff overlooking the sea.*

Gradually one idea followed another until I had enough to fill a page...then two pages.

That's how ideas come. One follows another, you pose questions to yourself, you put yourself in a character's shoes and ask what he or she would do, and in trying to answer your own questions, more ideas follow.

My ideas are not any more stupendous than yours, or anyone else's. That's why I say that everyone has within himself or herself all the ideas necessary for a great book. Learning the techniques and craft to put those ideas onto a printed page, that takes some work. But the *ideas* themselves are the free currency of the creative mind. I am thoroughly convinced that new novels are being born every day, and perhaps new novelists with them.

That is how the succession of ideas that began this doublet

called *Angel Harp* and *Heather Song* originated. I had no more notion where it would lead than you did when you began. As you have discovered by now, the path, the bench, the cliff, the gull, a harp—even the cyclist in his blue-and-yellow biking clothes!—all come into the adventure.

Michael Phillips